Published in the UK in 2023 by NJ Miller Books

Copyright © N J Miller 2023

N J Miller has asserted her right under
the Copyright, Designs and Patents Act, 1988,
to be identified as the author of this work.

Paperback ISBN: 978-1-7393792-0-9
eBook ISBN: 978-1-7393792-1-6

The author has taken creative liberties in crafting the story,
including the development of characters, dialogues, and
plotlines. While certain historical, cultural, or geographical
references may be included, they are intended to enhance the
fictional narrative and should not be regarded as factual or
accurate representations.

Cover design and typeset by Nick Hunsley

23

N J M I L L E R

For 'The One'

"I could have been someone
Well so could anyone
You took my dreams from me
When I first found you
I kept them with me babe
I put them on my own
Can't make it all alone
I've built my dreams around you"

The Pogues

The Neighbours

I know I'm not a bad person. Although I've done some pretty iffy stuff of late, I'm certainly not rotten to the core and my intentions are good, mostly. It's not like I actually meant to put my entire family in jeopardy.

It started with a small mistake, but that triggered a chain of events creating bigger mistakes and, before I knew it, I made nothing but mistakes. I think they call it the snowball effect; one small ball of ice gathering momentum can actually end up taking out the Trafford Centre, if you let it.

My mum's friend Denise, a wealthy woman by marriage, was the proud owner of an ITV Heart of Gold award. Very kindly, she allowed the naughty kids from the local comp to use her garden as a playground at lunchtimes. There had been a spate of biting and somebody had set fire to a prefect's hood, so Denise stepped in and offered these little assholes a place where they could let off steam. That award, the one she was so very proud of, was revoked within six months after Denise was caught shoplifting lasagne sheets in Waitrose. Apparently the temptation was too great as her new anorak had really big inside pockets.

So, I figured if it could happen to kind-hearted, selfless Denise, if she could blow up her life with one misdemeanour, then it could happen to anyone. And it did; it happened to me.

My name is Raquel, intended to be said in a demure French way. Sadly I don't look like a Raquel; I don't have flowing dark locks, a perfect red pout or a wardrobe from Paris Fashion Week. I am five-foot-fuck-all with frizzy blonde hair, but I do have a perfume that makes me smell of croissants.

I am a married mother of three, clinging onto sanity by my fingernails and wondering where it all went wrong. I think many women who reside on the shitty side of forty wonder this very thing and apparently, the magazines rejoice in telling us, the answer is not in the bottom of a bottle. (But there's no harm in checking – regularly.) I went from being a slightly windswept cheery mother with three beautiful babies to raging hag with three sulky teenagers in tow. I was happy in my thirties, throwing muddy Hunter wellies into the boot of my car and heading off to the beach to collect shells. I was an absolute whizz at making last-minute outfits for school concerts and baking wonky cakes for coffee mornings. I thought it was just another day at the office when all three kids got chickenpox in the same week, ha ha ha, these things are sent to try us.

Fast forward a few years and a cloud descends, a grey cloud that rains irritability and intolerance all over my parade. I blame the kids, each one took a chunk of my positivity and smeared it on something, something I had to clean afterwards with a baby wipe.

Child 1 – now seventeen – Suzy. Named after my mother, is very judgemental and makes me feel like the child. Says things like, "Is that a good idea?" when I am having a very weak Buck's Fizz at 11 am on a Sunday.

Child 2 – now fifteen – Michaela. Thinks she is named after my grandfather Michael but it's actually my unhealthy obsession with Michael Jackson which pushed that one through. Super clever, answers all the questions on The Chase before The Chaser. Puts education above fashion and thinks spending money on designer handbags is embarrassing.

Child 3 – just turned twelve – Sam. Named after nobody. Had too much morphine after my C-section and went along with my husband because I was off my tits and thought he was a Catholic priest.

And then you have my long-suffering husband, everybody's favourite class clown, Dave. Good solid Dave who was a police officer by day and dickhead by night.

That's my family and a year ago we were pretty normal; living in Cheshire, close enough to the posh bit to have a hot tub but far enough away to drink Jacob's Creek. Dave had provided much excitement over the years and his stories about front doors being smashed down and drug dealers being dragged in underpants across their lawns were highly entertaining. Dave was high up in the drug squad but he was hands-on, no sitting behind a desk for Big Dave. He always had someone by the scruff of the neck and called everyone 'son'. When he wasn't infiltrating drug cartels and flushing big bags of cocaine down the toilet, Dave would be in the pub telling stories at the top of his voice and making everybody laugh. All very laddish and banter-based and there was clearly a good bond between his team, a sort of code between comrades. Always sniggering at inside jokes, they seemed to have their own language, winking and nodding instead of actually speaking like us civilians had to do. I was an outsider and they were Dave's other family. I sound like I minded, I didn't really, it was good that he had his own world and I had mine. But all that was about to change.

My job is to write – to write endless articles about food. I used to be a chef but, when the kids came along, the hours just didn't suit a young family. So I started reviewing food for a local rag and from there I managed to get myself a half-decent contract working through an agency. At least I have kept my hand in the industry, and I can work from home and be there for the kids. I have my own little office looking out on to the cul-de-sac, I keep wine in my filing cabinet for creative purposes only and I write about food. Winter warmers for Waitrose, summer salads for Sainsbury's and how to feed a family for 80p from Aldi without shoplifting. Blah blah blah goes my keyboard four days a week, telling people about the benefits of baked beans (there really are none), but it earns me a decent wage and I am essentially my own boss. Perhaps if I had been in an office on a daily basis, I wouldn't have got myself into the mess I am in. We can't call it a pickle, it's too serious, even a fiasco is a bit light for this one. I was in the shit, a massive steaming pile of it and it all started when a new couple moved into Number 23.

She was slutty looking, always wearing something leather whether it be a boot, a skirt, a jean. Alarm bells ring when a woman needs something shiny and black to make her presence known. He was slimy looking; too much gel, skinny jeans and a slight belly hanging over the waist. Perhaps an estate agent, a football agent, maybe even a car sales rep in an oily Saab showroom. I imagined him with a fake Greek accent wearing a silver suit, pushing a blonde into the passenger seat, "the seats recline sweetheart, down you go." Do Saabs still exist? A friend's dad had one back in the day and he is now on a register for 'inappropriate behaviour'. Something involving a camera on a stick and a woman in a floaty dress.

They were both brown – not in the ethnic sense, they were just extremely tanned. Could be the sunbeds or bottle brown but to me it looked like they holidayed A LOT. Probably Marbella, I was getting that vibe. No carbs before Marbs types, fake Chanel passport cover, pay for speedy boarding and act like they are First Class guests on Emirates. I can see them rolling out a cheap red carpet on the driveway for a family BBQ.

I made all of these observations over three days of watching them out of my window. I was happily the most judgemental person that ever lived. I sat there at my judgy desk sneering and letting my imagination run wild. I didn't hate them, I didn't know them, I just found Turkey teeth and beach-bought Rolexes something to chuckle at.

That week, a story popped up on my phone about an incident that had caused much disgust to the distinguished readers of the Daily Mail. An 'Arab guy' with a rucksack was walking through Stansted Airport departures with a look of determination in his eyes. Apparently, a crowd of terrified people had thrown themselves out of his way; one broke her shoulder after hitting the revolving door in a bid to escape the inevitable blast, another had a fat lip from attempting to take seven Valium at once because she was "bad with her nerves". It was reported that someone's nan had soiled herself and completely destroyed a silk pair of trousers that she had only just had taken in. Total and utter carnage! Eventually, after all of this mayhem, a "brave citizen" pinned this lunatic to the ground and hurled the mystery bag into the madding crowd at Starbucks. When no blast actually happened and many questions were asked, rather mortifyingly this guy turned out to be a Spanish student wearing headphones. You know, the small ones that Apple made to screw my bank account at Christmas. 3 x £250 = Pissed off. This poor man simply didn't hear somebody ask him a basic question – "Where's the bogs matey?" – so he just kept on walking, as you would. Immediately red flags appeared and security were alerted. The term "security" was used loosely since it was actually the highly trained bin-emptiers that trudge the airports like sloths on tramadol who fuelled the fire. Pure panic set in for a group of sun seekers; Sue and Steve, Jason and Chantelle, our baby Rhianna and three people who preferred not to be named. This lot convinced themselves that this was a suicide bomber, no doubt from Syria, heading to Terminal 2. Most of the flights from here were Alicante-bound or similar – the mind boggles. They apparently prepared themselves to be "blown to powder". Sue's actual words.

Andre, the nineteen-year-old student from Seville, was very forgiving and chilled. He did suffer some semi-permanent sight damage after having a bottle of bubblegum-scented Impulse sprayed into his right eye but, in his words, it was "all good". He was mostly focused on his confiscated rucksack which had some very interesting edibles in the front pocket and a dummy from Blackpool Pleasure Beach that he was saving for the plane. The investigation continues and he remains under the supervision of an eye specialist.

So, on the back of this, I decided to not judge a book by its fur gilet and to stop being such a wanker. I approached Number 23 with a couple of wines inside me, the kids were all in their various lairs doing homework or chatting to strangers online. I wore my slippers and jeans hoping to offer a down-to-earth and friendly approach, I didn't want them thinking I was a snobby bitch going over for a nosey. With a chocolate torte, made by my own fair hands, on an antique plate and a bottle of fairly posh Prosecco under my arm, this snobby bitch was in welcome mode.

It was the smell that hit me first, the overpowering, eye-watering odour of cheap candles that slapped me straight in the face. She stood there, black silk pyjamas and a matching gown, full face of make-up and a wide and jazzy smile.

"Hi babes." She kissed me on the cheek. I blushed; I am not used to these intense physical interactions with strangers. The scene was actually quite intimate. Black silk, scented candles, a cheek-snog and an affectionate pet name all within a nano second.

"Good evening," I said in a very serious tone that surprised me. Why was I starting like a newsreader? "I am Raquel from across the road."

She was still beaming at something, was she drunk? Did she think I was from the Postcode Lottery?

"Oh my god, so nice to meet you." She had a Liverpool accent, a soft Scouse accent like the rough ones on Hollyoaks. "Come in babes, I'm Gina and me husband's inside, name's Matt."

I shook my head quite vigorously.

"I really shouldn't, I don't have long, I've left the kids ..." I started to turn around but she wasn't having it. She threw a long brown arm around my shoulders and ushered me into the house.

"Don't be daft, you're coming in. Is that for us?" She pointed a very long and manicured nail at the torte.

"Yes, and this." I offered up Tesco's Finest Prosecco like the baby Jesus.

"Ahh thanks babes, so kind of you."

Another kiss was heading my way, this time it landed awkwardly on my forehead because I looked at the floor at the wrong time, a cheap floor that was masquerading as real wood.

I stood in the hallway in my dog-chewed Ugg slippers and Mum Jeans and felt horribly underdressed. She had painted toenails the colour of claret and black fluffy slippers to match her bedtime get-up, lipstick to match her toes and a nearly-black, crisp bob. Her eyebrows were as sharp as a knife and sat very high up on her forehead. I looked like a jacket potato in comparison, one that had been in the microwave.

The hallway was all white and it was lit only by candles, about twenty of them. There were no coats hanging on the banister, no scuff marks on the paintwork and no evidence of a banana being dragged up the wall by a greasy teenager protesting a curfew. The stairs donned a very thick white carpet; it was a poor attempt to be plush but it wouldn't last five minutes on a rainy day. This place was like an advert for Jacky Malone – Jo Malone's less successful cousin. I walked behind her, wondering how much more affection I would have to endure as she led me into her kitchen. Glossy and white, a glittery central island with a huge glass bowl filled with what could only be fake fruit. Unless it was genetically modified – the banana was the size of my arm. There were two cream leather stools with the labels still attached to the arms and chrome appliances so shiny they blinded me. Everything was placed, everything shone, even the hob was pristine, it had clearly never been used. I scanned the walls for a plaque saying Love, Live, Laugh, but I am pleased to say it was a negative.

"Babes, babes come and meet our neighbour." From behind the fridge door – a huge double Sub Zero no less, with glass doors and a full-length wine section – emerged a freshly showered six-foot man with a towel turban on his head wearing just a pair of tight grey jogging bottoms with white socks and sliders. He was holding a ready-made lasagne from Asda with a 'whoops' sticker on the front. Nice.

"Alright luv." Another Scouser, I would need a phrase book at this rate.

"Good evening," I said again, like a total dick.

"I'm Matt, what's your name, luv?"

Babes and Luv were now on my 'things people say' hate list. 'Cool Beans' would probably always be at the top, with 'unprecedented' a close second banded about during the pandemic by every man and his dog. I did make a promise to myself to sneeze in the face of the next person who said it. I am still waiting with baited mucus.

I shook Matt's hand very firmly, creating a tension in my arm to stop any physical ideas of him coming in for a kiss.

"I am Raquel. Raquel with a q." They both looked horribly confused as to where this q would actually go.

Matt was also into the eyebrows, his were just as sharp but luckily thicker. He was bulky, bit of a dad bod but he was the same colour as a Curly Wurly so it was sort of fine. He took the turban off and revealed very dark, wavy hair and he did have nice green eyes.

"OK Raquel with a q, we having a drink or what?"

My mother would be horrified at all of these missing words and absent letters; luckily Dave was a cockney so I was acclimatised to strong accents. My accent had been fairly straight, coming from the Manchester side of Cheshire, so I managed to put a sentence together without confusing people or spitting on them. A scouser saying 'Raquel' was like a ride on the log flume.

"Thanks for the offer, Matt, but the children are home alone so I really have to get back. I just wanted to say welcome and if you ever need anything we are just across the road at number 18."

Matt sniggered and winked at me. "I know where you live, luv, I've seen you twitching your blinds and looking at me arse."

Really! Well, I am no prude but come on, we had only just met. I was dying inside because I had been twitching my blinds but I thought I had gone undetected. I replied with the well-known witty and clever retort, "Ha ha, very funny." He was clearly one of those banter kings that would have a whoopee cushion in his pocket at a wake – Bit dead in ere eh la – and all that.

Gina was completely oblivious to this embarrassing exchange because she was too busy pouring three glasses of Prosecco. I glanced at the door and wondered whether to make a run for it. Would they keep me here forever, had they slipped the date rape drug into my glass and would they cover me in slobbery Scouse kisses whilst I was unresponsive? To be fair, I had no make-up on, a very slack bra and my breath was quite sour from hyperventilating. They wouldn't waste their perversions on me even if I wanted them to. Which I didn't, of course, but it would be nice to be considered for the position.

Anyway, crazy thought process over, I followed them into their luxurious show lounge. Wooden floors, fluffy rugs, more candles. There would be no rotting grapes down the side of the sofas here, no way. Gina sashayed over to the larger sofa and patted it. I took a large gulp of my drink and just as I was about to say, "I love what you've done with the place," a pocket of air caused by the Prosecco travelled with velocity up my windpipe and turned the word "I" into a massive burp. A burp so loud and manly that Dave and his mates would have high-fived me. There was a moment of shock on all of our faces as we processed what had just occurred and then, as mine turned purple with embarrassment, Matt started laughing uncontrollably.

"Bloody hell luv, you nearly blew me windows out."

Hmm the laughs just kept on coming. I was furious and mortified that Matt had not let this slide but I had to keep it cool and just very Britishly said, "Excuse me." His shoulders still shook for a good two minutes afterwards.

Gina sat next to me on her pink velvet sofa, she sat very close and I could feel her analysing me. "I'm a Botox nurse, Raquel, got my own clinic in town. Matt's a professional gobshite aren't you, luv?"

Matt had, at this point, stopped laughing at my expense and was shirtless whilst lighting a faux flame glass-fronted fire below the massive telly. I imagined his chest hair catching alight. My shoulders would have been shaking then, oh yes they would. He turned around, having sparked up The Ambience 1200.

"I work in IT actually Raq, all very boring, just a desk job in town." He clearly had no interest in his job which was bloody marvellous because I did not want to hear about it. Nobody who works in IT should ever talk about working in IT to a non-IT person. It's just rude. Also very presumptuous to chop my name in half without asking, I noted.

"Ever had Botox or fillers babe?" Gina was still running her eyes all over my face and neck, I wished she wouldn't. Her skin was as smooth as an apple, not an imperfection in sight.

"Not yet," I said, "but I'm sure the day will come when I will give in and have eyebrows like yours."

She slowly nodded whilst attempting to frown. Very unnerving and I felt a sense of pity toward me.

"Well I am a food writer and my husband is a police officer."
Matt immediately stood up and said "Evening all" and bent both
of his legs. FFS.

Gina rolled her eyes at Matt, I think she could feel my
annoyance at his relentless attempts to be funny. She put on a
serious face in an attempt to be the clever one.

"So, what do you actually say about food Raquel?"

I imagined I was talking to my son when he was three days
old and spoke very slowly and deliberately.

"Well, when you see an article about food – like perhaps
a piece in the Mail on Sunday about aubergines – I could have
possibly written that."

"Oh, we don't like aubergines, do we babe?" She checked this
with Mr IT.

"Do we fuck." Matt screwed up his face.

So I tried again. "Well OK, any vegetable, or meat or fish or
sometimes a starter, dessert. Anything to do with food."

They looked blankly. I felt this could take a while.

Gina looked at the ceiling for a moment, "Do you do ...
grilled chicken?"

"Erm possibly once or twice," I humoured her.

Matt's turn next, trying to be clever – a pointless endeavour.
"Do you do minted lamb chops? I bet she doesn't." He smirked at
Gina. I suspected he thought this was a very stylish and rare dish
that a layperson had never heard of.

I sit forward and try and catch both of their attention
simultaneously like when you try and train two puppies at once.
"You understand I don't write menus, I write articles about food?"

Blank faces. Then Gina looked suddenly excited.

"Have you ever written a menu in The Sun, Raquel?"

I pulled that Donald Trump face that basically calls someone
a tit with your mouth and cheeks.

"No, I have never ever written anything the readers of The
Sun could, should or would cook."

They both looked very deflated that I was not a paparazzi
person who hid behind bushes taking photographs of unsuspecting

cabbages for the front pages. Idiots, just as I thought. This was my cue to leave so I stood and put my glass on the table, ignoring the coaster. The eyebrows of Gina slightly rose. "Well, I really must go and it was lovely to meet you both." More kissing took place and a weird pat on the back from Matt; maybe he was trying to wind me. They stood in the doorway in their posh nightwear and watched me walk across the road. And just as I thought I was home and dry, the male one shouted, "You owe us for the windows you broke with your big dirty burp."

I didn't turn around, I just put my thumb up above my head and shouted, "Ha ha, very funny."

I was drenched in Scouse saliva, had lost my dignity thanks to Tesco putting too many bubbles in their shit plonk and I had never felt so plain and ugly in my life. My house was a shithole and my eyebrows were, quite frankly, substandard. I had spent half an hour of my Friday night feeling incredibly uncomfortable with a couple of morons who I had absolutely nothing in common with but, here's the thing, a curveball if you will, I sort of liked them.

The Fam

The weekends in our house are always reserved for relaxation. The kids have their social lives and, apart from the odd drop-off and pick-up, they generally leave me alone to drink wine and to tidy up. Dave's shifts are sporadic so it was rare he ever had a whole weekend in the house. It was a Saturday morning when my oldest daughter, Suzy, told me she was planning to spend the summer with my sister Mel in Dublin. My sister is basically just a worse version of me but not as bad as my mother – we'll get to her at some point. When I say worse, she was more angry, much fatter and had a husband I would have greased the stairs for. They hadn't had children because apparently they wanted to live their own lives and have no ties. But I knew my sister and she had wanted children, she had fawned all over mine since the day they were born; it was him, Roger, who was the selfish one. Roger was in his fifties when he met my thirty-year-old sister while she had been browsing in his stupid Irish bookshop during my hen weekend. That pretty much paints the picture of my sister's character; sober and book shopping as I was at eye-level with a stripper's penis in a rowdy Dublin bar. She was simply too grown up for this sort of malarkey and stormed off in disgust when Magic Malcom appeared with a bulging crotch and a stick-on moustache. According to Mel, she and Rog had a connection on a deep level over an Enid Blyton original and from that moment on, Roger had her under his pensioner's spell. Roger did not like me. I could see into his black soul and he knew it; his facade was an intelligent book dealer, a scholar, a gentleman but Roger was a little bitch and I told him that by text when I was particularly drunk so from then we were done.

My sister is successful, she is a lawyer, a saver and has brains. They live in a very palatial town house in the centre of Dublin, they have a housekeeper called Nancy and they travel in style – from the outside looking in, it was perfect. So Suzy wanting to go and take up in one of their large spare rooms with an en suite and a view of the river was not hugely surprising.

"I will go to the theatre, I can join a gym, I will probably make some new friends." Suzy was selling this to me like she was on a zero hours' contract. I sat at my kitchen table weighing up the pros and cons. Roger could radicalise her like my sister and turn her into a sour lemon. My sister could convince her that I was a no-good scruff with the morals of a sewer rat. But ... she could also become more independent, meet a plethora of different nationalities and you just don't get that in Cheshire, a very backwards place if truth be told.

Perhaps she would become more rounded, perhaps she would miss me.

"OK, I will agree to this and I will fund it but only on one condition."

She sighed heavily. "Go on ... what is it?"

"That I can visit you halfway through the trip."

Her shoulders relaxed. "Fine, that's absolutely fine."

She was relieved that her sales patter sufficed. So the deal was done, I hadn't even consulted Dave but he was chill and always said, "We never have to worry about Suzy, she's a good girl."

Suzy was blessed in the looks department, she had height – god knows where from, Dave was as wide as he was tall and I was basically a garden gnome – she also had good hair, blonde ringlets, not the frizz that I had been gifted and Dave didn't even own hair, it walked out on him in the 90s. She had wonderful blue eyes and she was quiet and strong. Not really witty, not particularly articulate, very matter of fact. But Suzy did have opinions and she delivered them like poisoned darts, quickly and quietly. One Christmas morning when she could only have been ten, I heard her whisper the words "utterly ridiculous" at the sight of my specially purchased Christmas Day outfit. I had come down the stairs in a red velvet jumpsuit, it was festive, it was fun. It looked fabulous on the tall, skinny model in the magazine and, after two sherries,

I added a wedged boot for some extra height and in my opinion I was good to go. It was apparently "not a look" and I put it into the fancy dress box with my tail between my legs. Suzy had a way of making you feel tiny (or in this case gargantuan) with just a look. Michaela, who insisted on looking like a vegan even though she wasn't one, was a witness to the Dublin negotiations.

"Am I supposed to just stay here all summer with nothing to do then?"

She sat on the floor cross-legged eating sourdough toast, scowling up at us. Michaela was more like me, she was petite, she was angry and she had the bog-brush hair. Her clothes looked like she was auditioning for Oliver Twist. Everything was made of hessian in earthy tones and frayed at the edges. She wore wooden jewellery, who does that? She'll make somebody a cheap bride if the solitaire originated from a tree trunk.

"I'm sorry we aren't going away on holiday this year. Dad is working on a big case and he really needs to be around."

She put her head between her legs and groaned loudly. "Why does she get to go to Aunty Mel's though and I am stuck in this house, in this village, while she gets to travel?" Her face was that of a slave living in squalor – she had her own en suite for god's sake. I was sure that Mel would take all three of them but I made it a rule never to ask Mel and Roger to look after my kids; they would need to offer, at least twice. This was so when the kids burnt their house down I could say "well ... you offered!" as Roger wept over his charred racist books and scorched neckerchiefs.

"You would need to talk to Mel but don't get your hopes up, you know what Roger's like, he can barely cope as it is."

Immediately Michaela started tapping on her phone, no doubt sending stories of child cruelty and 'save me' messages to my sister.

I looked around at my worn and battered kitchen, my sanctuary where I had served up meal after meal for the last fifteen years. My method was to feed anyone who entered at least a snack and that would limit their ability to talk shit to me. The one non-negotiable clause when we moved into the cul-de-sac was that I had a proper kitchen, spacious and practical, all the gear I would need to feed a family from scratch for twenty years. It was no use allowing the developer to put in a tinpot MFI kitchen that would need replacing after five minutes, I got the asking price dropped and picked my own appliances and worktops. It wasn't a show home, the pans were old and copper and the oven had the endurance of a world war tank, but this was my lair, my happy place and it would feel strange without the usual suspects sitting around the table. Without the girls for a month, Dave working and Sam, who really preferred McDonald's to actual food, I could be forced into part-time cooking. Apron still on and a cup of tea in hand, I sat at the kitchen table wondering how I would fill my time. It felt like fate when an email pinged through from my agency at that exact moment.

To: Raquel Fitzpatrick
From: Jane Aldgate

Morning Raquel, hope all is good with you and the fam. Just had a job in for a four-piece article to run weekly in *The Mail*. Thought of you straight away as they need someone who can cook to get involved. No budget for a celeb chef so we kill two birds with one stone and use you; it's a practical assignment! They are also running a piece on a fat lad doing some exercise with a PT alongside so the vibe is getting clueless people to look after themselves.
    Can you find someone who can't cook and eats shite? Need the details on what they spend, where they shop, calories, e-numbers, etc. And then you teach them how to do it better. We can wrap it all up with nice photos, etc. They will get a load of vouchers from the supermarkets and a probably low-key celebrity status in their local shop.

Have a great weekend, deadline for the first article is in a couple of weeks.

Ta, Jane

Hmmmm, there was a long list of doughnut-eating cops that Dave hung out with, in fact he was one of them, but they had no time to cook. My parents still lived in the dark ages and ate the same thing each week, they wouldn't listen to me anyway. They boiled their vegetables to mush and winced at anything spicy, my dad would almost throw up if we drove past an Indian (restaurant not person). My friends were all accomplished cooks and Dave's parents had pina coladas for breakfast since they had moved to Portugal because of Dave's mum's knees. I put it on the back burner and considered approaching some of the school mums on Monday morning, perish the thought.

Dave and I had booked a restaurant that evening for our anniversary. We rarely went out just the two of us because we irritated the shit out of one another but we'd been married twenty years the month before and it was the right thing to do. I jammed myself into a black dress, tied my hair back and sprayed up my skirt with Anaïs Anaïs; Dave had always loved that back in the day so the effort was made to be nostalgic. Dave had squeezed himself into a beige suit and off we went like a couple of Humpty Dumptys to Felicini's, a poor excuse for an Italian restaurant a five-minute drive away.

"So ...!" That was the start of our anniversary conversation.

"So ... what Dave?" I almost laughed at the fact we had nothing to say.

"How are you?" Oh my god, we were so out of practice. There was a time when we first met when we had too much to say. We would gaze at each other over candlelit tables and hold hands while we were eating, how times had changed.

"The girls are going to Dublin for a good chunk of the summer." Dave looked up from his garlic prawns.

"What about Sam?"

"Sam won't want to go there, he has football, his mates and he won't like being around Roger. Remember last time he went? Roger made him work in the bookshop."

Dave laughed out loud. "Shit yeah, forgot about that, poor kid." Images of a miserable nine-year-old boy in a fusty bookshop listening to Roger reading pages from The Importance of being Earnest in his soft Irish voice had me laughing too. Read the room Roger, read the room.

"Maybe you could take a few days off and go do something with him, father and son bonding time."

Dave nodded. "Yeah maybe, let me see how things are with Dachshund."

Operation Dachshund was a stupid name, god knows why or who came up with it but Dave had been heading this for a good year. The impression I had was that, at some point soon, Dave would be on the news telling the public that he had managed to stop ten tons of heroin hitting the streets and that he had arrested and charged a number of undesirables. That's how it normally went, but this seemed like the big one. This would be the equivalent of me being asked to cook for Michel Roux and him liking it.

By the time the coffee arrived Dave was completely pissed. He stumbled into a waiter, almost crushing the boy against the wall, and he kept saying "Twenty years – you get less for murder," to anyone who caught his eye. The beige suit jacket was now on the floor behind his chair and the buttons on his shirt were almost crying at the pressure they were under. Dave's head was big and shiny, his smile was infectious but all in all I was married to a boiled egg. When he smacked my bum and said, "Not bad for an old bird" as I put on my coat, I made a firm decision not to have sex with him for at least a month.

Sunday was a nice day. Dave was nursing his hangover so he was lovely and quiet, the girls had decided to help me cook and Sam was around. Sam wasn't often around, he was always at the park, out on his bike or at a mates. He was a mild-mannered lad and a proper boy. Eat, sleep, do boy stuff, repeat, I had never had an issue with him beyond lost football boots or a black toenail. He was my easy one.

I had invited my parents over for dinner, which I did monthly. It took me the rest of the month to get over it. Mum and Dad were a travelling comedy show. My dad had been a lothario from the minute he was able to wink but he had been a good dad. He was at every netball match, he always waited up when we went out clubbing and he was pretty good at housework. He let himself down by acting like a dog on heat for most of their marriage and at his retirement party the only females in the room he hadn't slept with were his daughters. The room was full of retired PAs, cleaning ladies, even a lollipop lady and he had a special wink for them all.

Mum was an absolute nightmare, she had no filter, no compassion and no time for anyone apart from Mary Berry and Sean Connery. Everybody else was "just insufferable". Mum had been a legal secretary, a very efficient one and not a hair was out of place. She and Dad had their routine and they existed alongside each other quite nicely. Suzannah and Phillip read separate copies of The Times at either end of the dining room table with their glasses on their noses. That's who they were.

"Hello Mum, hello Dad." I opened the door of the burgundy Mercedes and my mum got out side saddle and smoothed down her skirt. "Why the headscarf, Mum?"

She looked at me as if I were stupid. "Because of the wind, Raquel, and your father's breath, I washed my hair last night." She looked like the queen when wandering the gardens at Balmoral.

"Hello darling." Dad walked around the bonnet and gave me the biggest hug. "What are we having for lunch? I am starving."

"Will you stop! Just stop thinking about food for one minute. We talk about lunch at breakfast, dinner at lunch, it's quite unbearable." Mum scolded Dad for everything and Dad just ignored her.

"It's pie day, Dad. Steak pie or chicken and leek with lots of vegetables and crumble for dessert." Dad rubbed his hands together and went into the lounge where Dave was lying on his side, sweating.

"Pie followed by a crumble, it's a good job I have Gaviscon in the glovebox. Honestly, have you heard of a light lunch, Raquel?" Mum looked at my stomach and walked stiffly into the house. Jesus Christ, it would be one of those afternoons would it, Mum had left her manners at home, as she used to say to me when I involuntarily sneezed.

My kids knew what to expect with Grandma. They knew she liked clear talking, not mumbling, she liked to have her coat taken and to be hung up not on a hook but on a hanger and she liked a gin and tonic, double with ice. Between the three of them they made all of that happen, leaving me to go into the utility room and punch a cushion as hard as possible.

"The garden is looking overgrown, has David forgotten about it?" Mum sat in the lounge looking out of the window to the front lawn.

"No, David has been working actually and David will get round to it soon," said Dave, who had managed to sit up by this point and was already sparring with Mum.

"Why are you talking about yourself in the third person? It's very odd." Mum doesn't even look at Dave when she asks this, she doesn't think he is worth the muscle movement. "You should get a gardener, you can afford a gardener. Phillip, give them the number of Old Tom, he can get this sorted."

Old Tom was the grumpiest and most depressing person in Cheshire. He was my dad's second cousin and was one of those blokes that did all the shit jobs nobody wanted. Never married, no wonder, had no friends, wore the same clothes for at least the last thirty years and I am sure he lived in a war bunker. I could not find a reason to feel sorry for this guy, very unlikeable. He said one word when I wrapped my new mini around a set of temporary traffic lights and wrote it off. "Clumsy," that was it.

"No way is Old Tom coming here, Mum, he makes me want to cry just looking at him."

"I am sure he feels the same way darling."

See what I said about Mum and Suzy? They are the same person.

We sat down to eat around 3 pm. Dave had a second wind and managed to keep half a bottle of red down so was much less spicy with Mum. Dad had tucked his napkin into the V of his jumper and was waist deep in pie crusts for forty solid minutes. The kids told my parents how they were getting on at school, all exaggerated on my instruction, of course. Mum would not be impressed with average grades or making the B team so I always said to the children, "Add 25% on to all of your achievements when talking to Grandma, it's just easier that way."

When the burgundy Merc pulled away, I finally felt I could stop holding in my stomach and start swearing again. "Drive fucking safely!" I shouted down the driveway, knowing she couldn't hear me. I had just finished the last of the washing-up when I heard lots of laughter and commotion from the lounge; the laugh was a cackle that I would recognise anywhere. CeeCee, Dave's Mum, had mastered the art of Zoom during lockdown and made it a thing to call us from their sunny balcony at least twice a week.

"Last week, David, your old man and his pétanque team won the regional finals, what a larrrf." She cackled again, it was infectious. Pétanque was basically a bowling game that old people did so they could day drink with a good excuse.

"Fantastic Dad, have you got a trophy?" Dave's dad, Gary, loomed over his mum's shoulder pointing to a big gold medal around his neck.

"What do you fink this is son, a necklace?" On closer inspection, the medal was a replica of a chocolate coin on a red ribbon, it was hardly Olympian but Gary seemed well chuffed.

"Allo darlin." CeeCee waved at me from her wicker chair. She was wearing every piece of jewellery she owned, it was surprising she could lift her arm up. I love Dave's parents, they have the ability to make anyone feel safe. They are everything a London cabbie and a M&S customer services supervisor should be – down to earth, friendly, kind, see the best in everyone and live life to the full. They took that nest egg, retired and make the most of life. Sure they are creaky in places and both have skin like a snakeskin handbag, but they are glass half-full people with a cocktail umbrella and a glazed cherry to boot. They literally give no fucks about appearances; Gary once used a bin bag instead of a suitcase for a trip to the Caribbean because it reduced the weight of his luggage. "Those bastards have had enough of my money," he told the people behind him at check-in. He arrived in St Lucia with two pairs of Y-fronts and one Hawaiian shirt, the rest of it was never seen again. But even then, they had the time of their lives, made friends for life and used this a lesson learned. Next time, he double-bagged.

"How many drug dealers you caught this week then, David?" CeeCee is so proud of Dave, he is the apple of her eye. Dave is an only child, or at least he is now. Dave's older sister Julie had sadly, very sadly, died from a drugs overdose as a teenager. She wasn't a druggie, she was actually quite an introverted young girl, quiet and timid. She was one of those people that just got unlucky, went to a club in the early 90s, took a pill she bought for a tenner to try and fit in and it wiped her out. By the time CeeCee and Gary arrived at the hospital she was being kept alive by a machine. They turned it off three days later and, from that day, all their eggs were in Dave's basket. David did not disappoint, he is a warrior for what's right and good, no-nonsense Dave who is good to his mum and dad and joined the police force. It was the best outcome to a tragic story; I admire all three of them.

"When my operation finishes, Dad, we will fly out and I will smash all you old codgers at bowls or whatever it is."

Gary put his hands behind his bald head and chuckled. "In your dreams, son, in your dreams."

We had a few laughs and a stupid game of 'Who am I?' with the kids and the in-laws on Zoom. They had never heard of Greta Thunberg and Michaela got a right bollocking from Dave after the call had finished for being a clever dick.

"Next time do Paul Daniels, someone they know for Christ's sake, Mic."

Michaela googled Paul Daniels and looked appalled.

A nice family weekend ended with my dad calling to confirm

they had arrived home safely.

"Beautiful pie, Raquel, absolutely marvellous."

"How's Mum?"

"She is lying down with a hot water bottle on her stomach, she said that pastry is not a friend of hers."

I rolled my eyes. "Oh Dad, god bless you."

My dad then slipped into the conversation very sneakily, or at least that's what he thought, that he was going on a two-day trip with his metal detecting club and could I keep an eye on Mum. So the following week whilst my dad was "detecting boobs", I would have to keep Mum busy and off his case.

Monday morning was, as always, absolutely stupid. "Where's my gum shield?" "What time is it?" "Who's farted?" A thousand annoying questions all being shouted out at once by three people. Once they had all been answered and I had filled up my car with hockey sticks, bags and kids, I did the two school drop-off. Two of them to the local comp and one to the local college. I could not bring myself to get out of the car in the rain and search for my non-cooking subject, but I needed to meet my deadline. The mums at secondary school are less offensive than they are at primary. They don't stand around for hours talking in bitchy whispers and sneering at one another. Secondary school was more like a drive-by, the cars barely stopped moving as teenage kids were literally kicked out of the car by hungover and menopausal mothers. I knew some of the parents because they had come through from the lower years but I liked to keep interaction to a nod or a short wave. I kept my windows firmly up in the car park and lay low in the seat in case one of them came up to the window with a sponsorship form or, god forbid, the suggestion to socialise. I had once made the grave mistake of accepting an invite to a dinner party at one of Sam's friend's parents. I knew when I saw TTFN at the end of the invite, I should not have agreed. I will start with the food; spaghetti Bolognese on a Saturday night made from a jar and with mince that I know for a fact was Quorn. The portions were so big that even Dave couldn't finish it, he didn't want to.

The company was even worse, the whole night was spent talking about sex with three other couples I had never met before; sexual positions, anal sex, sex with vegetables, don't ask. There was a carrot in that pasta and the visions I had kept me awake for weeks. Their Irish wolfhound Sadie took a shine to me and I spent the whole night with its smelly wet head on my lap. "Never again!" I said to Dave in the taxi on the way home. And I used so much mouthwash that night, my gums burned.

I called my sister from the car on the way home from the school run to confirm the arrangements for the girls over the summer.

"Melon!" She hated that.

"Raquel, I don't have long, I am in court in twenty minutes."

"I'll make it quick, then."

"Please do!" God she was short.

"Suzy and Michaela want to come on July 20th, they are staying for a month?"

"Yes, I will have everything arranged for them, Roger will collect them from the airport and I have taken some holiday so we can do some cultural things together."

"Well I will come over for a couple of days halfway through, OK?"

"Yes fine but can you please try and be civil towards Roger, he is still very upset about the text you sent to him."

"I have apologised, I sent a silver fountain pen."

She sighed, "That really doesn't cut it, Raquel."

"OK, I will try."

She sarcastically replied,"Will you really?"

The year before Roger had purposely blurted out that Dave and I were going to Portugal for Christmas. I was breaking the family tradition of going to The Falcon, a restaurant we had frequented every single Christmas Day for years. CeeCee and Gary had joined us for the few years they had before they moved abroad but after the pandemic it sort of broke the tradition. I knew that The Falcon meant a lot to my parents so when we were out of our bubbles and had all been jabbed, they presumed we would resume as normal. I had, however, agreed with Dave that it was only fair to give his parents a Christmas with their grandchildren. I had discussed this with my sister and she completely understood – in fact I think she fancied having Mum and Dad in Ireland and all to herself. We were very apprehensive about how my dad would take it. We agreed to leave it until November, giving him less time to feel sad about it. But Roger had other ideas and, on a point-scoring mission, he very spitefully announced that he was looking forward to a "child-free, stress-free Christmas". He said this in July. My dad was heartbroken, Mum shook her head and Roger took pleasure in what he did. So yes, I called him a little bitch on a message and sent it to him from across the table whilst looking at him menacingly. Of course he made excuses that he was trying to make it easier by ripping off the plaster, but there was malice in his actions and I called him out. The thing with passive aggressive people is you can't ever really nail them down when they have done something nasty. They always leave the possibility that this was your mistake and the interpretation is wrong. I hate that about him. "Don't you look well" means you are rosy and massive. "Gosh that's different" means the hair you just had cut makes you look like a mental patient. "This cake is moist" means it has the consistency of a wet sock, and so on, all delivered with that Tony Blair smile – would they murder you or kiss you? So, I would need to somehow be nice to Roger and pretend that I was sorry; it wouldn't be hard, I would do it in the evening after a day on the sauce.

To: Jane Aldgate
From: Raquel Fitzpatrick

Morning Jane, love the idea. Will need to start looking for my victim so I can get on with this. Can you send me the photography dates so I can get things in place? We will need to use a studio kitchen as mine is hammered, won't look good in a mag and always full of people.

Will come back to you soon with something written down.

Have a good week,

Raquel

I booked the girls' flights, ordered three-hundred quid's worth of loungewear from Zara to go to the shops in, cleaned out my fridge and made a lamb stew for that night before eventually starting to write an article with the subject name pencilled in.

Inserting the name 'Matt' into my article felt quite risky. It was when Gina had brought back my antique plate (which had obviously been through their dishwasher) that I had the idea. I felt the plate as she handed it to me and I thought about the Victorian potter who had created it by hand, probably by candlelight, whilst his family fought the consumption. Sure he would be thrilled to see his pattern fading away in a metal machine whilst being pummelled with boiling water and detergent. However, looking at the positives, at least it was clean.

Gina was visibly disturbed by my kitchen, there were veg peelings on the table and a pile of lamb fat on a plate on the island. She asked where she should put her handbag because it was Michael Kors and it meant a lot. I hung it on the back of a chair. She had told me that Matt had parted company with his IT job and was taking a break before going back to work. There were differences of opinion with his boss and a monitor was thrown plus somebody dropped the c bomb so they decided that it would be best if Matt left the building with a security officer to ensure he drove away. Gina was not perturbed by the loss of a job or that her husband was unable to control himself. She said, "It wasn't meant to be" and found it all quite hilarious.

I had made Gina a peppermint tea which she sipped through black lips. Black lips, black fingernails and the black tunic which she wore for straightening out faces. She was on her way to work and she, yet again, looked flawless if not demonic. This poor girl really had her hands full with the dimwit whose only plan for the day was to watch Lorraine and do a hundred sit-ups.

"He can't cook, you know, I've had to make him sandwiches with clingfilm over for his lunch, Raquel."

The cogs had started turning – can't cook, lives close, has a kitchen that looks camera-ready, has plenty of spare time on his hands.

"What if I gave him some lessons whilst you were at work?"

She looked genuinely grateful. "Really, you could do that?"

"Yes, in fact, I would make it a project."

She was thrilled, so thrilled I had to accept a hug.

"Ah babes, that's ace that. Can we have grilled chicken?"

"Let's not run before we can walk, Gina."

And she left having sent me Matt's number so I could make him a chef by the time she got home from work.

Work

During my time with my agency 'Eat' I had been given a large number of mind-numbing projects. In the early days, when everybody drank smoothies instead of food, I almost stabbed myself in a main artery with a courgette just to let people know I disagreed with the concept. There were literally three years when solid food was deemed a criminal act and if you were seen with a sandwich or a bowl of pasta you were deleted as a person. Turning up outside school without a green juice in your hand was about as bad as feeding your kids Turkey Twizzlers so, as a former chef, it was a very difficult time.

For instance kale, don't even get me fucking started on this 'superfood' that could cure anything from Parkinson's to big ears – they gave this fuzzy green nonsense more kudos than Jesus Christ himself. I had to work with these fads and trends because that's what the people wanted, I was forced into following the science and we all know where that gets us.

I am ashamed to say I wrote a twelve-week programme on eating lean protein and any vegetable that was more than fifty percent water. Bella magazine received endless photographs of slim brown legs, tape measures around waists and pictures of couples who had "got their lives back". But six months on those photographs just stopped coming and the success stories tapered – the mailbox was empty. Nobody at Bella gave a shiny shite until one day, one of these dutiful readers sent an image of the truth. Sandra of Bristol, who had lost six stone and three chins due to my advice, had one day walked past Greggs the bakers and was drawn to a vanilla slice like a lamb to the slaughter. To say the flood gates opened was an understatement. She spent most of the day sitting in a car park in her Ford Fiesta, ploughing through various pastries having what she called "a well-earned treat". Fast-forward just a matter of weeks and Sandra of Bristol was buying underwear in a size 18, fast-forward a few months and the fire brigade took the side of her house off to get her out of the bath.

"Bella magazine has a lot to answer for," said Sandra whilst having her bedsores dabbed with TCP.

I felt slightly responsible, but I was prepared to divide my guilt equally with Greggs the bakers, NCP car parks who really should have moved this woman on, and Ford because they should have stopped the seats reclining so far back. Plus, of course, Sandra herself who should have punched herself in the face before sausage roll number fourteen. The point here that I am trying to make is that diets only work so long as you adhere to them for life. If you stray from the path, the weight will be waiting down an alleyway like a Salford mugger to rob you of your waistline. So no, I did not always agree with what I wrote but I wrote it anyway.

I'd also had some fun along the way – a well-known chef who I must not name but who had rubbery lips and a boring wife invited me to the opening of his new restaurant chain. My friends and I had a fabulous meal, mediocre wine and a bird's-eye view of said chef behaving like a two-year-old without its dummy. A front row seat watching this tosser have a full-on meltdown over balsamic vinegar was a joy. It's not that deep, chef, chill the fuck out. I got on with my job good or bad and I used my money for the fun stuff. Like the time I flew Dave and his cronies up to Gleneagles to play golf for a few days for his fiftieth. I put a grand behind the bar and booked them three twin rooms. They had a ball! I doubt the staff did though. Six grown men wearing tartan skirts with not particularly attractive knees singing "Ya cannae throw yer granny off the bus" in the clubhouse at 1 am was possibly not what The Gleneagles Hotel was about. However, I paid for that without touching the joint account and it was nice to be able to do that.

My work also keeps the kids up to date with technology, they always have the latest phone, iPads, laptops … we live in a culture where you get cyberbullied if you're not on trend with Apple. In my day we just got our heads kicked for having a shit coat or spat on for having a Matalan shell suit (true story). Nowadays, in fear of my kids being targeted, I just keep up with the Jones' and buy them what they want. Possibly a parenting mistake that will come back and bite me but I am sure we'll trawl through it all with an online therapist called Janet at some point.

Matt was in a tracksuit when I arrived at Number 23, the sort of tracksuit you would see a celeb wearing as they were going into rehab. Soft and grey, like a babygrow really, and he had his signature socks and sliders to complete the 'One more for the road' look.

"Alright luv." He led me into the kitchen which smelt of bleach.

"Have you been cleaning? It smells fresh in here."

Matt smirked. "No luv, the cleaner's been cleaning." He pointed to the floor where a very small old woman was wiping the skirting boards on her hands and knees with a jay cloth whilst grunting.

I was startled, I almost stood on her.

"Hello." She looked up revealing a crumpled and sad face, she lifted her hand to acknowledge me, but said nothing.

"She can't speak a word of English, she's from abroad." Matt grabbed both her shoulders and almost lifted her up. He then said very closely to her face, "Go upstairs please," and pointed to the ceiling. The old lady nodded blankly, took a bottle of bleach and left the room. It was really quite odd. She looked like she had wandered out of a convalescent home and come to the wrong house.

"That's Barbara that is, she's our cleaner. She's dead old like but she does a good job."

This woman did seem too old to be doing such a physical job and, quite frankly, since Matt was now bone idle he could have done the work himself. I was annoyed at him already and we hadn't even started working together. This was going to be tricky.

"OK, well can we sit down so I can ask a few questions, please?"

Matt smiled, his eyes were actually amazing, mesmerising even. Damn!

"Let's ave it then girl, fire away." I took out my laptop and started to get an insight into what this man put into his stomach.

"What is your favourite food?"

"Lasagne."

"Can you make that yourself?"

"Yeah, three minutes in the microwave and bingo."

I winced.

"What would you normally have for breakfast?"

"Frosties or Coco Pops."

"Do you like vegetables?"

"Roast potatoes, mash potatoes, boiled potatoes and ... what's the name of that creamy one?"

I raised my eyebrows. "Smash?"

"Nah mate, you get it in restaurants, dead creamy."

"Ahh, you mean dauphinoise?"

"Yeah that's it, but I can't say that so I just ask for creamy ones."

"Of course you do. Can you cook a meal from scratch? That means without using anything that is ready-made?"

He shuts his eyes for a moment. "I once made a roast dinner for me and Gina's mam."

"OK, what did that consist of?"

"Beef, potatoes, peas, gravy, carrots and Yorkshire puddings, I love them I do."

"So you cooked the Yorkshires from scratch?"

"Yeah I put them in the oven."

"Did they come from the shop already looking like Yorkshire puddings?"

"Yeah but they were cold and needed heating up."

"Okey dokey then." I died inside. I shut down my laptop and had a rethink. "Matt, I think that we should start by making something, a simple dish and let's try and gauge if this is something you enjoy and could actually do."

Matt looked positive, energetic even. He got up from his seat and started opening the cupboards and chanting, "Pasta bake, noodles, soup, beans." He was listing the terrible things he had in his cupboard that all either needed to be microwaved or have water added to them. "Rice pudding, sweetcorn ..." I put my hand out to stop him.

"I think we should take this to my house, I have the stuff that we need."

Matt and I, a most unlikely combination, went across the road where Matt could begin his training. This guy had no limit to his comedic talents. When I bent over to get a saucepan from a low cupboard he blew a raspberry and then laughed at his own joke.

"Does your husband like football?" he asked, flicking at a photo of him and the kids on the fridge.

"Yes when he has time."

"Is he a red?"

"He's an Arsenal, whatever colour that is."

"Arsenal, how come?"

"Because he's a Londoner."

"Shame."

"Shall we get on with the cooking, Matt?"

Matt was relatively quiet for the next couple of hours, he concentrated, he listened, he was willing to learn. Look at me writing a thirty-five-year-old man's school report. He found the whole one-pot concept absolutely genius. I explained he could make a delicious dinner using only one vessel hence less washing-up and brownie points from the missus.

"Who knew?" he screeched in his silly accent. "Nice one."

We high-fived a lot that day.

I sent him back to Number 23 with a coq au vin and a Tupperware of mashed sweet potato that he had peeled and mashed himself. He wasn't too bad, he was actually the perfect subject, blank canvas and all that.

I decided to try and put pen to paper before the school pick-up and sat in my office with a coffee pondering on what to teach young Matthew next. A blacked-out Range Rover pulled up outside 23 and a guy in aviators let himself into Matt's house. It was all a bit Men in Black as the engine continued to run whilst this man was in the house. I went down onto my knees and looked through

37

the bottom slit of the wooden Venetians, it actually hurt to stay in this position but I was intrigued. Within ten minutes the aviator came out of the front door and was back in the car which sped off fairly quickly. There was no sign of Matt, I wondered if he'd been roughed up. Had he been dipping his pen in the company ink? Is that why he left his job? I could see it, he wasn't clever enough to embezzle fifty grand but he was certainly capable of giving the boss's wife one in the disabled toilet. Yes, that was probably it, he would have a fat lip by tomorrow. I hoped the swelling would go down before any photos were taken.

That evening Dave and I had parents' evening for Michaela. Rather disgustingly, we now had to drive to school in person and discuss our daughter's education. The past two years I had worn pyjamas to these events from the comfort of my lounge, Covid-19's greatest gift to mankind was the lack of effort required to meet people in person.

Dave met me outside St Mary Magdalen's School, a colleague dropped him off as they had been working until late. He smelt of lager and cigarettes and was quite short with me as we waited outside the maths department.

"You could have made an effort, Dave, you have a noodle on your shoulder." Dave swiped it off and it landed on the empty chair next to him.

"I've been working, Raquel, but we still have to eat."

"Were you working at a brewery or in a tobacco factory?"

"We had a working dinner, people smoke and people drink, that's life."

I sensed he was stressed, perhaps the dealers had slipped through his fingers. I imagined Robbie Coltrane in Cracker puffing on a cig at the docks and the criminals sailing away on a ferry with their middle fingers firmly up.

"I hope things are going well with Dachshund?"

He put his arm around me. "Things are going to plan, it's just been a tough day. Sorry, I am up against it at the moment."

Our names were called and we went into the classroom to

see Mrs Bayley, Michaela's super pretty maths teacher. The classrooms stank of children who had worn the same uniform for a week. I don't know how Mrs Bayley could endure trying to control a bunch of fifteen-year-olds whilst inhaling this odour.

"Michaela, Michaela. OK, yes, she's doing fine." She browsed a single piece of paper with three sentences at the top.

"Just fine?" Was that it? I had got dressed and left the house for this shit, a little more description please.

"Yes, fine, she's average across the board. She is on time, homework is done, no disruptions in class so I would say fine."

Dave was looking at his phone under the desk because a message had come in. I nudged him.

"Thanks very much, darlin." He stood up to leave.

"Sit down. We still have four minutes." I pulled his sleeve towards the chair. He sat back down looking disorientated. "So how do we get her to a level above fine?" I was going to squeeze her for more, that was her job, to get the best out of kids, right?

She flicked her short brown hair and sighed far too deeply for my liking.

"Mrs Fitzpatrick, I like to use the term, 'if it ain't broke, don't fix it'. We are happy with her progress and there are no concerns, I think that's a good thing."

"Do you?" I was annoyed at her beauty and calm attitude. I tilted my head to one side. "Have you seen the film Dangerous Minds?" Dave shook his head and looked at the floor.

Mrs Bayley screwed up her face. "Remind me, what is that about?"

I leaned back into the chair and prepared to educate Miss Sassy-pants on how they taught kids in the 90s. "Tough inner-city school, kids running amok, Michelle Pfeiffer – do you know who she is?"

Bayley shook her head.

"Well, she plays a teacher who will literally do anything to get her kids to graduate high school, she gets involved in their homelife, she earns their respect, she goes all maverick and off piste. It really is very good. Anyway the point is …" and then I was interrupted by a horribly loud buzzer and it ruined my momentum.

"I'm sorry, we'll have to leave it there." Bayley had a smirk on her face that I did not care for, Dave was as red as he's ever been and was desperate to leave.

"If I get chance around all the marking, I will give that film a watch." She then gave Dave a sympathetic look which was absolutely unacceptable.

I shut the door and whispered to Dave, "Lazy cow!" and then as I stormed off up the corridor, I passed a man peeling a noodle from the seat of his pants.

The rest of the evening was much the same, these teachers had no oomph, no pizzazz. At primary school there would be piles of paintings with the kids' names on the bottom and charts with gold stars to show how utterly adorable not to mention intelligent they were. Somebody once described Sam as a young Stephen Hawking and I had never been prouder. I immediately called my mum to tell her the news and she said, "Yes I can see that, he does dribble rather a lot."

These teachers were bland as hell, churning out the same words in a different order with no thought, no personality. It made me want to send my kids to downtown Detroit to be educated by Michelle Pfeiffer at gunpoint. At least there would be passion.

The following morning, I had planned to take Matt to Waitrose for some shopping for his next lesson. I tooted the horn outside 23 and he waved out of the bedroom window, he wasn't even dressed and it was 10 am. At quarter past he got into my car.

"Soz about that, I had to have a shower."

Was this man ever dry? I scanned his face for injury after yesterday's visitor but there was nothing to see. Interesting, I thought, they must have been body blows.

It felt quite naughty to be wandering around Waitrose with a man ten years my junior, people were looking, or at least that's how it felt. Matt insisted on pushing the trolley, every now and then he jumped onto the handles and free-wheeled in the aisles. It pissed everybody off but he didn't notice. I did a couple of selfies at the fish counter for the article and we both put our thumbs up in front of a monkfish. It caused quite a stir and I got the impression people thought I was his carer. I heard one lady voice her concerns over how I would handle him physically if he got nasty; it amused me.

At the till, Matt told me a story of when he was little and how his nan would always let him go on the children's ride after the big shop in the foyer of Morrisons. But because she was skint and lived on a state pension, she would just rock it with her hands and sing a song instead of putting in the twenty pence, it was the highlight of his week apparently.

On the way home I made polite conversation.

"How did you and Gina meet?"

"At a club in Ibiza about nine years ago, she was on holiday with her boyfriend. What about you and your fella?"

"We met at a wedding. He was best man, I was chief bridesmaid."

"Dirty dog," Matt sniggered

"So you stole Gina off some poor sod, then asked her to marry you. Where did you get married?"

"We got married in the Maldives, just the two of us, what about you?"

I recalled my wedding day, it was a bit of a shitshow to be honest. My wedding dress was far too tight and gave me crippling stomach pains, Dave's so-called friends had waxed his eyebrows off on his stag do and they hadn't grown back in time and he gave me the creeps. My sister had insisted on bringing Roger, who she had only known a few weeks and he had a 'fall' on the church steps so at least half an hour was all about him and his pussy elbow. And then, the cherry on the cake; the best man's speech was delivered by a very stupid person who told a sordid story about Dave, a Bangkok ladyboy and blow job that went on far too long. My mother was green.

Matt howled at the whole debacle. "That's fucking boss that is." Tears were streaming down his face. "Maldives was alright, we had one of those floating breakfasts and a couple's massage from two midgets." He cracked his neck as he told me. "Then at night, cause it was too hot in the day, we went to a beach and did the ceremony, like. We got matching tattoos when we got back as well, you know, to mark the occasion."

"Whereabouts?"

"About three mile from Heathrow."

"No, where is the tattoo?" I wondered if he had 'Gina 4 Matt' on his forearm.

"Oh right, soz." He undid his seat belt, pulled down his jogging bottoms and turned to the side revealing a very tanned buttock and thigh. I nearly hit a tree.

"Can ya see it? Bottom left." I glanced down and saw a tiny green dolphin winking at me from underneath his boxer shorts. Give me strength!

"Yep, got that, thanks for that, please belt up again. Why the dolphin?"

He looked a bit sad. "Well we went on a dolphin hunting tour in the Maldives like and we didn't see any. Six hundred quid and fuck all. So, when we flew back into London, we thought sod this for a game of soldiers and now we can see a dolphin whenever we want … in the mirror, like."

"Excellent, genius."

We grappled with paella that afternoon – another one pot wonder – while Matt and I enjoyed talking about his childhood trips to Spain and how he lived on chicken, chips and Fanta Limon. He was visibly shocked that this fishy rice was Spain's national dish. "Fuck's sake, they kept that well hidden." He looked annoyed but I suspected that his palate would probably have rejected it at the time. A selfie with the paella and off he went after what I would call a pleasant day's work. He did ask me to stop the prawns from looking at him so I peeled them all before he left.

The last couple of weeks at school before the summer holidays, everyone lets things slip. I had stopped soaking the girls' white socks in Vanish and checking the kids were off devices before 10 pm. We were winding down and I was drinking on a school night which I tried extremely hard not to do. The problem was that Mum was staying for a couple of days and it was hard not to have at least something to take the edge off when she was around.

"Does David even live here, Raquel?"

"Mum, Dave is very, very busy at work, he works late most nights."

"That's just the spiel I used to get from your father when he was fumbling with his secretary in his office with the lights off."

I don't know how she knew they turned the lights off, maybe it's because she turned the lights off too.

"Dave is not having an affair, Mum, he is actually at work."

"You're probably right, he's not the looker your father was, he'd struggle to find a buyer." She chuckled away to herself, imagining loser Dave on Take Me Out with no takers.

"Mum, can you actually help me please, go and test Sam on his science, he has a test tomorrow." Mum took her Hendrick's and tonic and headed upstairs to Sam's bedroom. He would be furious but I had just about heard enough about her distrust and dislike of Dave.

Mum chose to ignore all of Dad's indiscretions, she had come from a world where everybody had a mistress and the wife got the good bits. She would never lower herself to ever approach any of these ladies with a 'keep ya hands off my man' slap round the face. She was dignified but I think this was why she was always so angry, she held things in. One day I was sure she was going to snap like a twig and murder one of these tarts with a broken bottle, the wheels would come off and she would be on a year-long killing spree. She came close to reacting once when Dad let the two worlds collide. We were at the golf club, the four of us, I can only have been about fifteen. We were sitting down for lunch when a well-dressed lady with a large chest who wasn't afraid to show it walked over to our table and said, "Hello Phillip, how are you? Is this your wife?" My dad immediately stood up and threw his napkin down. I heard him whisper, "Not here Sheila, not here." Mum did not even look up at this woman, she just dabbed the sides of her mouth and looked directly at Dad.

"You know the drill Phillip, get it done."

We all had a banana split for dessert and Mum shut the door on Dad's fingers as we were getting into the car. After that, Dad didn't work late for a while.

I decided to write more of my piece for 'Live Well' that evening whilst Mum watched Joanna Lumley pretending to get down and dirty with the locals in India. The kids had been forced into doing the same so I slipped away and wrote in the dark with a warm glass of white under my desk. Just as I was getting into my flow, I heard a car horn honk outside. I reversed on my chair wheels and assumed my position. Matt was getting into the mystery car I had seen the day before; into the back which was weird. Gina must have been going to bed as I saw her close the curtains to her bedroom with her nightgown on. Where was he going at … I looked at my watch … ten past nine? I mean it was none of my business and I wasn't his keeper, but we had a breakfast thing happening in the morning, I had hoped he'd be fresh. If this was another pummelling from a disgruntled husband, he was being very cooperative. I sat writing for a good couple of hours and Matt never returned home, all the lights were out at his house so it looked like he would be gone for the night. I went to bed feeling uneasy, don't know why, it was just a feeling.

School's Out

Within two weeks I had taught Matt seven dinners and seven lunches that were made from fresh and healthy produce. I had sat down with him one afternoon and gone through a budget for the week. He wasn't the slightest bit interested and wrote boobs on the calculator with two zeros and a couple of eights whilst I was trying to explain cost per portion. He was certainly more into the practical side of cooking, he liked to roll pastry and massage marinades into meat, he said he found squeezing the meat out of a sausage very satisfying and pulled an orgasmic face whilst he did it which I found very uncomfortable. He really was a big kid and I don't think he was allowed to make a mess at home so I tried not to be too strict. I had plenty of content for week one, we just had to get some amazing shots of him in his sparkly kitchen to create the illusion he had done it all in there.

Gina had popped in a couple of times to thank me for giving her husband a purpose. She said she had never eaten so well and patted her skeletal ribs through her tunic. This woman worked hard, she left the house before eight and some days she didn't return for twelve hours. Those Michael Kors totes would soon be Chanel if she kept up this pace. It was hard to believe that Manchester had so many crumpled foreheads and I did make a note to self to consider having mine done.

I had given Matt the task of choosing a dish that he had always wanted to cook and told him to text it to me so I could write a shopping list for our next meeting.

Suzy had manipulated me into holding a BBQ to celebrate the end of term, I had agreed reluctantly. I had come to realise that teenagers are more trouble than toddlers. At least toddlers went to sleep … eventually. At least you could wipe their faces with a cloth and strap them into a pushchair tightly when the shit hit the fan. The drama, the mess and the attitudes of teenagers sapped all my positivity and I ended up just scowling at them all and hoping they would be arrested and sent to a boot camp. So although I agreed, I only agreed to a guest list of ten.

Luckily Sam was staying at a friend's and Michaela had gone to my mum's to get away from the party. She preferred a cheese board and an evening with Attenborough.

It was a Friday evening on the last day of term and the weather was a bit gloomy, Dave was in charge of the grill so black sausages with a salmonella filling were top of the menu. The garden was littered with idiotic teenagers all called Gracie, Poppy, Molly, Daisy, etc. and they all looked exactly the same; poker straight hair, highlighted cheekbones, cargo pants and crop tops. Every single one of them pouted into their phones on the hour and then sent their reflection to TikTok. They nibbled the food, not one full item was eaten and they looked disgusted at the fact that Dave and I were present in our own house, even my own daughter.

"Go for a walk will you, stop watching us." Suzy hissed at us to go away.

Dave was swigging from a can and flipping burgers whilst scanning the garden for the possible passing of a bag of pills.

"We're not going anywhere, Suzy, you are seventeen, anything could happen." He was having none of it. Suzy fumed, her style was cramped and she had some strange idea that this was going to become her crib for the night and that we would book a B&B and give her free rein.

"Oh my god, this is so embarrassing. Gracie had a party at Christmas and her parents went on holiday, actually left the country."

I tried to calm the situation down. "Actually Suzy, her parents didn't even know about the party until her mother found a used condom in the bread bin."

She glared at me. "That was her brother's actually Mum, nothing to do with us!"

I very much doubted it was as I saw the little oik itching his scrotum at the bus stop the following week.

"We will go upstairs if that helps but we are not leaving the house." Suzy flounced off back to the teenage coven and whispered awful things about us.

Dave and I lay on the bed and scrolled through our phones, the terrible music from the garden was turned up even louder and I checked my watch willing midnight to arrive, it was flipping nine o'clock for god's sake, three hours until I could eject them all.

"How's it going with the Scouser and your feature?" This was a very rare moment, Dave taking an interest in my work, Dave lying on the bed not snoring and farting intermittently, Dave actually being in the house was all unfamiliar territory to me.

"He's alright you know. I think the readers will relate. He's gone from buying everything ready-made to actually buying veg from the Farmer's Market."

Dave looked unimpressed. "He's not gonna keep that up after you've finished, though. He might be doing that now whilst you're involved but he'll be back on the ready meals the minute you're done. Remember that woman Sandra from Bristol, you're lucky she didn't sue." Negative Dave strikes again.

"He might … he's not working at the moment so he has plenty of time on his hands and for your information, this is not a diet thing, this is a cook from scratch thing."

Dave eye rolled. "There's a difference? What's he like? Do you get on with him?"

I found myself smiling, really smiling, another rare thing to happen that day. I thought about the giggles we'd had when I explained that Welsh rarebit wasn't a flattened bunny with cheese on top. How we'd belly laughed when he had thrown the tips of the asparagus in the bin and kept the stems. It was silly really but perhaps the banter king had lifted my spirits a bit, made me feel younger, he actually seemed to like being around me.

"We work well together, he fits the brief."

Dave went back to his phone and that probably would be the last time he talked about my work for a long time.

I had dropped off with my phone in my hand when the door burst open. Holly, Molly or one of them was standing crying at the bedroom door.

"I need to go home now and the taxi line is engaged." I rubbed my eyes and realised there was a crowd of them on the landing.

"What the fack is going on?" Dave stood quickly, his pyjama bottoms were riding very low and the group of girls all gasped in unison and disgust.

"Pull those up for chrissakes." I pointed to his trousers. He did immediately but so high he made himself into a Tellytubby.

Suzy appeared looking very bleary-eyed. "Mum please take her home, she liked Tom Branford's post on Insta and he is going out with Chloe, she's a snake!"

Holly or Molly started howling at this point, basically because she'd been rumbled. Chloe, the woman scorned, had her arms folded and a face like a slapped arse because it turned out Tom Branford had posted a heart in response to the like. Some of the other girls were starting to cry and I could smell a mixture of Prosecco and sick that made me want to cry too.

"Right, everyone downstairs right now please." Dave was completely bewildered and didn't even know what Instagram was. I told him to go to bed and to shut the door, the last thing this lot needed was a Tellytubby with its willy hanging out to add to the drama.

Taxis ordered and coats on, the girls sat in silence trying not to spin out apart from Suzy who was being annoyingly lairy.

"Who does she think she is? Stalking Tom on social media. She should get her own boyfriend." She was whispering this 'mean girl' style very loudly to another mean girl who was swaying.

"Can you shut up, Suzy, you are making this worse. Dad and I have put a nice evening on for you and this is how you behave." I gave it to my daughter because I expected more from her and she was normally quite reserved. She was incensed, threw her arms in the air and shouted, "Oh my god, it's not my fault, it's hers." And then she pointed at Molly/Holly who was retching into a frying pan on the back doorstep.

"How much have you had to drink?" I strong-armed Suzy over to the cupboard where I kept all the booze. It was almost empty bar some red wine and a bottle of Amaretto that I used for cooking. I had allocated three bottles of Prosecco and a weak punch for the evening – these girls were underage and I was married to the police.

"Wow, just wow. Your dad will hit the roof about this." She looked at least a little worried.

I poured ten glasses of tap water and demanded that all the girls downed them and before I managed to get them into two taxis and a minivan, I handed out paracetamol to numb the pain they would feel in just a few room-spinning hours.

"Get to bed! We will deal with this in the morning." Suzy sheepishly climbed the stairs in her mud-stained cargos knowing the following morning would not be pleasant.

I was wide awake by then so thought I would get ahead with the tidying up. It was quarter to one in the morning and as I picked up an empty bottle from the top of a rose bush in my front garden, the familiar black Range Rover glided passed quietly and stopped at 23. Matt got out and watched it drive away.

"Alright Matt, bit late for you this," I waved with the empty bottle in my hand.

"Err OK, just the one then." Matt, in yet another grey tracksuit, walked over to my front lawn under the illusion I had invited him over for a drink. It was too complicated to explain that he was mistaken so I took him inside and poured us both a whiskey, it felt like a whiskey type of night. I told him all about the party as I filled bin bags with uneaten meat and he kindly put all the dirty glasses on the outside table.

"Had a night out?" I enquired, it was the first time I had felt I could broach the subject without sounding too nosey.

"Err, just a bit of business." He squirmed a bit.

"Business at this time, what are you, an escort?" I laughed, he laughed.

"No, nothing like that." He sat down with his drink. "Just business, that's all."

And that was all he gave me.

"Is Gina OK?" I asked, wondering if she was aware of the

mysterious shenanigans. It seemed not.

"She's fine, she's at her mam's in Liverpool for the weekend, it's her sister's baby shower."

I imagined the Burberry pushchair, the Burberry babygrows and the Burberry everything else that would be pronounced 'Berberry' by a bunch of screaming women with skintight faces.

"That sounds lovely." I was not being genuine.

Matt and I sat on sunloungers looking up at the moon, me in my pyjamas, a top knot in my hair and no make-up, him in his grey onesie feeling completely at ease.

"It's been nice getting to know you and learning to cook and that." He looked at me right in the eyes when he said that, it was nice.

"It has, who knew, eh." We both smiled, we were both aware that this was a very unexpected friendship if I could call it that.

"So your daughter's party was carnage?" He changed the subject quickly.

"It didn't end well but what else can you expect, teenage girls are trouble – I know, I used to be one."

"When I was her age, it wasn't a party unless an ambulance turned up." He said this proudly.

"When I was her age I didn't even have a phone, or Instagram."

"But Raquel, that was a very VERY long time ago, luv." He smirked and I thumped him on the arm.

"Had any thoughts on this dish you want to cook?"

He picked up his phone and went to the photographs, a picture of James Martin slicing open a perfectly cooked beef wellington was presented to me.

"That's what I want to be me signature dish."

"That's a tricky one, but we'll get there." I was confident I could get him trained up with practice.

I saw Matt to the door after the whiskeys had been drained.

"I'll send you the shopping list and we can get to work on this wellington on Monday."

"Ah nice one Raquel." He went to hug me, I went the wrong way and our lips met momentarily.

He laughed it off, I pretended to be mortified but I went up to bed feeling extremely alive.

Good god.

Mum and Dad's house was a nice old, detached cottage in rural Cheshire. Lovely gardens, a thatched roof and a windy path to the front door. Inside it was always a bit cluttered, it annoyed me and I felt the need to tidy much to Mum's dismay. Apparently they knew where everything was so it really was nothing to do with me. "Sort your own mess out, Raquel, starting with your hair, your husband's wardrobe, oh and your front garden." My mother was not impressed when I moved a pile of letters from the countertop to stop them getting wet.

"You wouldn't like it if I was to interfere with your life now would you? Leave things alone."

Excuse me, my mother's middle name was interference. She had told everybody that Dave was a just a volunteer police officer and that he was planning on becoming a chartered accountant. Apparently it sounded better. She told the guests at my wedding reception, she even told his colleagues this, they almost had a goodbye banner printed until Dave put them right. She also had the audacity to ask my hairdresser to call her before I had anything big done because I didn't know my own mind.

Dad was wearing a blue cardigan with leather patches on the elbow and blue shorts. He completed the outfit with an exhausted and harrowed look on his face. The years of enduring Mum's sharp tongue had taken its toll.

"She's only trying to help darling, let her do it, the place could do with a tidy."

Mum glared at him. "Well why don't you do it Phillip, or are you too busy with other things?" Mum was particularly angry that day, her hair had just been blown into the shape of a storm trooper's helmet and she had a shirt on which was buttoned right up to the top. This look meant trouble.

"I'll give the place the once over later today, darling." Dad knew he was close to the guillotine and was trying to pacify the storm trooper. I had just come to pick Michaela up but inevitably would be caught in the crossfire of my parents' differences, again.

"Why don't you get a cleaner, Mum, just a couple of days a week?" I didn't think she would go for it because since she had retired she had done the housework all by herself, badly.

Mum threw down the plum she was peeling for her god-awful chutney and said, "Yes actually, fuck it, let's get a maid."

Now my mum didn't swear, she hardly showed emotion, so something had happened and it clearly wasn't good.

"Where can I get one, an ugly one that your father won't have sex with?"

Dad's head lowered and he mumbled, "I'm going to get the papers." And with that he picked up the keys to the Jag and left the room without making eye contact with either of us.

"What the hell, Mum?" I walked over to her. This wasn't like her. Mum opened a very full drawer in the kitchen and pulled out a piece of paper. "Read that," she said sharply and threw it onto the table.

I picked it up hoping it wasn't from an oncology department, a natural conclusion when your parents are old. But it wasn't a 'six-months-to-live message', it was from good old Barclaycard who had very kindly listed my dad's antics in chronological order. Why the fuck didn't he go paperless? Duh.

Selfridges £243.60 (probably new undies and a pair of Ray Bans)

Boisdale £140.45 (swanky restaurant in Victoria)

And then the crushing blow, The Savoy hotel, London. £890 (a night of passion and a full English).

"The fucking Savoy, Raquel. That's where we have lunch on our wedding anniversary."

Mum was wired but looked sad, I had not seen this before.

"So he shops, he lunches and he takes some cheap tart to a hotel in London whilst I do what, stay at your house and leave stinking of stew?" I laughed a bit, a nervous laugh.

"I'm sorry, that was uncalled for." She apologised so this was very serious. She put her head in her hands. "We are in our

seventies! When will this end? Why isn't he slowing down?"
I put my hand on her shoulder which was a big mistake because her blouse was white and she didn't like being touched. I quickly removed it checking I hadn't left a mark.
"Tell him Mum, tell him that you won't accept it anymore."
She looked at me, small and vulnerable.
"But what if he leaves me? This is the way it's always been."
There were no answers, I was skirting with danger myself, the thought of the lip brush had not left my mind since the night before. I said nothing to Mum because I couldn't guarantee he wouldn't leave. The silence must have hit a nerve because Mum quickly pulled herself together.
"It's about time I lived for myself and that's what I will do. Get me a maid for starters, I'm not washing his underwear anymore, this mug is on strike." With that she went back to the plums and I was left wondering how this would play out.

On the way home I told Michaela about the party and the dramatic events, we both hoped that Suzy had been given a good bollocking by Dave whilst being dreadfully hungover. Michaela did not like Suzy's friends and thought they were pretentious morons. She wasn't wrong but then again her crew were annoying in their own way too, bookworms with opinions on politics and lacking the ability to have a laugh. She was very much like my sister.

I arrived home to find Dave's car gone, he had left a note saying he had to go into work. Who leaves notes in this day and age, I ask you? Sam's bike was dumped on the lawn and I found him in the kitchen toasting Pop Tarts.

"Oh my god Sam, these things have no nutritional value." I scanned the back of the box, I could have made a bomb with all the chemicals and blown up Kellogg's. He nodded his head.

"I know! That's what makes them taste so good."

Sam was blond and petite, he was well covered but quite short. He would have his father's figure quicker than anticipated if he continued eating this shit.

"Let me poach you some eggs."

"No thank you!"

"Please Sam?" I put the kettle on.

"Mum no, it's fine. I have to go out soon."

"Out? You only just got home."

"I'm meeting the boys at the park for a game."

"You'll eat properly tonight?"

"Yes, I'll be back for six."

"Fine. Take your phone."

"Will do!"

See what I mean about boys, easy, simple, no drama!

I spent the rest of the day getting the girls' clothes for Dublin, their flight was Monday morning and I needed to be organised. I texted Matt his shopping list:

Fillet of beef (tell the butcher what it's for)
A selection of mushrooms including portobello
Shallots (tiny onions)
Thyme (herb)
Parma ham (Spanish ham)
Ready-made puff pastry
Don't forget to save the receipt so we can reimburse.
Speak soon, R

I waited for a reply. Only one tick for over an hour, I checked my phone an embarrassing number of times. What the fuck was going on with me? Eventually, after ironing the last crop top, I took it all upstairs ready to go into the cases. My phone pinged in my pocket and my heart skipped a beat.

It was my mum:

Please ensure we have a maid for next week. Mum

What was I, a recruitment agent? Did I have a black book of cleaners I could call on whenever I liked? I didn't even have one myself. I didn't reply, I had nothing to say and too much to do.

Still no blue ticks from Matt and by teatime I was quite

annoyed. I was snappy with the girls, I didn't make any dinner for Dave and left a pizza menu on top of his note. The next morning, I decided to take matters into my own hands after having a bath, blow-drying my hair and putting on an insane amount of fake tan. I casually started to clear out my car whilst keeping a close eye on 23. My mind was racing, was he so disgusted by what almost happened that he had taken to his bed to sleep it off? Had he become wracked with guilt and spilled all to Gina who had then locked him in his bedroom without his phone? Was he dead? Had black Range Rover man finally put a bullet between his gorgeous eyes? I shuddered, not at the thought of the assassination but at the very image of me, a middle-aged woman, obsessing over a married man who didn't even own daytime clothes. I blamed the menopause; this must have been the start of it. I would be found in just my knickers wandering around a shopping precinct singing Abba songs, I have heard this can happen.

The old lady cleaning woman who I think was called Barbara made an appearance as I was locking up my car. She was cleaning the outside windows of 23 – what on earth, who has a cleaner on a Sunday? But, it gave me an idea. She was ugly enough for my dad to keep his hands off and she didn't speak English so she would not understand how rude my mother actually was. It also gave me an excuse to go over there and smell Matt's neck if we had the chance to hug. God I was pathetic.

"Yahoo, hellooo." I waved and shouted at the old woman who looked over and looked afraid. I jogged over, smiling.

"Hello there, remember me?" I spoke very slowly and loudly just as Matt had. The woman nodded, her wispy ginger hair came loose from her bun as she did so.

"Would you like another job?" Again she nodded.

"At my mother's house fifteen minutes away?" She just kept nodding. I started to realise that if I asked her if she would like shit on toast, she would still nod.

Is Matthew here … or Gina?" I pointed into the house. She opened the door and ushered me towards it; how very accommodating I thought, perhaps she had a CV in her cauldron.

The bleach was certainly being used without dilution by Barbara, the house was cleaner than an operating theatre, I would happily have a leg removed right there in the hall. Mum's house would be pristine and Dad wouldn't give this woman a wink, no way. She had more of a beard than he did.

I shouted for Gina and Matt but there was no sign of either of them. Barbara stood looking up at me, waiting for something to happen. We then played a frustrating game of charades where I acted out the well-known movie 'Will you come with me to my mother's and be her cleaner?'.

When I acted out the hoovering motion, she went into the kitchen and then handed me a cordless Dyson. It was no use, absolutely pointless.

"No, no no." I scolded her and handed it back.

"You," I pointed to her. "Hoover." I did the movement. "At my mother's," and I pointed at the front door. She then went outside and started hoovering a load of gravel up from their driveway. Give me strength.

I wrestled the Dyson, which was now smoking, from her hands. Her fingers reminded me of Twiglets, another favourite of Sam's. I had just managed to turn it off when she started to shout at me in a language I couldn't work out. Gina pulled up on the driveway just as this was all happening, looking quite annoyed. She said one sentence to this lady from her car window in what I think was Klingon and immediately Barbara scurried inside.

"What's going on here, Raquel?" This was a side to her I hadn't seen, she put on an official and attempted-posh accent. Odd!

"So sorry, I wanted to poach your cleaner for my mum but she couldn't understand me and, well, there was some confusion so she hoovered your driveway and–"

She stopped me. Her smile appeared but seemed somewhat fake, "Ahh babes, you should have just called me." I felt embarrassed, she was right, I really should have checked with her first.

"Yes, apologies, I didn't know there was nobody in, I thought Matt may be around." I checked the back seat of her car in case he was hiding from me and my wandering lips. "Matt's out at the moment sorting a few bits out for the salon. Tell you what, I will try and get your mum one of Barbara's friends, leave it with me." She didn't invite me in, she took a small suitcase from the boot of her car and just headed inside. She still looked amazing in her weekend clothes – jeans, a jazzy top and some very glittery flip-flops with toes perfectly painted. She didn't look back, she wasn't as friendly as usual. I wondered if she had started to feel uncomfortable about Matt and me. Maybe I did still have it, maybe I'd never lost it. The door shut abruptly and, as I walked away, I heard her shouting at Barbara quite aggressively in that language again. The dimwit was bilingual. Interesting.

Arif

Arif was a dark-haired, dark-skinned young man who spoke pretty good English and had diabolical teeth. Mum and I had taken him to Asda to get some bits and to show him around the place; not the Science Museum, not Tatton Park; we took our tourist to Asda, the big one just off the dual carriageway. Quite honestly, this whole debacle could not have been more ludicrous. Gina had somehow, without my knowledge, struck up some kind of friendship with my mother via text and between them they had organised for Barbara's nephew, Arif, to become my mother's new housekeeper. Dad had agreed to everything without a peep and had given the boy a key to their house and a ride in the Jag. Arif was smiley, willing and attentive and during the interview process he even unblocked the downstairs loo with a wooden spoon and a whisk.

"He is just the ticket!" cried Mum and after throwing the shitty utensils into next door's skip, she offered him the job. He called her Mrs, just Mrs, and seemingly, she was OK with that. He was eighteenish and had no clue about anything connected to old houses or old people as far as I could see but Mum said he would be "fun" to have around the place.

We wandered the aisles of Asda and Mum insisted on taking all the lids off the cleaning products to check their smell and suitability, she would then offer them to Arif for his opinion, he used the thumbs-up, thumbs-down process as the decider as to whether he could take them to 'Judges' houses'. We had a trolley full to the brim with Brillo pads, Brasso, descaler and some personal items for my parents – Anusol for dad and some pastel-coloured padded pants for Mum in case she was thinking of trampolining. We bought a Freddo for Arif for the journey home and with that he was ready to begin his new life as their skivvy.

"Just look at him. Breathe in the smell of youth, Raquel." I looked into my mirror to see Arif licking the Freddo and gazing out of the window.

"Are you sure this is a good idea, Mum, what teenage boy knows anything about housekeeping?"

"Don't judge people by your own lazy children's standards, Raquel, he needs a job to pay for his studies and I have one to offer, it's a suitable arrangement for both of us."

"Where are his parents? Do they know about this?" I was a parent myself, would I be happy if one of my kids stabbed other people's poo with a spoon for a living?

"His Aunt Barbara is responsible for him and he is from Uzbekistan or Kazakhstan or something like that, something ending in 'stan'. His parents live there and have nothing to offer him in the way of money so he has come to the UK for a better life."

Not really knowing much about the stan countries, my mind wandered to freezing cold winters, turnips boiling in pans of piss and children drinking milk straight from the teat of a goat; perhaps this was a better option for the boy, particularly if he could get an education.

I dropped Mum and Arif back at the cottage, I had no time to go in so I waited until Arif had carried all of the bags inside and then drove away feeling quite cool about the whole thing. He was too young to be a serial killer, his eyes were kind so I ruled out the possibility of him transferring their savings to his Uncle Borat's offshore account and the very fact he carried in the bags without Mum or Dad lifting a finger was good enough for me. It felt a little crazy but I had a good feeling about him.

Back at home I noticed there were no cars at 23 and no movement either. My feelings about the lip brush had calmed down, I hadn't seen Matt for a few days and the last message I had from him was quite unremarkable.

Been a bit busy, will see you soon. M

I had already sent over a good chunk of our work so far and we had pushed the wellington lesson to later that week. Gina had waved a couple of times from her driveway but I felt I should keep my distance since my altercation with her cleaner. Dave had been particularly grumpy and had been no help whatsoever with getting the girls off to Ireland – he wasn't even there to wave them off. He'd left before any of us woke and I found a pair of his underpants on the kitchen table which had definitely been worn. So, I was left to get two hormonal girls out of the door and four weeks' worth of luggage to drag down the stairs.

There was the usual almost missing the flight because somebody left their passport on the hall table debacle but, eventually, I handed my daughters over to the mercy of Ryanair and then on to the feckless wonder, Roger, who picked them up from the airport in my sister's car.

I spoke to Suzy on the second night and she was already struggling with Roger's ways.

"He's got a septic toe, Mum." She had spent the first evening being told a very long story about how Roger's big toe had started throbbing around January time, from there it swelled to the size of a Cumberland sausage – his description apparently – and by the time the podiatrist had got to it, it was oozing pus and he was sent straight down to Clarks for a pair of prescription sandals.

"It's disgusting, I can barely eat. He takes off the bandage in the evenings to let the air get to it." Her voice was whiny and weak.

"Just tell him that you have a foot issue and ask him to put a sock over it."

"As if, Mum, it's his house."

"It really isn't," I said bitchily. "What are you doing at the weekend?" I tried to divert the conversation.

"We are going out on a boat with a friend of Mel's, they have their own boat." She sounded excited.

"Nice, you'll love it."

"And then on Sunday we are going to a big posh house in the country for lunch at one of her colleague's homes."

"Fantastic, sounds wonderful. Put Michaela on the phone a minute, please."

"I can't, she's making a soufflé with the cook."

"The cook? Is there a cook?"

"Yes there's a cook on weekdays."

"I'm jealous."

"You should be, they don't even wash up, Nancy does it."

"Make sure you offer to help, we don't want them thinking you're lazy."

"OK, bye, call me tomorrow."

So my daughters were living it up in splendour and I was vanishing skids in underwear whilst being ignored by my husband. I had insisted that Dave meet me for lunch on the Thursday. We had not had any interaction for a while and I had surmised that my unhealthy obsession with the neighbour had come about as a result of this. So I booked a restaurant, nailed him down to a time and waited at our table in anticipation for a romantic lunch. He turned up to Swish Fish twenty minutes late and almost broke the chair as he crash-landed onto it. He was panting like a Labrador, which I did not find endearing.

"Can't be long." He wheezed as he said it. I was instantly annoyed, turning up late is one thing but to then announce that he was leaving very soon after pissed me off.

"Great, nice to see you too."

"Sorry, sorry, just been busy that's all." Dave was sweating, he had clearly been running which he was not really built to do. His phone was constantly buzzing and he was doing his absolute best not to look at it.

"Shall we order?" He waved his hand at a server and without even looking at the menu he said, "Whatever you think."

The waitress clearly got the vibe. "What about I bring you the lunch special, it's a mix of everything? Any dietary requirements?"

We both shook our heads.

"Can I ask how long this will take?" Dave tried to hurry the situation along.

"We make everything fresh so about fifteen minutes at a push." The waitress was very patient.

Dave looked at his watch and then looked at me. I folded my

arms and huffed.

"What, what do you want me to do? Bring you a fucking packed lunch, why do I bother?"

I was furious, I had driven to town to a restaurant near Dave's work, I had put on jeans which, by the way, felt like a straitjacket for the legs since my lockdown pastry problem. I had washed my hair, painted my nails and flossed every tooth in my head and for what? To be hurried along and be treated as an inconvenience.

"You know what, send me an email and let me know the next time you have a slot for me." And with that I flounced out of the restaurant without looking back. One thing I could guarantee is that Dave would have taken both lunch specials back to the cop shop and necked the lot.

Sorry Raquel. Will make it up to you. Will be home early tonight.

Extremely childishly, I replied:

Going out. Don't wait up.

I picked up Sam from the local leisure centre around 4 pm. He was dishevelled and muddy, his jogging bottoms had holes in the knees and he could have passed for a homeless person. I nipped him home so he could have a shower and change and then we made the journey over to my parents where we were to sample some of Arif's cooking. I ate two bananas and a packet of crisps in the car because there was not a chance in hell this was going to be edible.

On the drive, Sam told me about the amount of keepie-uppies he could do, how one of the lads from his year was trialling for City and how he wasn't interested in girls at all; just football and food.

"You're only twelve, mate, you don't even need to think about girls at the moment."

I think that a mother should call her son 'mate' whilst they are young to create a bond.

"Yeah don't call me, mate, it's weird."

"Oh OK, what do you want me to call you then?"

"Err Sam, cause that's my name."

"OK mate."

"How come Dad is never home?"

"Work, that's a priority right now."

"I never see him or get to speak to him."

"I know, I feel the same, I tried to have lunch with him today and it went tits up."

"Please don't say tits. Can he take me fishing?"

"Fishing, since when did you like fishing?"

"I like the look of it, so I want to try it."

"I could take you, there's a tackle shop in town."

"Err, no thanks. It's not a woman thing."

"That's pretty sexist actually, Sam."

"It's not just about the fishing, Mum, it's like a man thing, talking and stuff."

"You can talk to me, I can talk man stuff."

"Just ask Dad to take me, will you?"

"OK, I will ask him later. Now eat this banana or you'll regret it."

Sam took two bites from the banana and put it into the glovebox. Great.

Mum opened the door before we even got to it. She stood head to toe in a matching green kaftan and headscarf, with one arm leaning against the door frame. My dad hovered in the background wearing a velvet blazer, holding a tray with some pink drink in old crystal glasses. Had I passed through a worm hole and ended up in Marrakesh 1969?

"Mum, this is interesting." I stroked the fabric of the costume.

"This old thing, this is just something I threw on." Her hair was not as stiff that day, it was softer, it was blonder, she had dyed it. She seemed high.

Dad offered me what was described as a rosé-infused gin with elderflower tonic. I sipped it nervously wondering what the actual fuck was happening.

In the kitchen the table was laid and the strong smell pungent, North African spices filled the room. Candles were burning, the place was spotless – no letters piled up, no newspapers on the sofa, no sign of trouble either. Both my parents seemed gloriously relaxed if not a little mental.

"Come and see what I have found in the garden, Sam." My dad put his arm around Sam and took him out of the French doors onto a perfectly green and smooth lawn. The gardens at Duck Cottage were pristine. Mum and Dad had both become green-fingered in their retirement and trawled garden centres and nurseries endlessly. According to Dad, a man's garden said a lot about the man. If this was the case, my dad was green and bushy and smelt of peonies.

Arif appeared wearing one of Mum's aprons from her Mary Berry merchandise collection.

"Hello Mrs."

I offered him my hand to shake it and he kissed it – interesting and unnecessary. Mum held up six fingers and said, "We eat at six, yes?"

Arif nodded and pointed at the door with his spatula. "You go drink now."

Mum and I went outside where a selection of olives, dates and walnuts were sitting in little glass bowls waiting for us with napkins and cocktail sticks.

"You look great, Raquel, you really do." I screwed up my face waiting for the insult that would surely follow, but it didn't happen.

"Gosh, Mum, you've gone to a lot of trouble for a Thursday night tea."

Mum sat down, all hippy-like and chilled. "Not me darling, Arif. He has done all of this. He's a wonderful help."

"What, everything?" I glanced back into the house. The windows were gleaming, the place seemed so fresh and energised.

"Yes, your father and I have had the most amazing week. We went to lunch, we've had afternoon naps, we had a drive over to the coast yesterday and Arif packed us a picnic, we have been living life, not letting the small things get us down." Maybe Mum had been reading Gloria Hunniford's autobiography again but the first time she told me it was only good for killing spiders with.

At the bottom of the garden, I could see Dad and Sam in deep conversation over what I think was a dead mouse. Dad looked animated, perhaps even happy, there had certainly been a shift in the mood at Duck Cottage.

"Wow, Mum, what a turnaround. I was worried last week … for your marriage."

Mum chortled, "Oh that was just a blip, we've talked, I think we will be fine." She looked back into the house at Arif. "Now we've got him, things will be perfect."

We sat at the table whilst Arif put piping hot portions of tagine onto our plates. We had a crisp green salad from the garden and delicately flavoured lemony couscous. I marvelled at the fact my parents – my meat-and-two-veg-eating parents – were consuming something that originated from beyond the North Sea. I wondered how Mum's bowels would react to the shock, I really wish I hadn't.

Arif silently bustled around the kitchen ensuring we all had what we needed. I was seriously impressed with this boy. After dinner, and that included a plum tart that Mum had insisted upon, I met up with Arif in the hallway as he was leaving.

"Where did you learn to cook like that?" He reddened slightly and looked at the floor.

"I work in restaurant at home."

"Where is home?"

He pondered for a while. "In the Turkish hills … originally."

I was confused. "Turkish, you're Turkish?"

He cocked his head. "A little bit Turkish and bit of other things."

I was left wondering what exactly that meant and whether the deeds for Duck Cottage were about to be transferred over to a splinter group.

"See you tomorrow, Mrs, my car here now." Arif sort of bowed to Mum as he put on his denim jacket and he shook Dad's hand.

"Goodbye, sir." Dad fist-bumped him which was just appalling if I'm honest.

Mum called out to him as he left. "Bring your account details tomorrow, Arif, so you can cash your cheques." Arif agreed with a nod.

"Mum, don't be ridiculous, you don't pay by cheque, it's not the eighties, you need to do a bank transfer." I imagined poor Arif waiting for five working days every time he wanted to access his wages. "I will set it up, just let me deal with it."

Mum shrugged and said, "Whatever." Christ, what was she smoking? I followed Arif down the windy path so I could explain about the bank transfer but I was too late, he was already getting into the back of a car. A car that I had seen before at Number 23.

The Row

Dave and I barely rowed; we preferred to sulk, ignore and avoid. There was no slamming of doors or nights in hotels, we just didn't have the passion, the energy or the need for these monstrous displays of emotion. That sounds problematic and I used to think if you don't have the fire in your belly to fight for your man then what was the point? For some people that works, I know friends who have ripped each other to shreds mentally and physically and then afterwards, in the debris of smashed windows and shattered wedding photographs, they would make love like wolves in the moonlight. For me that was bullshit, it was cringe, I couldn't buy into it, pretty much just grow the fuck up. However, I did have a boyfriend in my teens who I think I would have killed for – an arty type who was too cool for school (what does that even mean?).

His name was Xander, do I really need to go on? I met him in the last year of my A levels and I am quite frankly still not over him. He was interesting and mysterious, he had a top knot before top knots were a thing, he had wealthy parents but not in a crass way. His dad drove a vintage Bentley and his mum was a music producer; I mean come on, if Carlsberg made in-laws. He had been allocated the whole basement in this super weird multi-level house, custom built for bad behaviour and fingering girls.

His mum wore vintage everything and was a free spirit. Meanwhile my mum had an M&S store card and we were transported in a Renault Espace. His world seemed so unbelievably cool and mine … well mine was exactly what an M&S store card got you, boring as fuck.

Anyway, I fell for this guy. I mean skin-tingling, throat-tightening, heart-racing obsessive love and I thought he felt the same way. We lasted six months and that was mostly because of my stalking, I am sure we would have only had a handful of meetings had I not kept bumping into Xander at every carefully executed opportunity. He told me I was amazing, I was different, I was unique. The first three things the Top Shaggers Handbook tells a lad to say to get a girl's drawers down. And me, sarcastic, savvy Raquel, fell for it hook, line and sinker.

It all ended on an afternoon during Christmas week. I had turned up to the weird house uninvited with an early Christmas present for my Xander. After having taken a three-hour train to London, spent hours in dusty record shops searching for an old 12" vinyl of 'Riders on the Storm', I then headed back and prepared myself to present this to Xander with a note written in a calligraphy pen that simply said "You and me forever".

As it turned out it was Dylan Maloney, a dyslexic builder from the next village, who had got in first with the early Christmas present and the sight of him on his knees in front of Xander would never leave my mind. The worst of it was they didn't even stop when they spotted me in the doorway, apparently that would have been rude.

So Xander, my 1980s Jason Momoa, belonged to the other side and I was dumped on Christmas Eve in favour of a guy wearing a high-vis vest who couldn't even spell Xander.

Three months I barely ate, six months I still welled up when I saw him at college, a year on I still had issues with illuminous workwear, it took me an awful lot to get over him. I think this shaped my lack of emotion and passion and somewhere, subconsciously, I never really opened up again.

So I married Dave, an egg-and-chips kind of guy. He was intelligent in a practical sort of way. Dave could change a tyre, rewire a plug, he could make people laugh, he was not a threat to my sanity and although I loved him, my stomach never ever flipped when he looked at me. We'd met at a wedding and we sort of just never left each other after that. He got me, he ignored my weirdness, my wild imagination and when somebody doesn't run away when you expose your true self, you put a ring on it … quickly.

Mum was not impressed but unless I had come home with David Attenborough or a relation of his she was never going to be. Dad, on the other hand, was chuffed to bits to have a police officer in the family. He wanted his daughter and grandchildren to be safe and we were. Dave was never off duty, Dave was a natural protector so, actually, Dave was one of my good choices.

Watching my parents' unconventional arrangement made me want the total opposite. I didn't want a Top Shagger for a husband and I certainly could not have coped with the thought of him living it up with another woman whilst I was knee deep in nappies and sleepless nights. I was against this open marriage concept particularly when it was only one side that was open. I did, however, let my dad off so to speak because Mum was an absolute handful. Dad had his releases and they just happened to be big-titted women who wore stockings and a Wonderbra. Dave's release happened to be his career so that was his out and it left me wondering, aged forty-five, what was mine? It wasn't my job, that was piss easy and I only did it for spare cash and to fit around the kids, so what else did I have to get my pecker up?

This thought – what is my actual purpose? – had been visiting my mind on a regular basis of late and eventually something had to give.

It was a Saturday evening, Sam was at yet another sleepover involving six lads sleeping in tents in somebody's garden, a regular occurrence for twelve-year-old boys during the summer holidays. I had sent him off with a box of homemade sausage rolls, a sleeping bag and a bottle of wine for the poor parents who had to keep an eye out for any trouble. Dave was due back for 7 pm and I had cooked a meal, had a bath and set up the lounge for a night of Ant and Dec. At 8.30 Dave wandered in without an apology having had a Chinese at work with the lads. This was, as they say, the straw that broke the camel's back.

"Is this your hormones again, because if so, there's something you can take for that."

"What will you take for being a selfish fat bastard?"

"Fuckin hell here we go. Let me sit down for this one, and you're no Kate Moss yourself."

"You walk in and out of this house without a care in the world, washing done, meals made, kids sorted and what do you do? Fuck all!"

"Fuck all? I pay the bills, I work hard to keep this family."

"Work hard? All you do is eat, drink and make a few phone calls!"

"Is that what you think I do, is that really all you think I do?"

"I don't know what you do, Dave, because it's all very secretive, you could be doing anything."

"Secretive? Secretive! I work for the fucking drug squad you stupid woman, of course it's a secret."

"All I know is that you're late for everything, you're never here, you don't do a thing with your son … do you know he wants to learn to fish? You don't even know that, do you, because you never speak to him."

Dave stood up and got right into my face, something he had never done before.

"Well all I know is that you are a bitch to me and it's no fucking wonder I'd rather be at work, so leave me the fuck alone. Do you know what a pain in the arse you are? Moody, miserable, angry … actually I could go on all night but I have better things to do."

"Like what, Dave? What do you have beyond that job because this family has been living without you for a very long time."

Dave walked to the door and looked back. "Maybe I don't want this anymore. Maybe me and you … maybe we are done."

I felt hot, I felt angry, I felt humiliated, how dare he tell me he would rather be at work than with me, his wife, how dare he say that out loud. Dave and Raquel keep their feelings hidden, we don't say them. We keep them buried and we certainly do not scream them at each other in our front room like Mimi and Patrick Maguire.

Dave went up to bed after that. I sat at my kitchen table eating lamb chops with my bare hands and drank wine from the bottle. We had crossed a line and I didn't know how to get back and that is the problem with couples who don't row – when they do, it is apocalyptic.

The next morning, I woke in Suzy's bed feeling hungover and flat. It was after nine and the house was completely empty. Dave had left a note that simply said:

Picking up Sam and going fishing, staying at a lodge, back tomorrow.

I should have been happy that he was stepping up, that Sam would have got what he wanted and needed but I wasn't, I was jealous. He wanted to spend time with anyone but me and that hurt. We hadn't really connected for at least a year. We got on, we co-existed but we rarely talked about anything of substance. We hadn't laughed or slagged anyone off together, these are things that all couples should do and we had stopped. I feared we had become a statistic, grown apart, not put the work in and would end in divorce. He would then get a compliant Russian girlfriend and I would drink Pinot Grigio in my pyjamas. People would feel sorry for me and I would end up on the speed-dating circuit with the cast of The Undateables. I felt sick to my stomach, had I taken my eye off the ball so much that it was too late to salvage? As I sat on the floor of the shower feeling low, feeling unwanted, looking down at my jumbo thighs, my survival mechanism kicked in. Actually hang on, how many times had I tried to have a meal with this stupid man and how many times did he rock up late or never? What about the time I booked us a weekend in Paris and because of his work I had to go with my bloody mother? And what about the time I bought the sexy red underwear and he sniggered when I opened my nightgown?

I stomped out of that shower and went straight down to Budgens for more booze and a packet of fags – I didn't even smoke. "Fuck you, Dave, fuck you!" I shouted this out loud in my garden on a summer's afternoon whilst slowly getting drunk. A message came in from Matt as I had just about finished my first bottle.

Hi Raquel, you free?

Yes, I am! I am at home.

Coming over now.

I must have looked a state, I didn't care. I put on some sunglasses to hide the fact I had been crying to my wedding song just minutes before. He had dark glasses on too and seemed quite subdued. I turned down the music and got him a beer.

"So, the wanderer returns," I slurred.

"Just had a lot going on that's all. Gina's sister is in labour so she's gone over there as her birthing partner."

"Where's her man?"

"In jail."

"Right."

"You on your own?"

"Yep, girls are in Ireland, Dave and Sam are away fishing."

He seemed to relax a little.

"What's up?" I enquired with genuine concern; he did seem low.

"Nothing, just thought I would come and make a plan for our next lesson."

"You could have just messaged me."

"Yeah I could have."

And then there was a silence, awkward but necessary.

"So how have you been?" I flirted with the idea of telling him that Dave hated me but thought better of it. I couldn't dissect my entire marriage with Matt, the hottie neighbour with a shady side life.

"I've been fine. Just busy with family you know. What about you?"

"Helping out with Gina's business, shit like that."

"She got my parents a housekeeper, he's really good."

He smiled. "Arif, yeah he's a good kid."

"You know him?"

"Yeah, sort of."

"How do you know him?"

"I just do, babe."

I liked him calling me babe today, it felt nice. I didn't find it tacky or annoying, it felt like he liked me. I needed to be liked today.

"I think I annoyed Gina last week. I came over to ask your cleaner something and she didn't understand me, it all got a bit complicated."

"She gets a bit stressed and manic with the business."

"What, Botox?" I wondered what could be so stressful about Botox.

"And other stuff."

"What other stuff?"

He put his glasses on his head and looked straight into my eyes. He saw me, all of me, and I felt my stomach flip.

"I don't want to talk about it to be honest, Raquel, I just want to sit here with you and have a laugh."

So on that note, I turned the music back up and we danced around the patio and got very, very drunk.

The sexual chemistry between Matt and I that evening could have been bottled and sold to miserable people who were feeling flat, tired and over the hill. The fact was, I was feeling reckless. I had drunk enough to lose my inhibitions and any doubts I had about my looks had evaporated. It was dark so that helped, I looked better in the dark. We had talked, talked for hours about lots of things, not what the kids liked to eat or what day I was doing the big shop but about me, Raquel. I was a woman, not a mother or a wife that night, I was just me. I had interesting things to say, he found me funny, he said he liked my feet and apparently my intelligence was attractive to him. I told him I liked his grey jogging bottoms, the tight ones that were faded.

We were laughing at the time, laughing about when we first met and how awkward it felt. He said he liked that I was just across the road, it excited him.

The stage was set and I was a willing participant, I wanted to feel wanted so I did what people do and I made a mistake.

We were sitting on the floor with our backs to the oven, I can't recall why. He turned his head to me, he put his hand around the back of my neck, he looked straight at me with those eyes of his.

"You know what I am going to do now don't you, Raquel?"

My heart almost stopped.

"And you do want me to, don't you?" he asked provocatively.

Slowly I nodded before shutting my eyes.

"Look at me, open your eyes, I want to see you."

And so I did, and then, on the kitchen floor of my marital home, we kissed passionately for a very long time.

As much as it was tender, it was fiery and intense, it was exactly what I needed in that moment. He pulled at my hair and he bit my lip, not too hard but hard enough to take my breath away. He tasted like a man should and I could have gone on for hours just inhaling his scent. All of my anger, my sadness and my frustration with life melted away as I felt properly desired for the first time in years.

The kissing was as far as it went that night and that was enough. There was no denying that I wanted more, but more felt too destructive and something clicked that stopped me taking it any further. That was enough excitement for one night, as my granny would say after a particularly raucous episode of Heartbeat, so I let Matt out of the front door at midnight knowing that you should never eat the whole cake, always save a little for later.

The following day and by the time Dave got back, I was calm, calm enough to say hello and to put a dark wash on. Everything was normal and I was doing my thing. There was absolutely nothing I could do about my indiscretions the previous evening. I had to hope and pray that Matt was not the type to spill the beans and that it would never ever leave my kitchen. In light of what Dave had said to me, a drunken kiss was not going to take me down. I felt some sense of guilt but I was also still reeling from Dave's outburst, the anger and the shock I felt was still firmly sitting in my gut and not even my antics had diluted it. I am ashamed to say that this was probably a revenge kiss, a way of sticking it to Dave to show him I will not be walked over, a poor way to behave on paper but in theory it was genius.

I wondered what the readers of the Daily Mail would make of this quandary. 'Dirty old bitch, cheating scum, doesn't deserve a husband' versus 'You go girl, he doesn't deserve you, the fat pig'. Which one would I be if I hadn't been the subject? Would I have supported this wanton behaviour as an observer or would I have stoned myself to death? God I wanted to wash my brain, so many thoughts and nobody to share them with.

I had hoped that Dave would at least apologise or show me, via some sort of gesture, that he had been out of line; he did neither. He dropped Sam off, had a shower, made himself beans on toast and left the house, slamming the door so hard the windows shook. I watched him reverse at high speed and wheel skid before pulling away with a scowl on his face. He was on nights that week so I wouldn't see him again until the following day.

Shall we go shopping for the beef wellington? Raquel x

Yes! When? M x

In 30 minutes? X

See you then. M x

It was at this point, I knew I was in trouble.

The Crossover

Why does nobody ever talk about the positive side of an extramarital affair? We only really hear about the deception, the dishonesty and the downright disgrace of it all. It really does get a bad press and perhaps if we looked at the actual benefits of an exciting bunk-up with somebody other than the person you promised to be faithful to until your actual death then perhaps a little more understanding would be shown.

When love is not enough and the children you created together do not keep you bonded, is it so bad to fill the hole in your life with a little extra sugar? Well, I was about to discover the answer to all of this because I had experienced a small taste of this sugar and it had left me wanting to break into a Haribo factory with a napkin and a shovel.

Who knew that shopping for meat could be so exhilarating? Who knew that a short car journey to a supermarket could make my stomach feel as if a whole swarm of butterflies were trying to escape. This was new to me, feelings I could only recall from being seventeen had flooded my system uncontrollably. I was in lust, very much so.

A look, a brush of the hand, a knowing smile. I imagined these feelings were similar to lines of cocaine. I wouldn't know for sure, I had never indulged, but what I did know is that once you started you craved more, addicted to the feeling of what might be. Matt and I played with fire using every opportunity we could to create these moments. There had only been one kiss up until that point, the anticipation that there could be more was a drug in itself. Even my writing had become flirtatious and I was pulled up on it by my agency; it made me giggle.

To: Raquel Fitzpatrick
From: Jane Aldgate

Raquel, love the latest piece on beef wellington but you seem to have gone a bit Nigella. Can you rewrite this part and lose the suggestive description of the fillet, it got us all going when we read it. LOL
    "Matthew seared the juicy fillet in hot melted butter, he gently placed it onto the skillet and rotated it slowly for ten minutes, when he was done, he left it to rest."
    Mate, this is soft porn!
    Also, got the photographers coming out next week to do some shots, let me know when is good?

I had to get a grip, I was a mother, a wife, a woman whose food mixer was more important than her car and there I was imagining unthinkable things about a fillet of beef and hot salty butter. I wasn't planning on having any sort of relationship with Matt, I was simply enjoying the thrill of the chase. I knew it was wrong but really, in the grand scheme of things, unless we planned on running off together then what harm could it do? It was summer, the weather was tropical, the flowers were in bloom, what's not to love about a bit of a crush outside of term time? I had convinced myself that this is what middle-aged women did to keep their marriages alive, I was sure we were all at it. Pot-bellied husbands across the land were getting happy, smiley wives for reasons they would never need to know. This is what I had been missing all of this time – a focus, a release, a reason for my fanny to flutter. Dave blanking me and working twelve-hour days was the gift that just kept on giving, I literally had no reason to stop, no reason to address the downright stupidity of this classic mid-life mania. What could not be overlooked, and I found it extremely interesting, was the huge difference between Gina and me. Sadly, I was not the goddess she was. She was tall, skinny, young, childless. I was petite in height, not so much in the other direction, I was dishevelled, scruffy even, I was also saddled with kids and hems to sow back up. This man could pick up some young BooHoo model and have her eating out of the palm of his hand, all it would take would be a McFlurry and a Pandora bracelet, so why me? I put it down to distance – if you are going to start something naughty then what could be easier than with somebody a few metres away with a largely absent husband, I think they call it 'in plain sight'. The fact that I had an admirer only due to my geographical position didn't bother me one bit, a win's a win so fuck it.

Matt and I had exchanged some very immature messages littered with pictures of fruit and veg. I had to google why the humble aubergine had a sexual connotation and in response I said some very silly things about a cucumber. Of course I deleted them immediately after reading, the thought of Dave or the kids discovering what I had become was unbearable. Still, however, when my phone beeped, I got a rush.

With my trip to Ireland in less than a week, I needed to spend some time with Sam, check in on my parents and make sure the photo shoot went to plan. I invited Mum and Dad over for the afternoon mid-week and they brought Arif, who was very kindly going to tidy my garden. Dave had been on nights so he was in bed and, apart from seeing his stubby hand swipe the bacon sandwich from outside the bedroom door which I had placed there like a warden on B wing, there had been no contact.

It was a beautiful day, the air smelled of cut grass and roses, I had a real spring in my step, I was feeling positive, I was outfit-planning days in advance. My standard car washer's costume consisting of jogging bottoms and out-of-shape t-shirts were no more, and now I was putting earrings in and wearing heels during the day – the relentless reapplication of lipstick had actually given me chapped lips. I once got out of my car at the car wash to get something out of my boot and some cheeky twat in a van asked me for a deluxe wash and a polish. He either thought I was a low-rate hooker or one of the burly workers at Soapy Suds, either way my dress sense reflected my mood; knackered, under-appreciated and low in self-esteem; the message I was now sending was fresh, eager, up for it, possibly desperate.

I had only had the odd text from the girls and, by all accounts, Dublin was way cooler and much more them than this sleepy village in Cheshire they now called Boretown. I could understand it; big city life, living with staff and a selection of rich arty types to converse with completely overshadowed the monotony of home. My sister lived life to the highest of standards and had the time and the money to make every day count. Why she had Roger clinging to her coat tails, I will never know, it would always remain a mystery. She wasn't a stunner, granted, but she could do better than a gammy-toed old codger with a nasty streak.

I had put together some salads and summery bits for my parents and washed down the outdoor furniture. It was going to be a pleasant afternoon and I hoped my mother was still on cloud nine with her new assistant. Perhaps Dave would make an appearance, but I didn't really mind if he didn't. I watched a shirtless Matt cut his front lawn until my parents arrived, the best five minutes of the day so far.

I had only just got them all into the house, Mum in her sheer, shocking-pink blouse, Dad with a bow tie to match and their trusty steed, Arif, carrying their stuff when the doorbell went.

"Alright girl, how are ya?"

Matt stood there, bare-chested with a pair of shears in his hand, it was all very Lady Chatterley, set on an estate but one that had new builds and wheelie bins.

"Hi, my parents are here and Dave's upstairs." I was flushed, embarrassed there would be a crossover here that I had not prepared for.

"You look nice." His eyes smiled and his lips plumped.

I was flustered, I would have to blend the old me with the new me. I would be like a weird crossbreed; people would think I had been possessed.

"It's not a good time, I'm doing lunch." I shut the door but his foot was in the way, he waved over my head, "Hello there, I'm Matt from across the road."

Mum immediately sauntered down the hallway with one of her gins in hand.

"Good afternoon. I believe I have been in contact with your wife, so nice to meet you, Matthew."

And then that was it, he was in, half naked and talking to my parents about pruning roses of all things.

"Get him a drink, Raquel, gosh your hosting has really deteriorated." Mum flicked her hand towards the jug of Pimm's on the table and I was forced into pouring him a glass. Within minutes he was sitting down, eating the fruit from the drink with his fingers and showing no signs of leaving. Arif had nodded to him politely and shook his hand, there was little eye contact. Sam had wandered away from his Xbox to join us in the garden and before long had taken Arif down to the bottom to play football. This felt very odd, my parents with Matt and I sitting around the table whilst my husband snored in bed.

"What a fabulous accent he has Raquel, so authentic."

"Mum he's from Liverpool, he's not an actor."

"I know that, it just sounds so very … Liverpudlian."

"Ya think?" I shook my head and glanced at Dad, he was paying no attention because he too was enamoured with Matt. They reminded me of a couple of zoo visitors observing a gorilla's behaviour. I felt extremely on edge, this was all a bit too close for comfort, I wanted to keep everyone in a separate box, I was not a good juggler.

"The first time we meet her she burped, it was an accident, like, but it was so funny."

Mum found this hilarious. "Well she was brought up with manners, Matthew, but I am not responsible for her anymore." Mum laughed at my unfortunate ordeal and then went on to tell him about other embarrassing things that had happened to me with help from Dad to fill in the gaps and correct the most unimportant bits.

"The time she wet herself on that rowing boat in The Lakes."

"No, no darling it was in Yorkshire, Robin Hood's Bay."

"Ah yes I stand corrected, yes she couldn't row fast enough to the shore, she gave up and soiled herself. We had to go to BHS and get her some new pants." The tears rolled down her face.

"No darling, it was C&A, it's shut down now, gone bankrupt I think."

"Yes I think you're right, we went into C&A whilst she sat on a towel in Phillip's brand-new Mercedes."

"No, it was a BMW Suzannah, remember, it was gold."

I chipped in. "Not one bit relevant, Dad."

"Ah yes, sorry Matthew, my memory is shot, but what about the time when she went to the toilet in a field and fell back into a cowpat?"

Suzannah and Phillip laughed hysterically whilst selling me down the river like some incontinent moron and Matthew seemed to enjoy every minute. I squirmed in my chair wishing the show would just end; is this what they call being 'on form', this old lot?

A touch to my calf under the table stopped me in my tracks and then I felt a hand on my thigh. Although I hoped it was not my father, I did wonder if that would be for the best. A wink from Matt confirmed my dad did not fancy me so at least that was something. Just as the hand had reached places that made my top lip sweat, the doorbell rang.

"I'll get it, it's probably for me." Mum, who now was apparently using my house as a drop-in centre, went off to get the door spilling her fourth gin all the way. The hand remained firmly in place and I was glad I had started shaving my bikini line that little bit higher.

I could hear Mum laughing and giggling at the door, Dad had fallen asleep at the table, it happened a lot mid-conversation; it's an old man thing. Matt was staring into my eyes and saying nothing, he didn't have to, I could tell what he was thinking because I thought it too. I checked down the garden to see if Sam or indeed Arif had spotted the under-table groping but they were engrossed in diving headers.

Appearing at the back door and standing in the sunlight was a stunning woman wearing black hot pants, black wedged sandals and a – yes, you guessed it – black crop top. Her lips were bright red, the one and only colour she donned. Matt's hand retracted very quickly, Dad opened one eye and Arif rushed up the garden leaving Sam open-mouthed.

"Hiya babes." Gina the vision had arrived and boy did we know it. Matt knocked his chair over trying to get up to greet her and Dad's tongue flopped out of his mouth.

"Hiya babes, didn't know you were home." Matt picked up the chair and positioned it for his queen. She sat down and tucked her two elongated hot dogs under the table.

"Isn't she fabulous Phillip? What a beauty," Mum said to Dad, who was still acting like a spaniel.

"Hiya everyone, thanks for the invite." Gina was flashing her pearly whites in every direction but mine.

I glanced at Mum inquisitively.

"I invited her, Raquel, I have been dying to meet her and we really need to thank her for sending us Arif, he has been a godsend."

Arif was very oddly standing to attention at the table with his hands behind his back. He looked rather worried, perhaps intimidated. Gina did not look at him but said a very long sentence in a very complicated language. He then nodded and said, "I must go and visit with my aunt, thank you and goodbye" before scurrying away like a beetle.

"Don't worry babes, he'll be back in a bit." Gina assured Mum that he would not be long, god forbid Mum would be without him for an afternoon. She then turned to Matt and whispered, "We shouldn't be socialising with them."

"Would anybody like some salad and cold meats?" I didn't wait for an answer, I just headed to the kitchen for some respite from this hell. Mum was drunk, Matt was an absolute liability and Gina was getting cooler, more beautiful and more scary by the minute. I was sure she was on to me and why the fuck was she dressed for a beach club in Ibiza?

Matt came up behind me in the kitchen and I jumped.

"I've been told to go and put a top on even though it's roasting." He had clearly been ordered by GI Gina to cover up. I said nothing, just raised my eyebrows which was supposed to say 'Go away' without actually saying it. But he just stood gormlessly waiting for further instruction.

"For fuck's sake, go go go, what are you playing at?" My stomach had flipped for all the wrong reasons, my hands were shaking and rightly so, this was bad, too dangerous for me and then, as if things couldn't get any worse, I heard movement upstairs and the shower turning on. Dave's stomping indicated two things; he was hungry and he was coming downstairs.

I at least had time to position a chair away from Matt and to swig two glasses of wine in the utility room to calm my very fragile nerves. I leaned against the dryer and shut my eyes, I was flying far too close to the sun.

"Ah David, how are you?" Dad always stood and greeted Dave man to man, Mum barely looked up. Dave was in a pair of shorts and a very tight vest, he looked tired. "Good to see you Phil." He patted my dad on his back. "Suzannah." He nodded at Mum and she raised her glass.

"And you must be Gina." She stood, and put her glasses on her head, her long eyelashes fluttered.

"Hiya babe, nice to finally meet you." She kissed Dave on both cheeks and he visibly blushed.

"Well I am a very busy man so I'm not around much."

"We must have dinner one night, the four of us."

Dave looked interested.

"Yes what a great idea. Raquel, you can sort that can't you?"

I was about to say, "Oh so you're talking to me now, are you?" but I thought better of it. "Yes sure, sounds good." It did not sound good, I would have much preferred to fall down a well.

"Let's make it a six-some shall we?"

I glared at Mum. "No Mother, let's not."

"Why ever not, we can still keep up with you young-uns, can't we Phillip?" Dad was still gazing at Gina.

"Tongue in, Phillip." Mum scolded the dog. Dad jumped and shut his mouth tightly.

"I'll let you know, Mum." I shut it down, I was in all sorts of trouble. Matt was back at the door ringing the bell and Dave went to let him in. I heard them greeting each other and waited for the sounds of thumping or shouting. There were none, in fact they came in laughing and had all the makings of drinking buddies.

"Don't you need to get to work?" I watched Dave crack open a can and willed him to go away as soon as possible.

"No, I have a couple of days off. Today I am chilling, tomorrow me and Sam are off fishing again, aren't we pal?" Sam nodded eagerly, at least he was happy.

The rest of the day was about as comfortable as sitting on a cactus with my bare arse. Mum was completely sozzled and would not stop going on about Gina's beauty, Dad was desperately trying to be one of the lads and drank out of the can and openly farted which got a few laughs. Matt seemed to fall in love with Dave and completely forget about sexually harassing me, which was a kick in the guts; what I wouldn't have given for a smell of his neck. And then there was Gina who just lay around my garden looking demure whilst texting incessantly.

Dad was unable to drive home so, when Arif came back from visiting with his aunt, I had to ask for his help with these two idiotic pensioners staggering down the driveway. Eventually, when realising that the fresh air had robbed them of their balance, Mum ended up headfirst in my privet hedge. As Dad tried to pull her out by the backend, her skirt came completely off and she exposed her pastel pants to the whole of the street. I swiftly put it back on; nobody needs to see that. Dad's bow tie was now around his head like a headband because that's what drunks do with neckwear once they are smashed, and he and Mum lay on the grass laughing and rolling around like a couple of oversized babies. Arif very kindly helped me bundle them into the back of a taxi being driven by a horrified man. I assured him that if one of them puked we would pay for the valet, he was completely disgusted and apparently this was "not on".

As he drove away, Mum wound down the window and shouted "Whassssupppp!" with her tongue out like we did in the late 90s. Arif did it back so that was nice.

Embarrassing as they were, my parents had started to enjoy themselves in a way I never knew possible and if that meant them making complete tits of themselves every so often then I was OK with that.

Arif watched them drive away with a fond look in his eyes. "I will get to house at 8 am and make sure OK." I looked at his beautiful skin, glossy hair and innocent eyes. God knows what his parents would make of this. He was so far from home but seemed happy enough.

"Your parents, they very kind to me."

"Are they?" I could imagine Dad being half decent but my Mum was a right madam, or at least she was to me.

"Yes they treat me kind and I like being with them."

"Don't you miss your home?"

"I need work, no work at home."

"Who is the driver of the big black car, the one that picks you up?"

"It is my boss."

"Your boss? Of what job?"

"The boss of big company."

"What company?"

"Cleaning company, who I work for."

"Sorry, I thought you were a student?"

"I want to be." His eyes looked a little glassy.

"So you're not studying anything?"

"Not until papers come."

"What papers? University papers?"

"No, not university papers."

I was confused, this was not the information I had been given and what exactly did Matt have to do with this cleaning company? I wanted to get more out of him but Gina appeared behind us from nowhere.

"Thanks for a great day, babes. I love your mum, what a scream."

"Isn't she just." This had not been my experience until literally today.

"Oh, by the way, what time is the photo shoot on Friday? I will need to take some time off."

I was taken aback, this was nothing to do with her, just Matt, just me and Matt.

"Oh you don't need to be there Gina, it's not necessary."

She smugly said, "I don't need to be but I want to be."

"Ah OK, it's at eleven." What choice did I have but to tell her? It would have been weird if I didn't. "See you then, thanks for coming."

She called for Matt which meant screeching "Babe" very loudly. He came staggering out with Dave behind him, they were still talking very loudly about Sir Alex and how everything had gone to shit since his departure. "It's a fucking shitshow mate, a shambles." Matt spat when he said those words, Dave didn't care when some saliva landed on his head. "One man kept that place at the top and without him, it's nothing." They both nodded in agreement. God this was annoying, why were they getting on, why were they even speaking? This could mean Matt would stop making my stomach flip because he felt guilty. I would be back in my car-washing outfit and my summer of excitement would come to an abrupt end. I sneered as they shook hands and fumed that I had to share my new friend with my old husband. Bollocks!

Once everyone had left, Dave started clearing up which was unlike him. We moved around each other silently and awkwardly. Eventually he broke.

"Look Raquel, we both said things we didn't mean the other night."

I carried on filling the dishwasher.

"I mean, I shouldn't have said those things, I was tired."

I put the dishwasher on.

"I want us to be friends again, Raquel, this is not good."

I started handwashing the pans.

"Raquel, say something, for god's sake."

I turned around and smiled at Dave.

"Don't worry about it. I'm off to bed." And then, very coldly, I headed upstairs to have a very long bath and to think of Matt.

The fishing trip was starting early, I had made up sandwiches, flasks of tea and packed it all in a Tupperware for the fishermen to enjoy on their day out. The rods were poking out of the car window and Sam was busy checking his new tackle box. Dave was a little sheepish, I think by my lack of reaction the previous evening he had realised that something had changed. I was out of order in so many ways and had no right being this way but I didn't want an emotional make-up. My mind was now elsewhere and the distance between us suited me. This was a mistake and, in hindsight, I should have welcomed him with open arms, quickly getting us back on track, but I didn't. I regret that now. I waved them off and continued my diabolical obsession with hot neighbour.

You free today? R

Sure, what we doing? M

Let's do some work on desserts.

Be over soon

It was Thursday, I had the shoot on Friday and Dublin on Saturday. This was an opportunity for me to spend time with Matt alone. He arrived within the hour and I had set us up with all the ingredients for a cheesecake. A chimp could make a cheesecake so it would be a very easy and quick lesson with plenty of time to spare. Matt crushed biscuits with his bare hands, he whipped the cream, he even fed me a strawberry which was wholly unpleasant because it was from the bottom of the punnet and it had a mushy side. We eventually put the strawberry cheesecake into the freezer to set.

"So, what now?"

He smiled, I smiled.

"What do you think?" I wanted him to lead the way.

"We could go upstairs." He looked ready.

I shook my head. Hell no, there was no way out of upstairs apart from through a window.

"It's not safe." I opened the utility room door. "Let's go in here."

He shrugged, I got the feeling he would do it on a grave if need be.

So in we went and we started what can only be described as a heavy petting session, but this time it felt less spontaneous and more grubby. It was the middle of the day, I could see my son's football boots out of the corner of my eye, I kicked them down the back of the dryer because they were putting me off. He lifted me onto the washing machine, it was awkward and he made a heaving noise. It wasn't dark and I wasn't drunk, I was aware of everything, that wasn't good. He put his hand up the back of my shirt and unclipped my bra, visions of two boulders rolling down a hill flashed into my head. The scaffolding was off and the building wasn't secure. Why hadn't I had a boob job when boob jobs were cool? He was certainly ready for something, I could feel that he was ready, I wasn't sure I was. Whatever he was concealing inside those joggers wasn't as appealing as it had been in my thoughts.

Just as things were getting very heated, I heard the front door creak. I knew my house and somebody was definitely coming in. I pushed him away and jumped off the washer, I was too old to be doing that because my ankle stung when I landed. Immediately I picked up a basket of washing and walked back into the kitchen, a pro in every sense of the word.

Sam was standing in the kitchen.

"Oh my god, you're back, I thought you would be later, you've only been gone an hour."

Matt appeared behind me from the utility room, what on earth could he have been doing in there? My plan was to say we thought we heard a mouse.

"Alright mate." And then he ruffled Sam's hair which was awful.

Dave appeared with the rods. "Yeah, it started raining and nothing was happening so we thought we'd come home and watch a film … alright mate?" He looked surprised to see Matt.

"We've been doing cheesecake," Matt stuttered, opening the

freezer door and pointing to the evidence. Could this be any more obvious?

"Very nice, mate, well done you."

It felt patronising and quite the opposite of last night's lads-on-the-lash vibe. The sort of thing you would say to a child after they had made a plaque in woodwork.

"So I'll give you a shout when it's set and you can collect it." That was my hint that he had to leave.

"Oh right yeah, see ya later." I didn't even see him to the door, my heart was beating out of my chest.

Dave watched him cross the street from the bay window and then said whilst smirking, "Looks like someone has a little crush."

I quickly shut it down. "He doesn't fancy me, I am old enough to be his ... older sister."

Dave laughed his head off. "I think it's the other way round love." And then he patted me on the back and I felt like an old perverted aunty who needed a cold shower.

And there it was, it was big fat Dave who brought me back to earth with a humiliating bump. He had been the one who had made me realise that this man, this boy, was just a hormonal fantasy brought on by boredom and I had no business pursuing it. But Matt, well he had other ideas.

The photographers arrived early, about ten, so I was stuck with two women I had nothing in common with who had driven up from London to do about three shots. They were very London and could not believe there wasn't an artisan bakery on the road that I lived on. They found the whole street very American and they had their jeans tucked into their socks. This was now apparently the fashion and Londoners were catching tubes and turning up at meetings like hikers. Whoever came up with this disastrous fashion idea should be held accountable. One of the ladies, Stevie, identified as no gender at all and the other, George, was certainly on some sort of fence. I had to listen to them discussing how they thought that mandatory unisex toilets would be the only way to treat people fairly and to offer the LGBTQ+ community a level playing field. I wanted to ask if they would feel that way if a great big guy did a huge shit in the cubicle next to them whilst reading Viz magazine and eating a pasty. No no no, men needed their own spaces for that sort of thing but I was too scared to let them know how un-PC I was. I just made some agreement noises and tried not to speak so I didn't offend. They were also both vegan so I hoped to fuck they didn't want to stay for lunch.

Eventually we walked over to Matt's where the happy couple were ready for their shoot. Matt had skin-tight cropped jeans on, a white shirt that stopped his circulation and a brown loafer that I am sure had been fake tanned to match his ankles. Gina, much to my horror, had a black cat suit, longer lashes that I think would be legal to drive with and killer heels to no doubt stab me with.

Gina air kissed me and went straight into the 'studio' as she called it to boss people around. Matt hugged me for far too long and kissed my ear when nobody was looking. I barged passed him hoping he would leave it at that.

"Where do you want us?" Gina asked Tweedle courgette and Tweedle aubergine where she should position herself.

"Well, erm, you are not on the brief actually." Stevie dared to respond to the lady of the manor. Gina's look was dark.

"You what? This is my house, my kitchen, my husband."

She looked at me. I quickly interjected. "Well it's because you haven't done any of the cooking, Gina, but, well, I suppose it's OK because you have been somewhat involved."

She hauled herself up onto the island, arse in the air; this could easily have been a shoot for Nuts. One leg up, arm behind head; this was a game of twister I did not sanction. The vegans looked at me in horror.

"Just go with it," I whispered, "we can pick out what we want to use later."

So the following hour was spent with Matt and Gina on the island, Gina on Matt's back, Matt kissing Gina's hand, Matt feeding Gina a forkful of yesterday's cheesecake. It was awkward, uncomfortable, I wanted to puke. I don't know whether I was imagining it but this felt like a warning to stay away and I intended to. When the final shot had been taken, a more sensible one with Matt looking at a cookbook with Gina standing behind him, the vegans said they were done.

"It's a wrap!" Gina was certainly in her element, using industry lingo and thinking she was one of the greats. Matt looked alarmed.

"She's still going to give me cooking lessons though, babe." He threw a look my way, willing me to agree.

"Well, err, I am actually quite busy and I'm going away this weekend so …"

"She's too busy, Matt, we'll get you a proper chef to teach you." And by that I knew she didn't like me and this was not friendly fire. My trip to Ireland could not have come at a more convenient time.

Got to see the Funny Side

My sister was too busy writing some sort of legal document to pick me up from Dublin airport, so I was responsible for getting myself into town. The flight was harrowing – my seat was smack bang in the middle of a stag do full of absolute beer monsters who sang "Get your tits out for the lads" every time a female walked past rows two to six. I was in a window seat on row three, I was trapped and I did not dare go to the toilet in fear of the dreaded song. In fact I probably feared they wouldn't sing it, what would that have said about me?

They were told to quieten down twice by the campest steward I had even seen or heard, and once the gang realised the guy was gay they sang it to him too. Most of the passengers were hoping somebody would make a citizen's arrest but we were over the sea at this point so there was no landing of the plane, we'd be down before the handcuffs were on so the whole plane endured it with angry faces and itchy fingers ready to type a complaint.

Camp steward, whose name was Bobby, refused me a vodka tonic. He very rudely told me, "Your party will not be served alcohol due to the anti-social behaviour you have already demonstrated."

I glared at him. "I am not with this party thank you very much, so please get me that drink quickly." Bobby was suspicious and also the stupidest man ever to live. Did he think that these lads had brought their mother, a gym slip one at that, to a stag do? I was wearing an anorak for fuck's sake, not a t-shirt with 'RIP Jake lad' written on the back of it. Eventually, after me ringing the buzzer three times, the vodka arrived and I swigged it like a tramp and I did not care who was watching.

By the time I got into a cab outside the airport I was nicely oiled and more relaxed about the plane scenes. I was young once,

I even had my hen do here; boys will be boys, I thought, and hummed the tune to 'get your tits out'.

Driving through the city, I remembered the fun times I had enjoyed in Dublin. We had no family who were Irish, as far as I knew, but I had always felt an affinity with the place. Big plates of stew with colcannon mash, singing along to a man on a rickety old piano who also doubled up as a comedian; it was a fun place, a place where they made even sad things amusing.

I had been sitting in a bar waiting for my sister to finish work a few years earlier and a crowd of women all wearing black had sat down at the table next to me. They had black lace veils over their faces and they all carried an order of service with the face of an elderly lady. It simply said 'Mammy'. There were certainly three generations sitting around this table having just come from the funeral of a very special lady. There was a morbid silence until the drinks arrived and then one of them said, "She was a crabby old bitch though, wasn't she." Another said, "Aye, she was a right pain in the arse." Then another added an insult and within minutes this table was crying with laughter and completely desecrated the memory of their Mammy.

I later found out that Mammy hadn't even died of old age, it wasn't a peaceful goodbye in the comfort of a cosy Irish cottage. She had choked on a piece of gristle at the local pub and lost consciousness right there on the pool table. "Always the attention seeker," said her oldest daughter after doing three consecutive shots of sambuca.

The Irish had it right, you have to see the funny side or you would live in constant misery!

Roger wasn't this type of Irish, he was morose, depressing, a wimp. He didn't have the craic in him, that must have been left in the womb along with his testosterone. I dreaded seeing him and having to be pleasant, it's very tiring being fake, I struggle with it. But for my sister, my poor sister who I had taunted since the day I was born, I would try.

We pulled up outside 1 Riverside View, what a beauty. My sister had bought an entire town house, unusual for a city but she got it cheap when property was a good business. She renovated it slowly, it was taken back to the shell, the whole place was crumbling and rotting but Mel had the money to bring it back to its former glory. There was nothing she hadn't picked and placed herself, every bit of coving had been hunted for, the flooring was of the era, she was a perfectionist and she worked hard to be able to be just that. The stone steps leading up to the large oak door were super steep. You had to be a mountain goat just to stay upright; I felt the thigh burn on step three, I needed to go to the gym.

The girls were in the hallway to welcome me and they looked lovely, a bit different, maybe more grown up. Even Michaela had a bit of bronzer on her cheeks and had lost some of her Wednesday Adams complexion. It was wonderful to see them, I had been overrun with boys over the last couple of weeks and lived as a single woman. I shuddered. Seeing them just made me think about what an absolute tosser I was and how the risks that I took could have shattered their world. Distance from 23 and my own home and husband was exactly what I needed. I hadn't given Matt a second thought and, quite frankly, I felt grubby at the thought of it all.

Mel and Roger were both working until about seven so I had time to settle in and get the low-down from the girls. Nancy, the very accommodating and efficient housekeeper, took my case upstairs after making me the best coffee I had ever tasted. We sat in Mel's lounge on huge Chesterfields and enjoyed updating one another on recent events.

"So, I met someone." Suzy was glowing like a lamp.

"Go on …"

"Well, his name is Finn and he's Irish and he's a student."

"A student? Studying what? How old is he?"

She blushed. "He is studying modern art and he is twenty."

"OK, how did you meet him?"

"He's one of Mel's friend's sons. His family own the boat."

"Wow, you really like him I take it?"

She nodded. I remembered being in love at her age, it was a painful memory but that was my experience not hers so I would not piss on my daughter's chips, I would let somebody else do that.

"Well, I'm pleased for you. Will I get to meet him whilst I'm here?"

"As if, how embarrassing. I've only known him two weeks. God Mum, stop."

And that was the end of that idea.

"Michaela, have you made any friends?"

Michaela was such a home bird I imagined the only time she had left the house would be to join a human rights rally.

"Not really, I spent some time with Nancy's daughter and she showed me around, we went to a gallery and did some shopping."

I didn't even know Nancy had a daughter, I thought she lived in an airing cupboard upstairs and the towels were her children.

"She lives with her dad just outside of the city. She's half Spanish, same age as me."

I wondered how Nancy managed to be a mother whilst living at my sister's house and spent every waking hour polishing my sister's shit.

"What's her name?"

Michaela was reluctant to give me this information. "Why?" And then she thought better of it. "Her name is Connie."

"OK, will I get to meet Connie?"

"Dunno, maybe." She was a moody little devil!

I told the girls the acceptable version about the goings on back home.

"Granny and Grandad have been replaced by the Osbournes, Sam is now a fully-fledged fisherman, Dad still hasn't caught the bad guys and I have been working quite a bit."

The girls loved to hear about their Granny being drunk in a bush; they wished I had uploaded it to TikTok. They were also very intrigued by Arif.

"Are you saying they have a butler?"

"No, he's a cleaner with other skills."

"What other skills?"

"Well, companionship. Oh, and he can cook too."

They were both completely bemused.

"What are we doing for dinner, shall I take you both out?"

"We have booked a table at a steakhouse close by and we will meet Mel and Rog there."

"Oh lovely."

I found out the details for the evening via text from Mel:

Raquel – Dress code smart casual. Meet at Grillo: Argentinian steak house. Table booked for 7.30 pm, don't be late.

Okey dokey Melon, can't wait to see you and Roger Xxx

Really? That sounds sarcastic x

Grillo was a very busy, highly sought after city restaurant whose beef was of the highest standard. It was a place where you selected your own steak, not in a tacky way, and they only cooked it in the way chef deemed acceptable. I was good with that, that was a bit of me, the quality of produce was everything. The clientele annoyed me slightly only because everybody was dressed well and had an air of style about them. I wished I had packed something other than jeans and a boot. Perhaps I would go shopping and update my wardrobe, I was fed up of looking average. Mel arrived looking extremely professional as ever. A tweed blazer, tweed trilby and a very expensive-looking camel-coloured dress. She did scrub up well when she made the effort. Roger, on the other hand, had a crumpled pair of trousers, a V-necked jumper framing a hairy chest which blended into his beard and the sandals that I had heard about in advance. He would not have looked out of place on the set of Planet of the Apes.

"Hello Raquel, nice to see you."

"Roger, hope you are well."

We nodded at one another; I couldn't face a hug.

Official talk, stunted and fake. I really needed to loosen up and try with this guy, I would need a few drinks. I sat down next to Mel, we hadn't seen each other in a few months, it would be nice to catch up and tell her about the extraordinary transformation of our parents. The girls happily chatted to each other and Mel and I got stuck into a nice Barolo and chewed the fat, so to speak.

"The girls have been amazing, it's so nice to have bit of youth around the place."

"I believe Suzy has met someone?"

"Oh you mean Finn; nice kid, lovely parents, actually a great catch."

"She seems smitten."

"You'll see why, he is super cool, rich, clever, good looking. Reminds me of that gay guy you fell for at college."

"Do not! Just don't!" I covered my face. "I'm still not over it."

"I know!" She laughed. "That's why I said it. No, he's a nice kid, they make a nice couple. It won't last long let's face it, these things never do."

I looked over at Suzy who was texting under the table and I felt a sadness. She had no idea what heartbreak was yet but she would feel it when it happened.

"And Michaela says she has been hanging out with Nancy's daughter."

My sister looked flustered. "Yes, they are friends, they get on. They are really similar, in their interests."

"What's the story with her and Nancy?"

Mel sighed, I felt as though she had told the story numerous times.

"No real story, her dad got custody of her when she was little, she has always lived with him from being very small. Nancy had a few problems with postnatal depression and she wasn't in the right headspace to look after her. So, she lives with her dad and Nancy sees her on her days off."

"Poor Nancy, that must be awful."

"It was at the time, but she got through it." My sister was very matter of fact and sensible, her maternal instinct not quite on point.

"And how are you and Roger?" Roger's ears pricked up when he heard his name and I decided to change the conversation until we were alone. Instead, I turned to him. "So how are you, Roger?"

I decided to pull off the plaster.

He took in a breath, ready to unleash his wave of misery upon me. "Fine, apart from this toe." He started to raise the foot to show me.

"Put it down, please, I already heard about it." Roger looked disappointed that he couldn't unravel this septic sausage minutes before my rib eye arrived; he hadn't changed a bit. "Apart from the toe, are you well?"

"Well, I have had some trouble with my left ear, it all started one evening and I couldn't hear the commentary on the cricket …"

I mentally drifted away and nodded every ten seconds to appease him. The last line was "Just some olive oil and a cotton bud, that's all it took." And then I got back to my evening – I had done my bit for Help the Aged.

The following day, I woke in a huge sleigh bed wrapped in crisp, Egyptian cotton sheets with a thread count even royalty wouldn't sneer at. My room was on the top floor with stripped-back wooden floors dotted with various animal skins. There was an old cast-iron roll-top bath sitting alone under the loft-style window with old taps that came out of the floor and hovered conveniently just above. They thought of everything at Hotel Melanie, there was even a kettle on a tray with various herbal teas. Pure bliss! Taking advantage of my luxurious surroundings, I sat in a steaming hot bubble bath looking at the Irish sky and sipped a peppermint tea. My phone pinged.

Hiya babe, miss you. M

Jesus, this was all I needed.

Delete that asap.

I will but I wanted you to know. Thinking about you all the time. M xx

Can discuss when I get back, please delete these messages.

Aren't you going to say it back first? x

What the hell was he doing? If Gina got her hands on his phone, I would be done for. She would march over to Dave and I wasn't there to intercept her. Shit shit shit. I decided to calm things down temporarily.

You too. Please delete. Back in a few days. x

Gingerly I sent a kiss. Christ I had all this waiting for me back home, maybe I would just live at Mel's and send for my husband and son.

Sunday breakfast was a grand affair. Nancy did breakfast at weekends and she did it well. All the Sunday papers were laid out, fresh coffee was being served and we all had a different version of eggs; Benedict, scrambled, fried and poached, this woman was a master on the egg front. The girls helped Nancy clear away which I was really happy to see and the day started with much laughter and positivity.

We wandered around the city in the afternoon. Roger stayed at home with his foot up and a good book about cricket so the girls had some time together and my two allocated themselves an hour in Urban Outfitters with my credit card. Mel and I sat outside a cafe watching the world go by.

"So tell me now we are alone, how are you and Roger?"

Mel sighed. Her frizzy hair was straighter these days, something to do with a Brazilian and a blow-dry. She still had her side fringe that she hid behind when things got tricky.

"Stop hiding behind your hair and tell me."

"It's fine, it's always fine. We have our lives, we have friends, we entertain, we socialise."

"But?" I knew there was an obstacle.

"It all seems a bit pointless, without kids to share it with." I almost laughed.

"You want kids, with him?"

She gave me a look that usually came just before an arm punch.

"Even if I did it's too late now, I'm fucking forty-seven."

"Why didn't you do it before?"

"Because it never seemed like the right time and Rog didn't really fancy it."

"Didn't really fancy it? It's not a trip down the Rhine, Mel, that's a very wishy-washy way of deciding not to have kids."

"I know, I know. There's not much I can do now, is there?"

I shook my head. "No there isn't because even if you had one, you haven't got time to look after it anyway, plus Roger would be on a mobility scooter by the time it was five."

"Bitch," she said, but I knew she agreed. She then nipped off to Boots to buy some stuff and I had an idea, a pretty good one actually. A phone call later and the plan was in place.

"Where are we going?" The girls got into the back of Mel's car and I put our destination into the satnav.

"Just drive," I said.

Mel didn't like surprises, nor did she like being told what to do by me but I assured them this would all be worth it. Thirty minutes later we pulled into the place that would change Mel's life for the good although it would take a bit of persuading.

Dogs Trust was run by a lovely women whose life was all animals; she smelt like one, she even looked like a Jack Russell. Small, wiry and squeaky Mrs McDonnell led us down to the yard where at least twenty dogs were roaming freely inside a large pen.

"They're all pretty friendly, apart from the big black one – found him on the road out to the coast with a tag engraved with the name Sir Walter. He took a mighty great chunk out of me arm the other day, big bastard so he is." Her accent was so sweet, soft but peppered with much swearing.

"Fucking hell, Raquel. I can't have a dog, Roger is allergic." My sister immediately saw the negatives.

"Oh fuck him, get him some Piriton. I promise this is the answer, people prefer dogs to kids these days."

Mrs McDonnell opened the gate and the entire pack charged at us, yapping and squealing. The girls were delighted. My sister stood stiff as a board.

"I don't like any of them, have they even had rabies shots?"

Mrs McDonnell laughed out loud. "You need a dog to soften you up a bit, me darlin." And then she shut us in the pen and walked away.

All of the dogs were vying for attention, it was as if they knew this was their chance to live in a big posh house with the Sunday papers and full Irish breakfasts. They almost pleaded to be picked up, their claws dragging down our legs in desperation. The big black dangerous one sat in the corner with his big back to us, he was above begging plus he was probably full from the arm he'd had for lunch.

Mel looked at me. "Do you really think this will help?"

"Yes, hell yes! You'll have something to look after, a reason to get up, somebody who will listen without answering back, what's not to like about this?" She looked thoughtful. I went in hard. "My girls will be back home in no time and then it will be just you and him again."

She looked distressed. I detected that Roger was no longer enough to keep Mel happy, perhaps he was finally on his way out. I planned to call nursing homes next and book him in.

Eventually she broke. "I suppose I could give it a try, and I guess Nancy is there most of the time. Will you girls help me settle it in?" Both the girls eagerly agreed.

"OK then, let's do this. I'll take that one." She pointed to the beast in the corner. I was alarmed, this was more cow than dog.

"Whoa, really? Why not get a small one you can put under your desk at work?"

She shook her head. "No, I will take that one. That one is calling to me subconsciously." Sir Walter looked back at us, fully aware we were talking about him. I can't be sure but I think he raised his eyebrows.

So I went with it. I beckoned Mrs McDonnell back to the pen and told her the news. She was as shocked as me but after giving us a few tips like not to approach him from behind, not to look into his eyes for too long and not to dangle a sleeve near his mouth, we put a reluctant Sir Walter in the car. I shouted out of the window before we drove away, "By the way, what breed is he?" Mrs McDonnell shouted, "Fuck only knows." And we left with what could have been part sabre-toothed tiger dribbling on the shoulder of my sister's Armani coat.

"Sir fecking Walter! What sort of stupid name is that?" Roger was beside himself, I was in my element. "This is you this is, you and your crazy ideas." He pointed at me aggressively. Roger had never been this animated and I was loving it.

"Roger, calm down. Mel wants to be a mummy and now she is."

His face was red, skin flaky, his eyes bulging, there was spit sitting in his beard and Sir Walter was licking his elevated toe.

"Look, he likes you," I grinned.

Roger was livid, there were already muddy footprints on the kitchen floor and the girls and my sister were flying around the house looking for anything to make a dog bed from – one of Roger's cashmere V-necks was to be a pillow.

"How much does he eat? What the feck does he eat?" Roger staggered to his feet.

"I think his favourite is limbs," I smirked.

"You … honestly, you've only been here a day and Jesus Christ you've tipped this house upside down. I'm going out, I need a drink."

Nancy helped the situation and handed Roger his jacket and dreadful sandals. She then drove him down to a pub he frequented where he could vent to his fellow book people and other weirdos about his new black son. Sir Walter sat quietly, his huge head tilted to one side, weighing up his new family and no doubt planning to shred Roger like crispy duck when nobody was looking. After Roger had slammed the front door still grumbling, Sir Walter wandered over to the biggest and most expensive sofa and hopped up. He extended his body to full length and caught the last ten minutes of Antiques Roadshow before dropping off and snoring like an earthquake. He seemed peaceful; it was quite honestly like he had come home.

Meanwhile in the kitchen, my sister was frantically frying mince in a huge pan whilst asking Alexa questions about massive dogs. The girls had filled a mixing bowl with water and placed it in a corner next to the dog bed largely made up of Roger's wardrobe. Mel suddenly shouted, "Oh my god, we have no lead, he needs a lead, girls go get two of my belts from my dressing room and make a temporary lead, he'll need a walk tonight." The girls ran upstairs, loving the assignment.

Mel plopped down on the sofa next to Sir Walter and lightly sprayed the back of him with Febreze. Luckily he didn't notice.

"I'll take tomorrow off I think, help him to settle in."

Well this was new, she didn't even take the day off when my Granny died, she had her laptop on her knee in the hearse.

"What about work?" I asked.

She shrugged and said very casually, "What about it?"

And that was the moment that Mel became a mother.

Girls

The girls were thriving in Dublin. I really felt incredibly happy about them spending time with my sister who, yes, was buttoned up and snobbish but she loved the girls and she treated them like her own. What more could they want from their only aunt?

In three days, Sir Walter had become man of the house and my sister had finally felt what it was to love. Not care for because you felt responsible, not put up with because it had been agreed upon, just pure love without any agenda or reason. You have to love family, there is no choice, this was the reason that Grant and Phil Mitchell kept shagging each other's wives, killing each other and then reviving one another – they were literally bound to do so by blood. This is the reason that I put up with Dave's diabolical underpants and the girls' relentless meltdowns, they are family. But a dog? A dog is a choice and because you don't have to care, when you do it is appreciated. So, Sir Walter, the big smelly mutt that he was, showed gratitude to my sister's caring nature and he showed her with licks. This dog with a gigantic tongue would wake my sister in the night with a wet one on the cheek, he would lick the plates in the dishwasher so clean they needn't be washed. He even licked Roger, possibly knowing that if he did it Mel wouldn't have to, and so in a very short time he had become a solid part of the furniture.

After much whiskey and a night at The Hole in the Wall, Roger had just about managed the stairs up to his front door and had then spent the night with the room spinning in the dog's cashmere bed. Sir Walter had taken himself up to the master bed and was very comfortable in Roger's usual spot.

Roger had no choice but to get on with it and, for the first time ever, I saw evidence that my sister would not respond to her husband's whimpering. "Just get a bloody grip," I heard her telling him during one of his late-night crying sessions. So Roger must have realised which side his bread was buttered on and wiped away his tears, downloaded an app on how to communicate with dogs and darn well manned up. Sir Walter was here to stay and, unless he wanted to sleep on the floor of his shop, Roger had better get on board. Taking heed of the warning not to approach from behind, he would carry the dog food out of the front door, round the house, through the side gate and then in through the back so as not to take any risks. "I don't want to end up in A&E now, do I?"

And then minutes later he would appear at the back door only to find Sir Walter had turned around the other way, now with his back to Roger, leaving him flummoxed. Eventually he would slide the bowl across the kitchen floor and swiftly back away. It was all good fun, I enjoyed watching each meal time with great pleasure, wondering whether Sir Walter was being a belligerent beggar intentionally. I hoped he was.

I had managed to spend a decent amount of time with the girls. Walking a dog on two Gucci belts glued together through the main streets of Dublin got us quite a few stares. It felt wrong when Mel came home with a proper lead, dog bowl and bed – the end of a very short designer era.

My final two days before heading back to what I now deemed as hell was not without its own revelations. Finding out my youngest daughter was gay actually left me wondering why I hadn't seen it before, what had I been doing for the years when all the signs were there?

It all started with Connie, Nancy's drop dead gorgeous, jawline to die for, hair from the Head and Shoulders advert, ridiculously perfect daughter – even I fell a little bit in love with her. She was a young Penelope Cruz with a husky voice and could pull off a crusty hoody with torn hot pants. The way Michaela hung from her every word and was incredibly nervous around her had my rusty old gaydar spring into action.

I observed the interaction quietly from afar, just wondering and I suppose hoping I was wrong. I hoped I was wrong because this would mean she hadn't been able to talk to me; confide in her own mother about such a huge part of her life. I was fine with her being gay but I should have been the first to know.

Chef Stewart cooked us a lovely dinner on the Tuesday. Michaela was now showing a real interest in cooking, she had struck up a rapport with Stewart, a typically Scottish chef with ginger hair and a ruddy complexion. He was precise and organised, exactly the type of cook my sister needed. Apparently, Mel would send him an email monthly with her preferences and he would show up and serve up without any conversation. Michaela quietly observed and he would occasionally throw her an onion and would just say, "Dice" and she would oblige. All very military but quite effective, I think words are sometimes abused and used to excess.

So on that particular evening it was smoked fish risotto paired with a stunning Sancerre; the evenings were delightful in this house. Such class at mealtimes, although I did go a bit mental on the pre-dinner cocktails.

Connie had arrived earlier, briefly smiled at me then they scurried upstairs and spent at least an hour in Michaela's room apparently talking. After they emerged with raw chins, they gazed at each other whilst chopping vegetables. It was only when Connie almost sliced her middle finger in half did they snap out of this strange haze.

After a good few glasses of chef's recommendation, the penny finally dropped. My napkin had fallen on the floor for the third time, it was one of my clumsy days, and I witnessed a hand-holding session under the table between the girls. I stayed down there far too long before eventually Suzy nudged me.

"Are you asleep? What are you doing?" I came up red faced and dizzy.

"Damn napkin got stuck to the floor, who cleans these floors, so sticky."

Connie very cooly said, "I'll let my mum know."

"So, are you dating anyone?" I tried to trick the happy couple by outing them at dinner. Cunning Connie was good, she was smooth as chocolate.

"No, I am concentrating on my studies."

I raised my brows and wobbled my head toward my daughter. "And what about you, eh, anything you want to tell me is there?" I waved my glass of wine toward Connie, spilling a good glug on my sister's plate. Michaela was agitated.

"No Mum, you know I'm not. For god's sake, what's wrong with you?"

My sister was mopping her plate with a napkin and looking a little pressured.

I stood up, Roger stood up at the same time, either to catch me if I fell or to run away.

"Sid down, Roggy." And he did, the tit. Suzy's infamous eye roll was followed by a "Oh my god, you're so embarrassing". But I didn't stop.

"I'd like to make a toast!" I looked at the guilty party with fury.

"Raquel, stop it right now!" Mel attempted to ruin my flow.

"Ssshh shhh." I put my finger on her lips. Brave.

"To secrets, to keeping secrets from your mother." And with that the final dregs of my wine left my glass and landed on a very pretty looking cheeseboard. They all gasped, it was so dramatic of them. Connie looked down, possibly afraid.

"Right, you've had enough, we're taking the dog out, get your coat." Mel pulled my chair away from behind me and shoved me out of the room. Teenage eyes bore into the back of my head as I left.

Out on the streets, Sir Walter the bloody good boy walked very serenely alongside my sister. I linked her arm for support because without her I would have gone under a bus.

"So … you know then."

"Know that my daughter is a lesbian by getting underneath a table? Yes, I know, and it's not nice to be kept in the dark."

"So, are you cool about it?"

"Of course I am cool, I am a cool mum, really cool and open minded and cool as fuck, actually."

My sister smiled because deep down she knew I was not really cool at all, I was a blithering idiot blundering through life.

"So you know? You knew didn't you, before me her actual mother?"

"Because she told me in confidence and it's easier to go to somebody other than your parents with this sort of thing, to test the waters."

"I'm hurt, Mel, I can't believe I missed it."

"She wasn't totally sure herself until recently … and then she met Connie." I scowled.

"Well who wouldn't fall for Connie, the girl is a supermodel waiting to happen."

"She has a good head on her shoulders too though Raquel, not just a pretty face. And Michaela is going to be just fine – it's 2022, anybody can be anything without judgement."

"Maybe, but she's going to need me … being a gay woman still has challenges."

"And she's got you, so just be there for her and try not to out her when you're pissed again, yeah?"

I agreed. "Yeah, I will probably not do that again. Damn wine!"

"What do you think Mum will say?"

Mel was right to be concerned about Mum, she could be a sharp-tongued old goat.

"To be honest, Mel, Mum has changed quite significantly, you need to see it to believe it."

"I'll come over next month. I'm overdue a visit anyway."

So we made a plan for Mel to visit my parents and to see their new arrangement. Then I had an overwhelming surge of guilt that I couldn't hold in any longer.

"Mel, I have something I need to tell you, tell someone." Mel ushered me towards a bench by the river. She was concerned.

"Tell me!"

"I have fucked up Mel, I have created a disaster at home." I sat on a bench swinging my legs like a ten-year-old girl and poured my heart out to my sister about Matt.

"Are you fucking nuts?" was the first response, followed by "You've dug your own grave," and then a couple of eye rolls and a head in the hands for guilt trip purposes.

Sir Walter listened to the whole sorry tale with great interest and then turned his back on me, looking out across the river, pondering my impending demise.

"I know, Mel. I am all the things that are written in the mid-life crisis handbook. I was bored, I felt unloved, insignificant."

She was angry. "You sound like a middle-aged man who's been caught with his pants down, you sound like Dad, actually."

"Instead of bollocking me help me, help me make this go away."

"For the sake of the kids I will do whatever it takes to make this go away." I was glad of my sister's support no matter what her motive was. I moved to hug her.

"Get off ... unbelievable!"

There was no hug. She walked slightly in front of me all the way home to make me feel like staff.

I called Dave before I fell asleep. I had messaged him every day about Sam and to talk about the girls but I hadn't actually called him yet.

"Hello."

"Hi, where are you?"

"At the pub, why?"

"Just wondering. Where is Sam?"

"At your mother's."

"Oh OK, well I fly back tomorrow."

"Good good, err, just a minute, a lager mate ... and a chaser. Way-hay!"

"Who are you talking to?"

"Just Matt from across the road. He's a good lad."

I sat bolt upright, a nervous rash immediately made its way from my chest to my neck.

"Matt, from 23. Why are you out with him?"

"Can't hear you love. See you tomorrow."

Fuck my actual life.

My sleep was fraught, I dreamt of lesbian weddings which I was not invited to, I was peering through the church window in my knickers and bra to get a glimpse of my daughter on her special day. I had nightmares about Matt whispering into Dave's ear whilst smiling like a Cheshire Cat. I woke at least three times and paced around my loft suite like a madwoman on mushrooms, talking to myself in whispers. I had to get control of my situation and I had to do it fast.

My flight was early evening so I had an entire day to broach the taboo subject with Michaela. I didn't want to make a huge deal out of this so I went to her room under the pretence of needing a hairdryer. She sat in her bed surrounded by books, hair frazzled like Einstein, looking up at me with nervous expectation.

"So, Connie's nice." I dragged my fingers along the curtain fabric pretending to be interested.

"Yes, she is."

"Have you been seeing her long?"

I pretended to read the writing on the label of the hairdryer.

"Well clearly not as I only met her two weeks ago." She folded her arms in an impatient way. "Just get to the point Mum will you, this is painful. And it came across like you were some gay hater."

"Well, I think you make a lovely couple … funny thing actually my first boyfriend was gay."

"Are you sure he wasn't pretending to get rid of you?" She smiled.

"Well that's rude! No, I caught him in a very compromising position with … actually that is not important.

She stood and walked over to the window and leaned her elbows on the sill. "I'll make this easy for you Mum. She is not my first girlfriend. She is my third. I have always known that I don't like boys, not in that way. I thought I was asexual for a while and then I got some feelings. I am totally chilled about it and I didn't tell you because, well, you make things awkward sometimes and I don't want that weirdness."

My heart sank. I do make things awkward, I am a bit of a twat by the looks of things. I had to do better.

"I used to like Mel and Sue you know, back in the day."

"Mum, please leave!"

"Yep, sorry." I handed back the hairdryer, we both knew it was not needed.

Suzy had stayed uncharacteristically quiet during the episode that I would call going forward 'gaygate'. Normally Suzy, with traits of my mother, would not miss an opportunity to put down my mothering or to dog her sister and any of her difficulties. The silence told a story, one that I had not been a part of. Suzy knew that her sister was batting for the other team and had somehow kept it quiet. "Because I was asked not to and, to be quite honest, what are you, blind?"

Suzy the rude little bitch put me firmly in my place. Maybe I had been too caught up in my own shit, perhaps I was emotionally absent and, in essence, was just a housekeeper keeping out of the family's affairs. I needed to be more present.

We had the chance for one last lunch before I headed back to probably find Sam with a nipple piercing and my husband selling the house from under me. We all went down to Roger's local for a pub lunch – it was a dog-friendly pub and that was now top of the list of importance. No more swishing about The Ivy, no more five-star rooftops with white-gloved waiters. It was wellies and flat caps, it was dog hair in the Marie Rose, a whole new world for my sister who would need shares at the dry cleaners for her Chanel suits. She was becoming so attached to this dog that I could see him lying at the judge's feet whilst she gave her closing statement. "I put it to you, sir, that you are guilty of murder in the first degree." And then she would ask the dog his opinion on the length of the sentence. One bark for every ten years. Ooh the laughs I could have.

It was a bright and breezy afternoon as we trudged in a large group down the hill to The Hole in the Wall. Connie had joined us although hadn't made any eye contact with me and kept as far away as possible. Roger had acquired a soft pair of boots for walking, bought in a size massive to accommodate his dicky toe, and these were now his official dog-walking boots. My sister held the dog's lead across her body just as she'd been taught on the Crufts website and looked very professional in her racing green

Barbour and pearl earrings. Suzy was quiet, texting relentlessly and looking quite cross. Eventually her face broke and she exclaimed, "Finn's coming! He's on his way." So this slippery little looker that she had been chasing was joining us too. Christ, it felt like speed dating once we all sat down and got our menus.

Finn arrived in a vintage leather jacket that smelt of a horse. Remember the guy from Grease 2, I think his name was Michael because it rhymed with cycle. Well, this young man was his double – highlighted hair, a natural tan, blue eyes and a classic square jawline. He would have done well as a suit model for Jaeger and possibly some chunky knit advert for the sexy side of the Scottish Highlands. He had it all going on; parents loaded, seemed pretty intelligent, a fairly posh Irish accent and a shiny black Golf which no doubt was called 'The Shag Wagon' behind closed doors. My daughter was besotted; normally cool and a bit of a bitch when it came to boys but she was quite the Stepford wife with this one.

"Let me get you the specials menu, Finn, and do you want a drink? I'll get it." He had arrived a little late so by the time he had sauntered in, we were all sitting and drinking and had ordered. Suzy was fussing around him in a very embarrassing way. Michaela quietly observed, smirking and ready to drop a few of her bombs.

"You alright there, Finn, can you breathe?"

Suzy was incensed but trying to keep her cool. "Ha ha, shut up you silly little shit."

Back to Jaeger boy for more smothering. "Are you warm enough? It's freezing in here. Have you got a jumper in the car?"

He was clearly used to this level of attention because he just kept on patting her hand and smiling as if to say 'down girl'.

Michaela was lapping this up. "Be careful, matey, she usually snaps the heads off her toys once she's finished with them."

He put his arm around her and cooly said, "That's interesting. So do I." And they both looked at each other and smugly smirked. It was then that I witnessed the birth of Fuzy, a shallow pair with themselves as their specialist subject.

I wondered what Dave would make of this; both his girls

fully immersed in teenage dating life, leaving us oldies to make diabolical mistakes and act like the kids. A bittersweet pill for me to shove down my cake hole knowing that my behaviour back home was tantamount to relationship suicide – it would seem the kids were doing better and good for them, I think. Even Mel and Roger were laughing together, smiling naturally and, to be quite honest, they all looked like the perfect family out at the pub with their dog, enjoying life. And then there was me, the crazy relative wheeled out for a day trip from the asylum. Must do better.

I had managed to squeeze a conversation out of Connie and, bless her, she was a little wary but once I had managed to convince her I was not a gay basher and that I had a real soft spot for George Michael, she conversed with me about her dad, her extended family still living in Madrid and how she hoped to become a marine biologist studying whales in their natural habitat. I wanted to ask what their unnatural habitat was, the M6? But that humour would be lost on a half-Spanish, half-Irish lesbian who I had already offended, so I kept it in my funny jar for a later date. All in all, a nice lunch, I left in a taxi feeling as if everybody had grown. Not me but I was working on that. The girls had another fortnight of summer fun and I envied them; it was a shame that Sam hadn't joined them but between my parents, Dave and his mates, he had fished every fish in Cheshire and slept under the stars most nights so all was good. It was time for me to get home and clean up my mess, which I felt confident I could do if I could just get the nobs at 23 to emigrate.

My sister and I had a rather awkward conversation in her study before I left. I was sitting in the leather chair of shame with her behind her desk, looking over her glasses with Sir Roger watching from the corner like a bouncer waiting for trouble.

"So you're to tell Dave that you're sorry you haven't been yourself lately. It's the menopause and also a lack of self-belief."

I frowned. "Errr I do believe in myself, I just strayed from the path."

"Yes, yes whatever, I am telling you this in case it does come out; you need to plead insanity, get it in early as insurance."

I went to give her a high-five for her legal prowess but I was left hanging.

"OK, and to this Liverpudlian, his name is Matt, right?"

I nodded, shuddering at his name and the thought of him.

"You say the same thing, you are suffering from menopause; there is nothing less sexy. Tell him you have lost your mind and he isn't the first, you do this sort of thing all the time and you need to get help."

I cocked my head. Hmmm this could backfire. "Are you sure, this sounds dangerous, what if he flips and is annoyed he has been used?"

My sister sarcastically smiled. "Raquel, he is ten years younger, sounds like he is way out of your league, I am sure he'll get over it, you daft sod."

Firmly put in my hormonal place right there.

"And what about Dave and Mum and Dad, and then there's Arif, we're all intertwined. Plus he has the wife who is nice enough but I think she has a nasty side."

My sister slammed her fists onto her leather-topped desk that I am sure once belonged to Churchill. "Raquel, pretend it never happened, go about your business, distance yourself and he will soon forget about the whole thing. Concentrate on getting Dave back on side. Stop overthinking everything.

I nodded, I have my instructions and now I must get on with it. We hugged but she made sure her nose was pointing away from my hair as it hadn't had a wash in days. Sir Walter nodded as I left, I think he was wishing me luck.

As I drove away in the back of a taxi, they all waved from the grand steps of the house, It felt as if I was off to war. Who knew that Dublin would become my safe space and really, I did not want to leave the comfort of Riverside View. I imagined that as I turned the corner, they would all mutter things under their breath and open a bottle of Veuve. 'Thank fuck for that.' 'Nut-job.' 'Tart.' 'Homophobe.'

Mel was right, I was a chronic overthinker.

As the wheels hit the runway, I took a deep breath. Dave was collecting me from the airport and whilst this was not a scene from Long Lost Family, we had sort of been lost for a while. I wanted to rectify things, see the good in him, remember that I had once found him funny, attractive and desirable. I was forcing it a bit so I decided to focus on the fact he had been a loyal husband. That's the word I would keep on repeating when he humped up and down on top of me for a couple of minutes, loyal! And when he licked his plate clean, especially if I had made a chilli, loyal. Yes, loyal and dependable and that was enough, it had to be.

I stood outside Manchester airport in the drizzle. I checked my phone but I had no messages to say he'd be late. I eventually sent him a message.

Hi, landed!

Five minutes later, he started typing.

SHIT, SORRY I AM AT WORK. GOT CALLED IN. SAM'S AT YOUR MUM'S. WILL TRY AND CALL LATER. SORRY

This was not a great start, this was not loyal, not dependable and frankly not like Dave. Could I be annoyed? Should I be or should I just take it like a man because I had been playing up, the guy was at work. So I acted like a grown-up and did the right thing.

No worries, hope you are OK. Will leave you a sandwich, see you later xx

And then I ferociously kicked a bin and headed home in a cab pondering whether to butter the bread with dog shit.

Damage Limitation

Life at home in Cheshire was like a ride on the dodgems that lasted two whole weeks. Night one was not too bad; although the house was a shithole and the fridge had things growing in it that I could have sold as good bacteria to the wankers at Yakult. The mountainous washing pile was mainly jogging bottoms with remnants of half-dead fish and scotch eggs in the pockets. I could handle that, things we expect as a mother of boys. I had this in the bag. Twelve hours of laundry, cleaning and tidying and it was like I had never left. It was the other shit that I found difficult, the to-do list that Mel had given to me that was actually messing with my mind.

Dave had showed up at 4 am, dropped off by a colleague stinking of bhajis and lager. He crashed into bed next to me fully dressed and immediately started snoring. The old Raquel would have been less than impressed, but the new and improved nice Raquel pulled off his jeans like the skin of an unripe banana and placed a chilled bottle of water next to him, leaving him to sleep off his pasanda in peace. I made a cup of tea and sat in my office checking emails and paying bills. What a lovely time to be awake and alone. The world, well the world that was my cul-de-sac, was silent and although the sun threatened to appear I knew I had a couple of hours before the anxiety-inducing daylight tapped me on the shoulder.

Just as I was finishing reading an incredibly interesting junk email about 'Squirt club' which I was invited to join if I had decent enough squirting powers, the lights went on at 23. It was 4.30 am. Who has Botox at this hour? Position assumed, I watched the movement at the house of doom with the stealth-like skill of the SAS. Little yellow lamps created a glow in the lounge of 23 making the place look like a fortune-telling tavern.

The front door opened just as a number of cars pulled up outside, as usual without their headlights. Various people emerged from the house and filtered into the waiting cars. Matt and Gina, who both had caps on like American tourists, ushered people like tour guides into the motors. Finally, the boot opened on a particularly large 4x4 and one very small person hopped in. With all the cars busting at the seams, they did their three-point turns and glided off and out of my view.

Not being known for my skills of detection after making a burglar a cup of tea whilst he filled his van up with next door's silver, I did my best not to jump to conclusions. In my defence, said burglar did tell me he was on official business, he also proved this by providing his ID. Admittedly the word 'council' written in bubble writing was a little iffy, however it was laminated so I pulled out the big guns and gave him two custard creams to dunk in his tea. The officer taking my statement told me that it was an easy mistake to make and then under his breath he said, "If you were a blind man."

So just what exactly was going on in this house? I racked my brains for the various options. I did happen to know that doggers generally stuck to lay-bys and car parks so I ruled that out, although perhaps this was a dogging splinter group breaking boundaries and travelling en masse. I firmly decided not to google doggers and their habits as I was in enough trouble as it was.

Whatever dark and dingy underworld they were a part of, I had to distance myself and fast. I did not want to be associated with these people for many reasons and wanted no traceable connection with them at all.

Former chef and renowned food writer, Raquel Fitzpatrick, teaches non-cooking best friend Matthew Dennis to create healthy meals and to shop smarter

This was the headline I was faced with at 9 am. It was official. I was embroiled horribly. I couldn't get rid of it. This was the start of four weeks of articles with Matt and I cooking and shopping together, documenting our every move. This was the Curse of Strictly but with food and no dancing. People would say, 'One Shepherd's Pie and the knickers were down.' I had to stay strong, be British about the whole thing and just lie and deny until it went away.

Dave got up late and wandered into the kitchen rubbing his head.

"Hello love, sorry about last night."

I cheerily brushed it off and handed him a strong black coffee. "No problem, how is work going?"

"We're nearly there, ready to make some arrests and then I'm going to take a couple of weeks off in September. Perhaps we could go away?"

"Away, to where? The kids have school."

"Not them, just us, your parents can have the kids, or my parents could come over."

I thought about it. If Dave's parents came over I would prefer to be around. I liked them and I missed them, I would enjoy spending time with them. They could be a bit annoying, Dave's dad took his daily paper into the toilet with a pen behind his ear and did the crossword whilst pooing. He would hand it to me afterwards and ask me to finish the bits he couldn't do. His mum had a very alarming obsession with Aromat seasoning, once showering my six-hour slow-roasted leg of lamb in her magic yellow dust. They had their quirks, but a poo-stained crossword and chicken-flavoured sheep was a small price to pay for the kids to see their grandparents.

"Something to think about, could be nice."

"And the girls, how were they and your sister and the tit?"

I sat down at the table ready to fill him in on all that happened on my trip, leaving out the bits that made me look bad, obviously. By the time I had finished, Dave was open-mouthed and bulgy-eyed.

"So my youngest daughter is gay, my oldest daughter is punching but the most shocking thing is that your sister has a dog. Well, fuck me, that was one hell of a trip."

"How do you feel about Michaela?"

He sighed. "Honestly, I don't care, if that's what she wants or is then so be it. It's me and you I have been worried about, Raq, we haven't been good have we?"

I shook my head, guilt flooded into my face. I was uncomfortable but I remembered myself.

"I think I'm menopausal, not been feeling myself. A bit crazy actually."

He nodded sympathetically. "Yeah that makes sense, Pam from the canteen at work, you know Pam with the beard, she twatted a delivery guy round the face with a joint of meat because he was late with the order, that was the menopause you know." The fact I was being compared to Pam was quite painful but I nodded like a dog, knowing this could save me at a later date.

"Yes, I can see bad timekeeping could make a menopausal woman do terrible things, lots and lots of terrible things."

He smiled. "Don't worry love, it doesn't last long."

He had no idea, no idea at all.

"Hey, why don't you take some of those hormones, BLT or HMP, whatever it's called?"

"I'll look into it, Dave, and if things get any worse I will have a sandwich and check into prison."

"Good girl!" he said in his warm cockney voice, clearly not listening to a word I had said.

We went to collect Sam from my parents together. It was rare that Dave was off during the day so it felt quite alien to be in the car with him. He drove like a copper, adhering to the speed limit and eyeing up all other vehicles with suspicion.

"So, you went for beers with Matt from across the road?" I held my breath, praying and hoping there was no air of suspicion.

"He came over and asked if I fancied a pint. He's alright you know, he's coming out for the footie tomorrow night."

I felt sick, what sort of game was this guy playing? Maybe I could run him over – not kill, but just hospitalise and get him out of the picture for a bit. Hoping to scupper Matt and Dave's plan, I made a suggestion.

"Actually, I had sort of thought it might be nice for us to go for a meal tomorrow evening with Sam, you know because I've been away."

He frowned. "When Arsenal are playing in the Community Shield? Are you mad? Not a chance, Raq."

Crisis not averted, not at all. The rest of the journey I was narrow-eyed and full of a rash.

Mum's cottage was still spotless and organised, vastly different to the chaotic misery and staleness that had been there since they had retired. Fresh flowers from the garden were arranged in a cut-glass vase on the hallway table, there was the faint odour of lavender in the warm air, the downstairs loo had been painted in a lovely deep red and six of Dad's summer shirts blew away on the line outside the back door in symmetry. It was all so perfect. Mum came bounding in from the garden in a cream tracksuit, something I had never witnessed in all of my days on Earth.

"I've been power walking with your father." She stretched down and touched her toes. Dave, who was unfortunately positioned behind her, winced. "Crikey, I can see what you had for breakfast, Suzannah."

Mum shot him a look. "Too much David, too much."

I could see Sam in the garden carrying a bag of compost towards the shed.

"Has he been OK?"

"He is a wonderful young man, a real credit to you. And he's a great help for his Grandad, plus he gets on ever so well with Arif, they have a good bond."

Mum was so positive these days, not a snarl or a scowl, no mention of how much weight I had put on or the fact that Dave's fingers were yellow and curry-stained.

"So you're still enjoying having Arif around?"

"Yes, in fact we are thinking of offering him lodgings. We have four bedrooms and he lives in a hovel no doubt."

"That's a bit presumptuous, Mum, how do you know it's a hovel?"

"He has to go to a launderette to wash his clothes, and the

other day he brushed his teeth in the shed with a bottle of water and a mint leaf.'

"What, really?" I looked at Dave and he frowned.

"So what we thought was that he could stay here, we will give him a small allowance and help him with his studies. Like an adoption slash au pair."

I laughed. "I think the word you're looking for is carer, Mum."

"No it bloody isn't. Housekeeper, house manager, live-in caretaker."

Arif emerged from the laundry room with a striped pinny holding a pile of freshly ironed sheets.

"Hello Mrs, Mr," he nodded at Dave. "I go now and make up beds."

Mum whispered to me, "He sprays the sheets with rose water before he irons them, such a clever boy."

And off he went to make everything perfect upstairs. Dad came up to the cottage with a summery glow, he had a basket brimming with fresh veg for me to take home. Sam was, as all teenage boys, underwhelmed by my return. I hugged him and smelt him, as all mothers do. "Somebody needs a shower, young man."

He looked at his dad. "She means you." Dave chuckled.

"I'll take you down the pub to watch the footie tomorrow if you have a wash. The mighty Arsenal smashing Liverpool, you having that lad?"

Sam was laddishly sucked in, he beamed from ear to ear at the thought of the bantz, the back slapping and the roar of the pub when the Gunners put one in the back of the net. Yes, I got the lingo, sadly.

"What's this, footie?" Dad was now involved in this conversation. Dad could not be less footie if he tried. He would not fit in at footie and why was he even suggesting it? Dad was cricket, he was bowls and at a stretch rugger, as long as one of the royals happened to be on the team. Dad at footie would be like Eamonn Holmes at Ministry of Sound, it would not work well and would be cringeworthy.

"Tell you what, Dave. I will bring Arif along, he likes the football." Dave just agreed, he didn't give a shit who came as long as his team won and everybody sank twelve pints without puking.

"Dad, they don't do vermouth at The Kings Head, you should probably give it a miss."

"Very amusing, Raquel. I like the pub, I like football, I can drink a pint or two."

"Well, we shall have a girls' night won't we Raquel? Let's not let the boys have all the fun."

"Hardly a girls' night Mum, there's only the two of us."

"I'm sure we can drum up the troops, darling." And she began texting with her brand-new acrylic nails.

"No Mum, we will go to the pub and join them, women are allowed aren't they Dave?"

Dave had lost interest at this point now that his football match was being infiltrated by old people and Turkish adoptees. He plonked himself on the sofa, shut his eyes and folded his arms, his go-to position when the hangover kicked in.

"Right so it's settled, we will all go to the pub and watch football, do we need scarves?"

"No Mother, we do not."

During two frothy coffees with hearts on the top created by Arif the Barista – this boy's talents knew no bounds – I was regaled with some alarming tales from Mum about her new regime consisting of power walking, yoga, jam making and rekindling her sex life with Dad. Earlier that week she had downloaded an app that allowed my parents to get into positions that would make a Russian gymnast jealous. By the end I was ready for a bottle of gin in the bath.

"It got me thinking, Raquel, once I had mastered the downward dog in yoga, could these skills be transferable? And I was right, we did things that I hadn't done since my twenties." And then she nodded knowingly at Dad who rubbed his knees and winked.

My eyes, my eyes. It was unimaginable, unthinkable and downright disgusting.

I drove home, shuddering every few minutes.

Need to see ya babe. You free? M x

Another reason to shudder but also an opportunity to spin my middle-aged crisis spiel to Matt.

I could pop over, are you available to discuss the article? R

Yes! See you soon. MX

I slipped out of the front door shutting it quietly, leaving some potatoes on the hob on low, I would be five minutes and then back home to mash them. Dave was in the bath watching a box set, he would never know I'd gone.

"Hello gorgeous."

Matt had jersey shorts that clung to all the right places, no top and wet hair. I was wearing loungewear which clung to all the wrong places, crispy hair and no bra. Gorgeous I was not.

"Matthew, good evening."

He shut the front door and went in for a hug, I patted him on the shoulder keeping him at bay.

"Have I missed you babe, the street's been shit without you."

I walked into the kitchen where two glasses of rosé wine waited for us by a lit candle.

"Matt, I just came over to let you know that this thing, this friendship, whatever you think it is has to stop. I really like you but the thing is–"

He stopped me, he put his finger on my lip.

"I have thought about you and us every minute you've been away. Let's just enjoy the times we get together."

I brushed his finger away and stood back. "No Matt, I am serious. I am actually mental, mental and menopausal. I basically am not of sound mind."

He smiled. "That's what I love about you." I stepped back.

"What I am saying Matt is that I get these obsessions with people and you were just one of those and now it has to stop. So that's it now, no more."

"Have a drink babe, you need a drink, just relax."

I considered downing the whole glass. "No, I am not here for a drink, just to say it was nice working with you but now I have my own life and family and this is where it ends."

"We'll see." He smiled. What a menacing and unsettling response to being dumped.

"No we will not see, I am telling you no more texting, no more anything."

He was undeterred, unfazed, not listening.

"One kiss and then you can go."

"Absolutely not and, by the way, stop hanging out with Dave, it's completely inappropriate."

He sat on a kitchen stool and sipped his wine. "First I lose me girlfriend and then I lose me bestie."

I whisper shouted at him. "I am not your girlfriend and Dave is not your bestie, are you serious?"

He relaxed. "I am not serious babe, chill, it's cool. I'll miss you though."

I felt better, banter king was just messing with me. "Excellent, I will miss you too … as a friend and colleague."

He burst into laughter. "You actually are crazy, but I still love ya."

As I walked to the front door I couldn't stop my inner detective. "By the way, I saw you this morning, with all of those people. Funny time to have a gathering." His smile disintegrated.

"Family, babe, early flight. Bit of a curtain twitcher aren't ya."

I headed home and heard him wolf whistle as I walked away.

As dumpings go that went pretty smoothly and, quite honestly, I was starting to relax about my misdemeanour which was actually quite minor – a few kisses and a fumble, a few dodgy messages but nothing too serious. I would now concentrate on my family, my work and myself. Dave, Sam and I ate sausage and mash, watched a film and all was well.

Is it sorted? Mel

Yes, all sorted, phew! R

Act your age for god's sake. I am flying over with the girls next week, can I stay at yours? Thanks for the visit, it was enjoyable. Mel

Will do Melon! See you next week X

I went to bed that evening feeling positive, I had some work to do on my marriage, I had some effort to put in with the kids, but I had a clear mind so onwards and upwards. In the spirit of fresh starts, I allowed Dave to shag me from behind and I didn't complain once.

The King's Head was busy but Dave had secured us a table in the corner, the big screen projector thingy was down and the build-up to the big match was being shown. Mum and Dad, bless them, had attempted to dress for the occasion and had both been to Marks & Spencer's for the bluest jeans I had ever seen. Dad sipped beer from a bottle and Mum said "Oggy oggy oggy" when I handed her a G&T.

It was a dreadful evening weather-wise. The rain was smashing onto the windows like buckets were being thrown at them and the faint sound of thunder rumbled in the distance. The smokers huddled under a shade sail attached to a large oak tree. I didn't have the heart to tell them they would be fried alive once the lightning hit the tree. This was Dave's local; everybody shook his hand, bought him a pint and had a joke with him. The barmaids all knew him by name and were quite flirty with him. He was a 'Have one for yourself and keep the change' sort of punter. This was Dave's place, his second home. Arif sat next to Sam sipping a bottled water, I wondered if he had ever been to a pub before when a big game was on, he looked intimidated and overwhelmed surrounded by these big blokes wearing tops that were far too small for them. Mum stroked Dad's knee and whispered into his ear and then he choked on his beer and sprayed it everywhere.

"Cooey cooey, Gina we're over her."

I looked behind me and there they were, Matt and Gina, gatecrashing my table. Gina wryly smiled my way, Matt shook Dave's hand. This was their local, too. Liverpool were playing, I had no right to be annoyed, no reason to be worried, I had set him straight and I must act completely normal.

Mum was all over Gina like a bad rash. "I love your bag, really classy." The bag was from Marc Jacobs, I knew this because it had Marc Jacobs written in large white letters on the side. I doubted it was really from Marc Jacobs but that was because I was being catty.

Her eyebrows were higher than normal, her heels were insanely high, she looked like a boss bitch and I was glad that I wasn't kissing her husband any longer. Matt and I exchanged casual hellos and I did my level best to avoid any eye contact with him. He offered me a drink and I said "no thank you" to the carpet.

The game kicked off and everybody was concentrating. I had no interest so I wandered off to the bar because it was finally empty. As I waited for the barmaid to go down to the cellar for more vodka, Arif and Gina both walked behind me and out into the car park. He looked upset and she looked annoyed. "Just nipping to the loo," I told the barmaid as she fiddled with the optics. I sat in the cubicle side-saddle on the toilet and listened at the window. Arif and Gina were just on the other side of the glass.

"I fucking told you that you need to stay with the others, you can't move in with them. And what the fuck are you doing here? You could be working."

"This is work, Miss, they want me here."

Her Scouse voice turned to a hiss. "It's not work and you know it isn't, Arif. I am calling the car to pick you up."

"Please, I want to watch football game and try pint."

"Well, you can't, go inside and tell them you have to leave, tell them you need to help a friend out. NOW!"

I stormed out of the toilets bumping into Arif on the way in. Gina was tapping her phone furiously.

"Where do you get off bullying kids?"

She looked up coolly. "Excuse me, babe, I'm busy."

"Well, unbusy yourself. I just heard you bullying a young boy, I am not having it."

"Babe keep your nose out, he works for me not you."

"He works for my parents and actually he is going to move in with them and there is nothing you can do about it, you don't own him."

Gina stood over me and said, with a condensing smile, "If I were you, Raquel, I would run along quietly. Unless, of course, you want me to show all the messages between you and my husband to your entire family. Shall I let them all know that you have been messing with my husband for the last few weeks? Just a classic desperate housewife." I was silent, stunned and I felt physically sick.

"See you in a bit, babe." And she walked back inside with a sneaky smile.

The roar of a goal from the mighty Arsenal broke my shock. Fuck fuck fuck, did Matt know she knows? Would she kill him in his sleep? How had she got hold of this information? My head was busy with many unanswered questions, I needed to leave the pub, sell my house and run away.

I stood staring at the bar, listening to half the pub chanting deafening songs and the other half, the Liverpool fans, grumbling things about a referee being paid off. The game began again and the room fell almost silent. I stayed at the bar, I couldn't face her. I was frightened that she may blurt it all out. People do that when they've been betrayed, they grab microphones in pubs and publicly shame the cheaters. I looked back and saw her, she had sat right next to Dave and she winked at me, she actually winked. This was very, very bad.

Pondering my next move whilst considering lying under the whiskey optics with my mouth open, Matt appeared next to me almost touching my shoulder. I froze.

"Not a good idea, move away from me, she knows!" He stayed put. I nudged him with my elbow and said again, "She fucking knows Matt."

He tipped his head towards mine and he said in a very low voice, "Listen babe, just keep your mouth shut, yeah, and everything will be fine. You don't want to fuck with Gina, she don't mess about."

My eyes widened and I turned to him, I didn't care who was watching. "What are you two involved in?"

Shaking his head, he said "Always asking questions aren't ya? You need to keep quiet. We might have a couple of favours to ask here and there but stop twitching them curtains and our little thing will never need to come out."

"How long has she known?" My voice was shaky.

"She has always known, Raquel, it was her idea."

I was scarlet. They were in on this together. I was up against a wall and out of my depth.

The Irony

Following the football match, I kept the blinds of my office permanently closed. I had no intentions of being witness to any further shadiness. It would seem I had been the victim of a cruel prank at best, at worst the lead role in a blackmail plot.

Work had sent me a couple of small projects which I was happy to get my teeth into, anything to avoid focusing on the crushing humiliation.

From: Jane Aldgate
To: Raquel Fitzpatrick

Morning Raquel,

Great response to the feature with hot Matt! Wish he was my neighbour ⋯ lol!

Sending you a batch of ready meals from M&S, they want to boost sales. Can you write some nice stuff about them, big them up a bit, the health influencers have made a huge dent in their sales, that bloody Joe Wicks and his big mouth has got all their customers cooking from scratch. Dick!!

Also, we're hearing that gooseberries are making a comeback, no doubt heading for the superfood list. Can we get a couple of recipes together involving the little green bastards, we have to stay ahead of the game.

Cheers,

Jane

So a week of over-salted under-flavoured box meals to review and a conundrum with little sour berries that I didn't even like. The mood I was in, I planned to crush them up and snort them to see if I could get high.

Dave was full of beans after Arsenal smashed Liverpool; he celebrated with a full English, a pint of coffee and what he called a "grog log" which knocked me sick. His day at work sounded promising, his phone constantly buzzing as he chowed down on his black pudding. Lots of "Yes mate, we got them pal, and the eagle has landed" type convos. How I longed for the simple life of cornering criminals and throwing the net over the dregs of society, it just seemed so simple. Whilst still being unsure as to what part I played in this horrid fiasco at 23, one thing I did know was that my grasp on reality was certainly waning. I had taken my eye off the ball big time when I allowed my stupid self to be sucked in. I fumed. Did I think that three pumps and a squirt with a Saab salesman looky-likey was really the way forward for me? Me, an educated upstanding pillar of the community, OK well perhaps that was an exaggeration but I had children and a 4x4 Volvo, I owned my own home and actually happened to be respected in my field of work. My downfall could not be at the hands of a plastic gangster who had asked me if 'Osso Buco' was the leader of Isis. My sister was a lawyer, my husband was an officer of the law, her dog had been knighted, these fuckers would not take me down, not on my watch.

I was livid, pumped, ready to smash the shit out of anyone who got in my way, I was Raquel Fitzpatrick not some wallflower with a spine like Play-Doh. Fuck this and fuck them, I refused to take this lying down.

But later that day, I did lie down and I did take it.

Raquel, need you to take some people over to a warehouse this afternoon. Three of them, be ready for 3 pm. Gina

I'm afraid I'm busy. R

It doesn't work like that. Do we need to discuss recent events with your Dave? Would he like to hear about the utility room?

I imagined Dave's crushed face when he heard what I was doing whilst he was out with Sam, the betrayal he would feel knowing his wife was chasing after a man he had been for pints with. I had no choice. I could say they were lying but he would know, he would remember when he walked into the kitchen that day and how weird the vibe was.

Send me the details. R

Mum called to tell me that Old Tom had fucked up his back whilst trying to lift a tree trunk off the bonnet of his car. Apparently he had been parked up in the thick of the woods watching wildlife through his antique binoculars and the handbrake failed. A likely story, there was definitely more to it, there always was with him. "So, your father has invited him to stay here and recuperate. Normally I would have said no but with Arif here I'm sure we can manage. It'll be like boarding school, midnight feasts in the corridors." I cringed, it almost sounded sexual.

The story of Old Tom niggled at me that afternoon, Dad's crinkly old cousin had sort of crept in and out of our life for as long as I could remember. He was the guy who did all the odd jobs really badly but nobody said a word because he was unmarried. Being unmarried is not an excuse for mowing the lawn so badly that a specialist had to be called in, it also had no bearing when for eighteen months if you turned on the porch lights all the sockets sizzled inside my parents' cottage. To call an electrician would have been an insult, according to my ever-loyal father. When questioning Dad on why he refused to call this moron out on his clear lack of handyman skills in his actual handyman role, the story went a bit like this:

Tom had been quite the country gent. His parents owned a small but stately country home just north of Stoke. Tom was their one and only son and, when they both perished during a picnic on an unsteady cliff, he inherited the lot. He had absolutely no reason to learn a trade as running the family estate required two qualifications: a hoity-toity attitude and a good aim with a hunting rifle. Tom had it in the bag, he had the marksmanship to shoot a bluebottle between the eyes and he wore a silk cravat unless he was in the bath. It was all going so well until a young Tom fell for a scarlet woman; this was apparently the beginning of the end.

Dad told it best; my sister and I would sit with our hot chocolates of an evening listening to the appalling and dreadful demise of our randy old relative with a penchant for a bit of rough.

"She targeted him, you see, she made it impossible for him to refuse. She was a beauty, blood-red hair and milky white skin, a vampire's wet dream." Dad's eyes would light up at the very thought of her.

We loved this story, it was like an episode of Dynasty which, incidentally, we were not allowed to watch because Dad had to put a cushion over his trousers if Alexis and Krystal had a punch-up.

So, she and Tom planned to marry. She was his stable hand and had no means to speak of, no family and had no business bending over for the lord of the manor, but he was hook, line and sinker for the girl. Her status or lack of it had no impact, he was an olden day Richard Gere and she was his hoe.

On their wedding day, which was held in the grounds of the big house, ginger nuts was a sight for sore eyes in a waist-hugging satin dress cut so low you could see most of her double Ds. Her entire shapely back was exposed and you could just see a bite mark close to the buttock where she had been attacked by a bear … in Cheshire.

But just as Tom was about to crown his queen, a plumber from Warrington objected during the crucial bit of the vows. He claimed this woman as his wife of ten years and the mother of his very angry triplets. "She only popped out to get twenty fags for me breakfast, that was two years ago. I've given up smoking now." The crowd gasped as the plumber told his tale whilst holding a wrench.

It was actually the engagement announcement in an upmarket newspaper that had been the vessel for this deserted man's cod and chips that had alerted him to the impending bigamy. "I mopped up gravy with me barm cake and there she were."

Tom had pulled out all the stops with whole Scottish salmons, French champagne and a marquee that could house an army, so even though the scarlet woman was driven away in a van with an old toilet on the front seat, in true British style, the show must go on. It was sad, awkward and particularly upsetting to see Tom doing the first dance with an upside-down broom. To be fair to the band, they played the wedding song with passion and finesse right until the last note when Tom put the lips on Mrs Broom and the crowd gasped once more.

He never loved a woman again, the wasted love and his parents' cash was used on his second passion … Lady Ladbrokes. And so Tom lost the house, he lost his status and he put his last five grand on the second favourite at Uttoxeter – it lost.

The apple doesn't fall far from the tree. My stupidity of late would rival all of the above and then some. I would go down as the dumbest person in my family leaving Tom to bask in my misery. I was glad a tree fell on him, it made me feel warm inside.

Three men in retro Adidas tracksuits sat in the back of my Volvo looking tired and washed out. Not one of them spoke to me apart from a nod when I opened the car door for them to get in outside 23. The address I had been given was an industrial estate on the edge of Liverpool so for an hour and a half I inhaled their body odour with my hands shaking at the wheel.

I pulled up at a corrugated iron building and beeped my horn as instructed. A roller door ascended and Matt emerged with a smaller guy, one that I had seen driving one of the cars previously. Matt opened my door and the sweaty men got out and went straight into the building without any acknowledgement. I really should have detoured to Boots and bought them all a can of Sure, that would have been the correct and kind thing to do.

"Is this her?" The small bald one smirked.

"Yep, this is her." Matt cheekily grinned. "You can go now." And he banged the top of my car with his hand. In my wing mirror I spotted a sea of heads inside the warehouse lined up like a school assembly hall. There were certainly more than thirty people crammed in there and not one of them looked happy.

I now had a firm suspicion that this endless stream of foreign people were illegals; Matt and Gina were running some sort of migrant worker ring and they were the only reason she had nice handbags and good eyebrows. They were running this operation in plain sight of a police officer – when they realised that and how risky it was it was too late, they had already bought the house. I suspected they had hatched a cunning plot to get me involved knowing that it would be better to have me on side than outside, watching their every move from my window. And now I had helped with the transportation of these people just to save my sorry cheating arse from exposure. I needed Mel, she was the only person who could get me out of this.

I arrived home to another episode of 'Live Better' equipped with pictures sitting in my inbox.

Matt was proudly holding a sea bass with a glint in his eye and there was me chopping up herbs behind him wearing a wedged heel and lip gloss; we were both smiling, we looked close. I could have cried.

Mel listened to my predicament in complete silence, not even an oooh or ahhh. She paused before delivering a very sobering message. "This is going to get ugly." She offered no real comfort and she said she understood why I did the drop-off but apparently being in prison was not a better option than telling my husband I had been unfaithful. I guess she was right but it was too late now. "You didn't even sleep with him, Raquel. For god's sake, I am positive Dave has flirted with people in the past, he may have even kissed somebody. He would have got over it."

I doubted it, the old saying don't shit on your own doorstep was invented for situations like this. This would be a struggle without the fact it went on under his lawful nose.

She also brought up something I hadn't thought of, something quite dreadful. "You have an illegal immigrant working at Mum and Dad's; you arranged it and drove him there yourself. You have even handed cash over to them. There's a trail of you doing business with these people. This is going to look like you're all in on this."

I imagined Mum and Dad attending court with coats over their heads, civil rights activists pelting them with eggs. Dad would no doubt end up being the prison bitch because he said yes to everything and Mum would definitely be a grass. They were in no way good candidates for the nick.

How would I fare? It wouldn't be a picnic that's for sure. The food would be enough for me to try and break out and then I would be in solitary confinement getting kicked up the arse by the screws for no reason. A girl from college had an aunt in prison and she told me that they made their own sanitary towels out of cotton wool and mini cereal boxes. With this in mind and the large number of prison documentaries I had binged on, prison was not an option for any of us.

Dave called me from work. "You better get the champagne opened! We got them all, major success."

"Well done, really pleased for you, Dave, all that hard work paid off."

There was a raucous celebration going on in the background and, from the sounds of it, several portly detectives were ordering the takeaway to end all takeaways. "Six whole crispy duck, extra pancakes, chicken chow mein times seven, fifteen spring rolls ..." Some woman was shouting the order almost into the phone as I was trying to hear Dave tell me how they had done it. "Call me later, Dave, enjoy the Chinese." The line went dead as somebody probably rugby tackled him to the floor as a sign of affection.

I knew not to expect Dave back at a sensible hour, this had been the big one for him, equivalent to winning the league I was told on many occasion. He deserved to stuff his face with Chinese and do the conga round the office and I sort of hoped he would have a snog with a colleague to even things out a bit. Pam with the beard would probably be a good option on many levels. Besides having facial hair which she wore with a strange sense of pride, her cooking was of a level that would never get past a health and safety officer, he'd be back in no time.

I'd made soup that evening, something comforting to calm the nerves. Sam loved his soup with big sides of buttered bread so he and I sat with it on our laps watching bloopers from X Factor. This was what I was supposed to be doing, how my life should be. Just me, my son, leek, potato and Simon Cowell, and for a moment I forgot to feel the terror. And a moment was all I had because a knock at the door ruined my evening.

Arif tugged at my arm whilst pointing across the road. "Come quick, Mrs, quick." I shut the front door quietly, not wanting Sam to be witness to anything connected to the neighbours. "What is it? What's the matter?" His eyes filled with tears as he struggled to splutter it out.

"It's Barbara, she sick."

There were no cars at 23 so I presumed Bonnie and Clyde were out recruiting more slaves. I had to help so I shouted into Sam that I was popping to the shop for white wine, a very believable and likely event.

Barbara was upside down at the bottom of the stairs, the Hoover was entangled in her legs and one of her crocs was hanging from a wall light. She was moaning faintly as her eyes rolled around in her head like marbles.

"Can you hear me, Barbara? What happened here my love?" I used my Casualty voice, slow and steady, apparently that's how you did it.

No response, just more moaning and then a little bit of yellow vomit trickled from the side of her mouth and onto the collar of her violet cardigan. I turned to Arif. "We need an ambulance, call 999." He furrowed his monobrow.

"You help her, make her better."

I laughed slightly. "No my love (why did I keep saying that?), she's had a fall, she needs a doctor. Hurry."

Arif hopped from foot to foot. "Do you have your mobile? Mine is at home, you need to call for help." He didn't move, what was wrong with this boy. Barbara's eyes stopped rolling and she turned her head to Arif, she tried to say something but instead more yellow stuff spilled out.

"Ring a fucking ambulance now," I yelled at him, I felt bad but needs must. He turned and went toward the kitchen shutting the door behind him. I could hear him talking so I presumed he was going through the details with the emergency services, it was his aunt so he should know her full name and date of birth. God knows how long it would take as his English was extremely broken. I held Barbara's head with my right hand and held her hand with my left; it was tricky because I had an itchy foot. I wondered if I should put her into the recovery position so I could scratch it but if she had a neck injury, I would be responsible for a cleaner who couldn't clean. After what seemed like an age Arif emerged from the kitchen. "They be here soon."

"Get a cushion for her head. Cushion, quick." We wedged Barbara's head underneath a pink velvet cushion, her wiry little legs still clung onto the Hoover almost like a witch on her broom; had she tried to ride the Dyson, is that what had happened? She drifted in and out of consciousness and we just sat and we waited for the siren.

"Call them again, this is taking ages."

Arif went to the window of the lounge, "It's OK, Mrs, they here."

"Thank fuck for that!" I was relieved, I wasn't good in a crisis and my foot was still itching.

Gina, Matt and the other guy came through the door and stood looking at Barbara and then at each other.

"It's OK there's an ambulance on its way. Go get a blanket until they get here." I urged one of them to help instead of staring. Nobody got a blanket.

"We'll take it from here babe, off you go." Gina dismissed me immediately. I took offence to that; I had sick on my shirt so I intended on seeing this one through until the end.

"No, I'll wait and explain to the paramedics what happened."

Matt opened the front door.

"Off you go babe, Arif can explain. Ta for your help."

The three stooges bore into me with their cold looks and I was forced out. I turned back to Arif. "Can you let me know how she is?" He nodded and before he was allowed to speak the door was slammed.

I rushed upstairs to my office, got on my knees and watched through the thinnest slit possible, willing the blue lights to turn up outside 23. It never happened, instead I watched a limp Barbara including the Hoover being carried like a sack of spuds over the bald one's shoulder out to the car. They poured her into the back seat without much care if I'm honest and, within seconds, she was being driven away.

The warm white wine came out of my desk and I swigged it from the bottle in the dark, my heart pounding. Surely to god they had taken this woman to hospital, surely that was where they were going? They must have thought it would be quicker if they drove her there themselves, that was it, I was sure. I said a prayer that night for Barbara and one for myself, of course.

The following day I invited Mum and Dad over to eat their own body weight in ready meals. I didn't mind tasting them but, being a former chef, I could taste every single chemical they added to this stuff to make it last a week in the warehouse. There was nothing too spicy so I told Mum to leave the Gaviscon at home. I asked Mum if Arif would be joining them but she was leaving him with a rug cleaner they had hired from Homebase. It took me a moment to realise that this was not a person. I surmised that Barbara must have been OK as he wouldn't have been at work if she wasn't. I wondered if he had contacted her family to tell them about the murderous Hoover and I hoped to god she was recovering somewhere nice and quiet. Perhaps she would buy me a new shirt when she was better, I couldn't bring myself to keep the one she had soiled.

Mum and Dad pretended they were on MasterChef as I plied them with meals that came in boxes. The chicken stuffed with porcini was apparently "exquisite". Dad said "Bravissimo" and wiped his mouth. I wondered if he knew that was a lingerie company. Mum's favourite was the Icelandic cod mornay, apparently she could see the Northern Lights if she shut her eyes. When we got onto the vegetarian option, Dad had lost interest.

"Cauliflower as a main course, what is going on here?"

"Dad, the cauliflower is the most popular vegetable right now, people love it."

"Are you suggesting people who aren't vegetarian eat this for their dinner?"

"Yes, they have it marinated and baked."

"The whole thing?"

"Yes, or as a steak, rice, anything."

They both looked at each other and shook their heads.

Mum was flummoxed. "A whole cauliflower for dinner … my bowels wouldn't thank me for that." She shuddered, so did I. So the pesto cauliflower went down like a shit sandwich, literally.

Desserts were a success, Dad had chocolate on his chin which Mum wiped off with her wet thumb, the treacle tart was apparently an "oldie but goody" and the Eton mess was exactly how it was described, a complete shambles, a lazy dessert that had been created in a factory by someone wearing wellies.

"All in all I think M&S have done themselves proud." Dad threw down his napkin and rubbed his belly. "I bet you wish you could cook like that, eh love?" Dad patted my arm and headed off with his paper, unaware of the insult he had just landed.

"Are we having a little drinky?" Mum eyed up her bottle of gin on the kitchen worktop. "Mother, it's 2 pm, bit early don't you think?" She sat back down, deflated that her daughter would not get 'on it' on a Tuesday afternoon. I put the kettle on and probed her a little about Arif.

"He's been very quiet actually darling. Still working like a Trojan though, just not as smiley."

"Is he moving in with you?"

"He hasn't mentioned it, I don't want to push him but it would be great for Dad and I."

"Has he mentioned his parents or family?"

"Only that they are poor and they don't have the resources in his country that he needs for an education."

I put a cup of tea in front of her and she scowled at it.

"Who does he live with?"

She got impatient without the gin. "I don't bloody know, what's with all the questions? You're not stealing him from me, we couldn't cope without him, Raquel. Get your own cleaner."

Little did she know she would be sewing mail bags soon and there would be no G&Ts where we were going.

Dad had an hour on the sofa sleeping off the M&S hoard whilst Mum walked around the garden sneering at all the plants that needed attention. I pointed to the hose through the window urging her to do some gardening but she pretended not to understand.

Dave and Sam arrived home from the most successful fishing trip to date just as my parents were leaving, so they were subjected to many photographs of tench, carp and river trout, all absolutely furious to be plucked out of their homes to smile for the camera.

"Well done lads, keep up the excellent work." My dad was so desperate to get home and loosen his trousers he started reversing before Sam had finished scrolling.

As Dave was getting the gear out of the boot I heard a Liverpudlian voice. Christ, what the fuck did she want? I listened at the door not wanting to be seen. It wasn't to be, Dave shouted for me to come outside. My heart had landed in my knickers, I had no idea what I was about to be faced with. Sheepishly, I opened the door and saw Dave standing with his back to me in front of Gina who was wearing a black all-in-one with heels. A boiler suit and stilettos in the afternoon. Really?

"Hello!" I waved from the front door, not daring to take a step further. Dave turned around, he was smiling, that was good; not crying, smiling.

"What we doing tonight, Raquel?" I was silent. "Anything planned?" I still had nothing. "I think we're free aren't we?" Eventually my brain allowed my mouth to make a word.

"Sam, we have Sam."

Gina's perfect smile tricked my husband. "It's no problem, bring him along too." Dave nodded eagerly.

"Superb love, see you later. Can we bring anything?"

She looked right at him, sultry and sexy. "Just bring yourself." Dave went bright red and nodded way too fast.

In Too Deep ...

I lay in bed, looking at the ceiling in the pitch black with Dave lying sideways. It was 2 am and the events of the evening had no intention of allowing me to sleep. To say the plot grew thicker was an understatement. The plot was now so thick, it gave my thighs a run for their money.

Under duress I had showered, put on a very beige and dowdy dress with a pair of trainers which was a completely unacceptable combination unless you are over 5"6'. Dave said "Oh" when I came downstairs and nothing else. We were due at 23 at seven for drinks and nibbles, and I was hoping to be back home for eight. I planned a nasty headache or a bad stomach, anything to cut this night short. Dave was much more relaxed since his work had calmed down; he was cheerful all the time, it was annoying. The twats were all dressed up in jeans and white shirts and brand-new trainers, they looked exceptionally smug.

Gina was motherly towards Sam, which I hated. She handed him a can of Coke, which I also hated, and with her bony arm around him she pointed to the garden where I could see Arif kicking a ball against the fence. What was it about that kid? He was always around. Sam shot out happy as Larry that he didn't have to sit with the adults, he liked this boy's company. With deportation looming, I felt sorry for them both. Dave and Matt went out to join them with beers and I was left alone in the pristine kitchen with Gina.

"Nice to see you've made an effort, babe." She looked me up and down.

"I'm not staying long, I don't feel very well."

"Is that right?" She was staring at me for far too long.

"Your hubby's a nice guy." She looked out at Dave and cocked her head, I felt rage.

"Yes he is and I want you to leave him alone, leave me alone and don't contact my mother either."

"So negative Raquel, just relax, go with the flow."

I decided to be a grown-up.

"Look, I am sorry for what I did, I am really sorry for it all. I just want to get on with my life and you get on with your life, why don't we just do that?"

Gina hopped up so she was sitting onto the island and looking down on me. "I will tell you when it's time for us to part company and, until then, just keep your phone on and be available."

I was furious. "I am the wife of a police officer, I can't help you. I have children. Don't contact me again after today, this is it."

Gina looked at me with pity. "You just don't get it do you? You're already too far in now."

"Why, what do you mean? I kissed your husband a couple of times because I was drunk and stupid and hormonal. In fact, I am going to just tell Dave and get it all out on the table. I might get a slap on the wrist but you two, you're gangsters and what you're doing is wrong."

I walked towards the back door, I couldn't be a part of this shit any longer, but just as I was going to open the door, Gina jumped down and said, "She's dead you know."

I stopped and turned. "Who is?"

"Barbara ... she died. Why didn't you call an ambulance, babe? So careless of you." My neck rash appeared.

"Hang on, I told Arif to call an ambulance but he just called you. I begged him to get help. You knew that."

"Did I?" She was sarcastic in her tone.

"What did the hospital say, what was wrong with her?"

"She didn't make it to the hospital, sadly. She died at home. Well, at the warehouse."

"She lives in a warehouse?" My voice was reaching notes that would make Charlotte Church wince.

"Yes, it's very cosy."

"Did you even take her to hospital, Gina?"

She shook her head. "We have a doctor on site, there was

nothing we could have done by then. If only the ambulance had been called straight away. If you think about it, it was you that killed her, really. Any normal person, anyone not involved with 'gangsters' as you call us, would have called for help. Just goes to show you're as guilty as any of us, doesn't it?"

"I need to use your toilet, where is it?" I was wild, mind racing, throat dry.

"First on your right, top of the stairs. Please use the spray if you're planning on making a mess," she shouted after me.

Legs like jelly, I climbed the white carpeted stairs that had been the crime scene for the dead cleaner the night before. The lone croc was still hanging on the wall light, I reached up and placed it on the windowsill of the landing. How could they have walked past it knowing what they did?

I sat in their bathroom on the side of the bath rocking backwards and forwards, my brain pulsating with all of the possibilities. If this woman was an illegal immigrant then I don't suppose they could take her to a hospital without raising suspicion. But where would they take her body, was I going to be asked to put it in my fridge? Would I then be asked to chop it up with my dad's axe? I tried not to catastrophise but it was difficult. I'd been doing it my whole life and this was an actual catastrophe. To be honest she fell down the stairs, it's hardly murder, but then they might say I pushed her, I had it in for her. Oh my god. And then there was Arif. I mean his aunt was dead, he must have been devastated. He didn't look it. I heard a ping.

Darling, isn't it wonderful. Arif is moving in with us. Gina has confirmed it all this evening. I have agreed to pay a small fee for his papers and relocation but it's very cheap. Gina is sorting it all out for me. It's going to be a full house again, just like when you and Mel were at home.
Mum x

And there it was, the grip tightened. Mum was now housing one of them and transferring money to the ring leader. I had been driving them about in my car and DCI Dave was swigging lager in the garden with a man whose pants I had been rummaging in. Not even Jeremy Kyle himself could sort this lot out.

The rest of the evening was a blur. I did manage to ascertain that Arif thought Barbara was in a small hospital for old people and animals on the edge of Wales. He mentioned that a sick old badger was on the same ward. I was confused but Matt put me straight; "He means codger not badger." And then he laughed loudly and high-fived Dave.

The cocktails flowed and Gina put some crisps in a bowl and some tasteless cheese on a plate and that apparently Constituted as nibbles.

"You don't get a figure like mine, Dave, by eating all that fancy stuff your missus cooks." She continued her overly friendly flirting with my husband. What could I say, what could I do?

Dave was visibly disappointed at such a poor effort on the food front and I knew he would be planning a late-night fridge raid when we got home. I stuck it out until ten o'clock, by then I was close to tears and needed to get away from that house. I had fake smiled quite enough for one day and my aching jaw needed a break.

Back home I threw the beige dress in the bin, I knew I looked like a bulging paper parcel and, to be honest, it only sent a message to Dave that I was making bad decisions on all fronts. I listened to him rifling through the fridge like a pig on the hunt for truffles and hoped he would eat enough carbs to go to bed for thirty-six hours.

I called the girls and Mel whilst sitting on the back step since I hadn't spoken to them in a couple of days. They were both still with their significant others and both still enjoying Dublin life very much. I missed it, I missed them. Sir Walter would not leave my sister's side, he even sat in the bathroom whilst she took a shower or a bath and would basically guard the door. Due to this, my sister would be driving over to see us with Sir Walter and the girls would fly; she couldn't be without him and vice versa. I don't remember agreeing to have a massive dog in the house, but it was fine, anything was fine, I needed support.

At midnight I got a ping from a random number.

Hello this is Arif. We must talk, can you come to your mother's house tomorrow – Wednesday? Please don't tell anybody I contact you. This is friend's phone. Tomorrow please.

I didn't answer, it could have been the gang testing me. I didn't want another death on my hands, I would simply visit my mother and see what happened. There was nothing more that I could do without taking legal advice. I hadn't even had the guts to tell Mel about Barbara, I was becoming so paranoid even talking on the phone. I would go to Mum's to pick gooseberries for this bloody article and if he happened to be there, we could talk.

So there I lay, staring at the ceiling with a black cloud sitting over my head. How could I have spiralled into this mess and allowed a couple of thickos ruin my life? The problem was I had been led to believe they were stupid, but it was an act. They may not have been educated but they were cunning. They saw me for what I was and I played straight into their hands. It was at least another hour before I drifted off into what was a very unrestful sleep.

Mum and Dad had taken a trip to the big Ikea because old Tom needed new towels for his en suite. Mum said she couldn't allow Tom to use the John Lewis ones, not over her cold dead body. They planned to have lunch in a country pub on the way back and had left Arif to look after Tom and the house. I let myself in quietly, I didn't want Tom coming down to look at my tits and ask me what mess I had got myself into this time.

Arif was buttering toast and was making up a very nice tray to take to Tom. He had put jam in a small silver pot with a lovely old spoon, a pot of tea with a matching cup and saucer; his service skills were Savoy-esque.

He looked up and nodded. "When you've done that, I'll be in the garden." He nodded again and scurried off tray in his hand and tea towel over his shoulder.

I stood in front of the gooseberry bush with a colander plucking randomly and not concentrating at all. I had put my largest and blackest sunglasses across my knackered eyes and at one point I picked up a surprised bee and threw it in the pot.

Arif joined me picking the fruit, we were both behaving as if we were being watched, talking out of the corners of our mouths, looking over our shoulders and jumping at every noise.

"You need to stop them, Mrs, they have a new shipment coming in soon. Children and old people too, as old as Barbara."

"Have you told your family about Barbara's accident?"

"She is not my aunt, she came on same lorry. We got told to say that, it makes it, how you say … legit"

"So where is she? Where is she now?"

Looking like he really believed it, he said, "She in hospital, animal hospital."

"That's good." If only he knew she was probably in a wheelie bin round the back of a Spar.

"There are more people coming next week. It's so crowded in there, people are sick, can you help us?"

I sighed, perhaps I could have done if I wasn't so heavily involved. I would simply have shopped them to Dave and he would have swooped in with a SWAT team and sorted this lot out.

"It's difficult, I don't know what to do. Why do they agree to come here?" He teared up, the poor little guy was so young and here he was, kidnapped and trapped. "At home it is worse, we all come here to get a good life. They tell us we have nice home and good job, no war and we earn money for family. When we get here they put us in big warehouse and take all money for keep. They tell me I get education for free but they just send me to cleaning job."

"Where are your family, Arif? You told me you are Turkish, but there is more to it than that, isn't there?" I took my glasses off; it seemed inappropriate not to look this kid in the eye.

"My mother she in Syria, my father he dead."

"I am so sorry." I put my hand on his shoulder.

"No sorry, he bastard."

"Ah OK." I took my hand back.

"Can you help us?" He was desperate. "Please?"

"I can try to help you, I don't know about the others."

"Please you must try. Don't tell Miss Gina I tell you this, she has bad men to hurt us."

"I won't, don't worry. Stay calm, OK?" He nodded and looked at his watch. "I must go and give old man tablet."

"Nice watch!" I pointed to the vintage jewellery which looked strangely like my mum's sixtieth birthday present from Mel and me that I had spent three months searching for.

"Your mother she give to me, very cheap she say, not good style."

Mother was still her true self somewhere, after all. I was pleased. I watched as Arif scurried off to tend to dirty Old Tom. One thing I knew was that this kid did not deserve to be sleeping in a disused factory run by the Third Reich; I could at least do something about that.

Hi, My elderly uncle is staying at my parents and we need extra help. Can Arif stay from today please? Of course we will pay more. Let me know if you need any more help and I will be available. Sorry about last night, I wasn't myself. R

Good to see you're on board, babe. Shouldn't be a problem. £500 a week cash for him.
G

That sounds fine, I would prefer to pay Arif directly into his account. Do you have the details? R

Lols, he doesn't have an account. You pay me, I pay him.
G

Mum probably won't like that, it could have tax implications. Is there a way around it? R

Does it look like I give a shit about the taxman? If you want him, that's the deal. G

So I swapped a little bit more of my soul and at least £500 to keep Arif off the factory floor.

As I was almost out of the front door and just as I was about to become home and dry, Old Tom appeared at the top of the stairs in nothing but a silk dressing gown. I knew this was all he had on because the stairs were steep and I was looking up. His crinkly manhood winked at me in the most menacing manner. His silver hair was gelled back, his face was clean shaven, he looked better than he had in years apart from his penis; that still looked homeless.

"Trying to get away without saying hello, young lady?" He came down a few steps wincing in pain.

"Please don't come down Tom, you should be resting."

"I need some air, I want to sit outside."

He came down a few more stairs stiffly, my hand was on the handle of the door, I wanted and needed to bolt.

"Well help me then girl, come on." He waved his stick at me.

I had no choice, another pensioner falling on a staircase with me in the vicinity would land me in the same boat as Harold Shipman. I helped the doddery old twat down the rest of the stairs wishing he had chosen the underpants option.

Arif was vacuuming upstairs, none the wiser that the patient had escaped. I imagined the toe nail clippings and dandruff that lived around Tom's bed, no wonder the Hoover was screaming.

As he lay down on the kitchen sofa groaning and clutching his lower back, I thought up ways to cover his crotch area. The silk gown didn't even reach the mid-thigh.

"Let me get you a blanket Tom."

"No, no, it's too hot, I'm fine like this."

He relaxed, everything spilled out. I turned my back; it was the only way.

"So how are you, my dear?"

"Fine thank you. Sorry to hear about your accident."

"Yes, it was very painful." He moaned again and turned on his side so we swapped cock for saggy bum.

"If you need anything Arif will get it for you, I really need to go and work now I'm afraid, you're in good hands."

"Yes he is a very attentive and professional young man. What's his story, I mean where is he from?"

I stopped in my tracks. "He's from an agency."

And I headed out of the room.

"What agency?" he shouted me back.

"Not sure of its name."

"What country is he from?"

"Err Turkey I think."

"Where exactly in Turkey?"

"Not sure, the north?"

"We can have a good talk about that this afternoon, geography is my strong point."

"Is it?"

"Yes dear, it certainly is."

I drove home feeling weird, but then again that was normal these days.

My sister was arriving the following morning on the ferry with the dog. Roger was thankfully staying in Ireland so at least I didn't have him looking over my shoulder. The girls were flying into Manchester in the morning at 11 am. I had the remainder of the day to try and get my head straight, make some stuff up about gooseberries and write up nice descriptions of the M&S meals. Dave wanted to go for a picnic with the girls when they got home and went off to a local deli for some nice bits – it was also sample day so he wouldn't need any lunch.

Gooseberries are annoying as fuck. Maybe it was my mood but I was struggling to say anything good about them. With all the bad press sugar was getting, unless it was Christmas using a whole bag of sugar in anything was as bad as shooting up heroin. That put jam firmly out of the picture, and besides jam making was laborious and readers of the Mail were too busy trolling people for fun.

I settled on a gooseberry fool made with yoghurt so it was cool for the fatties, a gooseberry and elderflower mocktail, great for the winos and those on dialysis, and finally my pièce de résistance, a gooseberry chutney that would complement any cheeseboard (it is still basically jam but I was running out of time). The truth was, if the humble gooseberry was indeed a superfood full of antioxidants then the smart thing to do would be to eat them raw straight from the bush. But that's not article-worthy. "Don't do anything to them, just eat them!" The end.

So the trusty apron came out and I did what I did best, pottered around my kitchen creating stuff. Immersing myself in a world of bubbling pans and cocktail shaking, this was who I was or at least who I used to be.

Full House

It was 5 am and I sat in what was essentially my pyjamas in a lay-by on the M56. I had left Dave a note to say I had gone off early to get some fresh shellfish from a guy I knew at the fish market in town. It was believable enough, I had done that before, once.

My presence had been requested to help one person get from A to B on a crisis mission and I was apparently the only person for the job, according to Gina in one of her bossy messages late the previous evening. I didn't put up a fight, I was going to cooperate until I could sit in a room with Mel and hash this all out.

I sat with a strong coffee, my slippered feet on the dashboard, nervously waiting for my human delivery. After thirty minutes a car pulled up behind me and flashed its lights three times. These criminals were so obvious, who does that unless they are up to no good? Idiots, that's who. I waved my arm out of the window and Matt emerged with a girl in a big navy coat. He came to my window.

"Alright babe."

The humiliation sparked itself up in the pit of my stomach. There had been a time when those eyes and that aftershave and those jogging bottoms would have had me in a high state of passion but now, now that I knew it was bullshit, I felt disgusting.

A girl with her hood up got into the back of my car, quite a big girl wrapped in an oversized parka, around twenty in years. She had matted short black hair, quite a pleasant face and the same harrowed look that all the others had. I nodded to her, this was the international sign for hello these days.

"She needs to go to this address." I was handed a piece of paper. "Make sure nobody sees her. Open your boot, I got some supplies for her." I pressed the button. "Nice one babe." And he blew me a kiss with just his lips. The cocky, cocky bastard.

A couple of bags were put in the boot and then Matt hit the back of the car telling me to drive away, which I did immediately. I was complying with all demands – for now. The address was again close to Liverpool but not central, it was a semi-rural destination so the drive was quite scenic. I was silent but kept the radio on low.

We arrived forty minutes later at a very nasty-looking bungalow at the bottom of a very nasty-looking street. It looked derelict but I was definitely at the right place. The house had a name; Redwalls, but its once red walls were now brown. I reversed up the drive as close to the front door as I could, the girl leaned forward and handed me a door key. I wondered when a good time would be to let this person know that I was not part of the gang, that I was in no way involved in this fiasco, but it would have been pointless because I was.

The two carrier bags in the boot contained food and toiletries in one and clothes in the other. The only fresh item I could identify was a small carton of milk; she'd be lucky if she didn't have scurvy after a week of that. I ushered the girl out of the car and opened the front door.

"What the actual hell!" I said.

She looked at me with a frown, it was the first time I had spoken out loud. This place was dire, it was cold, damp and smelled of mould and staleness. A grey sofa, that had surely been thrown out and then salvaged, sat in the middle of an open-plan space. The kitchen was no bigger than my cloak room and it only housed a vintage microwave covered in bean juice, at least that's what I thought it was. I kicked open one of the cheap doors, not wanting to touch anything with my hands. Behind the first was a single bed with a quilt that someone had definitely wiped their arse on, the other door led me to an avocado-coloured bathroom where there was a corner bath with a couple of inches of stagnant water just sitting there like a swamp waiting for wildlife.

The curtains across the patio doors were red velvet of surprisingly good quality, but they were tied shut with some butchers string, presumably to keep any house guests undetected.

Lamp bases without shades and just the bare bulbs sat either side of the sofa; it was depressing.

I looked at her, she seemed OK, she didn't scream or run away, it made me wonder what horrors she had left if this was an acceptable place to stay. I placed the bags on the sticky, Formica worktop.

"I am going now. Will you be OK?"

She was blank, I don't think she had even basic English. I pointed to the door and then to myself and she nodded.

"Thank you," she said very huskily and slowly. I smiled and I felt genuinely bad for the girl but nothing was keeping me here any longer, I needed to leave. Besides, she looked exhausted, her weary eyes told me she had been on a journey not only physically but mentally too; we had that in common. With a bowl of beans and a good night's sleep, perhaps she would be able to join the others. I wasn't sure why she was staying there alone, it was not my business.

I shut the front door to Redwalls hoping never to return. I imagined this is what a crack den must look like and made a mental note never to do crack. It was only when I had my seat belt on and I was ready to leave that I realised I had left my damn car keys in the sticky kitchenette. I went back in and pushed the door open; the girl's parka was on the floor and she had put herself onto the disgusting excuse for a bed. She lay silently on her back but I couldn't see her face, not over the top of her huge and heavily pregnant belly.

My moral compass had taken a hammering that week and I was handling that, but somehow this was a step too far. Besides her going into labour alone there were many other horrific possibilities. Without medical help, both she and the baby could die. I had no choice, absolutely none. I would have to take her somewhere safe, somewhere she could be looked after; I could not leave here there knowing she was certainly in the last stages of pregnancy. I had to do something.

I couldn't take her to my house – Gina and Matt would see her, Dave would wonder what the fuck was going on – it would have to be Duck Cottage.

I left the clothes and the bag of beans, I even left the stupid big parka on the floor. I shut the door to the hellhole and I ushered her to the relative safety of my car. Before we set off, I tried to put her mind at rest. I turned to her, sitting there staring ahead like a deer in the road.

"I'm Raquel." She didn't respond. I pointed to myself. "Raquel." She was wary and rightly so, I could have been a baby thief or planning to cut out her kidneys to sell on eBay. Tentatively she pointed at herself.

"Sophia." Her voice was deep and husky. She sounded more like a Stuart.

"Right, Sophia, I apologise in advance but I am taking you to a house with three old cronies and someone quite nice you might be able to communicate with depending on where you're from. My mother is absolutely mental and my dad will probably try it on with you but anything's better than this shithole, my love. So buckle up and let's get you to somewhere decent."

I knew for sure that not one word was understood but it felt better to just say something.

Sophia and I drove all the way to the cottage with probably equal amounts of fear and dread in the pits of our stomachs; she did fall asleep for at least half an hour so she must have felt somewhat safe.

Mum, Dad and I talked in the safety of the garden shed whilst Arif took Sophia upstairs to the last remaining spare room. I had instructed him to tell Old Tom absolutely fuck all because he was a nosey old bastard and he needed to stay in bed. Arif was so excited to see Sophia, he said, "Yes Mrs" to everything I requested.

In Dad's shed there was one cheap old garden chair that Mum had bagsied so Dad and I leaned against various garden objects and I told them everything. I had no choice. For them to appreciate the gravity of this sorry tale they needed all the grit, it was excruciating. Using words like fumble, snog, indiscretion and sexting was a very demeaning experience. Even though Dad had been a tart his entire married life, at least he had done it with a bit of decorum.

I waited for their response, my head hung low. I braced myself for impact and it wouldn't be pretty. But it was sort of pretty, pretty bizarre.

"How exciting. You're like a modern-day Nancy Drew." Mum clapped her hands together and jumped off the floor slightly.

Dad picked up one of his saws. "Right, I'll make a cot, we can't buy one, it will be too suspicious."

"Yes darling, excellent idea." Mum put her thumb up to Dad.

"You need to get up to your attic, Raquel, and get all that rubbish down you had for your three." By rubbish she meant my children's precious things. Mum with the insults as usual.

"I'll take Dave for a pint whilst you do it." Dad again, with the beer drinking.

"Yes Phillip, good idea, good man." And the thumb went up once more.

"Whoa whoa whoa. Did you hear me, guys? I cheated on Dave with a criminal."

They looked at one another and both burst out laughing.

"I wouldn't call it cheating, Raquel, your head got turned momentarily. And no bloody wonder, he really is a charmer."

Dad nodded in agreement. "If I were your age ... and also a woman."

"Dad, is there anyone you don't fancy? For god's sake." I threw my hands in the air at the pure ridiculousness of their reaction.

Mum stood and pushed me down into the garden chair. She towered over me like a headmistress.

"Now listen up, pull yourself together for crying out loud. Melanie will be here soon, she can deal with the legalities, we just need to concentrate on saving all of these poor people. So stop feeling sorry for yourself and let's get this sorted."

They were a team, they were pumped, I think they thought they were on a TV show for pensioners solving mysteries.

The following hour was like being an extra on Downton. Sheets and pillowcases were being taken upstairs, trays of various food were being delivered to bedrooms, medication was separated into egg cups for the two incapacitated house guests, it was a hub of excitement for everybody but me. Mum had power walked down to the Co-op for some folic acid even though I told her this was only required for the first trimester. She was too caught up in all the drama and had the audacity to tell me to "Chill the fuck out". Dad had logged into my online H&M account and had filled the basket with maternity outfits and baby grows. I asked him to add a very long dressing gown for Tom whilst he was at it.

My head was pounding, my bad choices were having a real effect on my family. It was all very well having support and it did feel a little bit good not to be dealing with this alone, but I felt less safe. My parents saw this as an active game of Cluedo. I wonder if they had realised the severity of our involvement.

Arif was, as per, an absolute star and was beaming as he worked. When he passed me en route to take Tom a BLT and a hot water bottle, he grabbed my wrist quite tightly and said, "Thank you, Mrs, I knew you help us."

The fact that I was probably going to get divorced before being banged up wasn't of importance to any of these people, but at least I could tell the judge that even though I was slightly responsible for one death, I had just potentially saved two. So that should shave a year or two off my sentence and keep me away from the nonce wing. I would wear a t-shirt with 'I saved a baby' across the back for at least the first month of my hard time.

Sophia was settled into her new room looking over the garden, Mum had downloaded the Kurmanji translator app after establishing she was Kurdish. We also learned that she was due in a few weeks, so it could basically happen at any time. Her husband had come in on another lorry and she had hidden her pregnancy as they, the traffickers at the Syrian end, wouldn't have accepted her due to her inability to work. She knew the risks but she had to get out of the country and this was the only way. Her husband was wanted by the authorities and if they hadn't left he would have been executed. She did the pull trigger sign to her head to show Mum how they would have done it. Mum finished it with the explosion noise with her mouth; it was inappropriate but comical.

Mum ran her a bath and gave her a whole bottle of Head and Shoulders for her dirty hair and she told her to rub olive oil into her stomach unless she wanted it to look like a road map – all this was said by a robot in Kurdish through a smart phone; it was surreal to say the least.

With everybody settled into their respective cells, Mum handed me a cup of tea.

"Right, what time is Mel arriving? We need a meeting." I looked at my phone.

"FUCK FUCK FUCK!" Mum winced at my language. "I have to go, I didn't get the girls from the airport, oh my god. Do not open the door to anyone, do not speak to Gina or Matt, right? Just stay here!"

They all nodded as I flew out of the house still in my pyjamas and slippers. Nobody picked up when I called them back, not even Mel. One saving grace was there were no more messages from the neighbours so for now they didn't know Sophia wasn't at the crack den. That bought me a little time, time I needed badly. Right now, I had to be a mother, a wife and a sister with a plausible explanation as to why I had been missing since dawn.

The house was empty, Dave's car wasn't there and neither was Mel's big shiny black Porsche. I had visions of them down at the cop shop reporting me missing, pictures of my swollen face being stapled to lamp posts with the caption 'Have you seen this idiot?'.

Gone for that picnic at Tatton Park with the kids, the dog and Mel!

A sticky note on the fridge relieved my panic slightly. I had some explaining to do, I needed a story. I was in no mood for a picnic but a few sandwiches on the grass was possibly a good way to feel normal for a little bit. I chucked on a summery dress, a straw hat and drove to Tatton Park whilst practising my explanation for my absence.

"So, you lost your car keys and your phone at the fish market?"

157

I nodded as Mel pulled a very stupid face knowing it was a lie.

"Yes, it's so silly of me, I put them down and then spent the following few hours looking for them."

"And where were they?" she asked with such attitude.

"Under a bag of mussels."

"Were they really?" She narrowed her eyes.

"Mussels? Delicious, are we having the shellfish for dinner, love?"

Dave and his bloody stomach.

"No Dave, unbelievably, I left without the fish. Can you believe it?"

He mouthed "cuckoo" to Mel and raised his eyebrows.

The girls looked great; healthy, slightly tanned but they still both had their sour lemon faces. They were clearly missing their other halves and they were back in a place where they had to pick up after themselves. They tapped away on their phones throughout the entire picnic not giving a shit about anything but themselves. Sam also looked a tad annoyed, possibly put out that he didn't have his dad to himself any longer.

Dave had done a pretty good job at the expensive deli. I hadn't eaten a thing all day so I was surviving on adrenalin and shaking slightly. He had made a real effort with the spread, there were salads and sandwiches, cold meats and fresh fruit, he'd even bought some mini cans of pink gin and tonic which I would have skulled one after the other had I not have been driving.

"Sorry about today." I held his hand, I never ever did that, that was soppy.

"It's OK, love." He squeezed my hand hard. He was really nice my Dave, a thoroughly decent guy. I would have gone into silent mode if he had forgotten a family picnic, I would have sulked even if he was being held hostage. My lips would have been pursed for at least a week and I would have cooked a mince-based dish three nights on the trot and punished him properly. Yet Dave was chilled, he didn't sweat the small stuff, he was not an overthinker or a ball of anxiety, he was actually the perfect man for me.

Mel had insisted on taking me out for dinner that evening. It was the last thing I needed but I had to act as normal as possible and it would be better that I was out of the house and away from 23. The girls were happy to look after Sir Walter and Dave was happy to stay home and catch up with his daughters; they had a lot to talk about and he was completely receptive now his work on the big case was done.

Mel and I walked to a local Indian and sat in the corner, both facing the wall like a couple of weirdos.

"The walls might have ears," I told her in my paranoid state. She rolled her eyes. She would unroll them when she heard the latest.

Six Tiger beers later we both laughed hysterically at the absolute ridiculousness of what I had created. Tears rolled down Mel's face when I added in the details I had forgotten.

"So Mum is to deliver an illegal immigrant's baby in my old bedroom, Old Tom's cock keeps flapping about and Dad is making a cot out of the oak tree?"

She slammed the table and howled with laughter.

I hailed the waiter and asked for two more. In a whisper I said to her, "But seriously, what the fuck Mel, what are we going to do?" She stopped laughing and looked up at the yellow ceiling of the Bombay Palace.

"For the first time in my life, Raquel, I am actually stumped."

This was a worry, and momentarily sobered me up. If a criminal lawyer didn't know what to do then I was royally fucked. Mel beckoned the waiter and she said, "If this is nicotine on this ceiling, it's a disgrace."

He looked up and shrugged his shoulders. "I earn seven quid an hour love, I am not cleaning the ceiling."

The following morning, Mel went to Mum's first thing; she had to see it to believe it because the thought of Mum running a hostel for the illegal and infirm was so far from her usual stance on life. I felt utter relief to get the whole story off my chest but was acutely aware no solution was on offer. I also had to live in fear of the two scumbags across the road discovering the pregnant girl was AWOL but until that happened, I would just wait. For the time being it was business as usual, unpacking cases and doing breakfast for the family; something I actually enjoyed and had missed.

It was a gorgeous morning and as the family sat down to eat, the dreaded doorbell went.

"She's not at Redwalls." Gina's eyes bulged out at me and she looked slightly panicked. I shut the front door behind me and joined her on the step.

"What do you mean?"

"I mean she's not there, she has gone and she's left the supplies and her stuff."

"Oh wow, where do you think she's gone?"

Gina was red, purple even. "I don't know, you did take her there, right?"

"Yes, I dropped her off and I watched her go in."

Gina lit a long cigarette, this was new. She looked very stressed.

"I need to find her, she had no money or phone, she knows nobody, it makes no sense."

I shrugged, although I was shaking inside and my top lip was sticking to my gum.

"Well, I am sure she's not gone far, maybe a walk or something."

Gina inhaled deeply. "She was told not to leave that house, did she say anything to you? Anything at all?"

I frowned. "No, she slept the whole way and she didn't say a thing to me."

She threw the cigarette stump onto my step and crushed it under her stiletto boot. She looked like a drag queen that day, not beautiful, actually a bit panto. Her eyebrows looked like two sticks of liquorice.

"Sorry I can't help you, I delivered her to the place like I was asked."

She let out a huge sigh. "Right, see ya. Be in touch."

She stomped off back to her house but tripped quite badly

on the kerb once she got to the side of the road and her ankle bent outwards, it was no doubt excruciating. I turned away, I didn't want her to know I had seen it, it was best that way. A small victory, I felt, to see her bone almost snap but the battle was still larger than life.

I went back to breakfast feeling slightly smug that I had kept the wolf from the door for the time being. Mel called me late morning. I took the call at the bottom of the garden.

"Well fuck me. This is a real mess, Raquel. Mum and Dad are acting like hippies. They don't seem to care that they are neck deep in crime. This girl is literally about to give birth, she keeps on groaning which is quite unpleasant. Old Tom is a joke, I asked if I could get him anything and he asked for a bottle of brandy and a mucky mag. It's a mad house."

I shut my eyes, what had I done.

"What do you think of Arif?" There was a long pause. "He is the best thing to happen to Mum and Dad since me!"

I had to laugh; she was right.

Gameplay

Having been summoned to 23 with a rather snappy message from the Queen of The Pool, I once again went out in my slippers under the guise of borrowing some butter. Anybody who knew me would find this suspicious as I would never be without full fat butter, not ever. It was the afternoon and it was raining heavily when I received the message. I was quite used to the dreaded beep from my phone and almost always expected it to be bad news. That was the norm these days.

Luckily, the family were not listening when I left the house without one of them looking up from their phones. Dave was going out for early doors drinks for even more celebrations with his police family so he was very busy polishing his head and not in the rude way.

Mel had told me to keep my conversations brief if I did have to talk to Gina or Matt; she had said that if I acted mildly stupid they would see me as a liability and realise I was not a good ally. They had taken a big risk dragging me in. They didn't know me or how brave I was and, for all they knew, I could have been down the cop shop crying onto a statement at any time.

"Don't get cocky with them, you know that winds people up."

Mel had called to try and steer her dipstick of a sister in the right direction.

"I'm not cocky, I'm scared shitless, Mel."

"Yeah but you come across as arrogant, you don't want to rile them up. And try and get some information out of them, you could do with some leverage yourself."

I agreed. I must leave my attitude at home and act dopey. Nobody wants a dope on their team. I trudged across the road trying to look dazed and confused, a DPD van almost ran me over which made it all the more realistic.

Gina had no make-up on, her ankle was strapped in a bandage and she looked very pale and very tired. Matt was pacing up and down the hallway with a cap on backwards and not a lot else.

"Where the fuck is this girl, Raquel, you must have some idea? We have to find her."

"I've told you, I left her at the bungalow. What's the problem? She probably just changed her mind and went back home."

They looked at each other in astonishment.

"Do you really think that's possible? She has no passport, no money and she's illegal. Do you think she's just swanned onto an EasyJet flight with fuck all?" Matt was annoyed at my ignorance.

"Look guys, what are you so worried about? So you lost one, you've still got a warehouse full. It will be fine."

Gina lit a cigarette and then blew smoke towards my face with frustration. It stung my eyes but I continued to behave calmly. She wasn't calm, she was unravelling. Her Botox would take a real pounding if she continued to stretch her face to these unnatural dimensions.

"You stupid, stupid woman, she could have gone to the police, she could take us all down and that includes you!"

Matt put his arm around Gina, trying to soothe her. "Calm down babe, chill out."

She threw his arm away. "Don't touch me you idiot! She could be in hospital and she could be saying anything to anyone."

I frowned, my acting was pretty good. "Why hospital, is she unwell?"

Matt sat on the stairs, the very spot where Barbara had perished. I willed her ghost to punch him in the throat.

"Raquel, the girl is pregnant. We didn't know until we had her in the van, sneaky bitch has put us in a right spot." Matt shook his head in dismay. I feigned shock.

"Oh dear, I hope she is OK, what about the baby? This is just awful."

Gina stubbed the cig in one of her scented candles and let loose on me again.

"Fuck the baby, fuck the girl, what about us? All this hard work and she is out there somewhere and she could ruin everything."

Importing victims of war and putting them to work for barely any money was not classed as hard work, I think the term was exploitation. But I kept schtum, now was not the time for a lecture. I humoured them, appeased them, played their nasty game. I also tried to excuse myself as quickly as possible.

"Sorry to hear all of this but it's really got nothing to do with me. If the girl was about to give birth then perhaps you should call the hospitals. Good luck with it all, I have to go, I have a shepherd's pie in the oven."

Gina almost choked as I turned to leave, she was not letting me off that easily.

"Oi lady, you better try and find her, Raquel, you were the last one to see her. Me and Matt are under serious pressure here from our bosses, these are not nice people, we could all be in danger."

I shrugged. "What can I do about this? I did as I was asked."

Gina gave me a stark warning, intending to freak me out.

"Do you want your family in danger? Your husband to find out all of the things you have been involved in lately?" Her eyes were crazy and she pointed her dangerously sharp nail at my house. "You better get your thinking cap on because this girl needs finding and fast or things at your house could get tricky, know what I mean, babe?"

I scurried back to mine, my head ringing with guilt. It was all very well saving some people I didn't know but what about my own family, what about them? This was all getting very Soprano-ish and I was feeling the pressure. My slippers were threadbare from these endless trips across the street and trying to keep everything under wraps was exhausting. I was scared, but I wouldn't find a way out doing nothing; I needed to know exactly what was going on, who I was dealing with, and whether there might be some chinks in the armour. The only thing I could do without involving Dave would be to conduct my own investigation. Mel was right, I did need some leverage and something I could hold over them.

Mel and I had made the decision to use her car to have a little look at Redwalls, the hovel I had previously visited. Nobody knew her reg plate, nobody knew she was my sister. The plan was to see if any of the neighbours knew who owned that house.

We told Dave and the girls we were going to the cinema followed by Wagamama in Manchester which gave us at least four hours of detective work before anyone would start to wonder. There was an element of excitement, I am not going to lie. We had pretended to be detectives when we were kids and some of this felt like role play.

We turned into the road and parked across the street. We were dressed in all black and I had put a flask of coffee under the front seat with two cheese rolls and a packet of minstrels; an absolute must when playing detective with a sibling. A light at Redwalls turned on and then off in the bathroom; somebody was definitely inside. If it was a member of the traffickers then it was absolutely plausible that I was looking for Sophia as instructed and not for clues to get me out of the shit. This was the plan had any of the gang been present.

"But what if it's the police in there?" I bombarded my sister with possibilities. Mel thought for a moment.

"Nah, there's no police car, they've been in there at least half an hour, it can't be. Just knock on the door and ask if they know who owns the place as you're thinking of renting."

"Good idea, although who would rent that? Look at it." The sorry state of the shabby bungalow would not have been an attractive prospect to even a cockroach never mind two women in a very expensive motor.

"OK so how about we're property developers looking to pick up cheap homes, flatten them and build flats?"

I liked that idea, it was a good cover story. I imagined the types of flats I would build, a mock-Tudor development and the street lined with plane trees would be a start, and then each building would have a name; The Maltings, The Lodges that sort of thing. Perhaps I would do verandas like in the deep south where the residents would chew tobacco and sit in rocking chairs. Then I remembered that I wasn't actually a developer and to pack this overthinking bollocks in at once.

"Good good. I like that. Come on, let's knock." We parked up the road next to a patch of bare land with a rusty old swing that would have ripped the arms clean off a child had it been used. This area needed either to be nuked or at least cordoned off, it was hell.

We walked past one house that had a washing machine on the lawn with a skinny brown cat sitting on the top of it. It hissed at me nastily and I gave it the finger to try to fit in with my surroundings.

"Put your watch in your bag for god's sake." Mel raised an eyebrow and pulled her coat sleeve over her Rolex. A couple of skinheaded kids came out of the house and called us "a pair of fat slags" but we kept on walking without acknowledging; I couldn't get into a fight with two children and a cat.

There was a television on inside Redwalls, I could hear the music to The One Show quite low but I recognised the tune. The police wouldn't be watching The One Show, it was mostly about them being totally useless.

Mel rattled the door knocker but there was no response. We looked back to the mini skinheads circling her car on bikes. She shook her head. "I'll be minus my wheels soon so we'd better hurry up."

Nobody came to the door after a good few aggressive knocks but we knew somebody was in there. Perhaps they were frightened, they had probably been told not to answer the door by the powers that be. I bent down to the letter box and shouted.

"Hello, please come to the door, we just need a quick word, nothing to worry about." But, still nothing.

"Let's go round the back." I led Mel around the back of the bungalow. The passageway was overgrown and smelt of garlic plants, a child's scooter lay across our path forcing us to step over it to get to the rear of the house. The gate was practically pointless as it was rotten with damp and fell apart when I booted it. The back garden was carnage, white plastic garden furniture, stained and ugly, lying broken and bent in the middle of a very bare and sun-scorched lawn, a disposable BBQ that had been used for an ashtray sat just outside the patio doors and the hedge was so overgrown it was collapsing towards the house. The only sign of civilised life was a makeshift washing line tied between an outdoor light and a concrete post supporting a rotten fence. On the washing line there were three items; a pair of tan tights, a green corduroy skirt and a shabby lilac cardigan with a yellow stain on the collar. These clothes were Barbara's clothes, this was what she was wearing on the day of the fall. I relayed this to my sister, she narrowed her eyes.

"Do you think she's buried here?" I wanted to hear anything but a confirmation. Mel looked at me like the idiot I was.

"No, Raquel. I think she's in the house."

"Her body?"

"No Raq, I don't think she's actually dead. Why would they wash her clothes? Those shitty, shitty clothes?"

I considered it. To be fair, I had only been told about her death by Gina, I had no actual proof. I mean she had looked like a good candidate for death, with the yellow puke and rolling eyes, but I didn't know for sure. I walked back to the front door and shouted through the letter box again. "Barbara, Barbara, it's me, it's Raquel. Open up."

A few seconds later, the door opened slowly and there stood Barbara in a Nike tracksuit belonging to somebody a lot bigger than her. She grinned at me like she was pleased to see me, happy even that I was there and she knew I had actually tried to save her. Sadly, she had a black eye and the remnants of a fat lip, a tooth was missing but she was still smiling.

"Is this her?" My sister was fascinated by our find. "Is this the dead woman you've been stressing about?" I nodded, I was relieved, I was ecstatic, I was not a murderer or a manslaughter-er. This was an epic discovery, this changed an awful lot. Of course I was still a disgraceful wife, nothing would alter that, but this woman being alive would stop the terrible nightmares I had experienced since the so-called fatal Hoover ride.

It wasn't difficult to get Barbara to leave she thought I was one of them. She probably thought they had sent me. She handed me a small key and pointed to the door.

"Lock door."

I nodded, there was really no point as nobody would want to break in there, they'd need a hot bath after five minutes, but I obliged and did as she asked. I gave the key to Mel, at some point we could use this as evidence and, knowing my luck, I would lose it. I didn't even bother to explain anything to Barbara about where she was going, we both took an arm and led her up the road towards Mel's car. The little bastards were still circling it on their presumably stolen bikes; brown cat was sitting on the bonnet showing us its hideous yellow fangs. Mel pulled twenty quid out of her purse and beckoned the boys over.

"See that house? That's your house now. You can play in it, do what you like in it, here's the key." And she threw the key into the air trying to be cool; neither of them caught it and it landed on the pavement. The two boys looked at each other with confusion.

"Serious?" The smaller one questioned her.

"Yes, I'm serious. If you want this £20 then make sure you tell anyone that asks that you found the house unlocked with nobody in it."

They shrugged. "OK luv, sound."

"Oh and get this cat off my Porsche."

The bigger one got off his bike and elbowed the cat in the ribs. "Fuck off Pussy." And brown cat ran off toward the derelict park.

I had to ask. "Is that the cat's actual name?" They both nodded and I shook my head in disgust. Mel handed the twenty over and we were on our way.

"What now?" she asked, as if I were running the show. There was really only one option.

"Duck?" She nodded.

"Duck Cottage it is then, fucking hell this is mental."

Mum, Dad, Sophia, Arif and Tom were all sitting in the lounge, which never normally got used, with the lights off, bowls of popcorn on each of their laps watching *When Animals Go Mad Part 2*.

"What on earth is going on, Mum?" I had ushered her into the hallway to update her on the new arrival.

"What do you mean? They can't watch *Poirot*, it's too complicated."

"Mother, not the show, who does Tom think Sophia is, why are you all together?"

She chuckled. "He thinks she is Arif's friend. Stop making things so complicated, what a mood hoover you are, Raquel."

Dad shouted in hysterics, "Quick Suzannah, the polar bear is about to maul that man, get in here or you'll miss it."

"Pause it, Phillip, I am just dealing with your miserable daughter."

I pulled Mum's arm.

"Come into the kitchen, we need to show you something."

Mel was waiting with Barbara at the kitchen table. Mum was taken aback at the sight of this old lady in a rapper's costume. I think she said "Euurrghh" out loud.

"This is Barbara, the cleaner that fell in Gina's house."

Mum, blunt as ever, said, "I thought you were dead!"

Luckily Barbara had no idea what she was saying. Arif came into the kitchen to replenish the drinks and beamed from ear to ear when he saw Barbara. They embraced each other, he stroked her wiry red hair, she cupped his cheeks. It was a moment, and I imagined she had been through an ordeal, so to see a friendly face must have been a comfort.

"Are we keeping her?" Mum enquired, like we had found a dog on the street.

"We have to, she might not be dead but she nearly was. We found her in the same place as Sophia, it's disgusting."

No hesitation from Mum about what to do with the gangsta granny. "Right, let's run her a bath and make up a bed on Sophia's floor. Chop chop everyone, you know what to do."

Mel was open-mouthed, she could not believe that Mum, a woman who told a homeless man to "Smarten up his act" outside Kings Cross tube station, was actually being this kind and reasonable.

"Shut your mouth, Melanie, and heat up the soup on the stove, the woman's emaciated, she needs nourishment."

Mel did as she was told and fired up the hob with no hesitation. Arif showed Barbara upstairs and they chatted excitedly in their own language about god knows what. I buttered bread and Mum filled Dad in on the new house guest in hushed whispers in the hallway. He listened intently, kneading his hands together whilst processing our new situation.

"And no Phillip, she is not a looker so you can keep your eyes in your head." He looked ever so slightly disappointed.

"Where do we go from here, Mel?" I longed for my sister to have the plan that would get us out of the situation. She sank into the sofa completely exhausted.

"I guess we just keep quiet, I might talk to a colleague and get some advice. We are at least doing the right thing by keeping some of these people safe. What you do about the two cranks that got you into this, I just don't know."

Half an hour later Barbara came downstairs in one of Mum's turquoise kaftans, her red hair was shiny from probably the first dose of conditioner it had seen in years. She looked fresh, at least ten years younger and she looked less angry than before. Arif sat her down at the kitchen table and Mel put a bowl of soup in front of her which she ate very quickly.

"Just keep filling up the bowl until she stops, Mel." Mum was determined to fill this lady up and, three bowls later, she finally gave up, throwing her spoon down and heaving heavily.

Although Tom had devoured two large brandies and six paracetamol, he was still chuckling away to humans being mauled by wild animals in the next room and he was not comatose, which is what I had hoped for. We had no choice but to inform him of some of the situation.

"DO NOT tell him about me and the scally, he'll love it too much."

Dad agreed, he said that Tom could be a bit of a shit so we would give him the mild version of our torrid tale without the juicy bits. After five minutes with Dad I heard him shuffling in.

"Right where is she? Calamity Jane!" I knew he was referring to me, the old twat. He was smirking. "Well young lady, you've really done it this–" And then he stopped mid-sentence and turned to Barbara with a wry smile. "Enchanted I'm sure," and his curly eyebrows went up and down an alarming number of times. He bent down on one knee and kissed Barbara's gnarly hand in a very creepy manner.

Barbara wasn't perturbed, she nodded cordially to him even though he was dribbling and had lost control of his bottom lip. Mum pushed him onto the sofa next to Mel and put his stick out of reach so he had to stay put. Sophia waddled in wearing quite a stylish maternity onesie my dad had picked for her. Apart from the fact that it said 'Don't mess with the Mama bear' across her stomach – I was sure H&M had Holly Willoughby working in their design department – she looked one hundred percent better than her parka phase and she was smiling, which was a real breakthrough. Mum had established, through the powers of the translator app, that she was a positive person and really quite nice. She and her husband had run a very successful upholstery business and, until the trouble, they were quite well off. War had torn their lives apart and her husband had been a rebel. "Quite the hero by all accounts," Mum had told me proudly, like she knew him. Sophia was convinced they would be together again before the birth and was confident he would not be beaten by the English crime bosses. I hoped for her sake she was right.

Dad took me to one side before we left, a bit sozzled and quite emotional. "You girls are my world and although you've made some quite questionable decisions lately, I will always be proud of you. This is brave, this is strength," he said, pointing to the house guests. He kissed me on the head and slapped me on the cheek softly. A memory I would take to the grave.

We left Duck Cottage busting at the seams. I had a weird feeling that anyone who was delivered there would be safe and cared for. A lot of that was to do with Arif, who just seemed to hold everything together with such a calm aura. His influence on my parents was something I could never have predicted. My thoughts of the crack den now being occupied by two little shits and Pussy the cat had me in stitches – those kids couldn't believe their luck being given a whole house to take over with a telly and hot water. I wished them well with the short time they would be given to enjoy it. The niggling worry was that the residents at 23 knew my parents' address and an impromptu visit would have been a disaster – they had half the workforce hiding out there and I would have preferred for my parents not to have been kalashnikoved because of me.

Mel was quiet driving back to mine; I hoped she wasn't too disgusted in me. Although she was a wanker, I did have respect for her and I did love her, I couldn't handle the thought she may be appalled by me.

"Are you OK?"

She snapped out of the haze. "I am OK, I'm fine. I am just trying to work out a way we can all walk away from this without consequence." She sighed, it was difficult.

"I feel like most of us can, Mel. I will need to take the heat on this and I know I will probably lose Dave."

She looked deeply upset. "I really don't want that to happen, it can't happen."

She wound the window down and shook her head in the fresh air. "I was so jealous of you and Dave, so horribly jealous, Raquel, back when the kids were little."

I laughed. "You were jealous of me? Me and Dave?"

She was almost shocked I didn't know this. "Yes! He adored you. Not in a smothering annoying way. Not in a desperate way like … Roger."

I nodded in agreement to the Roger comment.

"He totally gets you. It's really rare. No offence but you're fucking nuts. You are literally certifiable at times, always have been. He just goes with it, he doesn't get worried by it. I think he even likes it. That right there is true love, when someone lets you be."

I welled up a bit.

She continued to mentally assault me but in a necessary way.

"You once threw Dave's work laptop into the swimming pool at his parents' apartment in Portugal, do you remember that?"

I nodded. "Yes, well, he was watching football on it but pretending to work."

"Bit much though, Raquel."

"Yes it was but at the time I was really annoyed."

"And do you remember what he did after that?"

I shook my head.

"He dived into the pool and he put the laptop on a sunlounger in the hope that it would dry out … and then, the next morning when it didn't work and it had bubbles inside the screen, he put it into the bin and ordered a new one. And then we all went out for tapas and it was never spoken of again. This is fucking relationship goals, Raquel."

I shut my eyes, she was right.

"This man accepts you for better or worse, he is your person and that may seem boring at times but your soulmate is hard to find, and you did it. He still wants you physically, he still wants to be around you, be with you, give you what you want, just fucking appreciate what you have and treasure it because I … I settled for a man who is so needy that he couldn't stand the thought of kids taking the attention away from him and now I have to live with that." She was angry and sad and emotional, hot tears were streaming down her face. I put my hand on her shoulder. She put her hand over mine. "And that is why, that is why I have to tell you something. I hope, I really hope this will help."

I took my hand away, this felt weird, I felt a strange sensation of betrayal. We reached traffic lights and she looked me in the eye. "After Sam was born, just after and you were a bit mental, I came over to help out. I had never felt so broody in my life and my envy, my pure evil jealousy that you had three kids and a husband with a backbone made me do something so deplorable that I feel sick even telling you."

"Pull over! Pull over right now." I wanted to be stationary so I could land the punch without her wrapping the car round a tree. She did as I asked and we sat outside a kebab shop with a rowdy queue outside.

"Go on …"

She undid her seat belt and faced me.

"Well Sam was a few weeks old and you were breastfeeding. You were being particularly nasty to all of us, probably because you couldn't drink. Anyway, you went to bed early one night and Rog was being a cunt, he knew I wanted a kid and he knew this was a sensitive time."

"Cut to the chase, Mel."

She gulped. "Well, Dave and I had put the girls to bed and watched telly and we ended up … well we kissed." She put her head into her hands. "We kissed and it was, for me, shamefully, an amazing moment at the time. For Dave, he regretted it straight away and he barely looked at me for months. But it was something that we did and I know it was wrong. I was in a bad place, I wanted what you had, I lost my grip just for one moment."

I shut my eyes, imagining my sister and my husband snogging whilst I was upstairs with our newborn.

"That's all it was, just a kiss?"

She nodded. "Dave pulled away, he was knackered and he'd had a few glasses of wine, he was all over the place. We knew it was wrong and, well, I felt something for him for a bit."

"You felt something?"

"Yes, like I had feelings. I think because he was a good dad, a real man and a good guy. I just wanted what you had and I had a momentary lapse."

"And then?"

"And then nothing. We never spoke of it again and I would never have told you but I think this is the time, something you need to know."

I put my seat belt back on. "Let's go home."

She started the engine, tears streaming down her face. "Aren't you going to say anything?"

I held her hand and squeezed it. "Fat slag!"

She smiled through the tears and we headed home.

Shitshow

Dave had been called into a meeting with the big bosses. He wasn't sure what it was about but he got suited and booted and looked a little on edge. My mind raced with the possibilities; did they have footage of me, his wife, involving herself in illegal activity? Did they have footage of me going in and out of a known criminal's house? Whatever they had, I hoped there were no images of me running without a bra, I would be the laughing stock of the courtroom. Would they slam the evidence on the table in front of Dave and ask him how much he really knew about his own wife? Dave would be in utter confusion as he thought I was home baking muffins and filling pies not putting the lips on the neighbour and transporting foreigners here, there and everywhere.

Mel was working from the back garden on her laptop, typing like a maniac with the phone to her ear. She had barely looked me in the eye since the revelation that she and Dave had their thing. I felt a little sorry for her; this was out of character to say the least, she must have been in a very bad place. With everything that was going on it didn't really bother me, it actually made me feel less at risk of losing my relationship. Whether I would need to use it was another story, I really hoped it wouldn't come to that.

"Where's my tie? The red one? Is my suit clean? Do I need a shave?"

Dave charged around the house trying to put together a decent and smart look for the big guns.

"What do they need to see you about?"

He shrugged. "I really don't know, I am hoping there's not been a complaint or there's a problem with the operation."

I bit my lip. "What else could it be?"

Again he shrugged. "When the big boss calls you in with no meeting agenda to work from, it could mean anything."

I felt nauseous, I had no way of knowing anything until he told me so I would have to wait; wait patiently, not knowing if this involved me. Eventually, and without any breakfast so he must have been worried, he left the house leaving a strong waft of Davidoff in his wake. I watched the car drive away wondering if this would be the last time I saw him whilst he still respected me. I should have squeezed it out a bit longer. Perhaps one last glimpse of me in a white cotton dress and crucifix on a chain would make him remember me as a nice clean wife.

Suzy was excited, giddy even, and came to me with a proposition which was the last thing that I needed.

"Please Mum, he can stay for a few days and I can introduce him to my friends, Mum, are you even listening?" I put my head on the kitchen table. I didn't want her boyfriend coming over to witness this mess, I really couldn't be bothered to entertain anybody.

Michaela shouted from the sofa, "If he's coming then Connie is coming too, they can get the flight together."

Suzy agreed. "Totally. Amazing idea for once." And then she looked at me again. "Well. Are you going to let this happen? I have to see him again before the end of the summer."

Exhausted and mentally weak, I eventually agreed to Connie and Finn staying the following week.

"You won't be sleeping in the same beds, I hope you know that." Both girls pulled awkward and appalled faces at the fact I should even try to discuss what they got up to behind closed doors. "You'll make up beds on the floor or it's not happening."

Why did I bother, as soon as my eyes were shut I had no control over what they did in their bedrooms, although Dave would probably stay awake all night with a cattle prod to stop any potential shenanigans. I would rely on him to stop a teenage pregnancy and whatever it was that lesbians liked to do.

Mel came in and put her glasses on her head, she looked tired. "Well, I reached out to a colleague and asked them about our situation."

I was hoping for a legal loophole that exonerated me completely. "And what do we do?"

She smiled nervously. "We tell somebody in authority absolutely everything, we ask for help from the police. You may face some charges, Dave will have to know the situation in its entirety but the longer we leave it the worse it will be for all of us and that includes Mum and Dad."

I shook my head and made a fist. "No, no absolutely not. Shut up, just shut up." I stormed upstairs like a teenager not wanting to hear anymore. I could not face that, not today. There were too many possibilities for me to get off scot-free and we hadn't explored any of them. Stupid stiff Mel and her sensible wanky advice, she probably wanted me gone so she could get the kids to call her 'Mom' and wear my perfume so Dave would fall in love with her. It was me now unravelling, I had to get a grip!

I spent the rest of the afternoon in the office. I could hear pans jangling and plates being used, Mel was playing mother as she knew I was not up to the job that day. My work was piling up and although I had submitted my gooseberry stuff, it was apparently a little incoherent and I needed to make the recipes clearer. It was basically a big red 'SEE ME' on my homework and I had to do it again or risk detention.

I also received a copy of my 'Live Better' edition for the following week: the beef wellington episode which took me back to when the trouble had really started. Although I had to say the photograph of the rare fillet did it justice and never had I seen a sexier wellington, but it had come at a cost so I would probably never eat that dish again.

My next assignment was to come up with an autumnal cake for non-bakers, something easy that wouldn't flummox the most basic of cook. Something a student could do if their parents were visiting their digs for a coffee. I read this with fury. Why, why are we asking people who can't cook and who shouldn't cook to bake a cake? Why can't they go and do something that they are good at like drink snakebites or go into their overdraft. I wasn't in the mood to do my job properly that day so I found a recipe for a banana loaf in a cookbook for children, added a sprinkle of cinnamon to the mix for that October feeling and pretended it was one of my favourites. Lazy, but then again so were students.

Dave's car showed up just before four. He hadn't called me, hadn't warned me in advance. This was bad, I felt like he wanted to give me the full impact so I had no time to think up an excuse. The door slammed and he immediately shouted for me, a sense of dread spilled through my veins and it was almost too much, I nearly hid under the bed.

Dave was standing at the bottom of the stairs. He looked serious. He had something behind his back. I was possibly in line for a beating with a truncheon or he may have had the handcuffs ready.

"Well, what happened?"

He breathed in deeply. From behind his back he produced a huge magnum of Bolly, lifting it into the air like the FA Cup.

"I have been put up for a commendation, Raq, a commendation!" His face broke into a huge smile – his dream, his lifelong dream had finally come to fruition.

Legs shaking, I flew down the stairs and threw my arms around him. He deserved this, he needed it and he had done it for his dead sister.

"I can't believe it, I just can't believe it." He sat down on the sofa whilst the kids clapped, Mel went off to open the bottle and I stood in silence wondering how to feel.

"You OK, love?"

"I'm fine, just so happy for you and I am so glad that you have been recognised."

"Are you kidding? This should be your award. You've looked after the kids, the house, put up with me never being here and working all the time. Behind every successful man, there's a loyal and dependable woman."

I went into the kitchen to help Mel with the drinks, I could not listen to another word of that.

We went out for pizza that night. Even though I was supposed to go to Mum's and check on things, I had to go and be there for Dave. Mel and I didn't discuss anything else that day, it just seemed inappropriate. Everything was put on the back burner whilst we celebrated Dave's news.

The following day Dave was back in the office, probably working on his next case and daydreaming about getting an OBE. He hadn't moved once during the night, he was clearly at peace with himself. Must be a nice feeling, I was jealous. He had spent half an hour on the downstairs loo before he left and said, "Ooof, that calzone has done its job," before winking and blowing me a kiss.

Suzy and Michaela had gone into Manchester shopping together for outfits to entice their other halves to fall in love with them, and Sam had tagged along with the promise of half an hour in JD Sports. I was alone, apart from the big black dog that Mel had left with me whilst she took supplies to Mum.

I was filling the dishwasher when he did it first. I thought I had imagined it but the second time I stopped and put my head around the corner to the hallway. Sir Walter sat in front of the door and let out a howl, very wolf-like. He turned his head to me and then howled again. I had never heard this noise from him before. I had heard his bark of course, but this was high-pitched and long. As I moved closer to him, he put his paw onto the door and looked back at me again. I presumed the old thing wanted a walk so, to prevent him leaving me a big brown present on my solid oak floor, I grabbed his lead and put on my flip-flops. A walk was probably a good idea.

We hadn't even got to the bottom of my driveway when Sir Walter started pulling so hard that I was unable to stop him – I had no choice but to run with him. I couldn't let go of the lead, he would have hit the main road in minutes with this gusto. He dragged me across the road and straight over to 23 where he started to howl at the front door.

"What the fuck is wrong with you, Walter? Stop this." He ignored me. I tried to pull him by the collar away from the front door of doom but he stayed put. He just continued to howl until eventually a dishevelled Gina opened the door.

"What the hell?" She looked down at the dog. "What is going on here?"

I shook my head. "I have no idea, he dragged me here."

"You got any news for me?" I shook my head.

"Well go away then, I'm up to my eyes in it."

"I want to go but he won't let me." I looked down at Sir Walter, who was strangely cocking his head and looking around Gina into their kitchen.

"What's he doing, what's he looking at?"

I shrugged. Gina went to shut the front door, she clearly wasn't a dog lover, but Sir Walter had other ideas and he charged past her straight into her kitchen. I had to let go of the lead or I would have gone through the porch window. She wasn't amused and threw her hands into the air in disgust.

We both ran in after him and watched him growling and barking at a cupboard next to the dishwasher.

"Oi, get lost!" she shouted and jeered behind him. He wasn't interested, he continued to try and dig a hole in the kitchen floor in front of the cupboard and kept looking back to me and howling. It was very odd.

"Do something, get him out of here."

"He's not my dog, I don't know what to do, all I know is don't approach from—"

It was too late. She had grabbed his back end with her long nails and the black dog saw red. He spun around immediately, grabbed the sleeve of her satin dressing gown, dragged her to the floor, sat on top of her chest, dribbling and growling into her face. He then clamped her skinny wrist into his mouth and applied pressure.

"Help me, get him away from me." I was frozen to the spot, I had no idea what to do, I'd only seen three minutes of When Animals Go Mad 2 and I hadn't seen anyone escape alive.

"What's in the cupboard?" I pointed to the problem. It had to be some sort of meat, maybe a rabbit, perhaps a mouse was trapped in there.

"Nothing, nothing's in the cupboard," she yelled.

"Well why would he do this then? It has to be something he wants."

I slowly edged my way around the front of Sir Walter, stepping over Gina's bleeding arm and opened the cupboard.

As soon as the door was opened, I knew that smell. Everybody who had walked through a park in the school holidays knew that smell.

"It's just a bit of weed, Raquel, make this dog let go of me arm."

I didn't have to ask him, he was already in the cupboard dragging a big bag for life onto the kitchen floor.

"Eh, that's mine get off."

Sir Walter warned her to stay back with a vicious growl and she clambered up onto the kitchen island.

"Me fucking arm's killing me and that's my stuff."

Sir Walter would not let go of this bag, his huge teeth clenched the handles and there was no letting go.

"Get it off him, that's worth twenty K." I tugged at the handles but he only clenched harder, he was not letting go.

"You're going to have to let me take him back to mine, my sister will be able to get him to drop it, it's her dog."

Gina lay on her side on the island looking at the teeth marks in her arm whilst crying. "Is that a police dog, Raquel? Have you brought a police dog into my house?"

"No, he's a rescue … he's Irish … I can't explain it."

"Get him away, but get that bag back here as soon as possible and tell your sister I'm going to sue her."

I pulled the Donald Trump face, it was appropriate at that moment. "Okey dokey, I'll let my criminal lawyer of a sister know you are going to sue her because her dog stole your drugs."

She grimaced. I left Gina nursing six puncture wounds in her left arm and probably a wet pair of knickers after her ordeal.

"You'll need a tetanus, he could have rabies." Just a quick bit of friendly advice before I left delivered with a Tony Blair smile.

Sir Walter and I went back home with a big bag of drugs and the sleeve of an Agent Provocateur dressing gown. At least life wasn't boring. My sister arrived back after half an hour; Sir Walter was waiting for her at the door.

"Why is he carrying a Morrisons bag?"

He dropped it at her feet and then wandered off into the sitting room and lay down.

"What's this?" She bent down and immediately knew what it was. "Whoa, what on earth?" I explained the events of the morning as we both stared intently at the bag.

Movement at 23 kept Mel and I busy for half an hour. She looked through my bedroom blinds and I was in my office. The Range Rovers appeared and Matt put Gina into one of them, she had a bandage around her wrist to match the one on her ankle and she wore a fuzzy peach onesie that said 'Hot to trot' on the arse. Idiot. I received a text from her pretty soon after they had driven away.

Look after that stuff for me, DO NOT lose it. Going to need to take Arif back soon, we have some issues. G

They were clearly now reeling that another of their workforce had vanished, they couldn't even tell me because as far as I knew, Barbara was dead. Dead because I didn't call an ambulance and I had failed her. So they were scurrying around like nasty little insects looking for a woman that I had rescued.

I showed the message to Mel and she instructed me not to reply under any circumstance. "We're in enough trouble as it is, Raq, do not incriminate yourself on any more messages."

She was right, me confirming I would look after some drugs would be the downfall of me and no doubt Dave, his commendation would be flushed down the loo along with his career.

"We need to get this out of the house and fast." We both looked at each other and said in unison, "Duck!"

Mum and Dad were out when we arrived, apparently they had joined a salsa group that allowed cocktails in the afternoon and as much couple swapping as they liked. I wondered what sort of group this was and whether they would all end up in a huge bed at the back of the church hall. Dad's hips had taken a real hammering in recent weeks due to "certain stuff" so they wanted to find a healthy way to loosen him up.

Arif was sitting in the garden with Sophia who again looked even better than before. She had caught the sun on her face and was clearly continuing to wash her hair properly. I enquired as to where Barbara was hoping she hadn't wandered off to find another Dyson. Arif rolled his eyes, he went slightly red. He pointed upstairs to the window of Old Tom's room. "She in there."

I frowned. "Why? Why is she in there?"

He shrugged and looked away. Mel beckoned me back into the house and there was really no reason to go up the stairs. The noises I heard that day would never ever leave me and, short of watching my parents actually do it, this was nigh on close enough. There were a series of groans, a couple of loud bangs and then Tom shouted, "Here we go, Babs." Babs, as she was now called, screamed, "Yee-ha." And at that point I covered my ears.

We moved swiftly as far away from this revolting connection as we could get. They had a combined age of at least one hundred and fifty and this was the stuff of nightmares.

"Why are all the old people in this house on heat?" I shook my head at Mel who was pale and astonished.

We put the bag of drugs in Dad's shed underneath a trestle table that Mum only got out for large garden parties. It still had a tablecloth over it so it was vaguely concealed. Should a really clever badger be able to undo a padlock, flip over a table and roll himself a spliff then he was welcome to the lot.

We sat and had a quick cup of tea with Sophia and Arif before we were due to head back home to act completely normally.

"Gina, she wants me back at the factory by next week. She say they lost two people and she not happy." Arif knew that although he was currently living in a lovely English cottage with my moronic parents, his future beyond looked bleak. He was clearly hoping that I could make this all go away but he also knew that these people were dangerous and held most of the cards. His only hope was me, poor boy.

"Just carry on with what you are doing, leave the rest to me. If they say they are coming to this house, you must contact me immediately. If they find the other two here, things could get really nasty."

He nodded. "What about baby? It come soon." He pointed at Sophia's stomach which looked huge and uncomfortable.

"The baby will be fine, I promise you. We will make sure."

His shoulders relaxed. It was a lie, of course, I had no idea how things would be fine but there was no point in letting him know that.

Old Tom staggered out into the garden on his stick, beaming at the world. His silk gown, the one that was too short, had made a reappearance even though he had been given a new one. Babs trailed behind him carrying a brandy glass almost full to the top and the two of them sat on the same garden chair even though there were six spare. Babs had expanded her wardrobe even further and had somehow acquired a sixties tea dress that Mum had worn in her thirties. Her veiny blue legs wrapped themselves around Tom like ivy.

"For pity's sake." Mel couldn't hold it in. "Get a room."

Tom sniggered. "We already did." And he swigged back the brandy and stroked the blue leg with vigour.

"At least they happy." Arif looked fondly at the pair of them, I suppose he was right. If nothing else, at least the two least attractive people I had ever seen were getting some, all credit to them.

I showed my parents where the drugs lived after they returned from swinging club, again there was much excitement and no actual concern. Dad sniffed the bag and said, "Good shit." I was now used to this reckless attitude and snatched it away from him, throwing it back under the table. Mum was interested in the street value more than anything else.

"Twenty K, how exciting, we're like Paulo Nutini and his gang."

"It's Pablo Escobar, Mother, and he was a cocaine baron."

"Have we got any of that? Pablo's stuff?"

"No."

"Oh!" she said, quite disappointed. "Anyway darling, don't worry, we'll look after the gear."

We left the house with Arif making a chicken and ham pie, Mum and Dad were showing the two other old tits their new salsa moves, Sophia had gone for a lie down and the shed was full of drugs.

Brilliant, just bloody brilliant.

Too Many Cooks

My mother, although she had been a good mother in the past, was now becoming a liability. Without any thought or consultation, she had organised a big party for Dave in light of his achievements. I got to know about this on a group WhatsApp with the title 'Well done David'. Surely David's wife should be the one to throw a party and surely David's wife should be consulted on the guest list. But no, I was learning all about this at the same time as the other guests.

"Are you kidding me, Mother?"

"What now, what's up this time?"

I had called her with bleach on my top lip whilst sitting in the bath.

"What's up is this, you have invited Dave's parents over from Spain without even asking me. Where are they going to stay? I have two Irish kids staying next week. Oh, and thanks for inviting Roger, you know I can't be doing with him."

"Stop finding problems and start looking at solutions, Raquel."

"Have you been reading Gloria Hunniford again, Mother?"

She sighed. I continued my rant in a whisper because there was movement outside the bathroom door.

"And another thing, do you really think with everything that is going on that throwing a party for a police officer is appropriate? I mean, you've got a house full of illegal immigrants and a shed full of drugs."

"And whose fault is that? I'm going to put the phone down now, Raquel, you're flattening my mood."

"Mum, MUM!"

She put the phone down. I went back to the WhatsApp group Mum had set up behind my back – how on earth did she learn to create that? She had mentioned going into the Apple Store the week before and she must have demanded that one of the techies engineer the whole thing for her. They probably shut down the branch after she left and were having treatment for PTSD.

CeeCee and Gary had confirmed and had already booked flights, there was no way they were missing celebrating Dave's success. Roger had said he'd check his diary but within eight seconds he had confirmed he would attend as long as the toe didn't get any worse. There was no diary, his days were the same no matter what. Get up, look miserable, go to bookshop, moan about toe, go home, whimper until bed. That was his schedule and everybody knew it. And then there was Tom, since when did a million-year-old man have a smartphone and why was Mum messaging somebody living in the same house as her? Utterly ridiculous.

I angrily scrolled through the replies wondering what I could do to stop this going ahead. The bleach cream was starting to burn so I reached over the side of the bath to grab a towel to wipe it off before my top lip disintegrated. I am not sure how or why but when I looked back at my screen, there were a group of familiar faces looking back at me.

"Oooh what's that on your lip, Raquel?" CeeCee was peering into the screen.

"Is she naked? Good grief!" My dad screwed up his face.

"She could do with a bit of a lift I think." Old Tom had put his glasses on to get a better view.

Roger just sat with his arms folded shaking his head very slowly.

I threw the phone onto the bathroom floor and submerged my head under water. Fucking WhatsApp, I would sue whoever was in charge, how can it be so easy to video call so many people at once whilst naked and bleaching a moustache? The phone was pinging relentlessly for the next five minutes but I simply could not face the comments, my saggy boobs and moustache were not up for discussion. I had to hope and pray not one of these people knew how to screen shot, I shuddered at the very thought.

Dignity well and truly in the bin, I headed off to do some food shopping. I actually enjoyed that, it was almost like therapy. I hung around the spice section stocking up on the basics and looking for a few new things. Just as I was reading the label of some ancho chillies for a beef dish I was planning, somebody tapped me on the shoulder.

"Alright, babe."

I looked over my shoulder and groaned. "It's you."

Matt smiled, in a genuine way.

"Shopping for your slaves?"

He put his finger on his lip. "Shh, keep it down." He looked around nervously.

I looked into his basket; fresh veg, organic meat and actual herbs. I raised my eyebrows. "What's this? Where are all the ready meals, the tins of custard, the Pot Noodles?"

"You know, Raquel, I actually enjoyed our lessons. I really listened, I don't eat that stuff anymore."

"No you didn't, you used me, you know you did."

He shrugged. "I did what I had to yes, but I enjoyed your company, it wasn't all fake."

I believed him but I remembered myself. "Just fuck off, you have really messed things up for me."

"I know I have and I'm sorry Raquel."

"Sorry is not good enough. Sorry means nothing. Where's your gaffer anyway?" I scanned the area for Gina.

"Don't worry, she's not here. She's not good at the moment. That dog really messed her arm up you know."

I laughed sarcastically and said, "Oh dear, I do hope she's OK."

He didn't respond. I walked away from spices towards the bread section; he walked alongside me trying to continue our chat.

"What are you doing? Go away, I can't be seen with you." I shooed him away with my hand.

"I just want you to know that I didn't intend for things to get this bad. And what happened to Barbara, it wasn't really your fault."

I stopped in my tracks. "And what exactly did happen to her, Matt?"

He looked uncomfortable. "It wasn't your fault, that's all I'm saying, you shouldn't feel guilty, please don't blame yourself."

"Thank you, I won't, and I appreciate you saying that, I've been upset about her."

I finished my shopping knowing that he wasn't all bad. Although he hadn't been honest with me, he tried to take some of the pressure off. Perhaps he was the weak link that I could use to break away from these people.

I purposely spent ages filling my boot with my shopping and kept an eye on the doors for Matt. When I saw him leaving, I casually walked back with my empty trolley to drop it off.

"Ah, we meet again, Mr Bond," I said. He frowned; it was a stupid thing to say. "Walk back to my car with me, will you?" He obliged.

"Matt, I just need all of this to stop. I can see you're not into this lifestyle fully. You know you'll end up inside. It's only going to end one way."

He gulped. I saw fear, vulnerability and emotion, I think I had him.

"I know that this isn't you, I know you're just doing as you're told, you're not like the others."

He leaned against my car and folded his arms. "Gina had an ex-boyfriend, he was from Syria originally, they met in Liverpool and he was into all sorts. Before it went mental over there with the war and that, they set up a business – a viable business that did pretty well. They were together a few years and then it all went to shit, his family never accepted her, they split and she was crushed. He married a girl his parents approved of and Gina tried to carry on with the business but it was too tough for her. She ended up owing a load of cash to the wrong people."

"So?" Was I supposed to care?

"So, by the time we met she had started doing this and that to pay the debts back, helping them out and making them money using her UK connections and it all got a bit messy. It's not that easy to get out you know."

"You mean she's greedy, the money's too good, she doesn't want to get out."

"Yeah you make good money but there's a risk, always a risk. You live on the edge all of the time, it's not that great."

"Just walk away Matt, it's that easy, just leave her." He looked at the floor.

"I love her. I can't leave her."

I found this a little hard to believe. It wasn't that long ago when he was shoving his tongue down my throat. But then again I let him and I loved Dave, so no leg to stand on with that argument.

"She doesn't love you, if she did she wouldn't have pimped you out to me."

He got impatient, he was trying to get me to understand their situation but I had no sympathy, none whatsoever.

"Look, she needed my support, things were getting too much for her, they needed help. I wasn't supposed to be involved in the business at all, that wasn't our deal, but these guys were bringing more and more people in, it was getting unmanageable for her. This is the third time we've moved house in the last two years, I was hoping we could stay put, put down roots."

I hoped they wouldn't put roots down, I wished they would sell up and bugger off.

"You don't want to live across the road from a policeman especially now you have drugs in the house, it won't be long until he's onto you, even my sister's dog knows what you're all about."

"Raquel." He looked at me pleadingly.

"What?"

"It wasn't personal."

"It feels it."

"And, she would kill me for saying this …"

"What?"

He looked nervous. "Well, I couldn't say it wasn't fun, I did feel something for you, Raquel. I didn't think I would especially after our first meeting but I liked being with you, that wasn't fake."

I had no idea if this was genuine, I would not allow myself to be sucked in a second time but it felt real and it did take away some of the humiliation. I checked myself. This man, even if his eyes were outstanding, would not have me weak at the knees ever again.

I shut the boot hard.

"Look Matt, you're into all sorts, a quiet cul-de-sac is no place to do business like this, if you just move then we'll say no more."

He shook his head at my wishful thinking. "She won't let you go, she doesn't work like that. You know too much, babe."

I got into the car and put my window down. "Just think about it, Matt, think about how life will be when you're caught. You need to go, go back to Liverpool or something."

Liverpool was not Dave's patch.

I hoped that I gave him something to think about. I needed them gone, I needed headspace and a day when I didn't see them within spitting distance of my home and my family.

Fancy meeting up for a drink? 6 ish at the pub? X

Dave was on his way home and finally I was a good person to go for a pint with. I was happy enough with that, we hadn't done that in a long time, it was spontaneous and a bit romantic.

Sure, see you in there. R xx

The pub was quiet, Wednesdays were never busy anywhere. Monday was for the alcoholics that needed to drink away the weekend, Tuesday was usually the Zumba arseholes who had earned a cheap glass of Prosecco after waggling their big arses and calling it a workout, Wednesday was no-man's land – it was the day we all stayed at home waiting for the unofficial weekend to start on the Thursday.

So there was me, a man biting his nails on the fruit machine and a barman called Nate who was clearly on a trial shift.

"Sauvignon Blanc, please?"

"Is that a wine?"

"It most certainly is."

"What colour?"

"White."

"Do they keep that in a fridge? I'm new."

I had no time for that. "Look, Nate." His name was on a little gold bar on his tie. "I really think you should spend some time learning about drinks as you work in a pub and this is taking much longer than it should."

He sneered at me. "Jesus, I was only asking."

"And a pint of bitter." He looked confused. "Google it, Nate. I'll be over here." And I went and sat with my back to him at a table in the corner. "Fuckwit."

"Who is?" Dave had appeared next to me as I mumbled about Nate's incompetence.

"Him, he knows nothing about anything, I nearly got the bloody drink myself."

Dave looked back at Nate. "You OK, son?"

Nate shrugged, he still hadn't found the wine and he looked bewildered.

"Give the guy a break, he's just a kid."

Dave went over and pointed to the wine fridge so Nate could do his job, then very kindly he talked him through pouring a pint of bitter. He had patience, he was understanding, I was not. We made a good team.

"Finally!" I grabbed the wine from Dave and he grinned.

"You can be a right crank when you want to be, poor lad is all over the place." He sat down opposite me.

"You'll never guess what I heard today."

I turned to face him, this sounded juicy. "What?"

"After the arrests, all the guys within Dachshund are singing like canaries, they know they're facing long stretches. Slowly they are starting to grass each other up to get lighter sentences."

"Oooh exciting, I love it when they all implode." I clapped my hands together.

Dave started to whisper. "That's not it though, Raq, one name keeps cropping up in all the interviews, someone we both know."

I frowned. "Go on."

"Georgina Dennis!"

I shrugged. "Means nothing to me."

His eyes widened. "It's Gina from across the road. Matt's Gina."

"Fuck off!" My heart dropped.

"I'm serious, we think she's been running some immigrant ring – her and some Kurdish lads from Liverpool."

I scoffed and fake laughed. "No! Definitely not, she's a Botox nurse."

Dave leaned in further, his eyes excited and eager to deliver the news. "How can they, her and him, afford that house and that car when he's not working and she does a bit of Botox? It's not possible. They have to be getting money from somewhere."

I shook my head hoping the movement would just shake this conversation away. Dave became more animated. "And another thing, that kid Arif who works at your mum's? I think he is one of them."

"A gang member?"

"No ya daft cow, an illegal immigrant."

"Oh I see. I doubt it, he's a good kid."

"Most of them are, it's not them, it's the bastards who transport them."

I swallowed almost the entire glass of wine.

"So the plan is to do some surveillance on them, see what they get up to. We'll have to use our house."

Feigning confusion I asked, "But what has this got to do with you, Dave? You deal with drugs not people."

"Ahh but it's all connected, apparently some of these people have been used as mules – if there's gear involved then it's on me."

I slumped back into my chair.

"So, we'll need to have your office and one of us will get into the loft, it's perfect because they won't have a clue that we're even there."

"I'm going to need another drink, Dave, get me the bottle please."

He went off to the bar where Nate was standing looking blankly at the till.

I was absolutely fucked.

Dave asked me relentless questions during the remainder

of our evening. I was incredibly uncomfortable and three times I went to the toilet for a breather and a dry cry. I knew what it felt like to be interrogated, my mother had seen to that during my teens, but when it's you own husband and you are guilty as sin, it was nail-biting stuff.

Did I ever suspect they were dodgy?

Had I ever seen any evidence of drugs?

Had I seen anything suspicious at night, when apparently they moved people around?

Had they mentioned a second property or a warehouse where they could store people?

The questions were coming in thick and fast and I knew the answer to all of them was yes but I said no, no to it all. Dave was back into this operation and was fully invested; little did he know he was actually investigating me.

"We have to tie up the loose ends, you know. We might have got the big guys but there are the people on the side who make things happen, people like those two across the road – I can't believe I thought he was alright. We have to get everyone and clean up the streets." He was beyond excited and apparently wouldn't stop until he had everyone firmly behind bars.

The walls were closing in, I had no plan, the more I lied the worse it would be but how do you tell your husband you are an unfaithful criminal on a Wednesday night? Nobody did anything on a Wednesday, so I said nothing.

The following morning before breakfast, Stu, one of Dave's colleagues, pulled down the loft hatch and made his way up the ladder. Dave handed him his flask of coffee, a long lens camera and a pair of binoculars. "We'll throw up a bacon sarnie in a bit, mate."

Stu had a ponytail and was pushing fifty so there was no way he could be taken seriously. The loft hatch was closed and nobody else in the house had a clue he was up there.

Dave had set up in my office with his laptop and phone and he would be there until they had something. I paced up and down the lounge whilst Mel stared at me in horror.

"This is getting out of hand, Raquel, come on, you have to say something."

"Shush. Think, what do I do? I think I should text Matt and tell him, they can leave, run away."

Mel shook her head. "You know that is a terrible idea. You want to tip them off? That is insane, they will get the evidence from the phone at some point."

She was right, I was panicking and saying some stupid stuff.

"I don't know how much more I can take, Raq, this is going to affect my career too, you know?"

I glared at her. "Not helping, Mel, not at all."

I was going to need space, and some help from Mel to make that happen.

"You know you kissed my husband and that it was a very bad thing to do?"

She looked up warily, knowing there was going to be a request she would have to agree to.

"I think, what would really help, is if you take all the kids over to Ireland until next week. You can come back for the party, if we still have it, but for now they need to leave."

I didn't want them to leave but it was necessary. I could not let them see me, their dad and possibly their grandparents come apart like a cheap suit before their very eyes. I also wanted to spare Mel's career, not least because she was the only one with any real money.

She was relieved. I could have been asking her to source me a gun.

"Sure, absolutely, it's the least I can do."

"Correct, Mel!" Who would have thought her indiscretion would come in so handy?

By mid-afternoon they were gone, over to Dublin for table service and ironed bedding, it was better this way. Dave was behind the plan under the ruse that his stakeout operation would be safer with the kids out of harm's way.

There had been no movement at 23 and I wished Stu would

do one, but they were doing twenty-four-hour surveillance so, once he went off for a sleep, Dave would take over. I was stuck with the pair of them. I listened in to a few of Dave's calls from behind the office door. From what I could make out they now knew plenty about Gina, enough to send her down for years. There was not much mention of Matt, only that he was her sidekick and a bit thick. They knew the small bald guy as Malik, he was known to the squad in connection with other things and was a slippery fucker by all accounts. Dave wrote down a series of number plates in the back of his pad and I had a good look whilst he went to the loo. I was pretty sure they belonged to the Range Rovers.

Dave repeatedly asked me for copious amounts of black coffee that evening – he needed to stay awake for the stakeout. I responded to his request but I went with decaf, I really had no choice. When Steven Seagal's poor excuse for a double came down from the loft, a weary and exhausted Dave took his place. I knew from his body language that Dave would be dribbling and out of it within minutes. Putting all his faith in the caffeine overdose, Dave assured Stu that he had it all in hand, however the hand he referred to would be limp and his tongue would be too – sweet dreams, detective, see you in the morning!

With Stu tucked up in Sam's bed using one of my scrunchies, and Dave probably dreaming about handcuffing and pinning Gina down from behind, I hoped that all criminal activity would take place pretty much immediately and they would be none the wiser. They didn't disappoint. At 2 am Matt and Gina both arrived home with their crew. There was a brief conversation on the driveway and the pair of them went inside carrying a couple of holdalls. This could have meant one of two things, more dirty drugs or they were packing to leave; I prayed it was the latter.

Dave was confused the following morning and had a stiff neck from sleeping against the loft window. Stu didn't have anything to say about the wasted night's observation because Dave was the boss so he resumed his position in the loft without comment.

I made a decision not to let my parents know about the latest developments – about my house being turned into a one-stop cop shop – it would have complicated things far too much. I couldn't be sure what my mother was planning to do or say next and her new personality was far too unpredictable. I told them to stay at home and to stay safe, sounding like one of Boris's sidekicks during the Covid era – a time I now looked back on fondly. You can't get into trouble when you can't leave the house. I missed lockdown terribly, simpler times.

Whilst still portraying myself as the good wife, I decided to wow Dave and Stu with some good home-cooked food. Their usual stakeouts would have consisted of Subway sandwiches and cans of fizzy pop. They had never been holed up in a house with a chef so I made them a slap-up meal before they realised the target was on the inside … with them … cooking their lunch.

I spent ages perfecting the spicy beef with a pomegranate and chilli dressing, bright yellow turmeric roasted potatoes with caramelised onions, sweet and sticky, it was a work of art. Unfortunately the presentation was lost as one portion went up to the loft in Tupperware and Dave had his with a slice of bread on the floor of my office – not even a glass of Chianti was required. Keith Floyd would have done his nut.

It was about three in the afternoon when Matt and Gina emerged from 23. I watched them from behind the lounge curtains because all the other options were full. Gina started walking towards my house and I felt a sharp stab in the chest – she could say anything, not knowing she was being watched and listened to from just a few yards away. I was at the mercy of the gods and had no control over what happened next. However Matt, for some reason, called her back and said something in her ear, something that made her think twice. She glared at the house for a moment but then went and got into her car. They left and I was safe for a little longer.

Dave came flying downstairs on his radio. "Go go go, don't lose them." He then read out the number plate and handed it over to his lads on the road.

"What now?" I enquired nervously.

"Not a lot, we follow them and we observe them over the next few days, we wouldn't make any arrests until we have some solid evidence."

"Like what, what evidence?"

He laughed. "Do I detect that you are loving this excitement?" I nodded and pretended that excitement was the reason I was on the verge of a cardiac arrest.

"Like them with drugs, them trafficking people, anything like that. These things take time, you have to be sure or we could muck up the whole case."

I was very, very close to asking about phone tapping but I felt if I did I would put the idea into his head. I decided that the phone thing was the least of my worries for now, I had bigger fish to fry.

I tried my best that evening to get on with normal stuff; I watched telly, did some cleaning but it was hard to take my mind off things. I eventually drifted off on the sofa with half a bag of wine gums to take the edge off, hoping to wake up and discover this had all been a terrible dream.

"Oi, wake up. Raquel, wake up." I jumped. Dave was sitting next to me.

"What time is it?"

He looked at his watch. "It's just after ten."

I sat up and unclenched my hand, a red wine gum had fused with my palm and would take a good licking to remove.

"Listen, I have just had word, Gina and Matt ... they're at your mum's."

"Fuck, shit, why?"

He shook his head. "I don't know but I haven't told my lot that they are at my in-laws' address yet. I'm going to have to at some point."

I tried to defuse. "They will be there for Arif, probably to speak to him or get some money from Mum."

"I thought he lived there now, permanently?"

"He does but they know him so maybe they are visiting."

He frowned. "Visiting on a Thursday night at ten o'clock? They're pensioners. This is weird." He pointed to my phone. "Call your mum. Find out what's going on."

I picked it up.

"Put it on loudspeaker."

I gulped.

Mum answered the phone almost immediately.

"Hello Raquel."

"Hi Mum."

"Hello Raquel, lovely weather today, wasn't it?"

Dave shook his head, he could tell something wasn't right.

"Yes, very sunny. How are you?"

"Your dad, Arif and I, we're all fine. Just the three of us here, having a lovely evening, just us three."

I deduced from this obvious head count that the others – and that included Tom – were upstairs and out of the way.

"Your friend Gina and Matt are here, just passing apparently, so that's nice, isn't it?"

Dave screwed up his face.

"Yes, very nice. OK Mum, so long as you're OK."

"We're fine thank you. Goodnight."

"Night Mum."

Dave stood and paced. "What the hell was that about, you thought that was weird, right? She didn't even insult you or ask you why you called."

I nodded. "She is weird though, Dave, a proper weirdo, they're probably swinging."

"No, it's something else, she sounded on edge, don't you think?"

"Maybe, but they probably don't want Arif to leave and I think Gina saw this as a short-term thing, that's what this is about."

He sort of agreed although he knew something was off and he wasn't fully convinced.

He went back to his post and I texted Mum immediately.

Mum, what's happening?

> *They are looking for two people and they wanted to talk to Arif. She is very angry (angry emoji)*

Are you OK?

Yes fine, they are with Arif upstairs (smiley emoji)

Where are the others?

In the shed with the drugs (needle emoji)

Delete that now.

OK sorry (sad face emoji)

Message me when they leave and I will call you OK?

OK. Could you send me your recipe for fish pie? We fancy fish tomorrow (fish emoji)

No!

OK (thumbs-up emoji)

I was in all sorts of bother. It was so complicated that I had lost track myself. There was no way I could get out of this without telling Dave. In fact, even if I did tell Dave, I was still ruined. It was no longer about if I told him but when. I would need to pick a moment very soon to bring his world crashing down. I didn't know what to expect, I had never let anyone down on this level before.

A colleague of Mum's, a young married lady who put it about a bit before falling pregnant, gave birth to a beautiful jet-black baby with her bright white husband present in the delivery suite. When all of the nurses waited for his reaction and the wife hid behind a pillow, he peered closely at the baby and said, "He's got my eyes." This was the level of denial I was looking for from Dave.

The H Bomb

I thought it would be a cold day in hell when Dave was right and I was wrong. Husbands, especially the ones who had grown up as 'Mummy's little soldier', always lived through their marriages from one bollocking to the next; they were always in the wrong, making daft mistakes and their wives would just laugh through gritted teeth about it all later. Sons who were overly smothered with love and attention as children don't fully function like adults once the apron strings are cut. Particularly outside of their jobs, they were still kids at home and their wives had to bring them up alongside the children. This was the reason that Dave threw his socks and underpants on the floor, never changed a toilet roll and did not have a clue how to make a proper sandwich, with layered fillings – his mummy had always done it for him. The first time I saw Dave fold a sandwich instead of cutting it with a knife I felt ill; I gently removed it from his hand and remade it properly. I couldn't allow him to eat such a badly built snack, it would keep me awake at night, so I had stepped in as Dave's Mum's replacement and made it all better.

It wasn't a particularly sexy role but that's what I was, somebody who corrected things and put a plaster on it, so to speak. Looking back, so what if his sandwich was made without love, so what if he had to wear dirty socks every day? These details, they were unimportant, and women like me put too much emphasis on everything being proper.

I was a woman who had some self-respect. I had never done a poo in front of my husband, I had never broken wind voluntarily with him in the room and, now I was in my forties and not so fabulous, I had the good grace to dim the lights whenever we had sex. Dave, on the other hand, would wander around naked like a rhino at a safari park – he had no inhibitions, no shyness, he thought of me as his rhino girlfriend and presumed we would frolic in the mud together … forever. So, in essence, Dave was extremely comfortable with me. He thought he knew me, knew us, we were in tune and accepted one another's flaws so when the bomb actually hit, he was absolutely shell-shocked.

The saddest part of this whole situation was that it hadn't been me to tell him. He had to hear it from somebody else, somebody other than his wife. I think perhaps that if I had managed to grow a pair in time and revealed it all in my own words, maybe he wouldn't have been so crushed.

I was planning on it, of course I was, but it took time to put my pitch together, to plead my case. OJ Simpson didn't just rock up to court on the day of his arrest with an excuse ready to go, it was meticulously planned by a team of experts. They presented opening speeches, closing speeches, psychological reports on the attacker and the victim. Expert witnesses were teed up, not that I had any of those unless you counted Sir Walter who, lazily, had not learned to speak English in time for my hearing.

I didn't get that time to plan my defence because Roger, the little bitch, got in there first.

Dave had been at the office window all of that day, his ponytailed partner was having a fag in the back garden wearing sunglasses and a cap – this was apparently what they called incognito.

I saw Dave leave the back door and have a quiet word with him. I presumed it was a talking to about the hair-do – it wasn't. Stu stubbed out the fag and respectfully put it into his jeans pocket, still slightly smoking. He left the house without looking at me and was picked up in an unmarked car.

"Where's he off to?" I was busy making another pot of pretend coffee.

"He's going off duty."

"How long for?"

"Until I sort a few things out here."

"What things?"

"You tell me, Raquel."

I stopped the plunger on the cafetière.

"What do you mean?" I carried on plunging, it had to be plunged.

"Why don't you look at me in the eye and tell me what the fuck has been going on?"

Now, call me stupid, but I actually mentally went through all of the stupid stuff I had done lately apart from the obvious, hoping it would be anything else on the list.

Did I pay the gas bill on time? We barely used gas in the summer so that was a no.

Had I pranged the car? It was likely but he wouldn't use the word fuck over that.

Was Suzy pregnant? I hoped she was, that would really help.

He grabbed my shoulder and spun me round.

"Raquel, tell me it isn't true?"

I threw my hands up.

"You've lost me, what are you talking about?"

Dave sat down at the kitchen table, his hands were shaking, I knew that he knew something. His face was red, redder than ever before.

"Have you been getting off with him over there? Have you?"

He screamed the last bit so loudly I jumped.

My chin hit my chest and I shut my eyes. The time had come and I had to give him something.

"A bit, yes."

"A BIT?" He was yelling. "What the hell does that mean, a bit?"

In my warped mind, the word 'bit' would take some of the sting out. In hindsight, it trivialised what I'd done and it was not a good choice of words.

I breathed in deeply. I didn't know what he knew, I didn't know if he'd seen the messages on a phone, whether Gina had told him, I didn't know what to admit to, what to hold back. I still thought at this point that I could drip-feed this story to him and keep some of it back.

"Tell me what you know, Dave?" It was bold, it was cheeky,

but I gave a shit about this guy – I cared, I genuinely didn't want to hit him with the lot because, well, it was a lot.

"Why don't you tell me what you've done, tell me the whole story, Raquel? Because that is the only way; any other way will just not work for me, for us, for our family."

He had tears, this was the one thing I had been dreading, tears in a grown man's eyes because of me and my stupidity.

I had no right to cry, no damn right to have any emotion right now other than sympathy for my betrayed husband. And, if he was crying over Matt, what the hell would the rest of it do to him?

He was calmer now, he took the good cop approach, any more shouting and I might have bolted.

"Are you going to be honest with me or are you going to try and water this down, like you always do when things get too much?"

I felt physical pain on his behalf. Being honest would hurt him further but holding back was prolonging the agony.

He wiped his eyes and he talked directly to me; I knew he meant business.

"The truth is always better than a lie, Raquel, no matter how hurtful. No matter how bad it is, you have to tell me the truth and if you can't, if you are planning on lying at all for whatever reason, then I am leaving you for good, it's up to you."

He stood up and went to leave the room.

"Where are you going?" I was frightened he would leave the house without me getting a chance to stop him from hating me.

"I am going to get a beer to drink in the garden and by the time I am done, I want your decision."

He went out of the back door with a San Miguel, sat on a garden chair, and I watched him through the kitchen window sobbing into his cupped hands.

I considered texting Mel for instruction, I thought about messaging Matt and offering him two and a half grand to never reveal our secret – that's what I had in my NatWest savings, money for a rainy day, and today it was torrential.

I even had an idea to run away and go to a fishing lodge for a few days giving everybody the chance to calm down and hopefully, on my return, everybody would have long-term amnesia and I'd be off the hook.

None of these options were the right thing to do; appealing, but I was already in a hole, it wouldn't do to make it any deeper. I was a coward in many ways, I should have come clean about this a long time before that day but it's never too late to do the right thing, as my dad once told me. We were standing in a jewellers buying Mum a 'sorry bracelet' at the time, after some red knickers were found rolled up in his glasses case.

I took a toilet roll, half a bottle of wine and a blanket out into the garden. I sat on a chair facing Dave and I told my husband the whole sorry tale.

Dave had a way about him; he must have learned it during his time at police school or detective college, whatever they called it. He said nothing when it was really crucial to say something. He had managed to listen to every disgusting, sordid and criminal element of the story without even a gasp. Even I gasped at my own version, I was shocked as I explained all that I had done even though I was the perpetrator. He never moved a facial muscle as I told him the bit about the cleaner's death, the cleaner's resurrection, the people I transported, Sir Walter and his drugs bust. He was stony faced and silent. He kept completely quiet during the bit about the first kiss, which was irritating as deep down I had hoped he would break a tree with his bare fists in a jealous rage.

He never laughed or cried during the revelations; he had an emotionless face. It was unnerving and confusing; he was good at his job. The less he said, the more I did. I had to fill the silence and somehow, because he said nothing, I left no stone unturned. Eventually when I had finished and I was quite out of breath because, let's face it, it's quite the tale, he turned to me.

"You must really love me!"

I felt temporarily better.

"Aren't you angry?"

He looked at the sky and sucked his teeth.

"I'm absolutely fucking raging ... but to do all of that to stop me from finding out that you kissed another guy, you must really love me, eh?"

I nodded. I really did. I might not have had butterflies when he walked in the door, I may not have had the heart flips when he put on a suit, but I did love the guy probably more than I ever actually knew.

I stood and walked around the table and leaned in to put my head onto his chest, it was something I had done since we met and it made me feel safe. He put his flat palm out before I got close and stopped me by the forehead.

"No, mate. Absolutely not."

That word mate had a profound effect on me in that moment. Dave had used many affectionate terms when addressing me as part of our marital vocabulary – mate was not one of them.

Dave left the house soon after our chat. He didn't say where he was going or whether he'd be back. Part of my punishment was not knowing my fate. I was alone in the house without my family, having pretty much fucked up everything, and I only had myself to blame.

I called Mel, she answered immediately.

"Are you OK?"

"No."

"He knows then?"

"Yes, he does."

"How is he?"

"I don't know, he has gone out."

"I hope you will both be OK."

"So do I, Mel, but I'm scared. I don't know what is going to happen."

"It was Roger."

"What was?"

"Who told him."

"Excuse me?"

"It was Roger. He said it had gone far enough and Dave needed to know the truth to stop it going any further. For the kids' sakes, for all our sakes."

"You told Roger?"

"I had to, I needed to offload."

"To him? Why him?"

"Because he is my husband, we tell each other everything."

"Fuck you."

"I'm sorry."

I ended the call. Of all the people to tell she chose to tell him, that little creep who I knew would have taken great pleasure in delivering the news to Dave. I cringed, this was not how it was supposed to happen.

I had no idea what I was supposed to do, I had been given no indication by Dave. I wasn't sure whether to carry on as normal or hide in the loft. Was he at the station or was he on a flight to the Bahamas? I was stumped.

When Gina came over gunning for me the following morning, I wished I'd had Dave by my side. She was in nasty mode and I was feeling weak.

"Where's my stuff?"

She was smoking again.

"It's not here."

She attempted to raise her eyebrows. "Sorry, what?"

"I couldn't keep it here, Gina, with the dog and Dave, could I?"

"Well you'd better go and get it because we need it."

I agreed, I couldn't be bothered to argue.

"Another thing, Raquel, I have had some things playing on my mind, well a couple of things actually." She was close to my face now, too close.

"What?" My voice was shaky, I was too tired to play games so I let her see my fear.

"Firstly, when we spoke about Sophia, the girl, the one who's pregnant?"

I nodded.

"You said 'she was about to give birth'. How would you know how pregnant she was, I never mentioned it? I just said she was pregnant and you claimed that you didn't know."

I shrugged. "Just a guess, I guess."

She shook her head. "No, I don't think so. Because on top of that, I gave two kids a packet of fags and a five-pound note and do you know what they told me in return?"

I shook my head.

"They told me that they had seen someone who sounds very much like you leaving Redwalls with an old lady recently. Ring any bells?"

I said nothing.

"I'm onto you, Raquel. This is going to get ugly. You really don't know who you're dealing with."

She gave me a look, one I didn't like. I wanted Dave so badly right now to put a plaster on it all.

I arrived at Mum's just before lunch to collect the drugs. At least once I had given them back it was one less thing in my possession. Just three people to get rid of and then I would feel less at risk. Arif came to the door with an apron on and the smell of cakes was a comfort in my otherwise hellish life.

"We have been baking, I make banana cake, the one you put in your magazine."

"Very nice, well done." I patted him on the back. At least somebody had appreciated my lazy recipe that week.

Mum had been helping and they had quite the display on the kitchen table.

"Gosh it's like Mr Kipling's kitchen in here."

"He's not a real person, Raquel." She rolled her eyes.

"I need the key to the shed asap."

Mum pointed to the kitchen drawer. I hurried out and took the Morrisons carrier bag straight to the car boot without going back into the house, it stank. The packaging for this stuff was useless, I was probably going to end up stoned by driving around with it. Perhaps that was the answer.

"I can't stay long, I have to sort that out." I winked at Mum so she knew what I was referring to. She tried to wink back but ended up blinking twice very obviously. She was not a good criminal.

"Your dad is up at the osteopath with Tom, he has started

some treatment on his back, they are hoping to realign his–"

I stopped her. "I don't care, Mother, we need to talk about last night."

She ushered me into the posh lounge and she shut the curtains for no reason at all.

"Well, they came round, it was all very strange but luckily Arif spotted them when he was turning down the beds."

"Turning down the beds? Who are you, Lady Mary Crawley?"

"Shut up, Raquel."

"Sorry, go on."

"Well, he saw them pull up with no lights on but he knows the car. So, like lightning, he got Sophia and Babs out of the back door and into the shed. Old Tom insisted on going in there with them because he found it all a bit arousing … I think that's the word he used."

"For the love of god."

"Anyway, we let them in and they said they were just passing."

"What did they want?"

"To talk to Arif and, to be honest, they seemed to sniff around the place a bit. Asked if they could go upstairs for a chat which was quite rude."

I marvelled at the fact my parents had acted so quickly. For a pair of golden oldies they had really pulled this out of the bag.

"Anyway, they left shortly afterwards and said to tell you that they would see you very soon. What are we going to do, Raquel, do you and Mel have a plan?"

"Mel has gone back to Ireland with the kids, Mum, she will be back in a few days."

Mum looked disappointed; she knew that without Mel I would probably fuck it all up.

"They know I had something to do with Sophia going missing, they know that I took Babs from the horrible house."

"Oh dear, what a pickle." Mum had a very strange way with words.

"This is not a pickle, Mum, this is literally a disaster."

"It's a pickle and a disaster, Raquel, let's meet halfway."

I gave up.

Arif had told me that Gina had repeatedly asked him if he had seen or heard from Sophia and Babs. She had pinned him against the wall of my parents' bedroom and Matt had to intervene. She had called him a "little shit" and her breath smelt of cigarette smoke and raw onions. I appreciated the detail although it was not necessary.

Arif had bravely denied all knowledge of their whereabouts and held his nerve. If this debacle had been a football game, he would have got man of the match. I left the house without seeing Sophia; she was in bed in some significant discomfort. Babs was with her and looking after her well, according to Mum, so I put her and the baby to one side in my mind but it would need addressing soon.

I was surprised that Dave had not sent in a SWAT team to recover the drugs – at the very least I expected a policewoman/ midwife to turn up. I had heard nothing and, until lunchtime, I was kept in the dark about Dave's location. I didn't dare to message Gina about the stash so I had no choice but to go over there and deliver it like a shady dealer. It was a good job Dave wasn't still in the loft, he could have mistaken my drug drop for a quickie with Matt, perhaps even both. I didn't want to step foot into this house ever again but it was possible they had good news. Judging by the boxes in the hallway and the lack of shite ornaments on the surfaces, they were definitely on the move.

Matt was humping boxes around whilst Gina spoke in Kurdish on her phone. The Malik guy was standing in the kitchen and for once he wasn't smirking. Gina looked over and, without breaking her conversation, she pointed to the island and then to the bag. I placed it down and turned to leave. Matt blocked my path.

"She needs to speak to you."

"Are you leaving?"

He nodded.

"Thank fuck."

"Charming."

"When you two love birds have finished, I need a word."

I hoped this would be the last time I had to listen to this awful woman's shrill tone.

"What is it, Gina? Your stuff is there."

"What about my other stuff? I need that back."

I said nothing. She continued, "I don't just mean Arif, I mean the other two. I need them all back and it needs to happen soon. You want us gone? Well I need all of my belongings, no loose ends. Do you hear me?"

I had no idea what to do, I couldn't very well give these poor people up without at least trying to help them. What did I have to lose now anyway, Dave knew the horrible truth.

"If you are referring to people, they are not your belongings. You cannot own people, Gina, they are human beings. Just leave them, go without them."

She shook her head. "No, no! We don't leave people who could grass us up roaming the streets, we keep them all together where we can keep an eye on them. You seem to forget, Raquel, they asked to come here, they asked for this life."

"Why let Arif go to my parents if you don't like them mixing?"

She snorted arrogantly. "He's a one-off, he's just a kid. Plus, I know you won't turn us in seeing as though you hired him yourself, illegally."

"So you planted him purposely to keep me on side?"

"It all fell into place, babe, it was meant to be."

My heart sank for the kid. He had been given a taste of a good life, a nice home, people who cared. Yes, he worked hard at my parents but they paid him well and treated him like family. He had been used as a pawn and very soon they would pluck him from what he now called home and put him back in a warehouse where he would be treated like a slave.

"So, here's the deal. You get me my people back to Liverpool, back to the warehouse where they belong by Sunday and I will let this all go. I don't know where you've sent them and I don't really care but I need them back. Once that has happened, you can go back to your sham of a marriage and we will be gone. We fancy the coast, don't we babe?"

She smiled at Matt who nervously smiled back.

"So Sunday, Raquel, you have until then."

Her phone rang again and she answered it immediately. Whoever it was, shouted so loudly that I heard every word. One of which was 'bitch'. She definitely had superiors; this went much higher than her.

My heart sank when I saw Dave's car on the driveway, he had come home whilst I had been at 23. There were to be no more lies and I would need to tell him where I had been and what I had done, it wouldn't be pleasant. He looked tired and he was making himself a folded sandwich with rock-hard butter that didn't even reach the edges. He didn't even look up as he sat down, without a plate, to eat a terrible lunch whilst his terrible wife looked on in dismay.

"Been anywhere nice?"

I shook my head. "Nope, not really. I went to my mum's and then across the road … to Matt and Gina's–"

He looked up and glared. "I know where you've been, and what you have done."

"Do you?"

"Yes of course I do, I followed you."

"You followed me, why?"

He threw the sandwich down onto the table.

"Why? Because my wife is involved in all sorts, with dangerous people, my in-laws are harbouring people in their home and you are shifting drugs for a known gang and, well, because it's my job."

I gulped. Yes, it was his job, his very important job and I was now a suspect.

"I don't know what to do, Dave, I'm in it up to my neck. You know they are demanding me to hand those poor people over by Sunday or apparently bad things will happen."

"What bad things?" He pumped up his chest.

"I don't know, they are capable of anything."

"Why did you do it, Raquel?" he snarled.

"They made me, I wasn't thinking straight."

"I'm talking about the affair."

I felt flushed. Could we really call it an affair? It was a fling at best, we never even got past first base, not really.

"I don't know why."

"Would you have taken it further?"

"I really don't know."

"Did you have feelings for him or was it just sexual? Actually don't answer that, I feel sick."

He looked broken; I had broken him.

"How do I know that the next guy with a tan and a flashy smile won't be the one you jump into bed with?"

I was furious, how dare he. Was I so out of control and desperate that I was gagging for it with anyone who'd have me? I wasn't a serial cheater, the closest I had got in twenty years was when a fit gym instructor put his hand on my thigh to check for an injury I totally made up so he would put his hand on my thigh.

"Same question – if I leave you in the same room as my sister, do I need to worry that you might kiss each other again?"

He looked up and his face crumpled.

"She told you then?"

I shrugged. "She did."

He said nothing, neither did I.

Perhaps this was it for us as a couple. We had dented the armour and the damage would always be there. I went upstairs for a sit-down shower and left him with his folded sandwich.

Karma

A family party was stressful at the best of times and there was no way anyone planned these things and expected them to go smoothly. I had put these events on the 'things you have to do' list along with funerals, christenings and any birthday party for people aged seventy and over. I had been to fiftieths that would make Glastonbury jealous, but seventieths? They were like a dress rehearsal for the wake. They tried, did the oldies, but they always failed. No matter how many free drinks or wacky dress codes they came up with, it was always a depressing event with the grave beckoning in the distance.

My dad's sixtieth went on for five days. It wasn't planned to end in such debauchery, nobody envisaged that an all-inclusive package would end up in the hotel having to send out for extra booze. A large group of Dad's friends and family had descended on a small boutique hotel and we were on a mission. I had just stopped breastfeeding one of the kids so the milk shop was shut, it was the first trip without them and I was determined to make it count. Dad and his mates had ended up in a belly dancing club somewhere in downtown Marrakesh, apparently "the lads" drank tequila from belly buttons and got a camel ride home. The slut drop that my mother performed in the hotel bar at 3 am allowing her undercarriage to kiss the carpet was the last time she did shots – she had no recollection of it but the chaffing and a stiff hip pointed to the fact something untoward had occurred. It was utter mayhem, five nights in Morocco left us all with the heebie-jeebies. Ten years later at Dad's seventieth and you could hear a pin drop. Even with a free bar and unlimited cigars I had seen more life at the cemetery and, when I told Mum that, she nipped me under the arm where the sensitive bit was. The Lake District was really nice and all that but the presence of wheelchairs and people on statins prevented the party from ever really kicking off.

Dave's party was to be held at Duck; there was no point in holding it at my "new build" according to Mum, and she was adamant that all significant events be held in or within the grounds of a listed building or quite frankly they didn't count.

"Did you even hear of a coronation, a battle or an important awards ceremony being held in a cul-de-sac? Unless it's Number 10 Downing Street, a house with a number is not appropriate for important events. We'll hold it at grade two listed Duck Cottage, Raquel, that way at least the history books will have an appropriate address to use."

I just agreed with her, now that Dave was fully up to date with all of my hellish endeavours, there was nothing to hide from him. The drugs were safely back with their owners and I presumed that the other stuff was being dealt with by the squad. I was not in control of anything anymore and it did feel quite liberating, I just had to wait and accept my just desserts, whatever they may be.

I had spent a couple of days living alongside Dave without us saying much. He had spent most of the time on his phone and laptop but he had not once left the house. We had made each other drinks, I had done some food for us both but, apart from the odd nod, we talked very little. I had sort of accepted that Dave would probably leave me. I also had to somehow face the fact I would be interviewed and charged with a number of different offences. But I decided I would enjoy living in my home with my husband close by because that, for now, was as good as it got.

On the Thursday, I presumed Dave would be going for a drink or two with his work people. I ironed a shirt for him as I always did and handed it to him as he was going upstairs.

"What's that for?"

"For you, to wear tonight."

He frowned. "I am not going anywhere tonight."

"Oh, how come?"

"Raquel. Get with the programme, I can't leave you on your own with them … he gestured to 23.

"I'll be fine, you go out. I can look after myself."

He laughed loudly and shook his head in disbelief. He went up without the shirt, leaving me hanging. I followed him upstairs.

"Is that why you haven't been anywhere, because of me? You're worried about me?"

"Until I decide what we do next, I am not leaving your side and of course I am worried, you've landed yourself and this family in so much shit, Raquel, it's clear you cannot look after yourself."

"When you say we, do you mean you and the police?"

"No dickhead, I mean you and me, Raquel."

"Is there a me and you then?" I asked with the hope of possibility. He very coldly and without looking at me said, "There is for now."

A glimmer of something to build on, a chance that was as small as a mouse's eardrum, but still a chance.

We watched TV together that night, just the soaps. Interestingly, there was nothing on any of them that rivalled the dramatics that we were experiencing. We had no choice but to laugh at the fact that even Emmerdale seemed boring compared to our lives; it was nice to laugh with Dave.

I put my foot on his lap, it was a completely natural move. It went badly. He pushed it off and said, "No!" in a very cutting way. I would keep trying.

I had agreed with Mum that I would do some of the buffet for Sunday's party. She and Arif were in charge of the sweet end of the table. The theme was 'afternoon tea' so a few pastries and sandwiches was literally all I needed to do.

I made a start on the quiche mix. I felt the smell of bacon would put Dave in a good place; if that didn't then nothing would. My suspicions were correct and within minutes he was sniffing around the kitchen with his inquisitive snout.

"Bacon sandwich?"

"If you're making one."

"I'm not but I will make one especially for you."

He thought for a minute and then said, "No thanks, I'm going to bed." It was a fail.

I would keep trying, I would use sausages next time, the ones with nutmeg, hopefully that would get me closer.

Dave slept in Sam's bed with the door shut. I felt miserable without him and missed his nightly chorus of bodily noises.

About 1 am I received a message from Gina.

Raquel. The clock is ticking ... Or I will be taking matters into my own hands.

I ignored it, I couldn't very well round these people up and dump them back at the warehouse, it was cruel. I think I would need to just let Dave do his worst and hand them over to the authorities. They would still end up in the system and would be sent to stay at a Travelodge in somewhere like Peterborough before being deported back to hell. I had failed them and I had failed my husband. I supposed they could attend a nice party beforehand; I could give them that. So I put double cream in the quiche, it was the least I could do.

Roger and Mel were coming back on Saturday evening with my children plus two extra. I had no option but to allow Connie and Finn to come over as promised, I couldn't possibly let them down. It wasn't worth the sulking or the glares, although I was getting used to all of that.

CeeCee and Gary had already landed in the UK but, as luck would have it, they were visiting friends on the way up north in Birmingham so they would stay there on Saturday night and just come straight over to my mother's the following day for the party. I had one more day to try and make Dave realise how sorry I was, so I started with breakfast in bed.

He was bleary-eyed when I put the tray down in front of him. He sat up and I handed him a napkin.

"Eggs Benedict with sausages on the side! Your favourite."

"This doesn't change what you've done," he said quietly.

"It's a start."

"I can't get it out of my head." He stabbed the yolk of the egg and it oozed yellow.

"What?"

"You and him."

"It was nothing Dave, it meant nothing. What about you and my sister?"

"Raquel, you kissed him more than once amongst other things. You exchanged messages, it was not nothing."

I sighed, he was right. "I'm sorry you know?"

"I know you are, love. I am just so disappointed in you."

I blushed, that was worse than a slap in the face, so much worse.

I left him with his breakfast and carried on with the buffet prep whilst fighting back the tears. It was a busy day, as well as making sure the guest room was ready for Mel and the twat, I also made up the camp beds for the extra two and planned we would get a takeaway because I was all cooked out. Dave had ordered a people carrier to collect the kids and Roger, who had flown over with them, and Mel pulled up on the driveway about twenty minutes before they landed. Sir Walter sat on the pavement eyeballing 23 before he came in to greet me. If that dog could have spoken I know he would have told me to 'hang on in there'. His eyes also showed disappointment and he sighed heavily as he passed me.

Mel had started to look less and less like her usual self; less of the stuffy lawyer, she was shifting more towards outdoorsy dog-walker. She had lost some weight and her cheekbones had showed up; about time, I thought nastily.

"You OK?"

I shrugged. "Not really, I think he is going to leave me and I'm definitely getting sent down."

"Try and stay strong, eh?" She patted my back as she passed me.

I laughed; talk about flippant. I was very curt with her but Roger was the one whose toe I would stand on with a heavy winter boot just as soon as I got the opportunity.

The kids came bounding in, extremely over-excited and giddy. They disappeared almost immediately to their rooms, whispering.

Finn was keeping it cool and kissed me on both cheeks, then he shook Dave's hand and called him sir. Dave was impressed, I hope he hadn't forgotten what teenage boys would do to get some action.

Connie was certainly still a little cold with me; she had probably boxed me off as someone to keep at arm's length and she was absolutely right. I forwarded a copy of a Thai takeaway menu to them all and asked them to send me their order, suggesting that it was a nice evening so we would eat outside.

Roger was dragging a suitcase in when we first locked eyes, his face was particularly flaky that day and I was sure this was a guilt rash.

"Raquel, how are you?"

I fumed at his relaxed attitude. "I'll deal with you at some point but for now let's keep it civil."

He raised one eyebrow and then looked at the floor before entering the house.

"Yeah, you keep walking, mate."

He did.

I saw Dave and Roger talking in the garden soon after and I immediately opened the back door to hear what was going on.

"Look, I had to tell you, things had gone too far, Dave. With you being an officer of the law, I knew you'd want to know what your wife has been doing, she's a mess so she is." His delivery was insincere, he put his hand on Dave's shoulder. "Hope you're OK, brother."

Dave turned to him, grabbed him by the collar and spoke very closely to his face but I couldn't hear what was said. What I did deduce was that Dave was not falling for this act and he said something that made Roger go upstairs to the bathroom for the next thirty minutes.

Dave gave me a little smile afterwards, it felt good.

The Thai takeaway was due and the door went so Dave went off to get it with some cash for the driver. I was setting the table and Mel was doing the drinks. I nearly died on the spot when I turned to see Matt standing in my hallway.

"Someone here to see you."

Dave stood behind Matt looking at me with disgust.

"Hi Matt, everything OK?" My voice was high-pitched, hysterical even.

Matt certainly felt uncomfortable even though he had no idea that Dave knew everything. "Can I have a quick word please, babe?"

Dave's eyes flashed. "Her name is not babe, mate."

Matt got flustered. "Err yeah, soz, I just am so used to calling Gina babe, and my sister, and Gina's sisters and–"

Dave stopped him. "Her name is Raquel."

Matt nodded.

Roger came down the stairs halfway through this terrible conversation and observed it with interest.

"So this is Matt, is it?"

He just needed a cat on his evil little lap. Matt didn't even acknowledge him, thank goodness, so mercifully I didn't need to feel embarrassed by how stupid Matt sounded and that I had fallen for his charm.

"A word please, Raquel." He pointed to the lounge. I turned to Dave.

"I'll be one minute, it's about the article."

Dave said nothing. Matt shut the door to the lounge. This was horrible. I knew Dave was standing on the outside, he had no idea what was going on in his home.

Matt put his head in his hands. "We've got a big problem."

"What problem? Gina told me the deadline is tomorrow. What do you want?"

"It's not about the people, Raquel. It's about the gear."

"What about it? I gave it back to you the other day."

"Where's the rest?"

"What rest?"

He whispered. "There's a load of it missing."

I sat down, before I fell down. "That's not possible, that's nothing to do with me."

He looked at me with genuine concern. "You need to get it

back, I can't hold them off for much longer."

My mind raced; were they having me on, was this another curveball to draw me in?

"I swear, Matt, I don't know what you're talking about. I left it somewhere, it hadn't been touched."

"Wherever you left it, someone has been into it."

"Are you sure?"

He nodded. "I just weighed it, it's light." As he went to leave the room he turned to me. "Get it back, girl, for your own sake."

Dave was unpacking the takeout in the kitchen which had arrived during my chat, I wasn't sure whether he had listened at the door. As we were being open now, I had to tell him.

"So, erm, Matt came over to tell me that there is another problem."

Dave stopped me and said, "I don't want to know.' And that was it.

The meal was as fake as Gina's handbags. I smiled, joked and laughed even though I wanted to lie in my bed shaking. I couldn't bring myself to talk to Mel or Roger directly so I purposely overcompensated with everyone else. At one point, for authenticity and just to see what would happen, I stood behind Dave and hugged him around the neck. The kids were all around us so there was nothing he could do. He just sat in his chair as still as a statue and waited for it to end. I whispered "Love you" in his ear and he responded under his breath, "What a funny way of showing it."

We had no choice that night but to sleep in the same bed, but he lay right on the edge with his back to me.

During the night, I felt his warm hand up the back of my pyjamas and I hoped he had softened. He hadn't, he woke up and immediately removed it, grunting with annoyance that he had let himself slip. I wanted him to tell me it was going to be OK but the more this went on, the more doubt I had. I had to get through the party and then we would have to face up to things properly. This party was going to be a struggle and I deserved to struggle. I just had one thing left to do to keep everybody happy before things were certainly going to get much worse.

The following day, I arrived at Mum's with a boot full of food. It was a glorious day and the setting was perfect. Mum had tastefully set out the garden with rugs, tables and a gazebo – a fancy one in case the weather changed. She would not normally have gone to such effort for the likes of Dave but it was lovely to see she was actually extremely proud of her son-in-law. Dad had a short suit on with a bow tie and Arif was dressed as a waiter; it could very easily have been a murder mystery event with all the crazy characters in ridiculous costumes. This could have been a lovely afternoon for me had I not fucked it all up, but not everybody knew about that so the least I could do was put on a brave face for the sakes of my family. Dave was subdued but not enough for people to notice, it was only me that knew he was hurting and that was a punishment in itself.

Sophia was going to try and join the party but she was feeling tired and hadn't slept well; that was one less person for me to explain, at least. Old Tom, who had no real time for children, ignored everybody and sat in the corner of the garden under a tree with his trilby over his face. Barbara sat next to him and was clearly a bit squiffy because she laughed her head off when all I said was "hello".

Mum was lording around the place explaining to her guests her choice in cakes, earrings and what year the roof was re-thatched. Everything was as normal as it could be.

The kids introduced their partners to my parents. It was lovely until I realised that I had completed forgotten to tell them about Michaela being gay. I heard my Mum saying, "Come again, she's your what?"

Michaela repeated, loudly and boldly, "She's my girlfriend, Grandma!"

I looked at Dave for support, the last thing I needed was Mum to say the wrong thing and to make us look like a bad family.

Dave marched over and stood in between Connie and Michaela with his arms firmly over their shoulders. "This is Mic's girlfriend. We were going to tell you but we've been a bit busy with stuff going on and what not."

Mum slowly looked Connie up and down and then looked at Michaela. "What a beautiful girl, I hope she has the brains to match."

Connie laughed and then began to tell Mum about her whale obsession and how she thought that David Attenborough should be sainted. Mother did me proud, for once.

Dave's entire demeanour changed when his parents arrived. They always had on outfits that said 'We live abroad'. I don't know how they managed it but they did. There was no sombrero or anything like that, just a weathered tan and relaxed attitude which possibly stemmed from not having to deal with shocking weather and hoodlums on a daily basis. CeeCee was a cuddly old thing, once her arms were around you, you wanted to stay there for good. She smelled of washing powder and her soft blonde curls made her look like an elderly cherub. She was deeply tanned and wore a blue linen shift dress with earrings so heavy that her lobes sagged down almost to her shoulders. Her matching bracelet was as thick as a bike chain but it suited her, gold and brown went well together.

Gary was Dave's double – short, bald and wide, lots of gold jewellery including a signet ring his father had 'acquired' around the time the Krays were in power which sat proudly on his little finger. They both jangled into Duck Cottage beaming with joy when they saw their son in the flesh for the first time that year.

"My boy, love you son." Gary grabbed Dave around the back of the neck and they touched foreheads. CeeCee put her arms around Dave's waist from behind and the three of them embraced. I felt dirty, I had broken their trust too. They had left their boy in my hands and I had let them all down.

Mum and Dad really liked Dave's parents; they were quite different but just enough to get one another. I think they were fascinated by my parents and their stiff British way and my parents felt as though they were starring in Eastenders when they hung out with CeeCee and Gary, it worked quite well to be fair.

Mum had always hidden her intolerance of Dave in front

of them, never letting slip that she thought he was a bit rough and ready. Mum was a charlatan and sneak but it was best that way because CeeCee would have scratched her eyes out had she known.

All the grandparents reacquainted, chinking glasses and pretending they liked each other's outfits. Mum introduced Arif to them like she had given birth to the boy herself and CeeCee hugged him until his head nearly popped off. They had a presence, a really positive vibe that spread throughout the house and garden as they said hello to everybody. The only person they were a little wary of was Roger who sipped a non-alcoholic beer and hung around the kitchen sink washing glasses and being a brown nose to Mum. I heard CeeCee whisper to Gary, "She's still wiv him, Gary, can you believe it?" And Gary looked at Roger from behind and shook his head in disappointment. They all thought Mel could do better than him, they all thought he was a little odd.

I helped to hand out the food, passing it around on trays to everybody was a good distraction from my impending doom. Tom and Barbara had not moved once, not even to say hello to arriving guests. I know he had a back injury but he managed to get up and down the stairs and in and out of Barbara so I thought it was very rude.

"Quiche? Bacon and leek!" I offered the plate to them both. Barbara burst into laughter and then lifted Tom's hat revealing a pair of very bloodshot eyes.

He reached out, grabbed the pastry and placed it into his mouth.

"Good god above, Raquel, this is delicious." He licked his hideous lips with his unnaturally long tongue and then slithered back under his hat smiling. Barbara was now crying with laughter again for absolutely no reason. I stood looking at them, analysing them and wondered, is this booze? It doesn't look like booze, his trusty brandy glass was nowhere to be seen. Surely not, please let this be a mistake.

I got down onto my knees between the pair of them and lifted Tom's hat back off his eyes. "Have you two been smoking weed?"

Barbara looked at Tom, she had no clue what I was asking. Tom looked at me and said, "Why, do you want some?"

"No, absolutely not. Where did you get it?"

He pointed to the shed. "Found a ton of it in there, really mellow stuff."

My head dropped. "You stupid, stupid man."

He laughed really loudly. "That's rich coming from you, my dear."

"That's mine, idiot, I need it."

"Finders keepers." And then he laughed even more than Barbara and popped another mini quiche into his stupid, stoned mouth.

I nervously looked around the garden at the children, the parents and my drug-busting husband. I would have to address this later once things had died down. They couldn't have smoked it all, not ten grand's worth, they had probably had a couple of spliffs if that. I would pack out what they had left with some rosemary and thyme and hand it back later.

I sat in a garden chair with a giant glass of Pimm's ready to try and at least enjoy myself for five minutes. I got to twenty seconds before I heard a scream from the patio, and not a pleasurable one.

Sophia was standing in a pool of sludge, crying.

Her waters had broken.

Quiche!

The kids were thoroughly disgusted at the pool that spread beneath Sophia's ankles. Connie wretched openly and turned her head away; she would need to man up if she was planning on become a member of the Attenborough lot, being squeamish at some womb slush was not a good start.

CeeCee had pulled a chair up behind Sophia, one of the patio ones so at least they could hose it down at a later date. I had originally allocated Barbara as the birthing partner, A because she could understand the girl and B she had spent more time with her than any of us. It turned out she was neither use nor ornament and had fallen into a drugs slump on old Tom's shoulder. I looked at Dave.

"What now?"

He shrugged. "You tell me, Raquel, what now indeed?"

Sophia was groaning loudly and grabbed onto Mum's jacket, pulling at her in desperation and hoping for some guidance. Mum pulled it away and tutted, there was no way the stitches on a satin trouser suit from Hobbs would survive such force.

We all stood in shock, half of the group not knowing who this girl even was and the other half wondering how we could keep this situation under control.

Before I could stop him, Roger had lifted up Sophia's nightie, got onto his knees and peered up into the abyss. We all grimaced.

"What the fuck, Roger? Stop that, there are no books up there."

He stood quickly and instructed Michaela and Suzy rather authoritatively to take Sophia up to her bedroom.

"Be careful with her. Lie her down, hurry."

The girls did exactly as he asked and Sophia staggered off walking like a cowboy and leaving a trail of the stuff behind her.

He then became more animated.

"OK. I'll need fresh towels, clean sheets, rubber gloves and some surgical spirit, anything to sanitise the space."

I screwed my face up. "Now listen up, Roger, I don't know what you think you're doing but quite honestly you need to leave this to the professionals."

He looked over to Mel. "Tell her, tell her what I used to do."

Mel blushed a little.

"Tell her for the love of god."

Mel fidgeted before eventually revealing all. "So … Roger used to be a midwife, before we met, before the bookshop." She said it quietly like she didn't want anyone to hear but him.

I laughed nervously. This would normally be the time I would rip the piss out of the pair of them but at this moment in time I was just grateful for the freaking miracle.

"Are you actually serious? Why have you never mentioned this before?"

Mel put both of her palms up in disbelief. "You know exactly why, Raquel, because you would have said nasty things about him not being a proper man like you always have. You even said that he was a pussy because he has a satchel for work."

Most of the people nodded and grumbled in agreement, even Dave, even Arif and he didn't have a clue what a satchel was.

I defended myself. "Hang on a minute, he looked like Roy Cropper, you can't blame me for that."

Dad interjected. "That's fair enough, he did look like Roy."

Roger became impatient with the lack of urgency.

"There's no time for this now; she's crowning, the baby is coming very soon, no time for hospital. We need to help this girl deliver this baby, now!"

Roger was not up for the debate on whether he was a man or not, which was probably for the best because I had plenty more examples ready to go that would have sealed the deal. Being a midwife didn't make him less of a man, I wasn't that narrow-minded, it was the constant complaining and the fact that his man sack had a separate pocket for dried prunes in case he got bunged up – this was just a sliver of my evidence.

"Well go on then, sister, go do your thang."

He curled his lip in disgust, I think he would have preferred matron.

So with that, the baby-deliverer went upstairs with his sleeves rolled up ready for action.

Mum and Dad fought off questions about who this girl was and they seemed to both go down the route of a friend of a friend's cousin. They had clearly straightened their stories beforehand which was helpful. Nobody was too inquisitive because they were all a few drinks in, although Gary had furrowed his brow a little when he discovered that Barbara, Arif and Sophia all hailed from the same place.

"Are you running some sort of drop-in centre, Suzannah?" he chuckled but I could tell he wanted an answer.

"You know me, Gary, my home is welcome to everybody." Mum brushed him off with a blatant lie. But you see, Gary did know Mum and he knew she was not all that welcoming in his experience. There had been a time when she had asked if he could do his "number twosies" at the local leisure centre instead of her downstairs loo.

"We don't want to have to get Dyno-Rod out again Gary, do we, eh?"

It was quite mortifying because she actually meant it.

I pulled Dave out of everybody's earshot.

"Dave, the situation is getting tricky. This baby will need looking at by a hospital, plus some of the weed – the stuff I kept here – well, it's been tampered with and those two are high, I think they stole some."

Dave looked from the stoners, who were still away with the fairies.

"For fuck's sake, Raquel, you are a walking disaster."

"I know, I know, I literally have to hand these lot back to Gina by the end of today and now that will include a newborn baby too. I also have to get the weed that Tom has taken and return that or else …"

"Or else what?"

"Well, they said they would do bad things."

"What bad things?"

"Tell you about everything for starters."

"But you already told me, well Roger did."

That was actually true. "I suppose I did, he did, we did."

"You see that is what they are playing on, the fact that I could find out about all of this, but I already know. So what are we scared of?"

"They could do other stuff. They're gangsters."

Dave smiled. "I have had dealings with many, many gangsters and these two are small time."

"What if they burn the house down?" My mind was running away.

"Why would they do that?"

"I don't know, revenge?"

"I doubt it, and anyway it's just a house and we're not in it, we're here."

"What about your job, the operation? What happens when the police find out about my involvement?"

"I am the police, Raquel."

I sighed deeply. "I understand that but you can't exactly let them go, you have to bring them in and they will incriminate me, my parents, everything is about to implode. You will get into serious trouble for knowing the information and keeping it from them. You could lose your job, your commendation."

"I am fully aware of the problem, Raquel, you are in a real situation and you can't deny it or lie to the police. Besides, there's too much evidence. There will be CCTV, phone records, witness statements. If they incriminate you, you would need to face the music. Do you think they would incriminate you?"

"She would!" I said with venom.

"He wouldn't?"

I thought about it, he was not like her. There was still something I didn't hate about him.

"Not sure to be fair, he's not all that bad."

Dave raised his eyebrows; it was the wrong thing for me to say.

"Dave, you know I would say you didn't know a thing about any of it, I promise, I would never tell them you knew."

"Well, that's good of you."

He wasn't being sincere.

Dave put his sunglasses on his head and rubbed his eyes. The mood had switched and he was clearly fed up with my stupidity. He probably already had the 'new wife' brochure ordered. I was sure I would be replaced by a rock-hard-titted bimbo who couldn't cause him any further stress.

"I'm thinking, Raquel. Give me some time. You just need to carry on holding it together and try not to create any more problems."

"OK. I'm sorry, Dave, for everything."

"Go and check upstairs and let me know how it's going; we need to keep an eye on that situation."

I don't think he wanted to look at me for another minute.

I rushed past Connie and Finn who were deep in conversation and not remotely perturbed by the events, in fact neither of them had even offered to help with anything all day. They seemed to be getting along extremely well and if Michaela's girlfriend hadn't declared herself a lesbian, I would have been concerned.

Mum was holding court in the kitchen and Arif was holding the fort on the food and drinks front. It was all a balancing act, but we were handling it.

Upstairs, Roger had wrapped one of Mum's pillow cases around his head and he had the Mary Berry apron on. He had put two carrier bags over his sandals so at least bad toe was out of the picture for a while. Sophia was lying naked on her side. It was all very bohemian; somebody had put the radio on and Simon and Garfunkel played softly in the background. Roger was stroking Sophia's back and saying, "You can do this, you can do this," in his irritating accent.

My daughters were milling around the bedroom folding, organising and being extremely helpful. Michaela had put a napkin in my mum's table-top scales and was preparing to weigh the baby and record it on the back of a receipt. Suzy had a nappy and baby grow ready on the dresser and was boiling a pair of scissors in the kettle ready to cut the cord.

"How's she doing?"

Roger looked up. "Mum is doing well, baby is as it should be and she's nearly ready to push."

I moved closer and checked Sophia was still breathing. She was panting like an Alsatian so definitely alive.

"Are you sure you're a qualified midwife and haven't just watched lots of episodes of Call the Midwife?"

Roger shook his head. "Stop making jokes and start being helpful for crying out loud."

"What do want me to do?"

"Bring up a cup of coffee please, black with two sugars."

"Should she have caffeine, is that good for the baby?"

"It's for me, eejit."

Back in the kitchen, the mothers were chatting away about the times they had given birth and how they had it much worse than we did.

"I was in labour four days with David, he was a big bugger too."

"You think that's bad, I was torn like a piece of paper from one end to the other, I couldn't sit down for months." Mum tried to outdo CeeCee and added, pointing to me, "That was you, that was. Your ears got stuck and you weren't for budging. I can still feel a sting when your father puts his–"

"That's enough info, Mother, please shut up." I put the kettle on.

CeeCee giggled. "How's she doing up there Raquel?"

I had no choice but to admit that Roger was doing a really good job. "It's all under control, CeeCee, you have another drink and try not to worry."

"Shouldn't you call an ambulance?" Gary was getting concerned about the handling of this strange set-up.

Dave stepped in. "No Dad, with Covid still hanging around,

home births are for the best as long as there are no complications and it all seems normal, doesn't it, Raquel?"

I nodded.

"Where's the father, shouldn't he be helping out with all this?"

Mel answered for me. "He's in the army, Gary, we'll get word to him and let him know as soon as possible."

Nosey Gary went back to his scone and jam and I hoped the questions would stop for a bit. I saw movement under the oak tree. Tom had rolled off the chair and was on his hands and knees in the long grass. Barbara was trying to lift him up but with no success, the two of them fell about each other like Weebles.

"For fuck's sake, state of them." I pointed to them so Dave could see the result of pensioners on dope. We both went over to help get Tom back to his feet.

"Good afternoon, officer Dave!" Tom grinned cheekily.

My moron of a second cousin thrice removed or whatever they call it was high as a kite at a party to celebrate the success of the head of the drug squad.

"You couldn't write it," Dave said, looking back at me rolling his eyes.

"You take her and I'll take him. Let's tell everyone they're pissed up and get them upstairs to bed."

I took Barbara's arm and led her towards the house. She resisted slightly until Tom caught up, then she grabbed his hand and was good to go. These two had become literally inseparable and, had it not been illegal, I would have encouraged them to go onto This Morning and tell their love story to Schofield.

Dave tied the belt of Tom's dressing gown in a triple knot at the bottom of the stairs.

"I don't want to see that thing again today." He ticked off Tom and then assisted him up the stairs. I did the same with Barbara and we bundled the pair of them into the back bedroom and put them to bed.

"Shall I look for the stuff?"

Dave looked at me in horror. "Don't discuss that with me, do what you need to do but keep me out of it. I'm going downstairs now, OK?" He tutted as he left the room, I really was an idiot.

I looked at the two oldies tucked up in bed, still holding hands, and I hoped to get some sense out of them.

"Where's the drugs?"

"What drugs?" Tom had completely forgotten he had told me.

"You know Tom, come on. The weed, the marijuana, the blow."

"Oh that." He laughed. "It's under here." he pointed to the mattress. "But please don't take it all."

"I will take it all because it's actually mine, you old fool."

He groaned. "Just leave us a little bit, please, we've had a wonderful few days."

I ignored him and lifted the mattress up so aggressively that Barbara rolled straight on top of Tom and he said, without any hesitation, "Well, if you insist," and started kissing her very loudly.

Under the mattress, amongst some electrical items I cannot even bring myself to mention, was a big bag of green stuff, a pipe and a box of matches.

"Quite the party you've been having, Tom."

He leaned over the top of the mattress and said, "Well, you only live once."

On the way downstairs I popped into the birthing suite to see if Sophia had made any progression; she had. She was legs akimbo on the edge of the bed and Roger was on his knees with a torch in his mouth.

"She's ten centimetres now, I think we start pushing."

Sophia, bless her, was moaning softly, she wasn't screaming the place down like I did. She didn't call her midwife 'Halitosis Helen' like I did and she didn't look like the girl from the Exorcist like I did. So Roger was doing a sterling job and the girls were shining as his assistants. At least something was going well.

With the drugs under my blazer, I hot-footed it downstairs ready to stash the stuff somewhere until later. The plan would be to quickly blend it with some herbs to get it back up to weight and then to message Matt and tell him which rock I had left it under.

Just as I reached the front door, Gary came out of the

downstairs loo with his paper. Let's just say there was no danger of anybody smelling the weed.

"Right my dear, see if you can finish this." He handed me The Sun open on the crossword page and a biro that was unfortunately wet. I had one hand for the paper, the other holding the drugs in place under the blazer, there were no hands free for the pen. He slid it into the edge of my mouth and went off for round two of the buffet. I stood in horror before dropping the pen onto the floor. But I had no time to think about what germs I had just swallowed, that would be a head-wrecker for the middle of the night, I needed to get rid of this shit and get back to the birth of this baby and then to put another round of quiches into the oven.

I opened the front door and, before I had the chance to get out of it, I heard that familiar noise; a noise that I really could've done without. Sir Walter was behind me, howling and pawing at my jacket.

"No, go away, fuck off." He didn't listen, he had one thing on his mind and before I knew it he was on me, I was down, he had the package in his mouth and I was on my back.

"What's all the racket?" Dave and Mel had come into the hall to see what on earth was going on. Mel immediately clocked what was happening.

"Jesus Raquel, it's that stuff again."

Dave stood with his arms folded. He should have cuffed me and taken me right then and there. He touched his phone, I thought he was going to make the call.

Mel looked at him, grabbed him by the shoulders and said, "Don't, Dave, please don't."

"Mel, please sort her out," he pleaded with the better sister.

She turned to the dog. "Drop, give it to me, Walter." He dropped the bag at her feet and wandered off looking back at me in disgust.

"Give it to me, I need to take it back to 23."

Mel looked at Dave, he shook his head.

"Don't give it to him, Mel, I need to take this back right now." Mel turned and looked at the door of the downstairs loo, then back at Dave. He nodded and walked back into the kitchen, shutting the door behind him.

"Mel, that's worth thousands, please."

But she bolted into the downstairs toilet and locked the door. I heard flushing – it took four flushes – and then she came out. I was still sitting on the floor since my run-in with the dog, and I gasped at her in disbelief.

"Sorry, Raquel, but that needed to happen and you know it." She went and joined the others leaving me more annoyed than anything that she had done the right thing in front of Dave and I hadn't.

Michaela came to the top of the stairs and beckoned me to come up with her fingers on her lips. She whispered before we went into the room. "It's a boy, Mum, a baby boy!" She had tears in her eyes and she was trembling.

I was very proud of her and Suzy, they were good in a crisis, who knew! They acted as a team when they needed to and it was nice to see, they actually reminded me of Mel and I when things went well.

I had never recognised this in them before; in the past, they would slice the tits off of each other's dolls and do other mean girl stuff but today they were working together as sisters.

"Roger says you need to stay with the baby, Mum, whilst he helps Sophia. OK?" Michaela gave me my orders.

In the middle of the bed, surrounded by pillows and wrapped in a John Lewis hand towel, was the biggest baby I think I'd ever seen. This little man had a full head of thick dark hair and at least three chins. His chubby little hands clutched the top of the towel and he lay peacefully with his big brown eyes wide open, he wasn't even crying.

Sophia was being cleaned up by Roger in the en suite, the afterbirth lay in the shower tray like a jellyfish on the beach. Roger handed Sophia some of Mum's pastel pants, the mint green ones, and she smiled when she saw me, a huge grin before pulling the pants much further up than was comfortable for me to see.

Roger turned and saw me gawping; he kicked the door shut to

save Sophia's dignity and shouted at me to concentrate on the baby and nothing else.

I sat on the bed next to the giant baby and I leaned over and smelt his head. Sadly it wasn't very nice, I would need to buy some baby shampoo from the organic shop in town as a gift as a matter of urgency.

Suzy had gone into the forbidden room with some sanitary items and a white cotton nightie, Michaela had gone off to get the Moses basket from the boot of Dad's car and I was left alone feeling very humbled and quite emotional. This girl had given birth to her first child without one member of her family to support her. She was living with strangers in a foreign country, she had no passport and no money, she didn't even know if her husband was alive or dead. Despite all of this I actually saw genuine happiness in her smile; you know the smile is real when it starts in the eyes. She was grateful for everything she had, for the kindness that we had shown her and the fact that, in this moment, she had all that she needed, even if she did have incontinence pants on that were pulled up to her tits.

We settled Sophia into bed after Roger had cleaned her up. He even put her hair up and wrapped it in a silk scarf. He was very caring, very calm, he was a very nice midwife to be honest. The baby sucked at Sophia's breast with a ferocious hunger, he certainly liked his food did this giant baby. Roger put a muslin square over her to maintain her dignity but she threw it onto the floor, proud for us to see her sustaining her baby's needs. She was a natural feeder, no wincing in pain when the jaws clamped down on the nipple, she was just like a cow, accepting it as her role as a milk wagon.

Roger and the girls cleaned up the room, getting rid of all the debris and transforming what was once a ward into a nursery. When the Moses basket's mobile was finally fitted and was playing a tune, Roger ushered us all out so mother and child could get acquainted properly. Just before we left, he asked Sophia what she would call her new baby.

Sophia, without even thinking, pointed to the baby and said, "Roger." I did my best not to laugh.

Barricade

It wasn't often I was off my food. Normally if something horrible happened I would be straight down the deli and leaving with a boot full of calorific 'picky bits'. That's what I did when I had a bad feeling, I ate!

I once had an iffy result on a cervical smear and I was called back the following week for a re-test. That week was a dark week for my waistline. I had acquired a full organic pig a couple of months earlier from a local farmer and I pretty much ate the whole thing myself. I was in and out of the freezer like a woman possessed, ploughing through the carcass to block out the worry of the potential bad results. I made sticky ribs, bacon sandwiches, pork belly, it was only the snout I didn't eat. I wasn't a cake person or a chocolate addict, I liked meat and lots of it.

But this crisis, this affected me differently. The fear in my stomach had filled it up, my appetite had vanished. It was only when the kids mentioned it did I realise that I must be in serious trouble. Suzy had noticed that I had not even made an impact on a whole Spanish ham I had spent a small fortune on, I was certainly not myself.

The smear was eventually OK, by the way. I was told I had a 'shy cervix' and they wanted to take another look. Imagine that, a cervix that didn't like to be persued so it hid like Lady Diana behind a tree avoiding the paparazzi.

I was living in fight-or-flight mode almost every minute of each day; the thought of facing the police, the gangsters and much worse, my children, was enough to put me off eating full stop. I did, however, consider that at least I would look thin in my mugshot, I could be described as slender for once, even if it was in a witness statement.

The party had been a bit of a mess. Obviously with a baby

being born halfway through, the focus had been taken away from Dave. He didn't mind, he had enough on his plate, but his parents minded and they were insistent that we had to give him an opportunity to celebrate, to show off and to make a speech to mark such a monumental occasion.

CeeCee and Gary were staying at The Falcon Hotel halfway between my parents and home. We decided to get together for lunch the day after the party and Gary made it quite clear it was to be just us. He had called to make sure he didn't have to endure any more births in the middle of his meal.

"Don't bring any of your mother's houseguests, for god's sake, we had a bloody gutful of them yesterday, Raquel."

"No problem, it will just be us."

I heard CeeCee in the background. "She's not invited that smelly old Tom and his girlfriend, has she?"

"I'll check, Cee. You've not invited that smelly old–"

I interrupted. "No, he is in bed with a bad back, he won't be coming and neither will she."

"Strange set-up that is, Raquel, all these random people everywhere, has you Mum lost it or what?"

"Probably Gary, she is a mental old witch, we both know that."

Gary laughed out loud. "Yes we do! Totally insane she is, absolutely cuckoo. In fact, she needs locking up she does."

"Alright Gary, that's enough."

He stopped abruptly. I had to defend Mum in this instance, she had been extremely kind of late and deserved some credit at the very least.

"OK then, love, see you at lunch, table is booked for one o'clock sharp."

Roger and Mel had made plans to take the dog off to the nearest beach early the next morning. Roger needed to be within thirty minutes of Sophia and baby Roger just in case he was needed. He said he was prepared to be on standby for a few days but after that the baby would need to be registered at a doctor's surgery within the week otherwise, ethically, we were failing them both. Even though mothers gave birth in Third World countries under bushes every ten seconds, that did not mean it was acceptable here. I agreed, although I struggled to come up with an explanation to feed to the NHS as to where this mother and child had come from. Mum told me to leave it to her.

"I will tell them I found them in the park and they are welcome to stay with me."

"Found them, in a park? They won't accept that as an explanation, Mum, they will want more information than that."

"Tough tits, it's all I have."

Mum thought she was above being questioned by anybody; she had been a legal secretary and she was over seventy and apparently that was enough to make her immune to investigation.

We had made it home after the party and everyone was off to bed safely without a peep from 23. Their lights were off and it looked like they were out. I had turned my phone off because, quite frankly, if they couldn't contact me I would not have to read any more of their horrible messages. A pathetic 'out of sight out of mind' concept but my only option to get through the night.

I woke at six in the morning knowing Gina's deadline had passed. Not only had I not handed back the elusive stash but the missing workforce still resided at Duck Cottage with no intention of returning to the warehouse. I was playing with fire, my fingers were literally melted flesh, but the drugs were down the bog and we now had a baby to add to the mayhem. I had absolutely nothing to offer Gina and Matt in way of compensation.

When we were ready to leave for the lunch at The Falcon, I scanned the street for a sniper. I checked under the car for an explosive package and I pushed all the kids into the car by placing a hand on their heads and ducking them in, something I saw Kevin Costner doing whilst he was 'protecting' Whitney and trying to get her to trust him enough to take off her knickers on demand. Connie was unhappy that I'd messed up her side fringe in the hustle, she tutted and smoothed it back into place with her perfect fingers.

Eventually, when we drove away from the street and no

explosion occurred, I had the stupidity to imagine Matt and Gina had moved on and forgotten about little old me and the missing stash, or perhaps they had thought better than to take me on? I was after all a middle-aged woman in a mood, was there anything more frightening?

I had allocated a new name for Michaela and Connie, Suzy and Finn. They were now to be known as the Dublin Four – I couldn't be bothered to say all of their names, I was too exhausted for that shit.

"We sound like a terrorist group, Mum." Suzy had tried to scold me when she first heard it but I carried on without caring. There were four of them and they met in Dublin, it was inevitable that I gave them a title.

So, the Dublin Four, who were secretive and sullen for most of the time they were in my company, were forced into a family lunch at The Falcon. Sam was nothing less than furious that he had to spend another day with his parents and sisters, Dave was just happy to be seeing his parents whilst they were still alive and I, well I was living on my nerves like my Aunty Pauline who smoked twenty-five Lambert and Butler a day and bit her nails until they bled; she was dead now, it was apparently the 'nerves' what killed her.

Mother had spent the whole morning from at least 5 am helping out with the big baby; her dedication to the cause was admirable but the woman was over seventy, I was not sure she was up to the task.

"I wanted to give Sophia a break so I took over and cradled him for an hour or two so the poor girl could get some rest. It was a struggle to stop him latching on, he was sucking at my chest with the force of a trade-strength plunger, hands grabbing at everything, he has a real grip. I had to give him a stern talking to."

She told me this on the phone whilst we were driving over in the car. I heard Dad giggle.

"Don't you bloody laugh, Phillip, I feel as if I've been attacked. Who's his father, Mr Tickle?"

"Apart from that, how is everything?" I tried to divert Mum's attention from the little groper.

"Well the two scumbags haven't been in contact, I have blocked Gina on WhatsApp. And as for Tom and Babs, they have been sleeping ever since the party. Just a couple of rounds of toast and a pot of tea and they're happy watching YouTube in bed all morning."

I shook my head and nudged Dave.

"Can you believe those two, the carnage they have caused?"

Dave pulled a face. "The carnage you caused, you mean."

A table in the orangery of The Falcon had been arranged for the family, they always looked after us in a traditional way. Coats were taken, chairs were pulled out and the women were told they looked "Absolutely stunning". They had been using this approach since the eighties and I swear if I turned up wearing a balaclava and a G-string they would say the same thing. It was frightening because people like my parents and even Dave's parents fell for it like the idiots that they were.

CeeCee blushed when one of them told her that he could tell she was a "wealthy woman" while he was pointing to her Elizabeth Duke at Argos earrings. Another told Dad that he had mistaken him for Michael Bublé from a distance, but that Dad was better looking upon close inspection.

"He's fucking old enough to be Bublé's father," I mouthed to Dave in disbelief.

When the well-spoken waiter got to me, I was ready for him.

"Go on, what you got?" I invited him to say something ridiculous, something along the lines of me being a swimwear model or a body double for Davina McCall. He looked at me for a while, he was certainly able to earn his tip with some bullshit he had learned in a team-building course for kissing ass, but instead he said something quite intuitive.

"You look really tired. Are you OK, hun?"

Never had I been disarmed in such a way and by somebody who was most likely studying textiles.

"Wine, quick!" I held my glass in the air and he filled it up to the top.

Mum smirked, she bloody loved it when someone got the better of me, she would tip him handsomely later for that and for that only.

After the meal which was a seventies mash-up of mediocre food covered in sugar-based sauces, CeeCee, who was very emosh about her son and his achievements, stood up and chinked the side of her champagne glass with a knife. Of course, she smashed the glass into her gateaux but brown-nose waiter came over and whisked it all away.

"I would like to say a few words about my David …"

She grabbed the hands of the two most important men in her life.

"Since my beautiful Julie got her angel wings, my David has made me prouder than any mother could imagine."

She leaned over and kissed Dave's head.

"I can't tell you what it means to me and to Gary …"

She leaned over and kissed his head too.

"That his efforts and his success have finally been recognised by the right people."

She dabbed her eyes with a handkerchief that had an embroidered flower on the corner.

"My David has devoted his life to doing what's right and fighting the fight against drugs. Those drugs took my precious daughter away from us and I, we, will never recover. It's people like my David who save hundreds of lives every day. Love you, son, the world is a better place thanks to you."

And she shut her eyes and put her head right back. Then she whispered, but so everybody could hear her, "This one's for you Julie, my girl."

Just when I thought this was over, just when I thought the guilt fest would stop, as she sat down Gary stood up, pint of Guinness in hand.

"Dave, my lad, my boy, never could a father be prouder."

Mum kicked my shin and rolled her eyes.

Dave looked up at his dad as if he were five years old, glassy-eyed in admiration.

"David, son, this is a proud moment for me, like the time you joined the force, like when you married this absolute superstar. Like when these kids were born."

He made eye contact with me and his grandchildren.

"What I am trying to say is that you have never failed us, not once! Thanks son, you mean the absolute world to us."

And then there was applause from everyone, there were tears from CeeCee and the waiter, Dave was proud as punch loving every minute of being his parents' little soldier.

Sam grabbed my shoulder. "Say something, Mum, say something about Dad."

I narrowed my eyes, this wasn't the Brits for crying out loud, but I had no choice but to speak.

I stood and lifted my wine glass which was almost empty. Over-eager waiter stepped forward and gave me a top-up, he now knew me well.

"Dave, Dave, Dave, what can I say about this guy? Kind, loyal, dependable, loving, attentive … sometimes."

Everybody laughed.

"He's just an all-round great guy and he deserves this award; he deserves that and more. The dedication he has shown to his role as a police officer in the war against narcotics is nothing less than outstanding."

Mum let out a huge laugh, she'd been holding it in for a while. "Listen to Moira Stuart, is she reading an autocue?"

Dad shushed her angrily, he was invested in my professional delivery.

"When Dave and I married we vowed to stay together through better or worse and that is what we have done and will continue to do. No matter what life throws at us, we are a strong couple with a good family. We literally are like concrete, me and Dave, nothing can break us. Through thick and thin, richer poorer, if one of us does something stupid, we're still Raquel and Dave, Dave and Raquel." I raised my glass to the table, most people raised theirs back, not Mum and not Dave but the rest did. Mum shook her head and looked at her watch, she could see I was rambling and that I was certainly buckling under the pressure, she didn't like people who buckled.

"So, to Dave and me and the fact he is a good guy who is very tolerant and also a really good guy and well done for the award, to Dave!"

There were some frowns at what was a very odd speech but I did what I had to do with the help of a few glasses of courage and pure desperation to keep hold of my husband. Observant waiter went to fill my glass and then thought better of it and just plonked the bottle next to me and walked away. Dave furrowed his brow and did a side smile; he must have thought I was completely absurd.

"You are a total and utter disaster."

Mum said it how it was in a toilet cubicle five minutes after the desperate speech. I sat on the toilet, head spinning from too much booze. She had shoved me into the cubicle after noticing me swaying at the mirror and putting my lipstick on my chin.

"Thank you, Mother, much appreciated."

"Well you are. Rambling on and on like a crazy women possessed."

"I am in so much shit, Mum. I'm a mess."

Mum twiddled with the collar of her stiff blue blouse. She was out of her comfort zone, it was normally me pulling her into line.

"I don't like this, you know."

"What, what don't you like, Mother?" My words were slurred.

"You are being weak, you're always the strong one, I hate this, sober up. Have a coffee!"

"Mum I need you, help me."

She flushed the chain of the toilet so nobody could hear.

"I love you, OK. I love you."

She stroked my cheek and I felt like a child. I knew she loved me but she never ever said it.

The older we get, when a parent says that they love you in a quiet moment with nobody else present, for some reason you think of how life will be after they are gone. You think, I will never forget you saying that because I know you meant it. After you are gone, this is the moment I will relive, this memory will be the one thing I will play back as a comfortable yet painful moment with my mother, the woman who bore me, the woman who fed and nurtured me and taught me how to survive in such a complex world.

"I love you too, Mum, I really do."

And then as she always does, she totally ruined the moment.

"I would wax that before I'd bleach it, you look like a polar bear darling." She ran her judgmental finger across the top of my lip with a curious look on her face.

When I finally emerged from my toilet talking-to, Michaela was angrily looking straight ahead trying to avoid eye contact with anyone. Considering I was just about to pay the bill for her organic sea bass with sides and a cheeseboard that cost the same as a full body massage, I expected her to be a little more grateful and cheerful at least.

"What's up with you?'

She sneered. "Take a look at those two."

On the other side of the table, Connie and Finn were yet again chatting like nobody else was there, the two abnormally gorgeous specimens were enjoying each other's company far too much for it to be innocent. Connie was laughing and she had her hand on Finn's leg, Finn had his hand under his chin and was inches from her face.

"She's gay though, darling, I'm sure it's nothing to worry about."

Michaela shook her head. "No Mum, she's not gay she's bi."

"Shit, oh OK, in that case we may have a problem."

Michaela looked defeated; she knew deep down she couldn't keep hold of this girl for long. It would just be a crying shame if she lost her to Suzy's boyfriend. That would be a whole mess I wouldn't like to witness. It would be me trying to mend two broken hearts along with my own.

Suzy probably thought the same as me, she didn't look worried at all because she was under the impression this girl was not interested in boys. She'd had a couple of champagnes and was regaling CeeCee with her wonderful tales of Dublin and how she and Finn were planning on travelling together the following summer – this was going to sting.

Dave planned to take his parents over to Chester for a day out the following day, to spend quality time with them before they went back. I told them I was working but they were welcome to take all of the kids, that way I would get a free day to sort my hungover head. I booked train tickets on line for the Dublin Four and Sam was going in the car with Dave and his folks. Rather selfishly, I couldn't wait for the break.

Dave and I had a brief conversation before we went to sleep which gave me food for thought.

"Any suggestions on what I do next?"

Dave turned over and faced me. "Stop drinking or drink less?"

"Anything not so dramatic?"

"You need to stay away from him and her across the road."

"I want to, Dave, but they want their people and their stuff."

"Well there is no stuff now is there? And as for the people, unless they can get back to their country and come into the UK through the right channels then I guess they will need to hand themselves in."

"And what are you going to do about the drug thing? Are you going to arrest them?"

Dave was very serious when he told me this and I knew he meant business.

"We have been watching and following them all week. We have a plan and they will be brought in very soon. I decided it was too risky to observe them from here especially with you and the kids so we moved our surveillance to another location. The policing has never stopped on this, my team are fully aware what Matt and Gina are involved in, we are just biding our time until we make the arrests."

"So when you do arrest them, I will be brought in?"

"Once we listen to their statements and go through all correspondence then yes, you will have some explaining to do."

I imagined the messages between Matt and I being scrutinised.

Can't wait to see you.

You tasted nice

Bring your big cucumber

A cloud of dread descended over me.

"OK, night then."

"Goodnight Raquel."

He turned back over and I knew that he knew this would be mortifying for us all.

I barely slept, neither did Dave, we tossed and turned all night but not once did he touch me.

I noticed Suzy being particularly clingy with Finn before they left the next morning. She tried to hold his hand as they were leaving but he was styling his hair in the hallway mirror. He looked irritated and claustrophobic by her advances, and he almost cringed when she took a selfie of them both without warning. Connie and Michaela were both in some sort of funk, they emerged from the bedroom scowling.

"Your flight is tomorrow so you might as well pack tonight." Michaela was being particularly rude and unfriendly to what was apparently her girlfriend.

"No problem, I will be so ready to leave."

"Good!"

"Yes good!"

Connie smiled her beautiful smile at Finn who was obviously doing his hair for her. I bet they couldn't wait to get back to Ireland to bang it out. I was furious with them for their lack of respect, I could have slapped them both silly for taking the absolute piss, but they were young, it's how it went and I wasn't about to intervene. So off they went for a day out in Chester which would be the last time they did anything as the Dublin Four.

About lunchtime, and just as I had finished my work emails, I saw Matt and Gina for the first time in a while. They came out of their house both on their phones and jumped into a waiting car which sped off in a real hurry. Coincidentally I had just received the last edition of 'Live Better' and I was glad it was over. The interview with Matt was like nails down the blackboard. He couldn't thank me enough for being a fantastic coach, we had really gelled and he felt confident going forward that he was going to 'live better'. Luckily, he said, because we were neighbours, he would know where to go if he got stuck.

The vegans had cut Gina out of all of the pictures because they said it was tacky and instead they used some of Matt on his own and one of the two of us talking and laughing over a wooden box of herbs. I resolved to buy every copy of this edition and burn it in the back garden, I could not allow Dave to see this documented record of my infidelity.

I had three missed calls from Mum's mobile and two from her landline in the space of a few minutes. I had left my phone in the kitchen and naturally thought the worse. Mum answered immediately.

"Stroke, heart attack or aneurism?"

"Don't be silly, Raquel."

"Why all the missed calls?"

"We have an issue."

"Go on."

"Well, the trouble is, Matt and Gina are camped outside, there's a bald man at the back door like the baddy from James Bond."

"What the fuck?"

"Try not to swear, Raquel. So they turned up and hammered on the door, they shouted to Arif through the letter box and demanded that he open up but he refused."

"Oh my god! What do they want?"

"They want Babs, Arif and Sophia – oh and they want their stuff, apparently."

"Have you called the police?"

"Of course not, Raquel, I'm not stupid. Anyway, Arif has locked Babs, the baby and Sophia in one of the bedrooms and they have barricaded the door with the wardrobe."

"Oh shit, Mum, I don't know what to do for the best, perhaps

I should call Dave?"

"No, don't worry, Dad and Uncle Tom are trying to negotiate through the bathroom window, wait a second we might have a deal."

"Negotiate how?" There was a pause.

"OK, no deal, Dad offered them the Jag for the weekend but they told him to eff off."

"For god's sake. What are they doing now?"

"Well they say they want what's theirs and they won't leave until they have it. Oh gosh, the bald one is jimmying the back door with a crow bar."

"Fucking hell, Mum. I am on my way. Tell them I am on my way."

I heard her shriek.

"My daughter is coming now and then you'll be sorry."

I jumped in the car, I didn't even shut the front door. It was a good twenty minutes to Duck Cottage at this time of day so I called Matt's mobile. He answered straight away.

"What the hell, Matt? What are you playing at?"

"I told you, Raquel, I told you this would happen. We answer to people, we can't have you taking things from us."

"Can you wait until I get there? I will explain everything once I am there, can you please just wait until I arrive? You owe me at least that, Matt."

There was a pause and a sigh. I heard him shout to Malik, "Leave it mate, leave it for ten." The banging stopped.

"Hurry up, Raquel. This will need to be good."

I was grateful to him for being at least slightly reasonable.

"Will you hurt anyone, Matt, you won't hurt them will you?"

"You know I won't but I can't talk for Malik or Gina."

I dropped the call and immediately called Mum. I told her to tell them all to sit tight and not to open the door under any circumstance. She told me the man at the back door had stopped trying to break down the door and was rolling a cigarette at their garden table with his feet on a chair. She wanted to pass him an ashtray through the window and a wipe for his boots. I told her to have a large gin and to settle down.

"He has flicked the ash onto the tabletop. The cheeky thing."

I heard her banging on the window shouting.

"That's solid oak, you bad man."

I arrived at the front of the house. Although the car was there, Matt, Gina and henchman Malik were not. I panicked; I wondered if they had managed to get in. There was a moaning coming from around the back and I prayed to god it wasn't my dad. I nervously made my way to the back garden and braced myself for pensioners strung upside down from a branch being tortured for info. However, my discovery could not have been more different.

Lying on the floor next to the table was Malik, there was blood everywhere, and Gina and Matt stood over him.

"What's happened, what's going on?"

Gina turned to me; she was fizzing with rage.

"They shot him, they actually shot him."

I looked up to the narrow bathroom window, a couple of foreheads and four eyes looked down at the casualty.

"Dad, is that you?"

"Yes, it's me. All OK down there?"

"Not really, apparently you shot this guy."

"It wasn't me, it was Tom actually."

Tom hollered, "Yes it was me, and he bloody well deserved it. Trying to break into my house, bastard."

I heard Dad dispute that immediately.

"Hang on a minute there, it's my house, Tom, not yours."

"Yes but you said I could stay indefinitely."

"Did I? I must have been completely drunk!"

Matt cradled the man on the floor and dabbed his head with the arm of his denim jacket.

"What sort of people are you?" Matt looked up at me. He still had great eyes.

"Ones not to mess with." Mum had opened the kitchen window at this point, and was having her say.

"You have a gun in the house, Mum?"

Mum laughed. "Of course not."

"Well who shot him then?"

The eyes at the window above appeared again.

"I shot him with a slingshot and there's more to come if they don't piss off. It was only a stone." Tom admitted guilt with pride.

Gina glared at me. "This is all your fault, all of this."

Malik sat up and shook his head trying to steady his vision.

"Look at him, they nearly killed him. Where's my stuff? And get me those three out of this house. NOW!"

Another stone came flying out of the window, missing me narrowly but landing another blow to the cheekbone of the man down. The flesh pierced and he screamed in pain, clutching at his face and writhing once more on the floor.

Matt shielded himself under the sun umbrella and waved his fist at the window. "Pack it in you lot, stop it now."

"Never!" shouted Tom. "You'll never take Babs away from me, she is my woman and she stops with me."

Matt and Gina looked at each other in confusion. They must have wondered who on earth would want crusty Barbara, although they hadn't seen Tom apart from his eyes and forehead. I'm sure it would all make sense if he came outside and showed his true self. I tried to explain.

"That's my Uncle Tom. They're in love, leave them be."

Gina half laughed. "Where's the other one, the pregnant one?"

"Sophia is not pregnant anymore," I was about to explain.

"She lost it then?" Gina had no emotion, nothing behind the eyes at all.

"No, she didn't lose it, she had the baby, she gave birth to a boy. His name is Roger and he weighed–"

"Shut up, Raquel, we don't want the baby, we need her and Arif. You can keep Barbara, she's no use anymore anyway."

"Hurray!" We heard Tom celebrating at the window.

Mum then yelled from her window, "Oh no, Little Miss Eyebrows, oh no. You are not taking Arif, not a chance. Fire another one, Tom, go on."

Another rock came hurtling out of the window and hit its target once more, he was really very good at this. I made a note to enter him for Bullseye if it was still going. Gina's elbow took the impact this time and she yelled in pain.

"I think he's chipped the fucking bone." She screamed for Matt but he stayed under the umbrella and appealed to my better nature.

"Raquel, get me the stuff and get me Sophia. I can't go back to my bosses with nothing. Keep Arif but we need one of them."

I shook my head. "I can't give you either. The stuff very sadly has been flushed down the toilet by my sister, she's a criminal lawyer you know, and Sophia has just had a baby, she is going absolutely nowhere."

Matt sat down on the chair and put his head in his hands. "This is a joke now G, we need to let this go."

Gina opened her mouth widely, if there hadn't been an audience I am convinced she would have slapped Matt hard around the face.

"No chance Matt, she owes me ten grand and three people and if I don't get that, I am telling her husband … everything."

Mum shouted up to Dad. "Go and get your cheque book Phillip and write these criminals a cheque."

Dad shouted back down. "How much do they want?"

Mum replied, "Ten grand should do it, you can also give them those leftover euros in the bottom of my straw beach bag too, the one I got in Corsica."

I threw my hands into the air. "Mum we are not paying for illegal drugs and human slaves. And definitely not with a cheque."

I turned and folded my arms, the time had come to face this head on. "Guys, you will have to tell Dave, tell him everything, I can't stop you."

Gina's face dropped, she had just lost her bargaining tool, the one she had held over me since those faded jogging bottoms had grabbed my attention.

Matt's body language told me he was exhausted with the whole thing and was ready to give up anyway. The guy on the floor had staggered to his feet and was using Gina's compact mirror to inspect his injuries. Gina walked over to me; she towered above me but I didn't move an inch.

"Wow so you're prepared to let that happen are you, madam?" She tried to make her voice sound evil but it was more stupid than anything.

"Yes, I am. I can't do this anymore, do your worst, Gina. I am passed giving a fuck and, quite honestly, I will not bullied by you for another minute. The drugs are gone, you have treated these people shockingly, I had no choice but to help them. You are an evil woman with the morals of a rat."

I stood my ground. The onlookers were silent, I think they would have enjoyed some popcorn for this showdown although, to be fair, they had played a very big part in my decision to man up. They had put up a decent fight; Gina had a bloody elbow, the other guy was concussed and I think his cheekbone was fractured. There was only Matt unharmed but I'm sure Dave had plans for him once he got a hold of him.

Gina beckoned to Matt and he stood up and walked to her, checking the window for any further attacks.

"Let's go, we need to make plans, just for us."

As they turned to leave the garden she gave me one last warning.

"Do you know what's going to happen to us now?"

I shook my head and shrugged.

"We have to deal with some very serious people, we must explain things to them and let me tell you, it will be you they come for – you and your family – once they know what you have done."

I gulped, I didn't like my family being mentioned by this dangerous woman. But then I remembered how Dave had told me that these lot were small time and that he would have them locked up soon, so I was brave and I was bold and I told her to "Shut the fuck up and go away".

Matt gave me a small smile; she didn't see him but I clocked it and I knew it was real. It was about time somebody stood up to this absolute bitch and her husband knew it.

Once the crims had driven away, the residents of Duck all rejoiced in the kitchen with cups of tea and malted milk biscuits.

It was only Mum who had a gin in her tea cup. They had kept these rotters at bay with a homemade sling and some rocks from the garden. Tom had used his marksmanship to maim Malik, who was particularly nasty and according to Barbara through the app translator, he was a "piggish brut" and she was glad to see he had almost lost an eye. She had been very vocal since she saw her captors bleeding and retreating. She was a happy old lady with a very happy old boyfriend. Sophia had come down and sat at the kitchen table, smiling away whilst feeding baby Roger with absolutely no attempt to hide her breast. In fact she let the other one flop out too, presumably in case it felt left out. Dad and Tom were absolutely fascinated and, at one point, Mum slapped Tom on the back of the head and told him that it was not feeding time at the zoo.

"You were brilliant too, Raquel, you really showed them, well done." Old Tom, for the first time ever, said something to me that didn't have a scornful undertone. The mood had lifted and, for them, the danger was moving further away. As for me, I still had a mountain to climb.

Old Bill

I watched my very first episode of *Poirot* during the school Christmas holidays with a cup of tea and a Pepperami. I remember it vividly because nobody was home and I was grounded. It was the early nineties and that was the punishment of choice.

I had been grounded indefinitely at the age of sixteen due to the fact I had fed next door's dog an entire packet of cherry-flavoured Tunes simply because he wanted them. That decision resulted in explosive diarrhoea, projectile vomiting and £78 in out-of-hours vets fees. Mr and Mrs Pritchard were "absolutely devastated" that the apple of their eye had been subjected to such cruelty. Mrs Pritchard said I was a wicked girl and Mr Pritchard said I needed locking up.

So my parents pretended to be massively bothered about Truffle the pedigree brown poodle who had a GCSE in arrogance, but it wasn't really the dog they were bothered about, it was their reputation and nothing else. The Pritchards were very well known at the local golf club and as a couple, they were in charge of everything that meant anything in the Cheshire golf community. Mum and Dad had to be seen to be dishing out a punishment that would crush my world and they didn't disappoint. I was instructed to stay in for the entire two weeks of the Christmas holidays and there would be no negotiation. I protested dramatically of course, I said I would end my own life and then I would kill Truffle. Dad said cheerily, "Okey dokey, good luck with that."

I then attempted to go on hunger strike but I only managed to miss breakfast and even then I paid Mel thirty pence to sneak me up half of her crumpet, which I know for a fact she had stood on before she slipped it under my door. Eventually I accepted that my Christmas would be a bag of shit and I settled down in an armchair with a mug of Baileys and my dad's pipe and spent the following two weeks watching back-to-back detective programmes on VCR.

And by the way, before you think what I did to Truffle was out of order, there was a Labrador who lived across the road who ate a pair of wellies, a box of paracetamol and an Arctic roll in one afternoon and she was absolutely fine.

Initially, I was fascinated by the continental glamour the portly Belgian detective's tales had to offer, I almost wanted to be murdered in a five-star hotel on a Dorset cliff edge just so I could taste the petits fours before I was throttled by a scullery maid with a dark secret.

I then moved onto Taggart, a hard hitter where Glaswegians regularly stabbed each other willy-nilly over tiny things such as bags of chips.

After Taggart came Inspector Morse which was aimed at posh people – the educated, the sherry drinkers. It wasn't as far-fetched as the others and had a bit more class. Generally, Morse focused on boys who had suffered at the hands of deranged house masters in private boarding schools. These pupils were now grown up and in therapy and wanted revenge; this revenge was normally delivered via an undetected dose of arsenic in a cup of Horlicks.

My absolute favourite, the one I felt most of a connection to, was Cracker; this was the daddy of them all, the one that commanded the most respect and is actually yet to be rivalled.

Criminal psychologist Fitz, played by Robbie Coltrane, was an overweight, super sweaty, whiskey addict who was also an all-round shit father and husband. But somehow, the combination of fags, booze and crime solving had never been sexier, this man was a genius! His mind games were second to none and his one-liners were superb. But it was the way Fitz took his suspects one by one into the interrogation suite and simply shouted into their faces, "You killed the bitch, didn't you?" until one of them started either wanking off or crying – sometimes if they were particularly disturbed, they did both. The series would always end with Fitz being empathetic, he would offer the suspect a shoulder to cry on and a fag to smoke.

I sort of wanted to marry a guy like Fitz and, in a way, I eventually did.

Dave left at dawn for work. He had a long shower, took an overnight bag and he was gone. I didn't ask but I knew that this would be the beginning of the end for Gina and Matt. Dave would be closing in and there would be nowhere for them to hide. He always went quiet when he was focused and he had a look on his face that said 'someone will suffer today'.

Mel and Roger were all packed up before breakfast. There was a bookshop that needed running and Mel had some serious catching up to do defending criminals who were innocent, allegedly.

The Dublin Four were quiet over their croissants; Michaela sat with folded arms and Suzy kept welling up when she locked eyes with Finn. He was leaving and she wasn't coping.

Connie and Finn were nothing less than ecstatic to be escaping the madness that was our family and it was pretty obvious they couldn't wait to rip each other's clothes off as soon as they were out of sight. Suzy, in a world of her own, had written a love letter to Finn and she slipped it into his leather bomber pocket for him to find at the airport. She had sprayed the envelope with at least a pint of her perfume, naively thinking this would deepen his feelings until they were together again. I leaned against the kitchen cupboard drinking my tea and watching my daughters' summer romances crumble to dust. Sad, but a necessary life lesson for us all at some point.

Roger was driving back with Mel and Sir Walter; they were keen to leave so were kindly dropping the Dublin Two off at the airport en route. Roger, for the first time in a long time, was wearing a full shoe. I didn't mention it, not wanting to tempt fate.

"Goodbye Raquel, it's been quite the trip." Roger and I stood awkwardly facing each other but not too close.

"Yes it has and, can I just say, what you did for Sophia and the baby was … well it was impressive … I was very impressed."

He shifted uncomfortably, one-on-one chats were not our thing.

"Well Raquel, even though I am not sure about some of the things you have done, you certainly have a good heart in there somewhere."

"Thank you for saying that, Roger, have a safe trip."

He went to leave but I felt he deserved a bit more.

"Sorry, by the way, for taking the piss all those times."

He smiled, he knew I wasn't sorry but he was grateful that I'd pretended.

I gave Mel a hug and told her I would call her later. By saying that she knew I had forgiven her for telling Roger my dirty secret – forgiven but never forgotten. Sir Walter rode in the front next to Mel with Roger relegated to the back seat.

"You don't have to go yet?" Suzy was trying to string it out by keeping Finn for longer than was comfortable.

"Yes we do, we don't want to miss the flight!" Connie was determined to make this quick and was standing at the door, headphones on and hood up.

Michaela pushed past her and went off upstairs and just shouted "Bye!" without even turning around. Suzy was offended on Connie's behalf; little did she know.

"She is so rude, Mum, such a moody bitch."

I said nothing. Connie said nothing. She knew I knew; it was best we kept quiet. Suzy was still wearing her pyjamas and a dressing gown; she wrapped her arms around Finn at the front door and stood on her tiptoes so they could kiss each other on the lips. Finn made himself taller so she couldn't reach, it was absolutely horrible to see. Connie stood next to me watching this awkward exchange, she eventually put her head down, at least she had the decency to look away.

"I really have to go, Suzy, let go please." Suzy clung on to Finn like a koala bear to a tree. Finn wriggled and struggled to free himself. I could take no more.

"Right off you go, lovely to see you. Hope to see you soon, goodbye."

I herded the pair of them off and shut the door. I turned to Suzy, who was in shock that I had cut short their emotional goodbye, and I told her woman to woman, "Respect yourself."

She frowned and then she pushed past me, opened the door and jogged down the street next to the moving car shouting "love you, baby". I don't think Finn even waved.

She was her mother's daughter alright. We were both a pair of absolute dicks.

Half an hour passed and Sam came in from the front garden with his football in one hand and an envelope in the other. Suzy was sitting on the arm of the sofa tapping her phone relentlessly, still smarting from my sharp advice. Michaela had come down to scowl at us all for no reason and to flick through a book on witchcraft she had ordered from The Pendle Hill gift shop. Sam stood in the doorway and started reading loudly from the piece of paper.

Finn, I want you to know that I love you with all my heart. I have never felt this way about anybody and I know you feel the same way, we will be together soon, try and be strong without me ...

Suzy flew off the sofa like a dog on the attack and snatched the paper from Sam's hand.

"Oh my god you little shit, where did you get this?"

Sam was laughing, he was uncontrollably laughing.

"On the driveway, it was on the floor."

Suzy cried out, "It must have fallen out of his pocket. Mum, take me to the airport quick."

Michaela looked up from her book; her face looked a little happier. "What's all this? You want to go to the airport to give Finn a love letter?"

Suzy screamed, "Yes, come on Mum, get the car keys, quick."

I didn't move, I couldn't do it.

Sam very reasonably suggested she put it in the post instead. "It would be easier," he said quite innocently.

"Just be quiet you, I want him to have it on the plane, I need him to read it on the flight."

Michaela looked up again from her spell book. "Why, in case the plane crashes?"

Suzy was getting impatient. "Mum come on, before they go through security."

I shook my head. "No, it's not a good idea."

"Yes it is, it's romantic!" She was pulling at my arm. "Please Mum, it will only take half an hour."

"No, it looks desperate."

She was completely shocked.

"Desperate, me? Excuse me, what are you going on about? We're in love, we literally are in love. We are getting engaged when we go travelling next summer, it's not desperate, it's lovely."

I looked at Michaela, who at this point was really rather enjoying this, but she was also tiring of the nonsense. "Mum, just tell her or I will. Put her out of her misery."

"Tell me what?" Suzy sensed all was not well.

"I just don't think he is as into this as you are, let it go Suzy."

Michaela put down her book and grabbed her shoulder.

"Mum's right, you are making a real fool of yourself, rein it in."

Suzy made the mistake of taking her on and went to a place she should not have gone.

"Just because Connie isn't interested in you, don't take it out on me."

Michaela laughed, a forced laugh.

"No, you're right, she isn't interested in me, and do you know why?"

Suzy's eyes were wide, her approach quite aggressive.

"Because you're a miserable bitch, something like that?"

"Nope it's not that. Guess again."

"Because you're boring and not much fun?"

"Nope, still no closer."

"Go on then tell me – why is a stunning, clever, gorgeous girl like Connie not at all interested in you then, Michaela, I wonder?" She put her finger to the side of her lip trying to be a smart arse.

Michaela picked up her phone and sent her a message.

"Check your phone Suzy and you'll see why."

Suzy's phone pinged, she picked it up and opened the message. She scrolled through what seemed to be an awful lot of text. She then looked at Michaela and said "Fuck you!" and ran upstairs howling.

"That wasn't very nice, Michaela."

"Oh, she had it coming."

"What did you send her?" Sam was intrigued and by this point, in absolute shock at the trouble he had caused with his big reveal.

"It was the messages I found that had gone between Finn and Connie since the day they came here. They realised they wanted each other and not us. They even met on the landing at 2 am in this house, our house, to kiss in secret."

Sam was all of a sudden privy to what could have been a plotline on Love Island.

"That's mental. Sly bastards."

"Indeed," I sighed. "But tone down the language, son."

This was the first of many heartbreaks but this one had been particularly tricky; it had to be a rarity that two sisters got dumped on the same day because their partners fell for each other.

"Go up and see her, do the right thing."

"Who me?" Sam was horrified.

"Not you, definitely not you. Michaela go on. You're both in the same boat and you're a lot stronger than her. Please?"

Michaela reluctantly trudged up the stairs to hopefully do what sisters did when they really needed each other. I didn't hear a cat fight or any screaming, just the odd sob from Suzy and somebody shouted "slut" rather loudly and then punched something. It was followed by laughter so I left them to it.

We had a nice evening after the drama. The girls came down later in the day, both with swollen eyes and bruised egos. They had both gutted their bedrooms, presumably to remove all trace of their lost lovers; the smell of polish and bleach wafted down the stairs. Sam had certainly felt some sympathy for them both and, bless him, he took them up a cup of tea and a packet of biscuits on a tray. I heard him say, "Bad luck girls" as a collective to the dumpees.

That night, I made a huge tray of award-winning fajitas and we ate a ton of them on our knees whilst watching Pitch Perfect 1 and 2. It was nice, it was quiet, it was normal.

I slept right through that night. I actually had a sense of peace and I wasn't as tightly wound up as I had been. I saw my children come together in the face of adversity, I had myself stood up to the school bully and actually had saved a few people from a life of hell. So it wasn't all bad, there were some positives that had emerged from the swamp of terror. The swamp, however, still existed and I needed to be very brave when the time came to face my own demons.

Mum had called to let me know that today was the day Sophia and baby Roger would attend a doctor's appointment to be examined. Mum had absolutely no concerns that they were both very healthy and she had informed the receptionist at her local surgery that she required an emergency appointment and would be bringing guests.

"What on earth did they make of that?"

"Well naturally they wanted more information."

"So what did you tell them?"

"I told them that if I wanted an appointment with a receptionist I would let them know but for now I wanted a qualified doctor, if it wasn't too much trouble."

"Ooff, what did they say to that?"

"See you at two o'clock."

I smiled. Mum got shit done.

"Oh I almost forgot to tell you the most fabulous news."

"What Mother?"

I really hoped this wasn't another sexual position she had mastered without the help of a blob of Deep Heat.

"Well through the powers of Facebook, Sophia and her husband have been reunited."

"You're kidding?"

"I wouldn't kid about that, Raquel. He is in Calais, somehow he ended up in France and has been working as a builder. It's wonderful, isn't it? Even if he did meet his first-born son on FaceTime."

I smiled, I was just glad the guy was alive, it could have been a very different story.

"So what now? How will they get together?"

Mum seemed underwhelmed at my response.

"Oh we'll sort it somehow Raquel, I think Mel has a contact who deals with this sort of thing. Anyway, isn't it brilliant that baby Roger has a dad?"

"Yes Mum, I am really pleased for them all. Does he know he's called Roger yet?"

"Well, it's a sore point. Whatever you do, don't mention that to Sophia; she got a real earful about it."

I laughed loudly. "I'll bet she did!"

I got a text from Dave mid-morning that was very strange. There was an attachment with three tickets to the cinema at 2 pm. The film was one of the Avatars and it was at the big screen in town.

What's this for?

For the kids

OK, I'll see if they want to go.

Make sure they go. OK?

OK!

My throat was dry and my internal shaking was bothersome as I drove the children into Manchester. I knew that Dave wanted them out of the way for the afternoon for a reason, but what that reason was I wouldn't know until it happened. I had no idea whether he would be moving out or whether he was making arrests. I could have been on the list to be brought in. I knew better than to send any questions on the phone, so I just followed orders and I gave the kids some cash for food after the cinema and instructed them to be ready for one o'clock. Suzy had been quiet but she was strong, there had been no tears for at least two hours when we left but I put a packet of tissues in her pocket just in case. Michaela had advised she didn't look at social media for a good couple of weeks for the sake of her own sanity. Connie and Finn had wasted no time – they had posted two selfies of themselves at the airport and a provocative TikTok dance which was both heartless and thoughtless. I thought the distraction of a sibling outing would do her some good as she couldn't face any of her friends after over-selling her new relationship and rubbing it in their faces. I waved them off and hugged them hard and I hoped I would be 'free' to pick them up later.

At two o'clock, I sat in my office at my viewing point watching 23 like a hawk. It got to 2.15 and still nothing happened. A message came in from Mum.

Saw doctor and he was happy after examining Sophia and the baby. They are sending social services around later this week. (Big nose emoji) Can you believe it, it's an insult! (Angry face emoji) I won't let them in, they will have to stay on the doorstep. (Punch emoji) Mum x

Although I had not had any personal experience with social services, I knew they were like bulls in china shops when they wanted to be. One of Dave's cousins, a cheeky little sod, was moved into temporary foster care for a week whilst they investigated her parents. Their ten-year-old daughter had recurring bruising on her wrists that could not be explained so the school called the Social and they sent a newbie in to deal with it. Too little too late, they discovered a cheap gold bracelet that she had bought on the beach in Faliraki leaked a green-blue dye after every shower. By the time the dumbass social worker had worked it out, Dave's aunty was ready to be sectioned. The little beggar knew what it was all along and just enjoyed the attention and the drama. All it would have taken was a baby wipe to save all the trouble, but oh no, that would have been too easy. Needless to say, I didn't have a good vibe about their involvement but I hoped to be proved wrong.

At 2.34 I witnessed a police raid. I had never seen a proper raid before and if it hadn't been a result of me shitting on my own doorstep I would have liked it much more than I did. From absolutely nowhere, at least ten police officers in bulletproof vests, riot masks and all the other gear you see on YouTube descended on 23. They came from the back, the front, it felt like some came from above. They had every exit point of that house covered and they all had guns, big guns. The rush of excitement and fear coursed through my veins making my heart almost explode. I just hoped and prayed they weren't coming for me next. I didn't want this, I didn't want my door to be smashed in and to be thrown into the back of a van, I would rather drive myself to the station like a civilised person.

The front door of 23 was knocked on once, there was one warning from a Scottish bloke who shouted, "Come to the door with your hands behind your head." Nothing happened for eight tense seconds.

From behind the Scottish bloke, a battering object was rammed into the door with a couple of guys on each side, the cheap door buckled and collapsed and they were all inside within seconds. Dave stayed outside leaning against an unmarked police car with his arms folded. After a few minutes, his colleagues emerged – one of them shook his head and put his thumbs down. Dave turned and looked up at the slit in my office blinds briefly before he got back into the car and sped off down the street. The other officers followed apart from one guy who stayed to secure the door with some wood and to put police tape across the front of the house.

I slithered down the wall and put my head on my knees; not knowing what was going on was the hardest bit. I would need to go to bed that night with a full face of make-up and wear a bra in case they came for me whilst I slept.

They have gone, no sign of them. If you hear from them call me immediately. D

I picked the kids up from town early evening and felt grateful for the small things. Just driving through Manchester, listening to music on a summer's night meant the world to me. Hearing the kids kicking off with each other and seeing Sam spill an entire Tango Ice Blast on the carpet of my car didn't bother me at all, not sweating the small stuff was liberating. I appreciated all that I had on that day and the very thought that I had risked it all was horrifying.

There was no word from Dave that evening; my old man was doing his job and I had to leave him to it. No point in looking out at 23 as that ship had sailed, they had clearly scarpered or perhaps they had been arrested at one of the other sites, it was anyone's guess. The police tape flickered in the wind and their house was completely dark.

It should have been a wonderful feeling knowing they had gone, but not knowing where they were was unsettling. The kids went to bed fairly early that night, the excitement of the day caught up with them. Three weary teenagers brushed their teeth with eyes almost shut, admitting defeat at quarter to ten. I shut all their doors knowing that would be them done until morning.

With time to turn around a couple of loads of bedding and to set some bones and veg boiling for a stock I had planned for a soup, I milled around the kitchen hoping for many more nights like this. Kids in bed, bones boiling, sheets washing. As boring as that may sound, it was exactly what I wanted and needed.

Not many people pegged their sheets out at night, but I did, especially in summer – the stunning odour of cut grass, moonlight and morning dew was a fitted sheet's wet dream. Jo Malone need only to sit with a test tube under my washing line to discover the holy grail of fragrance.

As the last pillowcase was pegged out on the line I inhaled the scent deeply before bending over to pick up my empty basket. I stood and turned to go back into the house when, before I could react, I felt a hand over my mouth.

In the Dock

I had no idea what it felt like to be helpless until that moment. The silence only added to the terror; I didn't move, I didn't shout, I did nothing because I presumed that would buy me more time. The hand slowly released its grip, the owner used their other hand to turn me around to face them.

The possibilities bounced from one side of my brain to the other, a random serial killer annoyed that his chips were cold? A sex offender with a penchant for clean bedding? I needed Fitz to disarm this maniac and to save me, I needed an overweight detective with a score to settle. I opened my eyes and focused on the face, I was dizzy from hyperventilating, and it took me a few seconds to realise who this was.

"Hello, Mrs."

Arif gazed at me with his big chocolate eyes.

"What the hell are you doing?" I hissed at him and he went to cover my mouth with his hand again. I slapped it away.

"Stop that!"

He stepped back and pulled me towards the house. "Please you have to be silent, this is very dangerous. Can we go in?"

I nodded, we both tiptoed into my back door and shut it quietly. Arif immediately turned the lights off and shut the blinds, clearly convinced we were being watched.

"What are you doing here, what is happening?"

"I needed to get a message to you and your husband. I can't use phone and Matt and Miss Gina, they somewhere close." He looked around the kitchen as though one of them was in the slow cooker, the other wedged in the microwave.

"But Arif, it's OK, they left, they are not in the house anymore."

He nodded. "I know this, they clear warehouse and move

people to new location. They need to get rid of evidence."

"Evidence?"

"Yes the people, my friends."

"Get rid?"

He whispered into my ear, "I think they plan to kill."

I stepped back. "What, all of them, how?"

"My friend he message me from secret phone. He say they going to get on boat and they go back home but he think that boat will sink on purpose, or maybe they throw them overboard."

I almost laughed, this sounded very far-fetched. "What murder them?"

"Yes I think so. Then when bodies are found it look like they were coming over here and drowned in sea trying to get into country, it happens a lot."

I thought about it. Would Matt and Gina and whoever else they worked for be callous enough to stick the whole workforce on a boat and watch it sink to hide the evidence of their trafficking operation? This was mass murder, this could have been Sophia and the baby, it was unthinkable. Arif grabbed both my shoulders.

"So you tell your husband, OK? He must stop them."

"But where are they? How will he find them all?"

Arif reached into his pocket and handed me a phone; it was some sort of flip-fronted Motorola that belonged in a museum.

"You take this, Mrs, you keep it. This is my friend's phone, his name is Kim. He will keep you updated by text message."

I looked at the phone, how would I even charge such an antique? Arif reached into his other pocket and handed me a charger that was heavier than my head.

"OK, thank you. What will you do now?" He zipped up my dad's jacket, one I had bought him for Christmas from Barbour.

"I go back to Duck Cottage, I am safe there. They not go there in case of police."

"But how will you get there?"

"I walk, in the shadows. Best way."

"Don't be ridiculous, it's fourteen miles, I'll call you an Uber." I reached for my phone.

"No, no Uber. It's fine, I walk. Please help, you must help."

He left through the back door and slipped through a gap in the fence. I stood staring at the brick-sized phone wondering if I could remember how to work it. I knew what I had to do and there was no way either Dave or me could let this little boat trip go ahead.

When are you home? I need to speak to you. ASAP. R XX

What about?

When are you home, make it soon? X

Is it urgent?

Yes!

On my way.

Dave never put a kiss on his messages anymore, I hated it.

I waited at the window in the dark willing Dave to turn up. He arrived within twenty minutes at about one in the morning, stomped up the driveway and into the house. He still had his stab vest on and he smelt of cigarettes. I thought Dave had started smoking again, it would be my fault if he had. I handed him the phone and he just looked at it in silence.

"You lift the front up if you want to look at the screen."

"I know how it works, Raquel, I'm 52!"

I told him the story of what had been planned. I explained that Arif had wanted me to hand the phone over to him specifically so he could save their lives. He still left it shut and was deep in thought before he said, "You know that once I take this in they will want to know where I got it from. You will be connected immediately."

I nodded. "But what other option do we have? We can't let this happen."

Dave opened the bonnet of the phone and began to type.

Where are you now?

Almost immediately a message came through.

In a big van. We are going to catch a boat.

Boat where?

They say to take us home but I know it can't be true.

Where are you sailing from?

Docklands, Liverpool.

Where?

I don't know.

We need a landmark. A building or a shop. Something to tell me where you are.

I try and find some information.

OK. Hurry.

Dave looked at me. "We're going to Liverpool. Lock up the house, let's go."

"What me?"

"Yes you. I might need you."

"But what about the kids, they'll be alone?"

Dave radioed through to somebody and asked them to send a squad car to keep an eye on the street.

"So, you ready?"

I gulped. Was I fuck ready, but I guessed I would have to be.

We sped through the streets and onto the motorway. Dave didn't use his blue lights but he said he would if he had to. It was impressive, he was masterful at the wheel. To be calm whilst hurtling along the roads at over one hundred miles per hour without breaking a sweat – these were skills I didn't know existed. I would need driving shoes, driving glasses, a bottle of water and a chewing gum before I could even attempt eighty miles per hour and that was during the day, never mind the pitch black. Dave was very quiet until the big ass Motorola buzzed.

"Read it to me now." Dave was aggressive. My hands were shaking so much, I dropped it on the floor.

"Come on, Raquel, come on, there isn't time for your clumsiness."

I picked it up, holding it with both hands at this point to be sure I had a firm grip.

We are in a building waiting for the boat. Royal Seaforth Dock. We get on fruit and veg boat soon. Hurry.

"Do I reply?"

Dave shook his head. "No, let's just get there!"

Dave spoke to his satnav with the same abruptness as he had me and it guided us in, told us we were quarter of an hour away. Fifteen minutes of stomach-churning hell.

"Don't you need to radio in so you can get back-up from the Liverpool police?"

"Nope, I will handle this."

"What, on your own?"

"I am not on my own, I have you. You need to do exactly as I tell you, Raquel, do you understand?"

"Me, are you serious? I have my slippers on."

I was definitely not a good partner. I was a joke when it came to confrontation and I'd already nearly wet my pants when we'd taken a corner at high speed. I would definitely mess this up, I was a gibbering idiot to be fair. "Dave, I am not good in situations like this. I haven't even had a glass of wine, I am not good without wine. Do you have any wine in this car?" I pulled open the glovebox, there was nothing in there apart from a spit hood which

I really hoped we wouldn't need.

"Funnily enough, Raquel, we don't carry wine in the police cars."

My shoulders dropped; I would struggle to be brave sober. Dave leaned over and shut the glovebox.

"Face it, girl. You got us into this mess so it's only fair you help out now."

My hands were shaking, beads of sweat formed on my top lip, I wasn't sure I could go ahead with this.

"Dave, have you got a gun in your pocket?"

"No, I'm just pleased to see you," he winked.

"Stop it Dave, have you? I'm so scared."

"Yes I have a gun, I hope we won't need it."

"OK so what's your plan, do we have a plan?"

"I dunno Raquel. Let's just play it by ear, see how things pan out."

I nearly choked. Play it by ear! What sort of approach was that to a set of gangsters who were planning a cull? What sort of attitude was this to a situation even Morse, Taggart and Cracker would struggle to handle between the three of them? I started to think Dave had properly lost it and I had driven him temporarily insane. Maybe he was going to drive this car straight into the Mersey and the kids would be orphans. I started panicking. I looked over at Dave, he had a silly grin on his face and I didn't like it, he looked unhinged.

I grabbed the radio and I shouted into it. "MAYDAY MAYDAY."

Dave slowed the car down a little, took the radio from me and placed it back into its holder.

"Raquel, love, it's switched off and we are not in a Boeing 747 about to crash." He burst into laughter, his belly shook, his eyes crinkled and he grabbed my hand. "You still really, really make me laugh … Mayday Mayday." And then he started howling again. I struggled to understand the hilarity if I'm honest but he was holding my hand and that was a win, so I laughed along at myself through gritted teeth.

We approached the docklands with Dave still holding my hand. He turned off his lights and glided down the side of the river.

"Send a message asking for more detail." I punched the message into the massive keys, it felt as though I was using a typewriter.

We are close, can you tell me more about your position, what can you see?

We in a building next to river. Big blue boat with a blue and white flag on the side. There's number on the building opposite. 369. We are going to get on boat very soon.

Dave pulled over and pulled up a map on his phone, scoured it quickly and within seconds he knew exactly where they were. He had worked out that if they were opposite building 369 we needed to be on the other side of the river. He was very clever, my Dave. He quickly manoeuvred in and out of the different lanes getting us closer to our target. Eventually he stopped and pulled up behind a large lorry.

"This is it. Brace yourself!"

I held my breath; it was very unhelpful and actually a terrible idea.

We watched as a crowd of people moved in silence and darkness down the dock toward a boat with a blue and white flag on the side. I recognised Matt and Gina, but they also had two other nasty-looking men hurrying the group along, pushing them at times to speed things up. The boarding walkway was lowered from the boat and another man in a red baseball cap waited on deck with a torch for his passengers to board the cruise of death.

A small boat, a speedy looking thing, was moored just in front of the bigger boat. Gina threw a holdall into it so she was clearly planning on taking some sort of trip herself.

"Why are you doing this without back-up?" I whispered to Dave, my voice shaking.

"It's your only chance, Raquel."

"My only chance?"

He looked at me.

"Yes! So do what I tell you, nothing else."

I had no idea what he meant but now was not the time for a lengthy discussion. I trusted Dave with everything I had; strong, dependable, reliable Dave and flaky, weak Raquel did not deserve him.

With the flick of a switch, the blue light on top of Dave's car flashed and the siren howled as he drove straight towards them and spun the car to a halt. It was very dramatic! The entire group of people froze, eyes wide.

Dave jumped out of the car shouting "Stop, police!"

He strode with confidence over to their captors. I cowered behind the car trying not to faint or vomit.

Dave shouted to the group of migrants, "Walk over there, to the car. Go now!"

They murmured to each other looking confused. It was clear they were a little unsure as to who to trust or who to listen to. Not one of them moved, they just looked at Dave and then back to their bosses, waiting for somebody to tell them who the good guys were. I needed to help Dave, I had to brave it and I had to step in. I emerged from behind the car and beckoned to the group. They must have thought that a woman in slippers was the lesser of all evils so they slowly walked towards me; in the region of thirty people shuffled along in single file hoping I wasn't the wrong choice. Dave nodded to me, I must have done something right finally.

"Take them back into the building, Raquel, and wait for the police. Hurry up, I have to keep an eye on this lot."

This lot: Matt, Gina, Malik and two other crazy-looking guys were stumped at this situation. I could see they were wondering where the rest of the police force was. I wondered the same thing but I had agreed to do exactly what Dave told me.

I herded the group back towards the building. They were a mixture of men and women but the majority looked under fifty, exhausted and malnourished. I heard Dave finally radio in and request immediate back-up.

"Urgent assistance required; I repeat, urgent assistance required." He stood in front of the motley crew, legs wide apart, hand on his gun. He ordered them to lie on the floor with their hands above their heads.

Gina, who was dressed as villain – black jeans, black beanie and a long black leather coat – stamped her foot and screamed out, "Are you serious? What the hell are you doing here, Raquel? Let us go or we'll tell him everything."

Dave shouted back, "Shut the fuck up and lie on the ground now. Don't speak to her, you're dealing with me now."

She sobbed quietly with her cheek in the dirt.

They lay in a line and looked extremely uncomfortable. Dave stood over them waiting for just one of them to even try to move.

"Raquel, go into the building and wait for me there."

I did as instructed, Dave had it all under control.

Inside the building, which was a cold warehouse with nothing in it at all, the migrants talked in whispers to each other. They were cold, tired and they were clearly incredibly frightened. They sat on the floor against the walls, looking up at me and waiting for me to do something or say something.

I flipped the Motorola open and thumped in a message.

I heard a phone beep to the left of me and a man with short grey hair and a goatee beard to match reached into his pocket. I held the phone up to him so we could put faces to the messages. He stood and walked over to me. I held my hand out.

"Hello, Kim?"

He nodded. He shook my hand and put his other on my shoulder. "Thank you."

I shrugged. "That was really brave, what you did. You saved all of these people by taking a risk and communicating with Arif."

His eyes filled with tears, it was clear he had really been through it.

"I don't know where they would have taken us. It didn't feel right. I think we may have all died."

"Please, Kim, can you tell these people that they will be safe and looked after? They all look frightened to death. Let them know that man out there is a good guy – the police officer – and he will bring help."

He immediately turned and spoke to them in their language, and he used his hands to tell them to calm down. They all murmured, some seemed unconvinced, but at least they knew now they weren't going to perish at sea. At least they knew this was the end of the hunger and the misery.

"What will happen to us, what will they do with us? We don't have papers; we are all here illegally."

I had done a little homework via google and I hoped this was correct. "Each case is individual. First they will find you accommodation and you will have food, hot water and a place to stay for now. Nobody will be deported immediately or left on the streets. You are all safe right now."

He still looked quite unsure, no doubt a result of broken promises from his captors. Just as I was about to crack under the pressure and invite them all to stay at Duck Cottage, I heard the faint sound of sirens in the distance. Help was coming for them, even if it did mean I would be in deep shit. I just hoped that they would go easy on me and that Dave wouldn't be slayed in the Daily Mail as Britain's dopiest cop.

"Kim, wait here, I need to check all is OK on the dock. Guard the door unless it's the police, OK?" I slipped back through the door and out towards the river but there was no sign of anyone – no Dave or the crims. I could see the blue lights of the police cars and vans on the other side of the dock heading our way but they would still be a few minutes, so I picked up the pace and started to panic. Where were they? Five people had vanished – there was no activity on the water in this part of the river, the boats that were moored bobbed about quietly in the darkness. The only light I could see was in the distance from the back of a small boat heading at some speed out towards the sea.

I ran to the side of the river to the fruit and veg boat with the flag. It was silent and the walkway had been retracted. That's when I realised that the boat I had seen heading into the distance was the one that Gina had thrown her bag into. I fell to my knees

– they had taken Dave, I didn't know if he was hurt, was he even alive, how had they escaped?

I screamed at the top of my lungs "FUCKING HELL" and it echoed around the docklands.

At my lowest ebb, I headed back to Dave's car so I could grab my phone and call someone for help, anyone. I opened the passenger door, sobbing, and reached onto my seat where I had left it.

It was Matt I saw first. He was sitting in the back of the car looking pretty fucked off. Dave was sitting next to him talking very softly.

"Oh my god," I squealed, "I thought you were dead. I thought they had taken you, are you alright? What the hell, what's going on?"

Matt didn't look at me, he stared at his knees and kept quiet.

Dave got out of the car and locked it. He came around to my side.

"The others got away, luckily I managed to keep hold of this twat."

I frowned. "They got away, how?"

"They overpowered me. I left my gun and spray in the car. Duh."

"Duh? I saw your gun, you had it with you."

"No I didn't," he said, with a funny look on his face.

"So how did you keep hold of him?"

Dave shrugged. "Just did."

The police cars were seconds away at this point, screaming up the road and almost with us. Dave grabbed my fist.

"Punch me in the face, hard."

"Sorry?"

"Punch me in the face right now, Raquel, hurry up."

"Why?"

"JUST DO IT!"

He yelled so loudly it made me jump and, to be quite honest, I wanted to punch him at that point because he scared me. I made a fist and cracked him on the side of the face catching his lip and his nose. My hand throbbed.

Dave felt his face with his hand and checked for blood, there was plenty.

"Good girl. Wait here."

I leaned against the car, confused. I had no idea what was going on, how had Dave lost the others but managed to keep Matt and why had I just had to give my husband a fat lip? I watched Dave talk to a group of police officers, he was animated as he told them his version of events, pointing down the river in the opposite direction to the way the boat went, and then pointing to the car where Matt was being held captive.

Three female police officers went straight into the building whilst the men stood outside making various calls on their phones and radios. Eventually, Dave shook their hands and came back to the car.

"OK, I'm taking care of this one myself," he said, nodding towards Matt who was wiping his nose on the window. With his hands behind his back, there must have been no other choice.

Initially we drove back to Manchester in silence; this was the most awkward I had ever felt in my life which is saying something. My phone went off at a crematorium once and the ringtone was circus music – boy did I know what awkward felt like.

It was Matt who eventually broke the silence.

"Dave, do you think she made it to the plane?"

Dave shrugged. "Probably."

Matt probed him further. "Will they know where she's gone to, will they try and follow her?"

"It's unlikely. She is on an empty leg flight and, if the passports are decent, she'll be on her way to sunnier climates."

Matt sort of smiled and then looked a little lost. Dave turned to him as we slowed down for a roundabout. "All you need to focus on now is doing and saying what we talked about and she'll probably be home and dry."

Matt nodded.

"What's going on, what are you talking about?" I asked.

Dave, with both hands on the wheel, looked ahead and said,

"Nothing for you to worry about. Text the kids, tell them you'll be home within the hour."

It was coming up for five in the morning, the sun was coming up and they would definitely be oblivious to the late-night activity.

"I'm going home?" I was shocked, I thought I would have to give statements and drink coffee from plastic cups.

"Yes, you are going home to be a mother and a wife; hopefully you can do a better job than you have lately."

I felt like a naughty child being bollocked by my husband in front of the hot neighbour, the one that had got me into this mess in the first place. I looked in the rear-view mirror. Matt looked like a frightened little boy, weak and possibly on the verge of crying. That wasn't sexy, anything but.

We pulled up outside our house and I looked back at Matt before I got out of the car.

"Goodbye, Matt."

"Bye, babe," he said wearily.

Dave rolled his eyes and shook his head. "You'll never learn will you, son?"

I walked into the house at just gone six. It was silent. I am ashamed to admit it, but I had a large brandy for breakfast. I needed to calm down and this is what they did on the telly.

I lay in a hot bath processing my thoughts and trying to make sense of all that had happened. I had been tempted to call Mum, Mel or anyone to get their take on things but I thought better of it. I had to try and not be such a catastrophe, I had to do better so, after the bath, I fell sound asleep on top of the bed wrapped in a towel. I was emotionally worn out.

I woke just after eleven. Dave was next to me fully clothed and drinking a cup of tea. He had an ice pack on his lip which was now like a bicycle tyre.

My towel had slipped halfway down the bed, I must have looked a complete sight. Dave seemed to clock that at the same time and said, "They found a whale in the Thames basin, once." And he laughed as he took advantage of my unfortunate position.

I quickly pulled my towel up over my unmentionables, god

damn all the quiches I had devoured that year.

"Very funny Dave. So, what happened?"

Dave took a gulp of tea and turned to face me. He spoke quietly, the kids were buzzing around on the landing. "He's in custody, we'll question him later … wanker."

I thought of Scouse Matt locked in a cell, his jogging bottoms would have been confiscated by now, without those he would be like Samson without his hair. There would be no beef wellington, just a Pot Noodle and a slap round the chops.

"Are you going to tell me what the hell went on back there? How come the rest of them got away and why did I have to punch you in the face?

"OK so when Matt is questioned later, which will be by me, he will cooperate. He will tell us all about the operation Gina and the others were running. He will explain that he was being controlled to an extent and that he didn't really want to be involved. A judge will look favourably on that, but he'll still get sent down."

"What about me, will he mention me?"

"No, not in a criminal way, absolutely not."

"Why?"

"Because he loves his Mrs."

"What's that got to with it?"

"I love my Mrs, he loves his. We did a swap."

"A swap?"

"Yes, she gets to go on a permanent holiday and he takes the heat. And I get to keep hold of you until you fuck up again."

"I won't fuck up again."

"I hope not." He rubbed his bald head and then his eyes.

"You let them go, Dave?"

He took a sharp intake of breath. "I did what I had to do for my family."

"I can't believe you let them go."

"What choice did I have? We couldn't have her in an interview room, could we? She'd take us all down."

"You did that for me, for the family?"

"Yes and I have fat lip and a sore face too, nice punch A. J."

"Who?"

"Nobody, forget it. It had to look like there was a struggle."

"And there was no struggle? He agreed to come with you?"

"Well it was either that or Gina languished in the clink forever more and she couldn't handle it – apparently she's not built for prison."

I disagreed, Gina would be top dog within a week in a women's prison, she would handle it no doubt. She just didn't give a shiny shite about Matt or anyone else, just herself. She would now be on a beach somewhere looking for her next victim whilst playing the dumb Botox nurse and sucking people in.

I was all over the place with this information, I was emotional, this meant everything. Dave was the most law-abiding person that ever lived. He took his job more seriously than I took my gravy. He had compromised himself and his integrity for me.

I was in awe of him that morning. He had sold his soul for me, he had done a deal with the devil, for me.

"I am so sorry; you'll never know how sorry I am."

He sighed. "Raquel don't say it, just show it. Don't let someone come between us again. For god's sake, the nightmare we have just gone through for some two-bit gangster with the brains of a slug. What were you thinking, Raquel?"

I racked my brains for an explanation. I really had nothing that could justify my actions. I tried to give a reason, not an excuse.

"I felt invisible, Dave, and he made me feel seen."

"So classic mid-life mania. My husband doesn't give me enough attention, blah blah blah."

I nodded. "Something like that."

He went to have a shower but gave me a warning before he left the room. "You better get dressed before Greenpeace turn up with a harpoon."

I smiled. I had my first glimpse that things could be OK.

All the Leaves are Brown

Packing the kids' bags ready for their return to school is the modern parent's version of Christmas Eve. Of course we all enjoy the lack of structure and the freedom the holidays offer but, by the end of August, most of us are on the brink of a colossal meltdown. Even the toaster looked forward to reducing its hours, the dishwasher – who was exhausted – was to go on a part-time contract until half term and my credit card heaved a huge sigh of relief because it wasn't being used and abused every three minutes by the bastards at Amazon.

That excitement, however, had to be contained until the kids actually got out of the car and went inside the school doors. It was never over until it was over. There was always still that possibility of somebody throwing up or, worse still, following through; the threat that one of them could develop a cold over night or god forbid test positive for Covid. I didn't want set myself up for a fall so I gave my three kids two paracetamol each before they went to sleep to mask any potential symptoms that could fuck up my meticulously planned week alone.

I craved solitude for three main reasons; the first was simply that I was all peopled out after a summer of pure madness brought on by my own ridiculous decisions. Second was that the house was starting to look tired – it was visibly sick of all the trampling and door slamming, it needed a well-earned rest. And thirdly, I was in sole charge of organising a wedding at very short notice. A wedding which, if I was honest, I could have done without but considering what I had put everyone through over the last few months, I felt obliged.

So on this Sunday evening, very early in September after a seven-week holiday, I swore to my family that if any of the kids were not fit for school the following morning I would piss in a tea cup and then drink it live on TikTok. Dave didn't even bat an eyelid but the kids furrowed their foreheads in unison.

It was only that week I had discovered TikTok. I was fascinated by the fact there were absolutely no rules. If you wanted to be famous, you simply could be and the week before I had watched with my hand over my mouth a dinner lady from school pole dancing in her front room wearing a very snug purple leotard and although I'm sure she believed it, she did not look at all like Jane Torvill. Her son had apparently put himself up for adoption the very next day and who the hell could blame him.

It had been an eventful week since the showdown at the docks. The police had deemed that Number 23 had been purchased with ill-gotten gains and the bank had started a repossession order. Matt made a full statement to the police throwing all of the gang under the bus and giving the police every piece of information they asked for apart from providing any clue as to Gina's whereabouts. I doubted he knew anyway, it's not like she had a forwarding address and she wouldn't have given him a second thought.

Matt told the police to forget Gina and not waste their time looking for her. He said she was like an iguana and that she could cleverly blend in anywhere.

"I think you may mean chameleon, you moron," Dave told him with a smirk on his face.

Eventually, Matt was charged with trafficking offences, possession of controlled substances, intent to supply and false imprisonment just to name a few. His only real crime in my opinion, which I kept to myself, was that he was easily led. Deep down, I hoped that the judge would take this into consideration when he was dishing out the sentence, but Matt was a grown man and his choices were his own.

Dave predicted he would probably do about seven years which he looked pretty chuffed about. He said, with a wicked grin, "Let's see if he's still so pretty after a long stretch in Walton."

Dave's heroics on the docklands had been accepted by his superiors, he had told them a colourful version of the truth, cleverly leaving out my involvement apart from the fact I was a good help with inside knowledge. They were intrigued to hear that, due to me working with Matt and having a 'friendly relationship' with him, Dave was able to use me as a sort of informant – his woman on the inside so to speak. Of course he couldn't reveal his source any earlier because, with me being his Mrs, he didn't want to put me at risk. The fact that Dave and I saved all of those people and managed to make an arrest was still deemed a huge success even if the others had scarpered.

One thing I did discover after the event was that Mel and Dave had been in cahoots for quite a while, plotting the route to my freedom together. Mel had also allocated an old university friend of hers who specialised in immigration law to assist my mum's four house guests. Paperwork had been prepared for them to apply for asylum and remain in the country without fear of deportation. It was all very good and very nice but I have to admit, I was a little jealous. My husband and sister had been secretly communicating and that didn't feel good, especially as I knew she had put the lips on him whilst I slept. But I knew that this was something I had to take on the chin and I showed nothing but appreciation.

Dave had been much warmer with me, though there was still some frostiness especially if somebody with a Liverpool accent came on the television. A documentary on Paul McCartney caused him to shout out the word "twat" before glaring at me and then going for a long walk. I had to accept that this would be a time thing; slowly we would heal and one day he might be able to listen to a Beatles album without self-combusting.

For some sick reason, after that, Beatles songs played on a loop in my head and I found it very hard not to hum them out loud. I stopped myself, that would have been a complete piss take.

So, the kids all went to school that Monday morning and it was as smooth as it could have been. I waved them off with a smile as wide as the car knowing that today I would have time with my own thoughts, something I had missed hugely and needed badly. I had allocated this one day to myself before I had a torrid week of planning, just one day with the sofa and coffee. After drop-off, I threw the keys onto the kitchen table, flicked the kettle on and lay down. I was just midway through an episode of Frasier when the doorbell went. I considered crawling on my belly from the lounge to the kitchen to avoid being seen.

'Who the fuck's that?' was my go-to expression whenever that damn bell sounded. I froze to the spot on the sofa hoping that whoever it was would bugger off and leave me alone. I stayed still and silent, praying that the visitor was a one-ring-and-leave kind of person. It was not to be.

"Cooey, Raquel!" I looked at the window through one eye; Mum, Dad, Barbara and Old Tom all peered at me through the glass. I quickly shut my eyes.

"She's playing dead, like a dog. Look at her." Tom thought I was playing a game.

I remained still.

"Raquel, open the door. We know you're pretending, come on you silly woman."

Mum knew me too well and my eyes started flickering so eventually and very grumpily I had to let them all in.

"What, Mother, why are you here and without even calling first?"

She walked straight past me, in fact they all did, and she plonked a huge shopping bag onto my kitchen table.

"We have come for a wedding planning update with the wedding planner."

I shook my head with vigour. "Oh no, you can't plan a meeting in my house without even telling me about it. I have my own plans today."

"What plans?" Cheeky Tom dared to question my movements for the day.

"Stuff that I need to do."

"What stuff?" Dad waded in with his two pence worth.

I gave in, it was futile.

"Come on then, what's this about?" I said, gesturing to the bag. I figured the sooner they got talking the sooner they would leave.

The week before, Mel's friend the immigration guy had

visited Mum's with relatively good news for what he called 'the refugees'. The mood was high and Duck Cottage was in full celebration mode. By then they were all aware that the threat from Miss Eyebrows and her sidekick was no more, so an impromptu cocktail party took place in Mum's kitchen which was becoming more like a nightclub every week.

Anyway, I got the whole story the next morning from my hungover mother who was resting her hip after attempting another one of the infamous slut drops.

Old Tom had waited until it was almost dark, you know that twenty minutes where it's sort of dim but still light. He had asked everybody to join him outside under the big oak tree. He had lit over a hundred tea lights with the help of Arif and he had put trousers and a shirt on which he had taken from Dad's laundry basket. He beckoned Barbara over to him and he got down onto both knees – his back wouldn't allow just the one – and then he proposed with a ring that he had fashioned in the shed with a hammer from the hook of a curtain. It was a real tear-jerker according to Mum.

"He asked for her hand in marriage, he said he was in his twilight years and he wanted to spend them with her," Mum told me with a gruff voice on the phone the morning after.

"What did she say?"

"Actually nothing, she just nodded. I actually wondered if she understood the question."

"Then what?"

"Well then we all clapped and celebrated."

"So they're getting married?"

"Yes, Raquel. Keep up, that's usually what happens after a proposal."

"Where will they live?"

"They'll probably get a little flat from the council. Tom has specifically applied for one with thick walls due to them being newlyweds."

"Gross!"

"Yes, it is a bit, isn't it."

"What's wrong with your voice?"

"Sweet Caroline, karaoke, last night." I grimaced, how lairy.

"Anyway, we have a proposal for you, Raquel, I hope you're feeling helpful."

"For me, what can I do to help?" My answer was already a firm no, but I humoured her.

"OK so, Tom, Barbara well all of us really would like it very much if you arranged the wedding ceremony and organise the whole thing."

I sat up, eyes wide. "You what? Why me? This is so unfair!" I slipped into teenage Raquel who made an appearance occasionally. Mum tutted; she always did that when she thought I was being insolent.

"Well Raquel, it's due to you that Tom and Babs met in the first place, it's because of you they are living in my house rent free and I thought, after all the trouble you have been in lately, it would be nice to redeem yourself by doing something nice."

I gave my mother the Vs down the phone. She was right of course, but the way she said things got my back right up.

"When are they thinking of, next summer? I could probably do June if I really pulled my finger out."

She chortled. "No, we've already booked the registry office for a week on Friday." I spat coffee onto the phone.

"What are you talking about, it's a bit soon isn't it?"

Mum heaved a large sigh. "Raquel, they are very, very old. If they both make it to the wedding it will be a bleeding miracle. No time to spare. Just a buffet, a few decorations, some music etcetera and try and make it about them and not you."

I slammed the phone down hard. I did not cherish the thought of another gathering at Duck Cottage, but over the course of the day, I mellowed a little. The fact we were all spared jail or deportation was reason enough to celebrate. So this wedding planning meeting, as inconvenient as it was, possibly did need to happen today.

"What's in the bag then?"

Mum emptied a crumpled peach trouser suit onto the table.

"Tadah, we just bought this for the bride, £20 from The Sally Army charity shop. There's some blood on the collar and what I think could be custard on the lapel but the colour will really set her hair off." I looked over at Barbara, who was bleaching my sink without even asking.

"Why are you showing this to me?"

Mum laughed and then said, as if I were completely stupid, "For the colour scheme, silly. Now you know what you're working around, you can create a theme."

My head was blown. A colour scheme based around a charity shop suit that was probably riddled with fleas. The entire morning was taken up by the uninvited guests throwing stupid ideas at me that would keep me busy from morning through night until the day of the wedding.

"Why don't we see if one of the Gallagher brothers can do the music? They live close by don't they, Raquel?"

"No, Mother."

"Raquel, could you get Marks & Spencer to do the food? It's top-notch fodder their stuff."

"No Dad, I cannot."

"Could we have our honeymoon here at your house, Raquel?"

"No you fucking can't, Tom."

My head was ringing by the time they left and I sat staring at the smelly peach suit wondering whether to take a flame thrower to it.

Mum's parting shot had been, "Idle hands are the devil's playthings. You'll do well to remember that when you're lying around on the sofa in the daytime. Best to keep busy."

Deep down I knew that I had to pull it out of the bag. People were relying on me to make this a happy occasion after what had been quite a traumatic time for all of us. So I did what all professional and conscientious event organisers did and I delegated the shit out of it.

That week I turned my house into a production line with Suzy on cupcakes, Michaela on decorations and Sam was instructed to learn 'A Million Love Songs' on his recorder and to make sure he was note perfect. When Dave got home from work that afternoon he was sent straight back out to the dry cleaners with the peach suit. I pushed my luck when I also asked him to make a playlist of love songs for old people but he said no chance and that he was going for a pint.

I managed to create the peach colour in the icing for the cupcakes and bought some ribbon in the same colour from a craft shop for the tops of the chairs. Arif and I liaised and he kindly agreed to mass-produce his Moroccan tagine for a hot buffet – I did an online shop and sent the ingredients to Mum's so he could start his marinating. By the Wednesday, I had it all under control, with the assistance of my assistants.

Dave and I went for a drink that night. He invited me by text at lunchtime and he put a kiss on the end. The last time I had sat in that pub on a Wednesday I had sweated my tits off during a hideous grilling from Dave; this would be a much better evening. Life was good without fear.

Daft Nate the barman, with zero knowledge of drinks, was still surprisingly employed at our local and he visibly winced when I approached the bar.

"Sauvignon Blanc please, Nate. White wine fridge, second shelf down, first on the left."

He smiled as he unscrewed the wine, it was probably the first thing he had got right all week. And then he went and spoiled it all by pouring it into a brandy glass.

Dave arrived huffing and puffing and rushing as usual with some paperwork in his hand. He shouted, "Usual Nate!" As he walked past the bar, Nate set to work with a cocktail shaker to create a pint of Guinness.

"Bringing work home?" I gestured to the paperwork.

"Nope not business, this is pleasure."

"Go on …?" I hoped it wasn't divorce papers, that would be ironic considering I had spent the week planning a wedding.

Dave took my hands, his eyes kind; his manner didn't seem like he was about to serve me.

"So I know you felt unseen, unloved and ignored."

I nodded.

"Well, I hope this will go some way to making you feel less of those things."

He handed me the papers and waited for my response.

I only needed to see the words, 'Santorini' and 'sea view' before I felt an overwhelming sense of love for my old man.

"We leave a week Saturday, my mum and dad are coming over to watch the kids, you will have my undivided attention for seven solid days."

I kissed him on the head. There were no words that would suffice to thank him for the way he had conducted himself during my Mad Period.

The wedding was, as you would expect, a complete spectacle and a total farce but amongst all of the silliness, which I'll get to very soon, there were two old people having a final stab at happiness before their time was up. I hoped they both stayed alive long enough to enjoy each other and I told them that outside the registry office after they had wed. Tom's reply was, "Oh don't you worry, we will!" before slapping Bab's arse leaving a greasy handprint on the peach suit. He really was a creature.

The vows had gone well, an interpreter had been brought in so that there could be no possibility that Barbara had got confused and thought she was attending a job interview. It turned out she definitely did want to marry Old Tom and she found him to be charming, handsome and amusing. The interpreter translated this and looked more confused than anyone.

We threw rose petals that Arif had collected from the beds at the cottage over the happy couple's heads, they were both smiley and elated. Barbara scrubbed up nicely that day. Her hair was smooth, her bruising and swelling had gone. A bit of eyeliner and some lipstick and she had a look of Anne Robinson. Old Tom wore a smart blue suit with a peach cravat, he was clean-shaven and he had brushed his teeth. He still swigged from a hip flask throughout the ceremony, but you can't win them all.

They were driven back to the cottage in the burgundy Jag with a peach ribbon on the bonnet by my dad, who was wearing one of Mum's woollen berets. We had forgotten to buy a chauffeur's hat so it was between that and a bejewelled Stetson from Mum's line-dancing phase. The lesser of two evils left Dad looking like a super posh and rather old Che Guevara.

Unfortunately, there were a few mishaps at what my girls called "the afterparty". Arif had totally misjudged the spices in his tagine and caused merry hell with the guests' gullets. He had multiplied the spices per person and given twenty-three people a bulb of garlic and a scotch bonnet chilli each, he was lucky he wasn't up on a murder charge. Roger had downed a litre of milk to try and calm down his throbbing tongue and Mum put a sanitary towel down the back of her trousers just in case of a mishap.

Sam's rendition of 'A Million Love Songs' was absolutely shite; he had not practised at all and ended up playing 'London's Burning' instead because that was the only thing he knew. I instantly blocked his GoHenry card; he only had one job and he managed to fuck that up.

The speeches were very unconventional. Tom mistook his wedding speech for a Bernard Manning sketch and he used that many double entendres that he was heckled and booed off the stage. I mean, who tells a joke at a wedding with the punchline "I only fucked the one goat". The girls were disgusted, Roger almost fainted, Arif didn't get it but Dave and Sam fell about laughing.

The fiasco continued. Inevitably we had a blocked toilet when somebody, I don't know who, managed to expel the tagine and three rolls of toilet paper in the very weary downstairs loo. I think that was the day we all realised it needed to retire.

Sophia got the udders out next to my cupcake tower and ended up spraying the whole thing with breast milk; she did say "whoopsie" but that really didn't help. We wiped them down and didn't tell anybody when we dished them out.

At the worst possible time, Suzy had decided to have a little peep at Instagram and was floored by what she saw. Finn and Connie had made a reel of their 'summer of fun'. Connie's skinny brown legs and Finn's fantastic torso intertwined as they rolled around on his parents' luxurious boat reduced Suzy to a velociraptor. I heard her up in one of the bedrooms making prehistoric noises and then I saw a curtain completely disintegrate. I knew not to approach – this was a teenage girl scorned, I used to be one.

The one moment I realised I was at an actual wedding and not riding the ghost train at the Pleasure Beach was when the first dance was announced. Dave delivered quite an emotional and tender invite for all the people who "loved each other unconditionally" to hit the dance floor, aka the lawn, with their partners in tow.

There was no playlist, because we hadn't had time, so Dave randomly asked Alexa to play a classic love song. At this point anything could have happened, with the way things were going I expected something by Gary Glitter. However what actually happened was very, very special.

Al Green and his silky voice gave us a direct instruction; "Let's stay together." It could not have been more appropriate. The pretty English garden, lit by candlelight, was occupied with a mixture of unconventional and odd couples.

In the centre of the lawn and just as it should be, the bride and groom did a tango-type dance which was out of time and poorly executed. Old Tom's hands were where they shouldn't have been, Barbara's blank expression led me to believe she had no clue what was going on but hey, she was still smiling.

Mum's emergency sanitary towel was poking out of the back of her trousers whilst she attempted to line dance with my sozzled Dad who was still sporting the stupid beret.

Mel was holding Sir Walter's paws whilst he balanced skilfully on his back legs and she allowed him to lick her face for the entire song.

Roger cradled baby Roger, gazing into the little fella's eyes and swaying to the music. He had an epiphany that night, realising that kids were actually what life was all about.

Sophia and Arif waltzed slowly with their foreheads touching. They had both been through so much and they were still so young. Their lives had barely started and they had faced things none of us would ever experience in a whole lifetime. These kids, and they were kids, were strong and resilient; they would be OK, I would make sure of that.

Dave held his hand out to me and smiled. "Come on then gorgeous, don't leave me hanging."

We danced under the stars like we did at our own wedding and, as the song ended and our eyes met, my stomach flipped.

About the Author

NJ Miller is your friend, your neighbour, the woman on the school run in her slippers. She is a slave to her hormones and blunders through life hoping for the best. Writing has always been a passion and she hopes her debut novel can make some of you smile.

She has decided to stay anonymous because she's just not that into people.

Acknowledgements

Thank-you to my wonderful family, although they have pushed me to insanity individually and as a collective at one time or another, I wouldn't have it any other way.

And to Murdock, a true friend who is brutally honest and actually quite rude at times. You say it how it is and make me laugh my head off.

Printed in Great Britain
by Amazon

43863636R00169